Since the publication of the now-classic THE DETECTIVE, Roderick Thorp has been considered a master of the police novel. He broke the mold cast by Chandler and Hammett, creating an entirely new kind of fictional detective and writing about crime and the workings of the police in a way that readers instinctively know to be true.

In RAINBOW DRIVE, Thorp does it again. From the first moments when a woman's piercing scream tells Mike Gallagher that something terrible is happening, to the riveting final pages, this tough, terrifying novel grips the reader and won't let go.

RAINBOW DRIVE

A story of murder and vice, corruption and cover-up in big-time L.A., where no one who matters ever goes to jail.

RAINBOW DRIVE

A Novel By

Roderick Thorp

IVY BOOKS • NEW YORK

Ivy Books
Published by Ballantine Books
Copyright © 1986 by Roderick Thorp

This novel is a work of fiction. Names, characters, places and incidents
are either the product of the author's imagination or are used fictiously.
Any resemblance to actual events or locales or persons, living or dead, is
entirely coincidental.

Library of Congress Catalog Card Number: 86-14408

ISBN-0-8041-0170-1

This edition published by arrangement with Simon & Schuster, Inc.

Printed in Canada

First Ballantine Books Edition: December 1987

FOR MY SON STEVE

1962

T HE UNDERTAKER WAS WORRIED ABOUT GETTING HIS money. After twenty-four years in the business in Southern California, he believed he knew when someone was thinking of skipping out on him. The deceased had borrowed heavily against his life insurance policy, and the widow knew there was not going to be much left of the proceeds after she paid the undertaker's fee. The widow was distraught and panicky, but she was thinking about finances, too.

The undertaker knew that because he had overheard a conversation between the widow and a sister from New York. The dead man's son, Michael, would be taken back East on the sister's return trip. At the age of twelve the boy was going to live permanently with the New York sister. The widow had said she was making an economic decision. Maybe there was panic in her choice, but she was trying to be realistic. Realism was a bad, bad sign for an undertaker. Upon the death of any man, guilt carried the day—the undertaking business was built on that principle—with anger setting in later. But in this case the anger was setting in early, and the undertaker had to protect himself. If the widow was beginning to think that in the initial hours of her grief she had spent too much money on the relatively opulent arrangements she had made for her husband's funeral, the undertaker would be firm indeed in showing her that there was nothing she could do about it now except pay the bill.

Apparently the deceased had been a man who liked to live high. According to what the widow had admitted to the undertaker, there was little in the estate besides the insurance—some equity in the house, no stocks, only a few small government bonds. Nobody in his thirties expects to die. This had been a hit-and-run death, and a real beauty, too: the man had been hit by a truck traveling at a speed of about fifty miles an hour.

Whether or not the widow thought she was going to pay too much, the undertaker did not believe she could complain about what she had gotten, including a clear day. The weather was perfect for a high-on-the-hill Forest Lawn burial. You could see for miles across the San Fernando Valley, across the orchards and bright subdivisions, to the purple mountains beyond. The mourners seemed to be enjoying the view, even the gangly son of the deceased, whose attention wandered from time to time from the business at hand. Maybe he was uncomfortable in his new blue suit, which must have been bought in a hurry. At the funeral parlor the undertaker had noticed that the cuffs were too wide and broke too much on his shoes. The undertaker wanted to like the kid, but he seemed to have nothing to offer, too quiet even under these circumstances, too ordinary, maybe he'd even become one of those men who spend their lives permanently lost.

The fact was, the undertaker did not like any of these people. There wasn't much to like in a man who left a woman and a child with financial problems. And the toughness in Mrs. Gallagher's voice was more than just her New York accent. Obviously she was a high roller, too, like her late husband. She was over thirty-five, a tall, full-figured woman who knew she was attractive to men. Gray was beginning to show in her jetblack hair. She was someone beyond the undertaker's experience, and he knew it. The undertaker was from Indiana, Hoosier born and bred, as he often said himself. A woman like her laughed at a man like him, fifty-five years old, fifty pounds overweight. He was not attractive to women, with pale, puffy eyes and thinning gray hair that was limp, like that of a corpse. The undertaker knew he could never handle a woman like her. That made him feel like a fool, and he could not help finding ways to despise her. At least he knew how to take care of his family, the undertaker thought.

He was more pleased with the perfect weather, if the weather was what had brought out the good crowd. All of the people at the graveside had been at the funeral service, and most had put down their addresses in the space provided when they had signed the guest register. The undertaker was having his secretary copy and verify every name and address in the book, to make it easier to find Mrs. Gallagher in case she decided to skip. That sort of thing happened often in Los Angeles. For that matter, she could be married again in three months. That sort of thing happened often in this city, too.

Standing next to his mother beside the grave, his collar too tight and his suit too warm, Michael Gallagher was not in tears. This morning the tall, thin, fair-haired boy had awakened resolved to show as little emotion as possible. He had thought he would fail, but now, in the last moments of the ceremony for his father, Michael was having difficulty keeping his mind on what was going on around him. It was strange, and he was very ashamed of himself, but questions were crowding into his head—too many questions—and he could not help being distracted by the view across the Valley. In the four years the Gallaghers had been in Los Angeles, Michael had never seen anything like it. He was hoping nobody would notice him turning his head toward the view.

He could not look at any of the adults gathered at the graveside without asking himself what they knew about his father. There were secrets. Maybe his father's death could have been prevented. A month ago Michael had heard him telling his mother as much. Everyone had his secrets, his father had said. Exactly that. Now he was in his grave.

"Prepare yourself," Michael's father had whispered across the kitchen table to his mother that evening, stopping at the end of every sentence as if he were out of breath. Michael was listening in the hall, sleepy and frightened, in his pajamas, curious about his father's late-night comings and goings, the car rumbling in and out of the garage. Michael was frozen into alertness, like a startled cat. "Something's going to happen. It was the way they looked at me when the meeting was over. I wasn't supposed to see what they're up to. There'll never be any public housing in Los Angeles like back East. You'll see. Too much money is involved—hundreds of millions of dollars. You have to understand, for that kind of money, people take no unnecessary chances. I saw the way they looked at me."

That had been a month ago. Now Michael was coming to understand that his parents had been living an unusual life here in California, one that had gone faster and faster. Two nights ago, he had overheard another conversation, in the funeral home, between his mother and his aunt who had flown in from New York, a conversation almost as chilling as the one he had heard a month before.

"I wanted you out here to take Michael back to New York with you. I have to get a job. It's the best thing for me."

"I understand that," Michael's aunt said.

"It's the only way I can help myself," his mother said. "If I put the house on the market and sell everything else, I still won't clear enough to go back East and start over. In New York, I can't even earn enough to cover ninety dollars a month for a two-bedroom apartment in a neighborhood in Queens that isn't full of the niggers or the guineas. So there you are. I can't think of another way out."

"We figured something like this," Michael's aunt said. She was shorter and plumper than Michael's mother, and now the tone of the voice was sharp. "You bit off more than you could chew out here. You two had everything while Joe and me ran around to doctors trying to find out why I can't have kids. We can't send Michael across the country every time you get lonely for him. Do you understand? It's too much emotional strain on me. If you want to stay out here, you're making a permanent decision. Everything has its price."

Michael's mother was silent.

"You like it out here, don't you?" his aunt demanded suddenly, her voice rising. "You have to be honest with me. If I know you're being honest with me now, maybe I can believe you're not going to give me trouble about this later. I won't have you tearing up my feelings. *You* like it here, even now, after what's happened."

"I'm being honest with you," Michael's mother said. "You don't have to tell me about the price of things. You be fair with me, I'll be fair with you, okay? I want what's best for him."

It was as if her words had floated out of the room, she sounded so strange and remote. For a moment Michael wanted to shout to his mother that he had heard his father warn her, but then he shrank back and stayed hidden.

"In the name of the Father, the Son and the Holy Spirit," the minister intoned on the sunny hillside and everyone in the sweaty crowd looked down except, as Michael observed, Michael himself. His mother held his hand. Maybe, like everybody else, Michael was supposed to pretend he didn't know what was happening. His father was dead, probably murdered by somebody, somebody he knew in business, that part of his parents' life that had really been so different from others'. Nobody was doing anything. Were they all too scared? Why did his mother want him out of town? He was old enough to take care of himself. Michael had made up his mind: he wasn't going back to New York, not now, not ever. They wouldn't try to get him on the plane if he was kicking and screaming in front of other people. That's what he would do if he had to, and he would tell them that this afternoon. Michael was scared, but he would be able to tell them, even though actually throwing a tantrum at the airport would probably be easier.

He knew he was not doing it for himself. He was not doing it for his mother either—she would know, but that didn't bother him. Michael was going to do it for his father, who wasn't supposed to be dead. Everybody knew it, but only Michael seemed to care. He wasn't going to say anything at all about it, not ever, but he was going to stay in Los Angeles and find out why his father had died, no matter what it took, no matter how long.

The undertaker was paid in full for the funeral before he left Forest Lawn. He had to wait until the last of the family moved away from the graveside before he could wave off the chauffeurs of the hearse and flower car, then he trudged down the hill toward the black Cadillac limousine in which the family was waiting. A few cars were still lined up behind, engines churning. The undertaker was perspiring heavily now, and it was going to be hours before he would be able to quit for the day. An old woman had been brought in and needed embalming, but even more unpleasant for the undertaker, he had to meet with his accountant in the evening to discuss taxes.

Twenty yards up from the service road, a sandy-haired man in an expensive gray suit and black tie walked toward him. The undertaker offered a small, tight-lipped professional smile. The man looked about thirty years old, but in Los Angeles he could actually be ten years older. The man stepped in front of the undertaker, blocking him from view.

"I want to thank you personally," the sandy-haired man said. The undertaker saw that he had a crooked, overlapping front tooth. "He didn't look like he'd been hit by a truck."

"That's the job," the undertaker said. The late Mr. Gallagher had sustained multiple fractures of the hips, thighs, and lower spine. From the waist down, Mr. Gallagher had been almost as shapeless as a pile of rags. The undertaker had had to wrap the legs with newspaper so they would support a pair of pants, even when the wearer was flat on his back. It had been a tricky job that had consumed almost a full roll of masking tape.

The sandy-haired man drew an envelope from the inside pocket of his jacket. "We took up a collection at the office.

It should cover what the widow owes you. If she calls you, tell her what I'm telling you, a collection we took at the office."

While the man watched, the undertaker opened the envelope. Inside was a blue embossed cashier's check for two thousand dollars, made out to the undertaker, Niles Eberhart.

"That should do it," the sandy-haired man said. "Any problems, Mr. Eberhart?"

Niles Eberhart kept his eyes down. Now he realized he understood the situation all along. Niles Eberhart was five feet eight inches tall and weighed 210 pounds. He was the first undertaker in America to wear muted striped suits to funerals, a real breakthrough. Niles Eberhart knew that the undertaker was an important part of the show he put on. "No, none at all."

"Well, you know what to tell Mrs. Gallagher." The man motioned toward the envelope. "It'd be a good idea to put that away."

Niles Eberhart tucked the envelope into his inside jacket pocket, and the man turned down the hill toward a four-door Oldsmobile 98 hardtop, a five-thousand-dollar car, not cheap. Gallagher had been some kind of an accountant or auditor, high up in the firm, and this sandy-haired man had implied he was a friend. Niles Eberhart had friends in banking who could help him trace a cashier's check, but he knew he would be making trouble for himself if he tried anything like that—asked so much as a single question.

The sandy-haired man with the crooked tooth had not been at the funeral home or at the graveside ceremony. Some people thought undertakers couldn't remember faces, but Niles Eberhart remembered everyone. Two thousand dollars, a nice round number. He was supposed to believe it had been collected in an accounting office. Hundreds more than the price of the funeral. The message was clear: forget about this. Niles Eberhart could remember everyone, the living as well as the dead, but he wanted to forget the sandy-haired man and everything about him.

In another minute he was sure he had all but forgotten completely. The two thousand was tax-free. Wife-free, too.

Niles Eberhart had just picked up a chunk of money he could spend on his own pleasure. He wasn't going to tell his accountant either. No, he was going to tell the accountant—not tonight, but later in the year—that Mrs. Gallagher had skipped on him, and that this year's tax return should show the Gallagher funeral as a bad debt.

Oh, hell, he was thinking a moment later as he approached the limo, if he was going to do that, he might as well rewrite the bill to show a twenty-five-hundred-dollar loss, maybe even three thousand.

Now the power window slid down—the widow wanted to have a word with him. The first eyes Niles Eberhart noticed were the boy's. The boy was staring at him, in that cold, distant way of grieving children. For just a second the boy's eyes dropped from Eberhart's own, dropped no more than eighteen inches or so, to the vicinity of Eberhart's inside jacket pocket, where the envelope was. The boy had seen what had happened on the hillside—he had been watching all along. Niles Eberhart couldn't help feeling a moment of fear, as young as the boy was, precisely because the boy's expression was so deathly—hating. . . .

But so what if the boy told his mother what he had seen? Niles Eberhart would simply tell her the truth as he understood it, exactly what the sandy-haired man had told him. And that would be the end of it. Mrs. Gallagher would not want more information . . . no, she would not want to pursue it at all. Niles Eberhart knew this dame: she would be happy if she never heard another word.

1985

BOOK ONE

1

MIKE GALLAGHER ROLLED OVER IN THE STRANGE BED
and smiled, his eyes still closed. He reached for Gretchen Heidl,
who was from Germany and a movie producer. Her side of the
bed was empty.

"Where are you?"

"In the bathroom."

Mike opened his eyes and stared at Gretchen's ceiling. He
had been running around with her for almost six months. She
was as bright as they came, but he was not in love with her, nor
she with him. They were marking time, and because they knew
it, they were friends.

It was four-thirty in the morning, still dark. Gretchen was
shooting her first movie in America, a big budget comedy starring Dick Albert and Connie Lyall, about a homosexual and a
lesbian who fall in love. Gretchen had told Mike that there were
actor problems, but she had not said more because of the names
involved. Only once or twice had they really discussed her work.

13

Mike loathed show business and the creeps involved in it. Gretchen agreed with him now—she had seen enough of Hollywood. She was here for the money, she said, and when she had it, she would be gone—another limit to their relationship, one that added to the respect between them.

This was Monday morning, and she had to be on the set very early. Mike liked getting up early anyway. Often he was at his desk at five-thirty. It was the Southern California weather, as close to paradise as the world could devise. The weather made you want to jump out of bed and get going. Construction and factory shifts started at seven, joggers were out with first light, and exercise gyms opened at six or earlier.

Now Gretchen came out of the bathroom and slipped back into bed. She was dark-haired and full-breasted, a little on the heavy side. They had met in Barney's Beanery in West Hollywood. Waiting to begin her first Hollywood feature, Gretchen had been exploring the city. She was a beer drinker, and Barney's carried over a hundred different brands. She had a slight German accent and still spoke English as if she had learned it in school, precisely, although she was almost completely fluent now. She was more surprised to discover that he was a cop than he was to learn she was a movie producer. She liked the idea of his being a homicide detective; what she didn't like was that he worked for the Los Angeles Police Department. If the newspaper accounts were right, she'd said once, LAPD was just plain vicious. Although she was from southern Germany, near Munich, home of the Nazi party, she considered herself a radical socialist. So they discussed his work as infrequently as they discussed hers.

Mike had done some bits in movies, fully satisfying his curiosity about them—making movies was like flying, hours of boredom punctuated by moments of stark terror. He had not seen her first movie, made in Germany—another comedy, about a pregnant girl looking for a husband—but at least he had heard of it. Gretchen was thirty-one and a tough cookie; she liked big, tough guys and wanted to have an affair.

"I have my own life," she had said. "I won't change my habits for you."

Mike was always careful, never fooling around with a woman

who had less to lose than he did. "Don't do your coke under my nose."

She laughed at him. "You sound so rough."

"Why don't you run around with crooks?" he asked.

"Oh, I do. The only difference between cops and crooks in this country is that the cops are better lays."

He smiled. "You have to explain that."

Gretchen had a husky, throaty laugh. She squeezed his bicep. "You cops are in better shape."

Mike crossed his eyes and Gretchen laughed again.

Mike understood the game she wanted to play. For as long as the game lasted, she would struggle and Mike would have to subdue her. The idea was to keep it light.

Gretchen was an aggressive, demanding lover who used her strength and nipped him with her teeth. She was curious about his failed marriage and surprised to learn that Judy was older than he was—thirty-six now. With the divorce Judy had quit teaching and gone into advertising. She had wanted to change her life. Mike never said more about Judy than that, and Gretchen professed astonishment that he didn't complain about his ex-wife, as so many men did. That kind of talk only made Mike's skin crawl.

In the predawn darkness, those thoughts faded easily. Gretchen liked to make noise in bed, and Mike loved noisy women. It was May, the windows were open, but that was no problem. This was Laurel Canyon, a rustic, aging, hilly neighborhood of hot tubs and cocaine, show business jerkoffs and hippies left over from the sixties. Mike knew it as well as he did because Judy had taught here, in the Canyon's only public school. Here people thought they could do anything, including fuck on the lawn. Mike knew that Gretchen loved that particular illusion of freedom, so he rode her harder. . . .

In another minute he heard the scuff of footsteps below the window. They sounded like an infantry squad running double time down the street. Joggers . . .

The sky was purple when Mike reawakened. Gretchen was out of bed again. From outside, and not far off, a woman cried out.

Mike sat up. "Gretchen?"

She stepped out of the bathroom, dressed in jeans and a T-shirt. "Relax. They're having a good time down the street again."

Mike heard the woman moan. She did not sound like she was in the throes of passion. Now furniture crashed.

"Which house is that?"

"Across the street, I think. I don't know." Gretchen turned away. "I'm never home."

"Don't kid me."

"They party," Gretchen called when she was in the bathroom again. "You're the cop, you figure it out."

Mike had his feet on the hardwood floor. For the moment there was silence, and Mike listened as he stood up. Gretchen rented this house, leased her furniture from Roberts Rents, dark oak Spanish colonial to complement the fake Spanish-mission exterior. She was a bit of a slob, with film scripts and clothing piled everywhere. He had to step over her high heels and then he put his foot down on a ball-point pen.

The wind had picked up, but through the rustling of the eucalyptus trees, Mike thought he could hear other sounds, so faint he couldn't be sure he was hearing anything at all. Another woman yelled. This time Mike heard a word, and there was no mistaking it.

"Don't!"

"Did you hear that?"

Gretchen stepped into the doorway again. "Was I supposed to?"

"This happens often?"

"Not so loud. But yes, it does. They yell. What are you going to do about it anyway? You're not supposed to be here in the first place. It's against department rules, isn't it?"

Yes, it was, because technically Gretchen was married. The marriage was nonfunctional and her husband was in Germany living as a single man, but the Los Angeles Police Department could tie the can to Mike's tail nevertheless. Mike had to forget about the noise across the street, much as it went against his instincts. He couldn't even phone it in to his own division without putting himself at bureaucratic risk. The Los Angeles Police Department's rules of behavior had nothing to do with the California Penal Code, the Constitution of the United States, or even the twentieth century, and the department had a gang of internal spies and squealers to make sure that the rules were enforced. An officer caught seeing a married woman was up for departmental charges. A captain would be in Chief Tom Cutler's office within the hour, and Mike, as an acting head of a Homicide Squad, whose job was insecure and still open to political infighting, could consider himself lucky if all he had to leave behind was his badge and pension rights. Mike and Gretchen had discussed all this when her disclosure of her marriage made it necessary. He'd told her about the Wednesday-morning meeting where his fellow supervisors discussed the personal lives of the people under them—no detail was too petty in the struggle to preserve LAPD careers. Gretchen thought it was disgusting and Mike couldn't argue with her. No matter, because the traditions, like Mount Rushmore, were there, and just about as subject to change.

Still naked, Mike was headed toward the bathroom when he heard footsteps out in the street again, this time going up the hill. What he had wanted to ask Gretchen slipped out of mind as he stopped and listened, holding his breath for silence. Gretchen stepped into the doorway and eyed him, but Mike remained focused on what was happening outside. The sounds beneath the window were not being made by athletes. Mike heard stumbling and hard breathing.

Gretchen threw her arms around his neck and kissed him on the mouth. "Put your shorts on and go down to the kitchen. Bacon and eggs are in the refrigerator. I made coffee. I will be down soon.

Downstairs Mike decided he wasn't hungry. When he had a cup of coffee, he went to the living-room window. Now the sky was bright enough to let him see into the shadows under the trees. Rainbow Drive was a straight, steep, tree-lined street climbing more than a mile to the rim of the canyon and a dirt road that led over the hill. Diagonally across the street from Gretchen's place was a row of two-story town houses. The garage door of the nearest house was up, showing a Jaguar sedan and a Datsun pickup truck inside. The gate to the little front garden was ajar, swinging against its wrought-iron frame. Mike was certain of his memory of the condition of the house on previous evenings and mornings: the occupants usually kept the garage door down, the gate locked. But there was nothing Mike could do after the fact of any crime committed in the house, never mind the question of putting himself in jeopardy.

The sunlight sparkled through the tops of the trees. On the other side of the canyon Mike could see the houses set on the top of the ridge, like teeth in a gum. Some of the roads at the top of the canyon were only ten feet wide, with sheer drops on both sides.

Gretchen came down in another few minutes. "I thought you would be making your breakfast."

"Who lives over there, where the garage door is open?"

"Are you still interested in that?"

"Then you know that's the house the sounds came from."

She stepped back, frowning. "What a snoop you are! I told you, the people there carry on—"

"Who are they?"

Mike had barely finished the question when his attention was distracted from an answer by the *whup, whup, whup* of a helicopter approaching over the jagged hills. He recognized the sound as that made by the helicopter used by several departments of the city of Los Angeles, including police and fire. Mike waved Gretchen back and peered upward through the eucalyptus to catch sight of the source of the approaching noise.

The helicopter swept into a slow circle—Mike could tell by the changing pitch of its sound. The machine swung into view, closer to the ground than he had imagined, below the rim of the canyon, over on its side, its spotlight housing poking from its nose like the mandible of a grasshopper, the familiar blue-and-white surveillance helicopter of the LAPD.

"What the hell are they doing here?" Gretchen asked.

Mike didn't answer, as still as an Indian listening to twigs breaking. Laurel Canyon was part of his division, Hollywood, and he thought he knew every major case Hollywood was working on. The helicopter could not have gotten here so quickly, so early in the day—if in fact something had gone wrong across the street—unless a police investigation was already in progress. Mike felt more uneasy than ever, because an investigation in progress meant that the action had originated at police head-quarters downtown, Parker Center. It was possible that the reasons at Parker Center for excluding Hollywood were benign, but Mike was too much a politician and knew Los Angeles too well to want to proceed on that assumption.

The helicopter made its fourth pass overhead. There could be no doubt that the object of its attention was the town house with the open garage door and swinging gate.

"They're not here to catch you fucking me, are they?"

Mike shook his head. "They would have telephoned while I had your legs in the air."

"I'm not in the telephone book."

"You're in our telephone book, just like everybody else. I'm going to drive you over to the studio this morning. Take a cab or have somebody give you a lift when it's time to come home."

"Why?"

"I want us to look like a couple going off to work."

Gretchen looked alarmed. "I don't want trouble with the studio. Will police be at the bottom of the street?"

It was a good question—he didn't know the answer.

"Let's just do it my way, okay? We'll be all right."

"You must think it is very serious if you want to use me for an alibi for getting away from here."

"I don't know," he said. "I'm telling you the truth. Is there anything *you* know about those people over there?"

He saw her stiffen with anger. "I've already told you everything, Mike."

At the top of Laurel Canyon Boulevard, where it looped over Mulholland Drive, Gretchen looked back to the helicopter slowly circling almost dead level with them, silent in the distance. She switched on the radio and turned the dial to KFWB, the all-news station. Mike thought it was much too soon for anything on the radio, but he said nothing. Neither of them had spoken since they'd gotten down to the foot of Rainbow Drive, where the only cop to be seen was Mike himself. He knew that the continuing silence between them wasn't helping, but he was afraid that anything he wanted to say would just trade further on the privileges of their relationship. He wanted to question her more closely about the people across the street. He liked Gretchen enough to want to avoid hurting her, and he disliked himself for the way he was finding it out, fighting his growing curiosity. But she was holding back—maybe only details, but they *were* something.

They were turning east on Ventura Boulevard when he said, "I'll call you later."

"Find out what happened," she said. "I want to know."

"You'll know. I'm sure you'll know."

"Should you have called the police? I know you *are* the police but should you have called someone?"

He drew a breath. "As it turned out I didn't need to. The helicopter was overhead before I had my underwear on. If I hadn't been with you, you would have thought nothing about any of it—that maybe someone else called the police. Let's not explore any other meanings just yet."

"You're saying that it could be serious."

"Yes, I think so."

"Damn it, Mike, I don't want to be involved!"

"In this context, Gretchen, that makes two of us." He glanced at her. "Got the idea?"

"The bottom line, as you people call it, is that I'm supposed to lie for you."

He never said "bottom line" and he knew that his annoyance with her phrasing was evidence only of his underlying tension. He had thirteen years invested in an ill-chosen career and waiting pension that could be gone in a flash because of her dead marriage, choice of residences, and that she had wanted to go to her place last night instead of his. He was tense, all right. "Just play dumb. We'll be talking."

"We'll be *talking*?"

"I hadn't finished." Now he was really controlling himself. "I had been going to say, I'll see that you know what to do and say to keep yourself as far from the situation as possible—okay?"

"What do you mean, 'as possible'?"

"You *live* across the street. The only way you can protect yourself during police questioning is to hire a lawyer, and even then he can only keep you from answering their questions, not them asking."

"I see." Coldly.

He took a breath. "You didn't see anything. You didn't hear anything that you hadn't heard before. The rest of the neighbors will have the same story to tell. That's all there is to it."

"I just hope it doesn't go any further than that," she said.

"It shouldn't." He turned in at the studio gate. To the guard, he said, "I'm going right out again." The guard peered across at Gretchen, recognized her, and nodded. Mike said, "We don't know yet what happened over there, do we?"

"We do know that *something* happened." She opened the door, but did not get out. "I know you're trying to protect yourself, Mike, and that's all right. Just don't push me around in the process. It just reminds me of what I don't like about Americans. You think you own the world."

He kept his hands on the steering wheel. Maybe she wouldn't see how tightly he was gripping it. "You've said that before and didn't get an argument out of me. You won't get one now."

"That's what I really care for about you." She managed a little smile and leaned over and kissed his cheek.

He wasn't paying attention. The traffic was still light—he could be through Cahuenga Pass in ten minutes. He wanted to see last night's reports. He wanted to see what kind of official business Hollywood Division had done in the hours since he had been there.

2

MIKE HATED THE NEW HOLLYWOOD DIVISION BUILD-
ing on Wilcox Avenue, a one-story, windowless building that
looked like a military bunker and told the neighborhood residents just how little the police trusted them. The new telephone company buildings were in the same "Future Siege"
style, and Mike wondered what the architects knew that hadn't
dawned on the rest of the world. In any event, Mike thought,
if you built for civil insurrection, you were going to get it,
because people weren't going to develop the internal mech-
anisms that prevented that kind of trouble. Mike knew from
what he saw going on inside the building that closing civil
authorities off like that created a certain paranoia in them.
Inside the building, where they couldn't see who they were
talking about, the racists and other haters said whatever they
damn pleased. Mike had stopped loving being a cop a long
time ago, and he knew exactly why: a lot of other cops, from
Tom Cutler on down.

The only human being in the world who knew that Mike felt as he did, as *intensely* as he did, was his partner and oldest friend, forty-year-old Dan Crawford. Dan himself was a little more than two years from retirement, and his plans were made. Good-bye Los Angeles, hello San Luis Obispo County. The Crawfords had owned a house near Avila Beach for years, and for the past five they had been fixing it up for year-round living. Neither Dan nor Marge cared what work they would do in San Luis, as everybody up there called it. San Luis was still the original California, full of bull ropers—cowboys—and less athletic drunks, as Dan described them. When Mike had expressed some reservation about Dan's ability to adjust down to that kind of slow pace—after all, if anyone could be called "Mr. Hollywood," it was Dan Crawford, who knew all the gossip in town—Dan had said that police work had never been more than a small part of his life, even if he had been the last in his family to realize it. Dan and Marge had been married the day they graduated from high school, almost twenty-two years ago. They had three kids, two of them already out of the nest and sharing houses with people their own age. "I'm really a suburban capon," Dan had said. "I couldn't wait to get married, settle down, have kids, and turn my paycheck over to my wife. Now I'm gray and turning to mush. I'm in terrible shape for a cop and I don't care a nun's fart."

Dan had trained Mike as a detective, letting him make small mistakes, then gently correcting him, in the process of teaching Mike how to *think*. Mike had made detective with the reputation for being the strongest white guy in the department; it was Dan who had made him know, as no other person ever had, that he had a brain. One night in Leon's on Victory Boulevard in the Valley, Mike had called him on that. Dan was more drunk than Mike. Mike had been a skinny kid, but he had filled out in his teenage years when he had played three years of varsity football for North Hollywood High. At six-three and 230 pounds, Mike could absorb as much beer as any of the six detectives who made up Hollywood Homicide, the only people with whom he ever did any real beer drinking. Mike hated whiskey. He had seen enough of it go into his mother to last him the rest of his life. "The most important thing I've learned since I've known you, you old turd, is that I'm probably crazy."

"Well, you're better off," Dan said. "Before, you were just as crazy, only you didn't know it."

"I'm not as happy as I used to be," Mike drawled.

"That's your reward for getting older," Dan said. "Besides, you were never really happy anyway."

"That's true. I wasn't even happy when my father was alive. I used to hear them fighting about some goddamned thing or other."

"All right, now that you have all the answers, shut up." Dan turned to Leon's piano player. "Do you know 'I'll Be Loving You in Hallways'? How about 'I'm Undressing 'Cause I Love You'?" Dan had a marvelous tenor voice he exercised mostly when he was well-oiled. That night, Dan had everybody in the bar in stitches with Tom Lehrer's "Masochism Tango."

Dan didn't arrive at Hollywood Division until a quarter to eight—not late, but after Juan Lopez and Bill Blair, which meant that Mike could not talk to Dan privately here. The six detectives of Homicide were stationed near the rear of the large anonymous room where all of Hollywood's detectives and plainclothesmen were supposed to do their paperwork. Homicide desks were pushed together, the large surface covered with papers, telephones, in and out baskets, and general litter. Calls were taken in rotation, and whether the problem was an old guy who had died in his bed without a doctor or a quadruple ax murder, it was your problem until it was cleared. The murder rate in Hollywood was nowhere near as high as people thought, only a fraction of the rate in South-Central L.A., the ghetto, but because Hollywood was the roosting place of transients, thrill seekers, the star-struck, ruthless fortune hunters, and other trash, some Hollywood cases turned out to be very difficult to clear indeed. Police critics loved to point out that the L.A. sheriff cleared a higher percentage of cases than Hollywood Division, but in many suburban areas the sheriff's deputies often arrived at a murder scene to find a wife standing over her dead husband with a bloody knife in her hand. In Hollywood, sometimes it took the coroner to tell detectives whether the pieces found in a motel room were male or female. Cases like that were solved with information. Every one of the six of Hollywood Homicide had his own collection of grifters, sleazeballs, scumbuckets, moochers, and just plain slime who supplied him with tips, only a few of which ever paid off. Everybody had had a case open for years that had been solved by a lucky break—a cellmate squealing for reduced time, an ex-wife trying to square accounts, a tip coming from another division or an agency outside the department. After all that, you had to go down to the DA's office and present your evidence to an assistant whose eye was squarely on his own career: if a case wasn't an easy win, he'd throw it back to you like an undersized fish, and the division was saddled with the lousy statistic.

Politics and careerism decided everything. Mike was *acting* head of Homicide because people downtown said that they weren't sure that he could handle the administrative and paperwork sides of the job. That wasn't it. The people downtown were concerned with their own statistics, which Mike had to deliver—and which he was too honest to fake. If the downtown people saw that he wasn't going to make them look bad, they would remove the stigma of *acting* from his title. To the best of his knowledge, there never had been an *acting* on this level before, but no one above him cared about that. It was Mike's problem, if he was stupid enough to allow himself to worry about it. He knew better than to do that: it just made him angry enough to tell people to kiss his hairy Irish ass. He wanted to keep the job.

Mike and Dan had a motel room murder, maybe an easy one, probably a rip-off, that had gone down last Friday, and a homosexual killing up in the hills that was already a week old. The victim had been a chicken hawk and one of his young prey had probably turned on him. Dan had the motel room murder autopsy to observe this afternoon, and Mike had caught a dead body call just minutes before the arrival of the others.

"I've got to have some breakfast before we hit the bricks," Mike said. It meant he had something on his mind.

"I can always eat again," Dan said.

"Mike's been waving his big dick again," the mustached Lopez said cheerfully to Blair. "Eat, fuck, eat, fuck: it's all he knows."

Blair looked up from a form he was filling out by hand, laboriously block printing so it could be read ten years from now, if necessary. A lot of cops never learned to type, in spite of all the reports to be filled out. "Don't you ever shit, Mike?"

"White guys don't shit," Lopez said. Blair was black. He was thirty-five, balding, one of those skinny blacks who seem to age rapidly.

"They shit when they die," Blair said.

"Maybe they save it up," Lopez said. "Maybe that's why they're white, from the strain."

"Where's Novak?" Mike asked. Nobody knew where Greg Novak was. The sixth man, Marvin Burgess, who was also black, had the day off. Novak and Burgess were partners, as were Blair and Lopez. Dan Crawford spoke Spanish, which gave Homicide two in that language. What was needed were people who could speak Korean, Vietnamese, Cantonese, Japanese, and Thai. Asian and Pacific peoples were rapidly outnumbering everybody else in Hollywood. Seventy percent of the motels in the division were owned by Asians, and most couldn't speak English. At least they cooperated with the police. "Hold the fort," Mike said. To Dan, he added, "We'll take the db on our way to breakfast."

Walking around to the parking lot, Mike told Dan that after he cleared the db, he wanted to take a quick run up into Laurel Canyon. "We'll take your car." Dan was already on full alert, and by the time they reached the apartment house on Romaine Street where the old woman lay dead, Mike had told him everything he had heard and seen that morning on Rainbow Drive.

"But you still don't know what happened," Dan said.

"No, but I'll have a better idea after a drive-by. The way things are laid out up there, we'll be able to get a look at what's going on, if anything, from half a mile away"

"Did you check our files this morning?"

"First thing. Burglary, narcotics. We have nothing active on Rainbow Drive."

"That's on paper," Dan said.

"On paper."

Upstairs in the dead woman's apartment, a young medical examiner was refusing to release the body to her niece's husband, who had already called the undertaker. The corpse was in the bedroom on the floor next to a dresser, a dental plate, an upper, two feet from the mouth. The woman had been dead at least a day, because the apartment air was thick with the smell of death.

"The guy's wife is working," the medical examiner said. "He says that they expected this, that the old lady had a heart condition. If she was taking drugs for her heart, I'll sign her off, but there are no drugs in the bathroom medicine chest or by her bed. If you guys can find her medicine, it'll be one less autopsy we'll have to do."

"Don't give us that," Mike said good-naturedly. "You love every one of them." He turned to the niece's husband, who was one of those fairhaired, pear-shaped guys who looked as if he shaved once a month. "What do you know about this medicine?"

"We weren't that close to her." He looked terrified of Mike.

"She took this stuff every day? Four times a day? She was an old lady. She must have told you."

"Wait a minute. Morning, noon, and night. That's it. I remember."

"Go look in the kitchen," Mike said. "Around the sink and in the refrigerator."

He left. Dan was smiling. "She had a heart attack and fell," Mike said to the medical examiner. "She was dead before she hit the floor. It was the force of the fall that knocked her teeth out of her mouth. That's all that happened. If she'd been alive, she'd have tucked them back in."

"I got it!" the young man called. "I have the medicine!"

The medical examiner passed over his form for Mike to sign. Mike wrote the medical examiner's name in his notebook while the medical examiner glanced around the dingy apartment. "How did you know where the medicine was?"

"She had to take it with meals. When you live alone, you arrange things to suit yourself."

"Another case closed," Dan said, not exactly suppressing his mirth. Going down the stairs, he said, "I think I'll pass that on to the others. Sometimes you're not such a bad little detective."

"I should have gone across Rainbow Drive this morning."

"It was already going down when you heard it. Were you going to enter that house in your skivvies? You heard a lot of guys, and you don't know that they weren't armed. Don't go looking for ways to die, kid; it's much too easy."

Mike had been thinking only of himself this morning. He knew it. He still was, hoping that Gretchen would keep him out of anything she might have to tell investigating officers, and, that in fact—as he thought—no one saw him leaving her place this morning. He had timed his steps from her house to his car to coincide with the seconds the helicopter's view of the street was hidden by the overarching trees.

Dan hated Laurel Canyon, and in that he shared the majority opinion. Outsiders always had a hard time understanding the Canyon, with its near-vertical hillsides, rickety, precarious houses, and incendiary vegetation. In the fire season the chaparral—mesquite, sage, and a hundred other types of low-lying shrub, in soft, muted tones of purple, blue, and olive—swelled with resins more explosive than gasoline. The streets were too steep for walking, the lots too rocky and angled for much gardening. In the winter rainy season came the more lethal danger of mud slides. But the Canyon was a bit of wilderness in the geographic center of Los Angeles, which in itself was desirable to some, and the contours of the land formed natural amphitheaters so that, from many sites, people could see each other from distances of a mile or more.

It made for neighborliness on a large scale. People moved here for refuge from the city and for informal living, but the rigors of life in the Canyon as much as its charms led to both cooperation and self-reliance. Neighborliness led to friendships that were healthy or unproductive depending on the people involved, and in extreme cases the privacy led to secretiveness that sometimes concealed criminal activity. As more than one dope dealer had explained, the police could be spotted a long way off. Laurel Canyon wasn't called Cocaine Alley for nothing. On the other hand, Europeans had told Mike that Laurel Canyon was one of the few places in America where creative people could find a sense of community with which they felt comfortable. For Mike that was the key—after all the analyses and judgments, one thing made Laurel Canyon unique among Los Angeles neighborhoods: it was always *intense.*

And by ten-thirty on this Monday in May, the Canyon atmosphere was so highly charged that a wise old hand like Dan Crawford warily slowed his car to fifteen miles an hour. The helicopter, or its successor, circled overhead, and people out on their decks or front steps to watch it turned their attention down to the passing car and its two occupants. Mike had hoped for inconspicuousness, but that would have been impossible for any two strangers, much less a pair of sport-coated guys who obviously were the heat. There was still nothing on KFWB, which meant that there had been no public announcement yet.

At the foot of Rainbow Drive, a T intersection, a uniformed officer was directing the driver of a station wagon to pull over to the side. Two hundred feet up Rainbow was a black and white, too far for any special markings on it to be read from the cross street below.

"Let's keep on going," Mike said.

"No shit, Sherlock." Dan stepped on the gas, but not too heavily, and kept his eye on the interior mirror. "He's not watching us."

"From what I've seen from Gretchen's place, we'll get a good view of Rainbow Drive from the ridge on the opposite side. Gretchen says that there's a road at the top that runs all the way around.''

"I've seen those fucking roads," Dan said sourly. "Some of them are about four feet wide. The Indians used to blind-fold their horses up there."

Dan was stretching it. City garbage trucks were up there every week. "Want me to drive?" Mike asked.

"No, thanks. I still remember Mexico."

So did Mike, who couldn't help smiling. Mike and Judy and Dan and Marge had driven down to Ensenada, and on the way back to the hotel after a dinner that had been awful because everybody had been trying to have a good time in spite of the impending collapse of the Gallaghers' marriage, Mike had missed a turn and put Dan's car in a ditch. No one had been hurt and the damage to the car had been minimal, but the Mexican authorities had acted as if the gringos had been using their country for a public toilet. The divorce had taken humor out of the incident for a while, but the divorce was now six years old, ancient history.

At the top of the hill Dan wheeled the car into a hard left and then followed the thinly paved track around toward the city, which revealed itself below them, glinting in the haze. Up here they were exposed to the helicopter, but there was nothing they could do about that except keep their attention roving naturally. People made the mistake of not looking at the cops, and that aroused a cop's suspicions faster than any-thing else.

From Gretchen's house Mike had noticed a particular brown-and-beige cliff-hanger house with an empty lot beside it. From the lot he and Dan would be able to see the full length of Rainbow Drive where it wasn't shrouded by trees. In the old days the spot must have been a nice place for a picnic. Now it was just another patch of dry weeds in the urban sprawl that stretched north, south, and east for a hundred miles.

Today the lot served as a viewing platform for a half-dozen men and women, all of them barefoot and in shorts. The women, uncombed and without makeup, were wearing T-shirts or tank tops. No bras. Mike recognized one of the men as a television actor who had been around for years, having graduated from playing teenagers to villains. When he turned away from the stopping car, he said something to the others, and they glanced back at its occupants.

"We're made," Dan said.

"Up here," Mike said, "we stick out like sore dicks."

"Why do they dress like that? They don't dress like that in Pine Fucking Bluff, Arkansas. Remember when everybody in L.A. wore suits and dresses, like back East?"

"I'm not that old," Mike said. "Let's stay in the car. We can see everything from here."

From this angle, Rainbow Drive was as straight and deeply sloped as the downhill plunge of a ski jump. Trees obscured about half of it, but on both sides, from the bottom, where the police barricade could be seen, all the way to the top, where the pavement faded in crumbling chunks into a dirt track, the roofs of the houses looked like the patches on a quilt, red and green shingles, gray tar paper, brown cedar shake. The steepness of the slope and the small size of the lots made all the houses multilevel, but that was the only interesting thing about them. They were junk, like the cheap houses in poor rural areas, painted the same colors. Here and there was a house slathered with stucco, soft concrete mix sprayed on turkey wire with a gun, and which had all the strength of the icing on a piece of stale birthday cake. The action was in the middle of the long street, where four or five black and whites gleamed through the foliage. You had to look carefully to see the uniformed officers and the plainclothesmen gathered in front of the house across the street from Gretchen's place. From here Mike could see the open window of her bedroom. The sun was shining on a portion of the sheet on her bed. Mike realized he was probably looking at one of his own pubic hairs.

"I'm not that old either," Dan said. "I have a good memory from my childhood. I can remember when the Korean War started."

"I was born that year," Mike said dryly. "You know, if I hadn't been across the street when the thing happened and the helicopter arrived, what I'd be wondering was how the case got downtown without going through Hollywood Division. I checked that, too. Nobody up here called the division from midnight on.''

"Well, it's a nice neighborhood," Dan said. "What do you know so far? Something violent happened in the house. The helicopter was overhead minutes later. Nobody called the cops. Therefore, the cops—*those* cops—were charting activities in the house before you heard the violence. Either they had a bug, or—"

"Say it."

"Or they had somebody inside. Wheels within wheels."

Mike wished his palms were as dry as his mouth. He felt strange and distant, almost sick.

"Or one of the guys I heard on the street was a somebody. That's nasty, but we have to keep our options open."

"Let's boogie," Dan said. "If they want us, they'll call us."

"Unless they're going to try to hang something on us. Remember just a few years ago they busted those plain-clothesmen guys for being a burglary ring? After all the publicity and the bullshit and reputations ruined and careers wrecked, every one of those guys was acquitted."

"And out of the department, not incidentally." Dan sat up. "Here we go."

Mike saw it. At the bottom of Rainbow Drive, crawling its way up to the house. Mike's palms itched. The vehicle wasn't going anywhere else: the sickly beige van of the county coroner. The Meat Wagon.

Mike was at his desk again at eleven-fifteen—he had decided to make a point of checking his watch regularly now, remembering times, what he saw, what he was doing. He couldn't take notes. If he took notes, he'd have to find a place to hide them. Greg Novak had come and gone. In addition to the division's homicides, Mike's unit had to cover everything else as time and manpower allowed. There was still no record of Hollywood having any knowledge of the activities in Laurel Canyon, which in itself did not mean anything.

LAPD was a welter of overlapping divisions, squads, teams—
at Parker Center downtown they were supposed to have it all
sorted out, but critics often said the department was top-
heavy, with too many brass. Top-heaviness was possibly the
least of the department's problems. The ACLU had been
fighting in the courts for years to get the department to stop
spying on the political activities of citizens, sending agents
to political meetings to stir up trouble, drawing law-abiding
people into crimes. Confidential police documents that should
have never existed in the first place had been found in the
computer banks of private right-wing watchdog committees
organized by the same people who sent guns to overseas
counterrevolutionaries. Before Mike had been transferred to
Hollywood Division from Devonshire in the west Valley, a
herd of Hollywood officers were charged with the seduction
of Girl Scouts who had been interning for merit badges. Mike
had been told that only a fraction of the real story had ever
been made public. And currently, a former meter maid convicted of pandering was claiming that she had been framed
by police because she had been writing a book—about what?
The sexual antics of her former colleagues on the LAPD.

The lesson to be learned from all that was clear to Mike.
Covering one's own ass could not be a passive activity. You
had to be careful about the people you took for your friends,
learn everything you could about them, and then *still* calmly
consider what you confided in them. You had to be careful
about what was going on around you, at the next desk, across
the room—if something was going sour, you could be sure
that those who had organized it were going to look for someone else to take the blame for the mess. And you had to be
careful most of all of the people with authority over you,
because while people sought authority and loved having it,
they never wanted to accept its attendant responsibility.

For them, you existed to serve not only in good times, but
bad: when the dogs came howling, you were the meat thrown
to them. Those who did the throwing never thought twice,
except perhaps to enjoy a moment of self-congratulation for
having survived another of their own fuckups.

Mike had three hours of paperwork waiting for him, and

then he wanted to have another look at the chicken hawk file. The one solid piece of evidence was a thumbprint on the headboard of the victim's bed. The coroner had found coarse red hair glued in lubricant on the victim's penis, and Mike and Dan had found fine, very short red hair in the brush on the sink in the victim's bathroom. There were a lot of young men with crew cuts out on the street these days, punks and other crazies, but the victim's friends had said that he liked the clean-cut boys—very cleancut. At first Mike had thought that the victim had been afraid of the disease that was all too easy to pick up from Hollywood's street kids. Moreover, no one in the division had picked up any street chatter about a local boy offing a faggot. There had been no robbery either, which would have been part of that MO. Now Mike was thinking something else entirely. It wouldn't be the first time: Hollywood could have a file of such cases if somebody could be bothered to put it together. Mike called Camp Pendleton and asked to speak to the commandant.

"Let me see if I understand you, Mr. Gallagher. You want the names of all the red-haired recruits who were on liberty two weekends ago."

"All the enlisted men, actually."

"Can we exclude the drill sergeants? It will make the job at this end a lot easier."

"Sure."

"Can we keep this quiet? It reflects badly on the Corps."

"We can't keep it quiet if one of your people did it. What I can promise you is confidentiality through the investigatory phase."

"Why did you call Pendleton?"

"It's the nearest base with unproved troops."

"The Corps is an elite unit, you know—"

"I know," Mike said. "I was at Khe Sanh."

"Why didn't you say so?"

"It's just what I did instead of going to college."

"I'm sorry you feel that way—"

"Don't misunderstand, Commandant. I loved the Marines. I just didn't like getting shot at. I don't even like remembering it."

"Were you wounded?"

"No." Novak came in and pulled up to his desk. He was twenty-eight and could hardly remember Vietnam, much less the siege of Khe Sanh back in the sixties. To the commandant, Mike said, "I got my love letters scorched. Don't ask me how, because even then I didn't know."

"We'll have that information for you as quickly as possible, Mr. Gallagher."

"Off the top of your head, how many men do you think we're talking about?"

"Off the top of *my* head, none. I'm white-haired. Maybe thirty or forty."

Mike grinned. "Semper fi, General."

"Semper fi."

Greg Novak was staring at him. He was one of those well-tanned, yellow-haired Southern Californians. He looked as if he spent all his time at the beach, but in fact he lived in the Valley not far from Mike and got his muscles and coloring from Nautilus machines and tanning lamps. Lopez and Blair kidded Mike about being single, but they had no idea what Novak's life was like. In those co-ed gyms, a healthy guy had only to mind his own business to have the women melting all over him, like butter on an ear of corn.

"What was that all about?"

"The chicken hawk killing. The victim liked them clean-cut. What's more clean-cut than a marine?"

Novak shook his head. "You have to grow into this work, that's for sure. I don't know if I'd have the balls to call the commandant at Pendleton and tell him I think one of his boys has been wearing a dress."

"Let's see if it gets the son of a bitch. What have you been up to?"

"I presented that vehicular homicide this morning—that female DUI who hit the carload of Mexicans? The DA says it looks like she can cop a plea to a reduced charge because it happened at an intersection and she'll claim that she was making a left turn."

"At fifty miles an hour and 1.7 in her bloodstream? A cop

could suck shit for some of these DA's and they'd tell him the stuff is nutritious for plants.''

"I'll remember that line," Novak said.

"Dan Crawford said it first."

"Then I had a db on Las Palmas, a young guy. Heroin overdose.''

Mike had forgotten he had asked the kid what he had been doing. Novak was being conscientious today. "Apartment or private house?''

"Parked car in the lot down from Miceli's. No ID. The car had a stolen Michigan plate.''

The telephone rang. "He gets the regular treatment, not the deluxe,'' Mike said as he picked up. "Homicide, Hollywood. Gallagher.''

"*Mike* Gallagher?''

A guy. "None other.''

"This is Bob Wills of the *Herald-Examiner*. I want to ask you about the five murders in Laurel Canyon.

Suddenly Mike could hear the air roaring in his ears. It was like being thrown out of an airplane, the shock was so intense and long-lasting. With what felt like the last shred of consciousness he remembered to look at his watch: three-fifteen. Novak was looking at him out of the corner of his eye, probably because Mike was out of his chair. Mike realized that the room was coming back into focus. *Five*! He spoke slowly: "Maybe you ought to call Lieutenant Whatley at the press office downtown for that kind of information, like all the other reporters.'' Mike hung up. Novak was feigning reading a report—if Mike had given something away to him, what had the reporter heard? "Tell Dan to hang around until I call him. I'll try to make it before five-thirty.''

3

THE ROADWAY AT THE FOOT OF RAINBOW DRIVE WAS squeezed by police barricades to a single lane, and three uniformed officers were checking the identifications of all who wanted to go up the hill, police, members of the press, elements of the coroner's team, and Rainbow Drive residents, most of whom were angry to learn that they would be told where to park, and then would have to walk the rest of the way to their homes—for some, almost a mile up a hill so steep they would be better off on a flight of stairs.

The climb took the fight out of everybody. More barricades kept people back from the area slathered with cardboard notices printed CRIME SCENE, and for good measure, two more uniformed officers and three plainclothesmen were standing at the gate of the house. The plainclothesmen were dragging on cigarettes, but looked no less purposeful. Mike saw that the coroner's van had not moved from where it had stopped this morning. Mike's badge was in plain view, but his palms were wet, and not from the effort of the uphill hike. This was all too carefully orchestrated for it to be pure police work— *good* police work. Fifty feet beyond the crime scene—in front of Gretchen's house, in fact—television, radio, and print reporters talked among themselves like dockworkers at a shapeup. Two of the three local network outlets had news programs starting at four o'clock; if, as Mike suspected, the release of the story was being timed for proper exposure, no one would think twice about it, because it was done all the time. The Los Angeles press was as uncaring about what it was fed as an old woman's fat dog. The local stations expected the networks to get first crack at the stories, and the *Herald-Examiner*'s and *Daily News*'s combined circulation was half that of the giant *Times*, which in 1979 sent twenty people to cover a brushfire here in Laurel Canyon and managed to report the blaze on Mount Olympus, the adjoining neighborhood.

As he stepped up to the gate, Mike recognized one of the plainclothesmen, a guy named Burke. The last Mike had heard of him, Burke had been working burglary in North Hollywood, busier than a McDonald's fries guy at lunch hour.

"Whattaya say, Burke? Moving up in the world?"

"Yeah, Mike. I hear the same about you. I didn't know Hollywood was being invited."

"Well, I got a call," Mike said, passing through. "How is it in here?"

"Forget your dinner plans."

As he entered the house Mike knew from experience the meaning of what he was feeling. The sensation started in his back and his bowels, and then spread out to the arms and legs, a kind of hyperawareness that didn't involve the brain. The brain didn't want to know, or maybe it already knew too much. Beyond the little entry, the living room was being slowly washed with the lights attached to a video camera— videotape was the modern way to record the evidence at a crime scene. Police had been in the house since at least tenthirty, to Mike's certain knowledge, but almost surely hours before that, and they were getting to videotape only now. They were being more methodical than heart-transplant surgeons. Why? Against the wall, sitting on the floor, was a male Caucasian, dead, in shorts, the top of his head so hammered by blows with an object like a crowbar or lead pipe that his brains bulged out of his exposed and fragmented skull like the meat of a broiled lobster tail. His tongue protruded from his mouth. His eyes were open. Thick spatters of blood and tissue arched up the wall and across the ceiling. A little while ago Mike had been sorry that he had reminded himself of Vietnam, but now he wasn't: what was fresh in his mind again was that he had seen worse than this, and in quantity. The stairs to the second floor were narrow, and more plainclothesmen stood up at the top, talking. Somewhere up there, a dog was whining. Mike wanted to avoid being questioned about his presence here, if that was possible, and so he stood back from the team videotaping the living room. Overhead, the joists above the ceiling creaked as the men moved around, and Burke entered the house.

"Ambulance," he said to the men at the top of the stairs.

"They saw it. They're coming down now."

Ambulance? Mike almost cursed aloud. Before Burke turned around, Mike slipped back outside, his heart pounding. The other plainclothesmen at the gate seemed to take no notice of him. He hoped not. He had to walk around the back of the arriving ambulance to stay out of the line of sight of most of the men in front of the house. Then he hiked up the street to the crowd of reporters. He recognized four or five of the television people, but none of the regulars who covered Hollywood Division. Mike didn't want to answer questions— he didn't want to be put on record in any way. As a group of plainclothesmen and Dr. Elmer Washington, the Los Angeles County coroner, emerged from the house and climbed briskly toward the reporters, Mike turned his back to them and tucked his badge into his breast pocket. As the reporters crowded around the officials, Mike eased to the back of the pack. He would hear what was being said at home on his own television set on the rebroadcasts at five, six, and eleven o'clock. He remembered that he had not called Gretchen, who would probably learn all this from the same programs. Now the young, mustached plainclothesman who was acting as police spokesman headed up the hill a little, swinging the attention of the reporters away from the house. Mike was breathing through his mouth. He knew what was coming—he was almost afraid to turn his head around toward the house. The best way to slide something past a group of people was to do it under their noses. Mike could hear the plainclothesman describing the carnage inside. The bedroom upstairs looked the same as what Mike had seen in the living room. Dead were three men and two women. No IDs yet. All the victims but one had been found in bed. Out of the corner of his eye Mike saw the back door of the ambulance swing open. Now the reporters had questions. Mike didn't have to see what was going on behind him, but he really didn't want to hear the young plainclothesman's bullshit either. Mike heard the door of the ambulance click shut—were they being *that* careful, closing the door quietly? The plainclothesman stepped back, and Elmer Washington moved into the center of the circle to take his place. Washington was a big, black man who perspired freely and was almost always disheveled. The ambulance motor was started and Mike could see it being swung into a quiet U-turn. From the gate, Burke saw Mike glancing at the ambulance.

"Is this where you want me to stand?" Elmer Washington asked.

All day. The police had been here *all day*! Of course Washington was doing what he had been told. The proof was in how quiet he was—for him. Last year, when an actress's body was found on the beach in Malibu and later proved to be overdosed on speedballs, Washington thought he could aggrandize himself by calling a news conference to condemn the excesses of "certain members of the movie colony." The actress had been loved too much, in spite of her bad habits, for important people not to resent Washington's comment. Washington received a public reprimand from Norman Birnbaum, the studio production chief who had guided the actress's early career—and was now, incidentally, Gretchen's boss. It was the soft-spoken Birnbaum's first utterance to the press in more than a dozen years, and his puffy, heavy-lidded, lizardlike eyes shimmered with what was supposed to be grief. Later a young comic at the Ice House in Pasadena

RAINBOW DRIVE   41

said it was one of the ten worst moments in Hollywood acting. ''Dr. Washington may be an authority on death,'' Birnbaum whispered hoarsely, glaring balefully at the handful of
gathered reporters, ''but he has a lot to learn about life.''

Apparently Washington was now willing to stoop to the
complete disgrace of conspiracy to commit malfeasance in
office, participating in the delay in getting the survivor of the
attack to the hospital. Mike's thoughts were focused sharply
on how he was going to get out of here, but that did not stop
him from hoping that Elmer Washington would choke to death
on his very next words:

''We have a survivor.''

Mike thought of Gretchen again before he reached Laurel
Canyon Boulevard, and called her office from one of the pay
telephones outside the Canyon Country Store, but she was in
a meeting. Movie people were always in meetings; it was a
wonder that they were ever able to make a movie. Mike told
her secretary that he would leave a message for Gretchen on
her home answering machine. He called Dan Crawford next,
but Bill Blair told Mike that Crawford had left early without
saying a word to anybody. Mike was halfway down the Valley
side of the hill heading for home when he realized that he
had forgotten to call Gretchen's machine at home, as he had
said. In the welter of miserable new information that had
come in, it seemed just too easy to lose sight of the fact that
he needed her to stand up for him now more than ever. As
slovenly as the Los Angeles press was, if the fact that investigating police had kept a survivor from medical care became
an unavoidable story, then the people responsible for that
moral disaster would be looking everywhere for someone or
something—anything—to obscure that central fact and the
reasons for it. An experienced homicide detective with a
medal for valor who had been just across the street and must
have heard the killings was made to order for sacrifice. Mike's
position was indefensible: he had been reaching the male
orgasmic plateau when he'd heard the killers double-timing
down the street to the house; his postcoital snooze had been

interrupted only by the louder screams of the dying. And to put a polish on his career's tombstone, he had not gone out into the street with his .38 because the woman who had been moaning under him was married to another man, a fact known to him at the time he had entered into the relationship. Bad luck had nothing to do with it. Gretchen's husband's activities in Munich were besides the point, too. Mike had known the rules in advance and the people in charge would zero in on that fact alone.

Under the circumstances, he was more than willing to tell those people to go fuck themselves—except that he didn't want to be fitted for the collar they alone had reason for him to wear.

They might go for it even if they never found out about Gretchen and him—his sex life was something he was pretty famous for already. The kidding he took regularly from Lopez and the others wasn't simply something he tolerated with good humor; it was unavoidable because it was based on what was known about him. Mike was a good-looking guy in a beat-up, sad-eyed way, and women liked him. He liked them back. As he had grown older, he had come to see that there was a world of difference between his attitude—and the attitude of the women he ran around with—and those of what seemed like most other people: if you wanted to get them pissed off at you, act as if you had a sex life and enjoyed it. Add to that the fact that on more than one occasion Mike had been offered shots at a career as an actor, and the little rat-brained bastards of the world saw a guy whose life was a roller-skate through the buffalo herd, no matter what the deeper reality. Appearances counted, and on the basis of appearances, the social, moral, and sexual teeny-weenies wanted to get Mike Gallagher.

And how did they have their opportunity without knowing about Gretchen and him? Mike would have seen the answer— or the answer *confirmed*—in that living room on Rainbow Drive without a corpse propped against the wall. The shoddy furniture, the filth, the Jaguar, what Gretchen had told him about the partying going on in the house, all added up to dope dealing, and not necessarily on a grand scale, but one of a thousand setups, estimated conservatively, in Los Angeles, or maybe just Hollywood Division alone. A quintuple murder in the house was only the window dressing required to make the deal look like the kind of sloppy law enforcement that could be hung on Hollywood Division, its key personnel, and its still-provisional head of homicide, simply because they were easy pigeons. Mike wanted to resist. He wanted to defend himself.

The quick arrival of the helicopter showed that there had been a police operation centered on that house, and the murders showed that somebody involved with the operation had fucked up. The importance of that somebody, or perhaps something else entirely, could be seen in the disgusting delay in getting the survivor to medical attention. A lot of people were involved already, a lot of people who had voluntarily or involuntarily put their careers on the line—for whom? That didn't matter as far as Mike was concerned. What mattered to Mike *right now* was that all those people, including the totally self-serving and clownish Elmer Washington, had already committed at least one criminal offense and had to be willing to commit more as necessary to cover themselves. They had gone to the limit already. Why had they kept the survivor from medical attention for *so long*?

Mike lived well. He rented a one-bedroom condo in Toluca Lake, almost a thousand square feet in a complex with a pool, hot tub, sauna, and game room with billiard tables. He used the pool and sauna, but otherwise kept to himself. He couldn't enjoy a hot tub if he had to wear a bathing suit, and he had given up billiards and variants thereof when he had graduated high school. Most of the people in the complex were drawn into themselves in the same way, or, if friendly, had all-too-obvious problems. Mike's unit was owned by a Japanese executive who had once thought he would have a lot of business in L.A., and the place was now either an investment for him or up for sale—Mike was never sure which. A Mexican cleaning woman came in every other week, and left the ticket for his shirts at the Chinese laundry for Mike to find when he came home. An Iranian owned the 7-Eleven where Mike did his incidental shopping, except for the frozen dinners he bought at Alpha-Beta for heating in his Korean microwave oven when he wasn't out for Thai, Indian, or East African food, his current favorites. He had told all this to Gretchen when she asked if he minded her being German, and then the next time they saw each other he gave her a bumper sticker that said, WELCOME TO CALIFORNIA—NOW GO HOME. She was giddy with laughter when she put it on her car.

The message light on his answering machine was flashing, but Mike called Gretchen's machine at once, asking her to call him back as soon as possible. Mike had heard that people on the East Coast were resisting these gizmos, which made no sense if the purpose of the telephone was communication. The message on Mike's tape was from Dan, another of their codes: "Call me back anytime this evening except between nine-thirty and ten, when I'll be out for hamburgers."

Dan would be at his local Burger King, where Mike had the number of the pay telephone. Dan would be waiting for Mike's call, which would be made from a bar on Riverside. Dan had been at the county coroner's building this afternoon; maybe he had picked up something about Elmer Washington's performance on Rainbow Drive. Given what Mike already knew about the murders—the murderers had arrived on foot, from somewhere up Rainbow Drive's steep hill—the problem of Gretchen's telephone security had already occurred to him. The telephone company *always* cooperated with the police—that was what Mike had meant when he had said she was in their telephone book. The telephone company supplied the police with schematics of telephone lines, back telephone bills, even vans and uniforms. A police operation working the murder house with sufficient juice to loft a helicopter would have no problem getting together the equipment for an areawide electronic surveillance. Evidence gathered in such a surveillance might not be admissible in a court of law, but it could be doctored to look like the kind of "information" on which judges issued orders for legal tapes. It would take a day or two to set up shop legally or otherwise, but no more than that. Cocaine Alley, after all. Mike was going to have to figure out another way to stay in touch with Gretchen—and given her fears this morning, he was going to have to find the language with which to express himself that would keep her from reaching the wrong conclusion before he had the first ten words out of his mouth.

The five o'clock broadcasts had nothing important that Mike didn't already know. No names of the victims. The detective in charge of the case was Charles Wheeler, the young plainclothesman whom Mike had seen earlier talking to the press. On a case of this magnitude, he was just a front man—but a good one, neat, soft-spoken, and half-surprised, like a .250-hitting ballplayer or one of the second wave of astronauts. It was pretty bad in there, he told us. Drugs? That was under investigation. Robbery? That was under investigation, too. Was this a Manson-type case? Wheeler looked taken aback, then recovered enough to say he didn't think so. It didn't look like it. Everything else was under investigation.

Then Washington and his "We have a survivor." Mike hoped the line would become famous. All five dead, the three men and the two women, and the survivor, another woman, had been beaten about the head with a blunt instrument— one. Mike had heard many assailants. Only one of the many had done the killings, it seemed, which explained the common mode of killing and the location of the bodies in different rooms. The other assailants apparently had kept the victims apart, telling each that nothing would happen to him or her, while the one with the weapon had gone from room to room and killed them all. There would have been more screaming otherwise. Only a certain kind of man was cut out for killing, but happily that type was rare. Mike hadn't enjoyed it in Vietnam, the times he had thought—but had never been sure—he had killed people, but he had served with the guys who had loved it. Sociopaths. Vietnam had explained a lot of human history to Mike.

His VCR on *record*, Mike dialed around the channels. They were all the same, even to style: after the interviews with Wheeler and Washington, the station's reporters became talking heads in front of the murder home. One said that a neighbor had heard the noise and called the police. The second said that the police had told him that a neighbor had heard the noise, and so on. Not that there could have been any point in asking the first reporter where he had gotten his information: he would have claimed freedom of the press and then braced himself for being carried off to jail on his shield law.

When the six o'clock broadcasts began, Mike was in his bathing suit, sipping a cup of instant coffee he had prepared in the microwave. He loved the microwave oven; when he had a muscle ache, he prepared hot compresses in forty-five seconds in the thing. He was pacing himself. A couple of laps in the pool before dinner would keep him alert until it was time to go out and call Dan. Channel 4 claimed an exclusive with the name of one of the victims, the owner of the house, facing trial next month on cocaine charges: Daisy Nunn. The reporter assured the audience that Daisy Nunn's next of kin had been notified. As for the question of this being another Manson-type killing, the reporter said, that didn't seem likely now. His grim, reporter-type expression never wavered, but Mike wondered if the kid was congratulating himself for single-handedly stopping a wave of terror— or at least another homeowner run on guns. Los Angeles was famous for that. Whenever some geek slashed three or four young women, boys, or old women, grim-faced, middle-aged mortgage holders headed for the gun shops and laid up a little more ordnance. Mike knew a guy from Beirut who insisted L.A. had more guns. Now Mike went to Channel 7.

A live broadcast, from the scene, in the deepening shadow. The reporter was standing in front of the house, where the action seemed to have simmered down. A couple of kids trudged up the hill behind him. This guy didn't have the names of any of the victims, saying that the police were still withholding them. The coverage was becoming too much like predicting a winner on election night. A uniformed officer stepped out of the house. He had a dog under his arm and motioned to someone off camera. One of the kids, a little girl, walked back toward him. Mike moved forward on the couch, the nubby fabric of the cushion rough on the backs of his thighs. The light on the VCR said it was working. Mike didn't know if an enlargement could be made from a picture like this, an enlargement of the kind he had in mind. This was the dog he had heard whining on the second floor—now the uniformed officer was giving the dog to the little girl. She was taking the dog in her arms. The uniformed officer was an old-fashioned nice cop and one really stupid son of a bitch. Didn't he see the collar on the dog? Didn't he see the tags on the collar? If Mike had been in charge, he would have kicked Mr. Nice Policeman's ass all the way down to Sunset Boulevard. Mr. Nice Policeman had just given away a valuable piece of evidence—and not just to the little girl, but to anyone who was watching the broadcast. The reporter returned us to Jerry Dunphy, who blinked and said, "Terrible." Mike turned off the set. He was chilled—stunned. It was time to swim. A good cop could find that kid and "her" dog if they were living in a tree house in Burma. Mike didn't think it would be that difficult. It had occurred to him that he had an easier way of getting to the kid if he had to do it— nuts! He would be better off if he did it now, before he was in trouble! But there was a problem.

He had to talk to his ex-wife, Judy.

It had taken Mike almost six months to tell Judy that he thought his father had been murdered, a long time in the life of a teenager. He had been fifteen when they'd met, Judy almost sixteen. He'd weighed 180 pounds, most of it in his upper chest and shoulders, giving him the appearance of a man until one got close and saw the peach fuzz on his apple cheeks. Mike still didn't like to think of the kind of kid he had been then, trying to sport a glib facade to conceal his terror of the world, about which he had known nothing. He knew that now—but he'd known it then, too. He'd wanted to seduce Judy, and he'd thought—somewhere deep inside him— that telling her his darkest secret would make her want to be a woman in the way that was important to him. True: the heart of a girl always melted before it broke—but that came years later. All teenage heroes are morons. Maybe all heroes in their twenties are morons, too.

Mike wasn't ashamed of himself now, not of that; he hadn't been ashamed of it then either. What bothered him still was that he had spent himself so cheaply in so many ways. He had set himself to a task and had failed completely. At thirty-five he didn't know any more about his father's death than he had at fifteen. He'd wanted to get away from his drunken mother, and then he'd wanted someone to come home to after his military service; after that, he'd wanted what he'd thought was a normal life, and later still he'd wanted relief from the life Judy had planned, orchestrated, and even schemed for him. She couldn't admit that last part even to this day: she was one of those women who insisted she'd never done anything wrong in her life, a will of polished steel cradling the most fragile of egos. Her pain at the end had been so intense that she had not been able to allow herself to see how she'd contributed to it. It rarely surfaced on his consciousness now. Doing laps across an otherwise-empty pool surrounded by the pink stucco walls of twilight created the kind of inner climate that could make him sometimes remember unhappy things. It was like being at the bottom of a well, or even in prison, the prison we all build for ourselves, the prison not of regret or lost joy or any other particular quality of feeling, just memory, the prison of memory, swimming laps, back and forth.

He still did not like looking at the reflection of the child he'd been in the days and weeks after his father's funeral, seeing himself in the anguished eyes of his aunt, when he had screamed that he wasn't going to New York, or in the fury of his mother, or in his own childish decision not to care about his mother any more than she seemed to care about him. He had pulled into himself, but not any more than she had done, he had told himself. Whenever the subject of going to New York was brought up again, he always wrenched away from her. She hit him a couple of times, but what she must have seen in his expression made her quit, and even, at times, weep. At the time he thought years were passing, but children are crushed by the burden of time. He would lie awake listening to his mother sleeping in the other room, awake because he wanted to go in there, into that closet where his father had kept the fraying cardboard boxes containing his files. But Mike was afraid, if not of his mother, then what she could do to him—what she seemed *willing* to do, which was to hit him, flailing with both hands, screaming at the top of her lungs, threatening to send him to juvenile hall.

Those were the months that Mike found out that there was such a thing as a juvenile justice system. North Hollywood, where they had moved into an apartment after she had sold the house, wasn't a bad neighborhood then, just at the beginning of a long decline. Eighth graders and high-school boys were taken away to juvenile hall regularly, and Mike was afraid of that. It seemed as if he did not sleep for weeks on end. He became not so much a tough kid as one who was self-exiled. He did not know when he became aware of his mother drinking, or being drunk. Her harshness turned ugly and stayed that way, pushing him further away from her. After a while he never relaxed around her, and thought carefully in advance about everything he told her.

She would get drunk alone in the living room, after he should have been asleep, but when he would hear her talking to herself, talking to people who were supposed to be there and weren't—Mike never found out who they were, or if they were real: he never had the courage to question her even when she was at her worst, setting the chair on fire with a cigarette, flat on her back on the floor, mumbling, smelling of vomit. . . .

It was when she was at work that he went through the boxes of papers. Most of it was beyond his understanding. His father had been an accountant, working for a large firm. One box was full of nothing but tax returns, the amounts Mike saw in the six and seven figures. He remembered what his father had said about housing in Los Angeles and that hundreds of millions of dollars had been involved. As years passed, the remark became engraved on Mike's brain because he saw that there *was* no public housing in Los Angeles, as he sometimes saw on the television news from back East. But how had *not* building public housing made hundreds of millions for someone—it must have worked that way. All of it almost obscured something else that Mike knew, that he knew no one else knew he knew: he had seen the sandy-haired man give the undertaker an envelope. And going through the boxes—and his mother's own records—again and again never produced a receipt for payment for the funeral. Someone else had paid for it, and even in her most selfcongratulatory stupors—which were always followed by periods of rage or tears—his mother never spoke of the funeral, how his father had died, or for that matter, his father himself. . . .

Years later, when Dan asked him why he had become a cop, Mike told him what he knew of his father's death: Niles Eberhart, now Niles Eberhart and Son, E. & H. Accounting, Airreal Development, no longer in existence, addresses on Third Street, Broadway, Figueroa, all buildings that were gone, paved over . . . by the time of the conversation with Dan, there were more pieces missing than ever. Mike's mother had died while Mike had been in Vietnam, and Judy, not Mike's wife yet, had not learned of her death for almost a month. The apartment had been vandalized, Judy had written, and the landlord had elected to clean the place out. Hearing that, and all the dead ends Mike had found since, checking everything he had been able to remember, Dan could only turn his palms up. . . .

Twenty laps—no real distance: the pool was only forty feet long. Mike spread out his towel and did his sit-ups, quitting at seventy tonight, but still perspiring freely. He was too big an animal to do this in his apartment. He'd tried it once, and had been able to smell his sweat in the place two days later. Better to sit in the sauna anyway, and let the poisons pour out of him. Older people were supposed to need less sleep, but Mike thought that that was a function of the amount of physical energy they expended. If they moved their bodies, they'd sleep better. He didn't think he was lengthening his life with exercise. The old guys he saw were mostly small, under 130 pounds. What Mike wanted to improve was the quality of his life. The worst of this regimen was still to come: after working up an appetite, he didn't allow himself to eat heavily. His microwaved dinners and favorite restaurant foods were all low in calories. He was used to being a little hungry most of the time. In his line of work, that was probably an asset.

Upstairs, there were no messages waiting on the machine, and then no one called while he was in the shower. As he picked at turkey Parmesan, spaghetti, and Italian vegetables, Mike watched the nine o'clock news on Channel 9: in the two hours since the network-outlet local news had gone off the air, another victim's name had been released: Frank Thomas, of Gardena. The survivor was in the ICU, in critical condition. At nine twenty-five Mike put on his windbreaker with the .22 five-shot revolver in the pocket. He was wearing faded jeans and a T-shirt which bore the picture of a famous county building, and lettered under it, L.A. COUNTY JAIL—THE OFFICIAL JAIL OF THE 1984 SUMMER GAMES. Mike never went out without a gun; he had been off duty when he had won his medal for valor and promotion to plainclothesman for stopping a guy trying to rob a bank with a note, shopping bag, and a bottle of acid. The bottle had been open and the guy had been raising it to throw when Mike shot him in the belly. The guy was alive—without a spleen, but alive. Being wheeled out of the bank, the guy had yelled that he intended to sue Mike. More than once since, Mike had thought that he would have had more peace of mind day to day if he had killed the son of a bitch. Mike figured that the guy was still crazy enough to want revenge, and there were plenty of others out there whom Mike had put in jail who hated Mike the same way—just crazy. So Mike always carried a gun, and he calculated that he would continue to carry one long after his police career was over. It took him five minutes to walk up to Riverside. Dan picked up on the first ring.

"You've been watching the news?" he asked.

"Yeah. I was up there this afternoon. They're already saying, if you know what to listen for, that one guy did all the dirty work."

"You know Ira Rosenberg, the pathologist who hates Washington so much?" Dan asked.

"Oh, sure."

"Well, when I was down at the facility, Rosenberg told me that Washington locked himself up in his office at eleven o'clock in the morning—that's when he knew about it. When I saw on the news that there was a survivor, I almost puked. Washington's secretary told Rosenberg that Cutler was on the phone with old Elmer for about half an hour. Washington was acting pissed off because Cutler kept putting him on hold.''

"Okay."

"This evening they're working overtime at the facility because thev're planning on an autopsy festival tomorrow. They want to make sure that they have the pathologists available.''

Mike said, "I can tell you what killed those people, if the one I saw was any kind of an example. A guy with a crowbar or a piece of pipe and a nice, over-the-top swing, like splitting logs.''

"Rosenberg told me that the secretary overheard Washington say 'nightstick.' ''

"Nah.''

"Why not?''

"Because I heard those guys in the street. What they didn't have was discipline. Or conditioning.''

"I'm guilty on both counts.''

"Dan, the guy who did the killing isn't important. He's just a psycho. What's important is how that helicopter got there so fast and why the people in charge kept the lid on all day even at the risk of that woman's life.''

"One other thing," Dan said. "Rosenberg says that this was some kind of dope deal that went haywire. I got that first name they released tonight. She was busted last year for dealing coke—pretty blatant, too. What I remember about that one was that the guy busted with her as her supplier had a funny name, and I remember thinking at the time that he was one of ours, an undercover guy.''

"I figured it was a dope deal," Mike said. "The undercover guy, if that's what he was, was definitely not Hollywood.''

"Definitely not Hollywood," Dan said.

"Still, forget that nightstick shit," Mike said. "There were too many guys, and the wounds I saw were a little too sharp and deep for a nightstick.''

"Well, then, what makes the nightstick theory interesting is that it seems to be official thinking, meaning that somebody who's supposed to be in charge really doesn't know what's going on—or wants people to think he doesn't."

"Either way, that could make it worse for Hollywood," Mike said.

"Possibly."

"If the people in charge really don't know what's going on, they could do some thrashing around."

"All the more reason to think twice, my friend."

"I hear you."

Mike headed straight home. Toluca Lake was one of the nicer neighborhoods of Los Angeles, clean, quiet on the side streets. He hadn't lived this well as a kid, even when his father was alive. It was Judy who was making Mike think these things or, more exactly and in fairness to her, the prospect of calling Judy again after almost two years. That was the last time he'd seen her, almost three years after their previous meeting. A chance encounter. He'd been startled by how much she'd changed and aged, but if she'd had the same reaction to him, she hadn't shown it. She was living well, too, in her own home in Sherman Oaks, what she'd always wanted. At the time of the divorce she had insisted on a court fight, looking for punitive alimony, her own lawyer trying to tell her that it was a waste of time. It wasn't until his lawyer had said that it could be proved that she'd been harassing his client, calling him after midnight, two and three times a night, that she had finally backed off. Mike had told the lawyer that, because they were in different toll zones, her telephone bill would show the six weeks' pattern of late-night, one-minute calls—one minute because Mike had been picking up the receiver and dropping it again only to stop the infernal ringing. He had felt sorry for her at the time, but in the years since, his feelings had congealed: he still felt sorry for her, but wary of her, too. Very wary. But that didn't mean he couldn't call her now, on his business: all she could do was say no.

Gretchen still hadn't telephoned him. That was all right: she had his message, and could call him at the office tomorrow—provided she was calling from her own.

He had to look up Judy's telephone number. He had known the woman twenty years, longer than anyone save his widowed aunt back in New York, and not knowing her number said something about him, he thought. He didn't know his aunt's number either. Still self-exiled.

"Judy, it's Mike. Do you have a moment?"

The tone of her voice dove two octaves from her chirrupy hello. "What do you want?"

"Maybe you saw the news tonight about the murders in Laurel Canyon. They were just up the hill from where you used to teach."

"I know. They haven't given the names of the people, so I can't tell you anything about them yet—if I know them at all."

He told her about the dog and the little girl. "The chances are good that she attends your old school. I don't know if you're still in touch with anybody there, but it would be helpful if I found out who that little girl is. The officer made a mistake that can be corrected without bothering people too much."

"I haven't talked to anybody at the school in years. Let me think about it. You call up after all this time and ask me for something like this—"

"You asked me what I wanted. Are you all right?"

"Oh, yes. Let me think about it, I said. It's late for me to be calling people I haven't talked to in years."

"I'll get back to you," he said.

"No, I'll call you," she said, and hung up.

Ten-fifteen. It wasn't that late—but he *had* been tired. Now Mike was wide-awake but, just as much, determined not to let her continuing bitterness disturb him. It was her problem, and it became his only when he let it get to him. He put on his jacket and went out again to walk. When he'd been living with Judy he'd been afraid of being alone, and for a year or so being alone had been difficult. Now he was beginning to believe that he had lived alone for so long that he had become a bad candidate for living with someone again. He remembered another bachelor saying that he wasn't going to put up with some dame telling him which air to breathe. Exactly—

that was what had happened between Judy and him. Mike had kept saying yes to her until he had had to say no.

Tonight Mike's timing was perfect: he was back in the apartment just as the eleven o'clock news began—and the telephone rang. It was Dan.

"Channel Four has been saying for the past half an hour that it would have the names of the rest of the victims. I was going to have Marge monitor Seven to see if anyone had tipped to what you saw."

Dan meant the dog. Mike said, "I've already called Judy. She said she was going to think about helping." Mike set the VCR to record Channel 7 while he watched Channel 4. "Tell Marge to punch out. I'm recording it. If they're onto it, I want the tape."

The anchor was finished running down what had been known earlier this evening, and now he turned to the reporter who had been outside the murder house. Two of the dead had come from the San Diego area, the reporter said, and one, a male, like the female owner of the house, had a record in illegal drug trafficking.

"Give us the names, asshole," Dan said.

As if on cue, the station cut to tape of Rainbow Drive made in the afternoon, and the reporter, voice-over, ran down the list of victims: Daisy Nunn, the owner of the house, in her forties; Frank Thomas, fifty, of Gardena, her boyfriend. The third man, from Chula Vista near San Diego, was thirty-four-year-old Billy Lansing, with a long criminal record, including an indictment for murder. The fourth victim, from National City, also near San Diego, was Marylou Brown, aged twenty-one. The fifth victim was twenty-nine-year-old Jerry Chambers, a show business fringe figure and sometime sound man. The survivor, now comatose, was also from the San Diego area, Ellie Gordon, twenty-eight. Channel 4 had learned exclusively that she had been the sometime live-in girlfriend of Lansing who had arrived in Los Angeles only yesterday afternoon to effect a reconciliation between them.

"Inquiring minds want to know," Dan said dryly. "We're going to have to have breakfast again tomorrow so I'll see you at the usual place. Bring your appetite. Hold on." Dan had something more, something important, on one of the victims, and Mike's curiosity *itched*. "Marge says she's going to charge you for overtime anyway. Channel Seven didn't even have the girlfriend connection as a heart tugger. I'll see you tomorrow at the usual place at the usual time."

That was Leon's at seven o'clock. "Let's make it an hour earlier," Mike said. "I want to attend that festival you mentioned."

There was a moment's pause. "Are you sure?"

"I'll explain tomorrow." Mike said good night. He had had plenty of time to think over the hours that had passed between the arrival of the police on Rainbow Drive early this morning and the use of the press conference in the middle of the street to divert attention from the survivor being packed onto the ambulance after four this afternoon. Coma? Somebody had waited all day for that woman to die, and it was only when it was seen she wouldn't that it was decided to get her to a hospital. That meant something else: that the somebody had decided she must have seen something she shouldn't have. Mike had heard something, the coming and going on foot of the killers from and to a location up the hill—possibly a car, but not probably—and the arrival of the helicopter. And then what? Mike was still getting glimpses of somebody having one hell of a long, bad day. Mike was at risk. And so was Gretchen. He would call her again before noon tomorrow. He was going to have to figure out how to tell her what to do without scaring the shit out of her. Mike started turning out the lights. If he waited around for Carson's monologue, he'd only be wasting valuable sleep time.

BOOK TWO

4

THE TELEPHONE RANG AT A QUARTER TO SIX, WHILE MIKE
was out in the hall locking the door. He knew who it was and
what the message would be, and he got back into the apartment
to the telephone just as the answering machine was kicking in.
"I'm here, Dan," he said over his announcement tape, and
waited for it to run through its cycle.

"I couldn't get to sleep at all last night," Dan said. "Wait
where you are; I'll bring in the eggs."

Dan lived in Valencia, fifteen or twenty miles to the north;
figuring a shower, shave, and a stop at a 7-Eleven, he wouldn't
be at Mike's apartment before seven-thirty. Mike had time to
walk up to Riverside and get the three daily newspapers.

All the papers had gone to press after last night's eleven
o'clock broadcasts, but what the papers had this morning that
Mike had not learned last night only filled out the broad outlines
of the story. Billy Lansing had been a Vietnam vet, Frank
Thomas a longtime smackhead with a history of petty offenses

to support his habit. Jerry Chambers's mother had collapsed when given the news of her son's death. Two neighbors reported what Gretchen had told Mike: loud parties late at night, and noises not very different from those heard at dawn yesterday. According to the *Times*, a neighbor had called the police because of the open gate and a dog crying—the only mention of the dog. The *Herald-Examiner* front-paged a columnist's observations of the affluent tranquillity of the Canyon having been disturbed by the violence of the city the local residents had tried to escape. Drooling nonsense. All three papers had photographs of the front of the house, and two were sharp enough to give Mike the license plate numbers of the two vehicles in the garage—whenever he felt like congratulating himself for his detective work, he was given this sort of reminder of how far from perfect he was. Those numbers should have been in his notebook yesterday afternoon.

At five to seven he turned on Channel 4, for the first local television news. The other network outlets would have similar broadcasts every half hour, but Mike doubted that any of them would have more than the story's bare bones. True. Mike made a cup of instant coffee in the microwave and turned the radio to an all-talk station. He wanted to see if the city really was cranked up about the murders, as people had believed yesterday.

People calling in wanted to talk about Rainbow Drive, all right. The show's host wanted to be careful in his characterizations of the victims, in spite of what was in the newspapers he must have seen before airtime, using qualifying words like "apparently," and "reportedly," in mentioning Daisy Nunn's arrest the year before for cocaine dealing. The *Times* had given the name of her supplier at the time as P. Vik, a name that looked pretty strange to Mike. The host went on tiptoeing around the established facts of the case as if the dead were going to rise up with an army of lawyers to sue him.

Mike was paging through the *Herald-Examiner* again when the next caller began drawling. One of those country boys with a deep, back-of-the-throat voice that usually went with the hillbilly Baby Huey, No Brain-No Pain type. "Those people in that house were friends of mine. I was supposed to be there, too. I'm a marked man. Billy Lansing was my best friend. We were up here in L.A. only two months. He was a little wild, was all. Those were good people, say what you want about them. We're talking *good* people. That little girl in there, she was so young, she was just in the wrong place at the wrong time. She was waiting for me. Marylou. I *loved* her, man. Marylou Brown, it sounds like a song title, know what I mean?'' He started weeping. ''I'm not going to answer any of your questions. I just wanted you to know what happened in there. Those were good people.'' And he hung up.

The host seemed a little rattled, then tried to cover himself by questioning the caller's authenticity. Mike was on his way to call the station. The telephone rang a dozen times before someone picked it up.

''Police. You just had a caller on the show on the air—''

''Sir, the switchboard isn't open. If you want to talk on the air, this isn't the number.''

''This is the police, I said. If you hang up, you're going to be arrested. Go get the engineer or the producer of the show on the air now, and let me talk to that person.''

''Very well.''

He doubted that he had interrupted her at anything more important than a long, admiring look in a mirror. Three or four minutes passed before someone picked up the handset. A very young woman.

''Yes?''

''This is the police, Detective Mike Gallagher of Hollywood Homicide. You just had a country boy call in. Do you tape your show?''

''Yes, we do.''

''We need his remarks—a copy of the tape will do. He gave evidence that may be valuable in the investigation of the Laurel Canyon murders. Under no circumstances should it be said on the air that our conversation took place. We don't want to make this man nervous. If you remember what he said, he described himself as a marked man. Do you understand?''

''Yes, of course.''

''A detective with proper identification will be at the station to pick up the tape before nine-thirty this morning. Who should he ask for?''

"We can leave it in an envelope at the receptionist's desk, if you like. I don't think anybody here can tell you anything. We have no idea who he was or where he was calling from. We don't check on them. We just have a seven-second delay in case their language gets out of hand."

"The receptionist's desk will be fine," Mike said.

He was watching Channel 7 local news when Dan arrived. He told Dan what he had just heard. "I think it was the real thing," Mike said.

"Are you going to pick up the tape?"

"Sure. I won't be sticking my neck out. Because of the time of day, I'm not sure that any other cop in the city was listening to the show. I'm just doing good police work, that's all."

"*If* you turn it over to those in charge of the investigation. And if you do, then they'll know that you're paying attention."

"Let's see how the wind blows," Mike said. "I think I can go to the end of the day before I have to surface. The gal I spoke to was more interested in protecting herself than remembering my name, and I'll bet you a dollar the receptionist turns over the tape just because I ask for it. She don' need no steenking bodge."

Dan grinned. He had taught Mike the line from *The Treasure of the Sierra Madre*, using it, in fact, when he had to pound on some asshole. Dan considered himself out of shape, but he was a true tough guy, with fast hands and the kind of instantaneous fearlessness that you see nowhere but on the streets. Dan had taught Mike how to hit people. "Just be quick, that's all. Introduce him to the idea that you're not fucking around."

Mike had needed instruction because he had hit a knife wielder so hard that it had taken surgeons seven hours to finesse one of his teeth out from under his eyeball. Tom Cutler had given Mike five days without pay for that one, saying with a straight face that it wasn't good public relations for the department for people to be worried about getting hit that hard.

Over breakfast Dan told him what he knew about Jerry Chambers.

"I have my notes on this at the office, but it happened only three weeks ago, so I'm very sure of the facts. Do you know anybody down in Palm Springs?"

Dan meant in their business, Mike knew. "No, I never had any call down there."

"A good guy to know is Don Grant. He helped me out about eight or nine years ago, and he's the kind of guy who stays in touch just to keep the lines open. He's always at the One Eighty-seven meetings." The number of the state homicide statute was also the name of the organization to which California's homicide detectives belonged. Its meetings were usually raucous. "One year I got a Christmas card from Grant that showed nothing but a set of handcuffs on the front. Inside, it said, 'Ho-ho-ho.' He's that kind of a guy."

Grant had called Dan three weeks ago because of an event in Palm Springs involving Hollywood assholes—it started when two bimbos checked into a motel one afternoon and paid cash. The clerk thought there was something wrong with them, that they were more than just dumb. Both of them were in shorts and light blouses. One of them, an attractive redhead, was showing just a little too much tit. She wasn't exactly coming on to the clerk, but he had the feeling that she was putting on a show for him. A nut. When the girls left the office, he was able to get a glimpse of their car, a '78 Caddie Coupe de Ville, white, and he thought he saw two more people, a man and a woman, sitting in the front seat.

Later, when he was reasonably sure they were all in the room or at the pool, the clerk went around to the car to check the license number as a precaution. The girl who had filled out the card had the license wrong by one digit. Since they'd paid cash, the clerk didn't have to worry about that end, but there were other kinds of trouble people could get into in motel rooms. When he went off duty, at midnight, the clerk told the lobster shift man what had gone down, and to keep his eyes and ears open.

At three in the morning, one of the girls called the desk. She wanted a doctor—when that occurred, the clerks had standing orders. The clerk went down to the room and found a girl unconscious on the bed. Naked. The other was in her panties. There was just the two of them and no car. The clerk called the paramedics and the police. Grant caught the call.

"Grant told me that the dame on the bed was a clear OD,"

Dan said. "Nothing could be found in the room, nothing stuck in the toilet, and the other dame—the redhead who had shown all the tit—says that the one who's unconscious took some kind of medicine. The paramedics got the unconscious one on the gurney and were prepared to load her into the ambulance when the redhead decides she wants to ride with her friend. Not family, no can do."

A helicopter passed overhead, and Mike had to wait for the noise to fade. "Names," he said.

"The redhead's name is Paula Rogers. She tells Grant that the other dame's name is Jane. He says, Jane what? She says Smith."

"Smart." Mike was wondering why the name Paula Rogers was trying to whisper something to him. "Go ahead."

"Well, when Grant told her that she couldn't ride in the ambulance, she threw a fit and spat in his face. He bounced her off the wall and threw the cuffs on her. He thought that would cure her, but it didn't. Before he put her in the back of the car, she did it again, so he punched her solidly, but not too hard, in the stomach. You can't spit when you're gasping for air."

Grant booked Rogers for battery and resisting arrest and put her in a cell until court was in session. He checked with the hospital and was told that the other girl would live. Grant returned to the motel and got the information about the Caddie, the clerk passing on what the afternoon man had told him.

"Now it's seven o'clock in the morning," Dan said. "Grant goes to the hospital to see if the girl is conscious and willing to tell him anything, but she's gone, and nobody seems to know anything. 'People' showed up for her just about at the time she was able to get on her feet and hold a pen, so she signed herself out and took off with them. Grant's working over his shift so he can appear with the Rogers dame, and he doesn't want to explain to the judge how this Jane Smith is already out of the hospital and gone. Grant doesn't like being spat upon, but he knows all Rogers has to do is say that he hit her first or put his hand on her breasts, and that's the end of it. So all he's really got is the Caddie license number."

"He ran it and called you," Mike said.

"First he had to appear in court with Rogers, where she acted up again and the judge held her on five hundred dollars bail. That's a long way from a conviction, especially since Rogers hadn't yet availed herself of the legal fraternity, any of whom will happily advise her on how to slip the hook. Grant says she has some knockers."

"Wasn't she covered up by the time he got to the motel?"

"No. But she's more than one of those uninhibited types. You know who she is. The *Herald-Examiner* runs ads for her movies all the time. *A Taste for Lust* was one title, I think."

"I was wondering why her name seemed familiar."

"Why are you reading those ads?" Dan was laughing at him.

"Looking to see what's on television. The *Herald* always puts those ads near the program schedule."

Dan laughed aloud now. "The Cadillac was registered to Jerry Chambers, whose last address was in Hollywood. That's what I wanted to tell you. I know Chambers. I owed Grant one, as I said, so I went around there and found that he'd moved, and at the new address I found that he'd moved again, so finally I called the telephone company and got his current address, one of those fleabag apartments on Franklin. When I went around there I found him wired to the eyeballs and totally paranoid, and when he heard that he was implicated in a drug overdose in Palm Springs, he opened up like a bad clam. He'd sold the Caddie six months before. Showed me the receipt. He'd never gotten around to filing a change of ownership form with the DMV, and the new owner hadn't registered the car in his own name. Chambers was scared shitless. He told me that the new owner was a friend and that he, Chambers, had been given reason to believe that there wouldn't be any trouble—like me.

"All right, tell me who the new owner is."

"You never let me have any fun. Donnie Jackson."

"Who?"

"Terrific. I go through all this fucking crap and you don't remember Donnie Jackson, the stand-up comic. He played the clubs around town a few years ago. Tall, skinny guy with jet-black hair down to his shoulders—at least it was at that time. He never made it. There was an angry edge to him. He didn't understand that people didn't have to laugh at him if they didn't think he was funny. I'd sort of wondered what happened to him, and now I know.''

"Yeah, he's a dope dealer."

"And a friend to Jerry Chambers. Not registering the car is another asshole's trick. He probably took it in trade for coke, or a coke tab. Chambers was clear about it being a friendly deal.''

"Assuming he was the guy the afternoon clerk saw,'' Mike said, "Jackson sounds pretty well-connected, if he could spring that girl in just a few hours.''

"I'm wondering about that myself,'' Dan said. "I'm going to call Grant in Palm Springs and find out what happened to the Paula Rogers case. Just the size of the lawyer ought to give us some information. Chambers gave me Jackson's address and I passed it on to Grant, but he didn't want me to bother to check it. I will, now. Are you still planning to go downtown to the festival?''

"After I pick up the talk show tape."

The corner of Dan's mouth twisted in a wry smile. "We may be closer to this than anybody else."

"We? I haven't done anything yet."

"Bullshit. If you hadn't been playing horsey with your Kraut—''

"That's enough,'' Mike said, feeling the color come to his face.

The Los Angeles County Coroner's Building is a new structure located not far from Union Station, and was designed for efficiency. The living enter the building from the north side, where the parking lot is landscaped; the dead are wheeled in from the south, several stories below, where the concrete-and-blacktop courtyard is without amenities. It is on that lower level, deep in the windowless interior, where autopsies are performed. The facility is not called the morgue. No one ever calls it the morgue.

The living arrive at that lower floor by elevator, and when the elevator doors open, they are assaulted by the odor of the dead, heavy, penetrating, inescapable, and profoundly distressing. More than a few first-time visitors can venture no farther, and for them, just as well. For all its efficiency, the facility is over-taxed, and the bodies, naked and not always covered with sheets, line the halls. Necessarily, the air temperature on this floor is quite low. Experienced cops wear old clothes because the smell clings to everything. Even after a change of clothes and a shower, the thick stench is still in your nostrils, in the mucus you cough up the next morning, and the morning after that. Caucasian corpses are grayish green, sometimes sallow yellow, with purple blotches of postmortem lividity where blood had settled. Many of the corpses have eyes that are partly open, lips drawn back in the rictus of death. These smiles cause the uninformed to believe there is peace in death, or even happiness. Many corpses have these smiles, but not all. Attendants call drowning victims balloons because they are swollen to the bursting point. Similarly, those who have burned to death are known as roasts. The attendants and those who pass in and out of the facility on business have no pity for the dead; if anything, the living hate the dead for showing death as the disgusting horror it really is.

An all-male crowd was in the hall at the examining room door, Mexicans and blacks in the green cotton uniforms of the coroner's department, Caucasians in plainclothes, all detectives. Flashbulbs were going off in the examining room, as bright as it was. Official photographs, part of the chain of evidence. The big police guns on the case were inside, their rank according them the privilege of standing as close as they wanted to the corpses laid out on the tables, the feet of which faced the door. A couple of detectives stepped aside to allow Mike to enter as the pathologist's electric power saw began its high-pitched whine.

The oldest of the three men was already opened from the neck to the pubis, his rib cage angled wide like the covers of a choirboy's hymnal, his ribs protruding like an artillery roast of lamb. The coroner's people called these bodies canoes, and not because they looked it, but because they needed bailing out. This was Frank Thomas's last public appearance. He was thin, but still full of the fluid being pumped out to the drain on the floor beneath him. On his first visit here Mike had asked where the fluids went. The answer was, into the sewer system and down to the beach. Frank Thomas's left index finger was missing, and the forearm bore a swollen slash. His head was mis-shapen, dented vertically above the eyes and on an angle above the left ear.

By the look of her, the woman was Daisy Nunn. Daisy's chest was open, too, and now her head was propped up and forward, her eyelids pushed down shut by the position of her head. Her long bleached hair made the next step easy. It was lifted up by the pathologist and pulled forward while her scalp was sliced to the bone above the back of her neck from ear to ear. The hair gave the pathologist a grip while he loosened the scalp from the skull and peeled it forward, dislodging and crumpling most of her face like the mask it was. Now the saw sang again as it made a neat cut around her skull, so it could be removed to allow the pathologist to take samples of Daisy Nunn's brain.

The whine of the saw stopped and the examining room filled with the sound of fluid gurgling down the drains. Mike looked up to find Larry Hammond staring at him. Mike almost stepped back. Hammond, a small, dark-haired, wiry man, five years older than Mike, was a deputy chief, but he was not to be con-gratulated for his high rank in the police department of the big-gest city in the American West. Hammond was Chief Tom Cutler's number one boy, part hatchet man, part gofer, and all conniver. Mike wasn't the only man in the department who hated Larry Hammond. Hammond moved behind people's backs—it wasn't possible to get a straight count from the guy. Now he stepped toward the door and, with an almost impercep-tible jerk of the head, indicated that he wanted to talk to Mike in the hall. Mike led him back to the elevator.

Hammond had a way of twisting the corner of his mouth downward. "You like autopsies, Gallagher?"

"About as much as the next guy," Mike said. "That clown Chambers was one of our informants, or had been, from time to time."

Hammond looked a little surprised, then he narrowed his eyes. "I was told you were at the crime scene yesterday."

"A call came in. It was my turn and I caught it."

"A call? From whom?"

"An informant."

Hammond stepped closer. "Don't *fuck* with me, Gallagher!"

"I'm not *fucking* with you!" Mike said through his teeth. "I'm down here because Chambers's name rang a bell with one of my people. It's my idea of good police work—"

"You're full of shit. You're trying to butt in. This is our case. If we want you, Gallagher, we'll call you—"

Maybe Hammond wasn't interested in what Hollywood Division could contribute, but now he couldn't deny that Mike had made the offer. Mike had covered himself well enough—now all he wanted to do was get away from the son of a bitch. "You had five fucking murders up there, asshole! You need all the help you can get!"

Hammond looked as if he were trying to stand on his toes. "If you were at your desk where you belong, smartass, you'd be getting word to pass on to each and every man in your fucking squad that we want them to keep their mouths *shut*! Do you understand me? This is from the chief. Anybody who starts bullshitting to the newspapers about this can figure he's an ex-cop. We want everybody quiet-*everybody*! What I'm talking about is butt out. Keep your distance—and your *mouth shut*!"

Mike jabbed at the elevator button and Hammond walked away. The elevator arrived and the door opened, but Mike was waiting for Hammond to turn the corner. When he did, Mike crossed the hall and entered Ira Rosenberg's office. It was tougher for a cop to put up with the crap a Hammond dished out than to go up against a dust-crazed rosebud armed with a .44 Magnum and a bread knife, but at least Mike now knew who was really supposed to be in charge of the Laurel Canyon case. He had not lied to Hammond about Chambers, but he hadn't told him the truth either. Chambers had been an informant only because Dan had had the drooling, coke-addicted little wimp by his prunes, and the last thing Mike would have told Hammond was the business that had brought that situation about—and not that long ago either.

Finding out who was in charge had been one of two reasons why Mike had come down here this morning, and now he had a third—as well as a fourth question no one here could possibly answer: if Hammond really was the guy in charge of the Laurel Canyon murders, where the hell had he been yesterday afternoon, during that all-important performance for the press and the gullible public it served?

The secretary who worked for Rosenberg and two other pathologists only glanced up from her typing. She was a young girl, fairly pretty, and while the smell was not so strong here, Mike had to wonder how she was able to stand it at all. But you never asked women such questions; they shot you a look that said you were the pervert for asking. Inside, Rosenberg was on the telephone. He smiled and waved to Mike. Rosenberg was a little, balding guy who wore octagonal glasses. He had a fringe of gray around his ears, and the kind of rosy cheeks you'd expect to find on one of Santa's elves. "I'll have to call you back, the mayor just walked in." To Mike, he said, "My wife always calls me in the morning to ask what I want for dinner." Mike remembered that about him. Now Rosenberg glanced around. "Does this look like the place for menu planning? Maybe for the Board of Education." He cackled at his own joke. "So what's new and exciting, Mike?"

"Hammond just gave me his Captain Queeg impression, that's all."

"The little prick. He thinks he's going to be chief someday. He's got some chance. You should have gone into an honest line of work, like me. Do you know I've never lost a patient? They're always right where I leave them." Mike thought he had heard all of Rosenberg's jokes at least four times. Rosenberg clasped his hands and rested his elbows on his desk. "Don't worry about that little shit Hammond. He's not going to be chief as long as Cutler is stuck in Los Angeles without a federal appointment."

Mike smiled. "You know more about this crap than I do."

"My customers don't hold my interest. I thought the story about Cutler was common knowledge. He wanted to be head of the Drug Enjoyment Agency, but the president doesn't want anybody from Los Angeles within a thousand miles of Washington. Except his old pals, of course, and that's because he's got the goods on all of them. The prez remembers only too well what happened to Nixon because he let all those Southern California boys run loose around Washington. So here Cutler sits, totally pissed off about all those duck-hunting trips he invested in Our Fearless Leader. In the meantime, that keeps you safe from Larry Hammond. Ipso facto.''

"Was Hammond here yesterday?"

Rosenberg sat back. "Ah. I thought this was strictly a friendly visit.

"Someday you may need my services, Ira. If I ever need yours, I won't give a shit."

Rosenberg tapped his head. "Good point. Nobody's tricking you today. To the best of my knowledge, Hammond never showed his ass around here yesterday. I didn't know he was here this morning until you told me."

"And Washington was on the telephone with Cutler as early as yesterday morning," Mike said.

"That's what I told your buddy Crawford," Rosenberg said. "Mike, you're acting too much like somebody who has his own ass to protect."

"Suppose you cleared a body as a heart attack victim and then somebody came along and planted four bullets in it?"

"That wouldn't work," Rosenberg said, "but I get the idea. There you are in Hollywood Division, all sweetness and light, with time to stop and smell the roses, and all of a sudden this septic tank backs up. You're afraid they're going to blame you."

"Something like that," Mike said.

"Are you going to keep me posted?"

Not the way Rosenberg gossiped. "We'll tell you the whole story, if we ever learn it."

"Well, Washington was grumbling around here yesterday evening, after he came back from Laurel Canyon. Kicked a couple of file cabinets. I was slicing through some of the backlog—I'm just now finishing the paperwork. My guess is that Washington got drawn into something he would have just as soon avoided."

Mike already knew that; he just didn't know what that something was. "I saw only four bodies in there."

"That's what Washington was doing here last night. He took care of the young girl. He's at a seminar in Phoenix. I think he felt he had to do one body to show that he was cooperating with Cutler, and he took the only one who wasn't really connected with the case.

"Anyway, you know I listen to the talk shows. This morning I heard some guy phone in to say she was his girlfriend. Well, she had a fresh load of semen in her stomach. What he doesn't know won't hurt him. Maybe she was on a diet. The stuff is pure protein and only a hundred and fifty calories."

Mike almost smiled. Country boys never believed stuff like that happened to them. The tape of the radio show was locked in the glove compartment of Mike's car. He said, "I've got to get out of here before Hammond sees me again and accuses me of hanging around."

"You were in here discussing that motel room murder Crawford observed yesterday. I've got you covered. We've got to have lunch. Is lunch still your big meal?"

"Yeah." Mike grinned. "Go out to dinner tonight."

Rosenberg winced. "You sound like my wife. By the time I make up my mind about what I want to eat, she says she hasn't got the time to get it together. I wind up having to take her out. If she'd just decide for herself, we wouldn't have all this bullshit and we'd save a lot of restaurant tabs, too."

"That's why she does it," Mike said. "Can she cook?"

"I've had better meals over my work."

Mike was back at Hollywood Division before twelve-fifteen. Juan Lopez, Bill Blair, and Marvin Burgess, who was the oldest man on the squad, heavy, balding, with a lot of gray around his brown scalp, were at the in desks. Mike went through his messages. There had been a call from Pendleton, another from Gretchen, and one from someone named Yolanda who had information on the motel killing last Friday night. No return phone number. Mike had forgotten about Gretchen—it had taken the message slip to remind him of her. There was no point in trying to call her before two-thirty. At this time of day the business side of the movie business had lunch—and then they went back to their meetings.

Marvin Burgess came around the desks and pulled Dan's chair over so he could talk to Mike without the others being able to read his lips. "We got told this morning to keep our asses *out* of the Laurel Canyon case," he whispered. "Captain Ruppert had us in the office before nine o'clock. He asked about you, and Dan said you were out on a case—you're covered. Ruppert is running scared. He doesn't want any bullshit with Cutler over this. The word is also that we don't talk to anybody, not *any-body*, about Laurel Canyon. This is heavy, Mike. Anything is likely to happen. *Any-thing*—you dig?"

"You bet."

"Now, there was a call for you while only Dan and me were here. He took it, wrote down the message, put it in an envelope, and didn't give it to me until he had to go out. He didn't say where he was going, but I have a feeling, okay? You two better watch your asses. That cocksucker Cutler has people everywhere. You wouldn't be where you are if you didn't already know that. Now make use of it." From his inside jacket pocket Burgess took an envelope and handed it to Mike. "I don't want to see what it says." He got up and returned to his seat.

Mike opened the envelope in his lap. *Cutler's office called. Call back for an appointment to see Cutler in his office ASAP. Be careful.*

5

B*E CAREFUL.* LONG, LONG AFTER MIKE HAD LEARNED TO
be careful about the people he took for his friends, to learn
everything he could about them, and then still think twice about
what he confided in them, his friend Dan Crawford took Mike
into *his* confidence. He told Mike something about himself that
not even Marge knew, something that had happened to him,
something he had had to do—the two together and the same
thing, *one* thing. Mike understood that—he'd had no trouble at
all understanding that. Dan had had no choice. Dan had to tell
somebody, he said, but Mike didn't exactly believe that, although he did not argue. He thought to this day that Dan wanted
to *educate* him in the way the awful experience had given him
the privilege to do. When Dan told him, unnecessarily, never
to speak of it to anyone, Mike resolved to forget it, or at least
bury it so deep in his memory that it would surprise him whenever it resurfaced on his consciousness.

Since then, Mike had been able to do it exactly that way—

except: like a dream or a fantasy or anything else deep in the dark places of the mind, what Dan had told him was the same as real. Mike could see it whenever it returned, clearer, better remembered than a movie he had seen in his childhood and forgotten until it turned up late one night on television—much clearer than that. He didn't know if Dan actually had said, *It could have happened to you,* but Mike believed it in a special way, maybe believing it even as Dan had told the story, voluntarily—more than that: *willfully*—slipping into Dan's shoes, behind Dan's eyes. When Mike remembered what Dan had told him, he remembered it as if it *had* happened to him, four years ago, when Dan and Marge had been living in the West Valley, where they had raised their kids, trying by then to sell their big house in the terrible real-estate market at the start of the eighties. . . .

Winter, the rainy season. Dan was headed north on a residential stretch of Tampa Avenue, north of Roscoe Boulevard, at ten minutes to four in the morning. He had the radio off. The wagging windshield wipers glinted under the streetlamps passing overhead. A flash of light in the rearview mirror snapped him out of his reverie. A car was bearing down on him at a high rate of speed, weaving from lane to lane. Dan was on the right, but even if he pulled over to to the curb, he could not be sure he was not going to be sideswiped. He could see he could not reach the next intersection and turn off before the drunken fool overtook him; all he could do was brace himself for a possible crash and hope for the best.

The car roared by, so close Dan shouted in terror. The car was a brand-new Datsun 280ZX, and Dan thought he saw a girl behind the wheel. She sped on across the next intersection, still weaving, closer to the curb. In the crosswalk a man flung up his hands. The girl hit the brakes and threw the Z into a sidelong skid. The Z hit the man broadside as it went on rotating slowly on the wet pavement. The rear wheels hopped and Dan's headlights picked up the man, on the blacktop on this side of the Z, which was stalled now, facing back toward the intersection, the headlights shining through the rain. Dan mashed his foot on the brake. His car skidded, and when it came to a stop almost on top of the man, the engine quit.

Dan looked across at the little brunette behind the wheel of the Z. She was smiling at him, blinking, her head nodding.

He drew his .38, put his car keys in his pocket, and got out his badge. She watched him step out of his car as if at a movie, her smile fading. The man on the pavement was dead. The rear wheels of the Z had passed over his head, which was flattened like a deflated football. Across the street a porch light came on and the front door opened. A woman in a thick terry bathrobe appeared.

"I'm going to call the police!"

"I *am* the police!" Dan yelled without taking his eyes off the girl behind the wheel of the Z. "Call an ambulance too!"

Dan opened the door of the Z. It was a T-Top, loaded. The stereo blared. The girl continued to watch him, her mouth open, eye makeup smeared on her cheeks. Her skirt was up around her hips and she was wearing no underwear. Dan reached into the car and removed the ignition key.

"Who the fuck are you?" she drawled.

"Police. Hands up where I can see them. Get out of the car."

"Bullshit! You want to fuck me! Are you in for a surprise!" She giggled. "My cunt's so fucked, I'm sitting on a swamp—"

Dan had her by the hair; he pulled her out of the car. She was so drunk and high she collapsed to her knees on the pavement, facing the dead man. His brains were puddling onto the blacktop, spreading with his blood in the rain. People didn't want to know that brains were mostly liquid. One eye was still swelling out of its socket, as if it wanted to see who had done this to him. She tried to twist around to hit Dan, saying something about not taking his shit. Dan pulled her hair until some of it ripped out of her head.

"I just saw you drive your car into this man and kill him! I'm a police officer! You're under arrest for vehicular homicide, driving while intoxicated, and resisting arrest! You have the right to remain silent! You have the right to have an attorney present at any and all questioning! If you can't afford an attorney, one will be appointed for you! Anything you say can and will be used in a court of law against you!"

A man came running from the direction of the house with the lighted porch. He was barefoot, his belt undone; his T-shirt was tucked in on one side of his belt line. He gaped at the body on the pavement.

"Police," Dan said, not letting go of the girl's hair.

"I know." The man had a country twang. His hair was thinning. "She's making the call. I'll set out some flares, if you have them."

"I think I have one."

Looking at Dan, the man motioned to the corpse. "That's the worst thing I ever saw in my life."

"Fuck you," the girl said to him.

"Fuck yourself, bitch," he said to her. "I wouldn't touch you with a pair of tongs."

She tried to swing at him, but Dan used her momentum to throw her facedown on the hood of her car and snapped his cuffs on her wrists.

"Don't move," Dan said. "I'm adding attempted assault to the charges. You move and I'll think you're trying to escape."

"You *hurt* me!"

"Shut up." Dan reached across the interior of her car to her purse on the passenger seat. The purse was oversized and very heavy. He tucked her wallet under his arm and went through the rest of the contents, tossing them into the car after he had examined them. A small plastic bag half full of marijuana went back in the purse. So did a paper packet that probably contained cocaine. A bottle of Black Beauties. A foilwrapped chunk of hashish. "What are you, the fucking Red Cross?" Dan opened the wallet. "Does Daddy know what you're doing with his—"

Daddy's picture was in the wallet, and Dan recognized him at once. The girl's driver's license confirmed the girl's identity. She didn't live in Reseda. She didn't even live in the city of Los Angeles. In her condition, she might not even know where she was going, but more likely, she had been headed to one last party for the night or even a place to crash.

The man appeared again. Dan motioned to the corpse.

"Do you know this guy?"

He shook his head. "I never knew anybody who looked like that. Is there anything else I can do for you?"

"Yeah," Dan said. "Go inside and stay there. I may want to use your phone in a few minutes. I'll need privacy."

The man hesitated. "Sure, whatever you say. I'll tell my wife we're supposed to go into the bedroom." He looked at the body again. "Pretty flashy car. He must have done a lot of damage to it. That's a shame." With a last glance at Dan, the man turned and headed back across Tampa Avenue.

"Don't move," Dan said to the girl. "Don't even turn your head."

His eyes on the corner house, Dan kept the purse out of view while he retrieved the Black Beauties and the packet of coke. He put the purse on the front seat of his own car and the pills and coke in the glove compartment, which he locked. His hand was shaking. A black and white was speeding down from Nordhoff, still a distance away. He took the girl by the arm and unlocked the handcuffs.

"Now listen to me. I'm putting you in my car." Dan could hear the breathless quaver in his voice. "When the police get here, have your head against the window, your eyes closed, and *don't move*! You can get out of this, but it's going to take a lot. Do you understand me?"

"You're a pig. You're all alike. You'll do anything—"

"You'll go to jail!"

She smiled as she turned toward his car. "And you'll lose your little fucking job!"

But she did what she was told, and when the Devonshire Division patrol car arrived, Dan told the two officers that he had seen the man step out of the darkness directly into the path of the girl's Datsun. The girl had collapsed and was probably going into shock, he said. He wanted to use a landline to call the girl's parents, whom he did not identify. Dan was not worried about the story; there seemed to be no other witness, and the rain on the street had made skid marks impossible. Then he thought that the officers would check the glove compartment of the Datsun for the girl's registration. He was the one who had the keys. The Datsun's door was still open. Dan waited until one of the officers returned to the black and white to call in to the station, and then told the other to check the body for identification. While the officer was bending over the man on the street, Dan closed the door of the Z and made sure it was locked. Neither of the uniformed police noticed what he had done.

In the house across the street Dan called Parker Center and told the captain on watch to call Tom Cutler—to knock him out of bed, if necessary. Dan gave the captain the house address on the girl's license, and told him to tell Cutler to meet Dan there as quickly as possible. The captain objected: like everyone else, he was afraid of Cutler's wrath. But Dan said that Cutler would recognize the address and the only additional information he needed to have was that the problem was vehicular homicide. The captain put Dan on hold, but not for as long as he expected: three minutes later, the captain was back on the line, with *detailed* instructions for all concerned.

When Dan hung up, he saw the man of the house standing in the doorway.

"We're not witnesses, you know. We didn't see anything. I don't think we even heard anything but you yelling at her."

"Don't worry about it," Dan said.

The man was the kind who prided himself in not taking crap from anybody. He said, his voice rising a little, "In fact, I sort of wish you had made that telephone call collect, or third party billing."

"Do you want me to leave you a quarter?" Dan asked sourly, as he headed for the door. He was still so frightened he felt light-headed, unsettled in his chest. Now he was trying to remind himself that he had no choice about what he was doing, that he'd be in desperate trouble if he did anything else.

Outside, the girl had remained quiet in the passenger seat of his car. Dan unlocked the Datsun and drove it over to the curb, the rear wheel scrubbing against the fender. He cleaned out the glove compartment and gave one of the uniformed officers the keys. The officer said they'd already received the call from Devonshire about the matter: they were supposed to do what Dan told them.

"Call the tow guy you trust," Dan instructed him. "Have the car put in the Devonshire lot. No gas stations, no impound facilities."

"Are you sure you know what you're doing?"

"If I don't, you'll be selling tacos in Pacoima."

"What we don't understand is, what was the guy doing out in the rain at this time of night?"

"Any ID?" Dan asked.

"Nope."

"Not our problem," Dan said.

Reseda was at least ten miles more distant from the girl's home than the downtown apartment Cutler used when he was working—Cutler's home, somewhere in Santa Barbara County, its exact location a secret to all but a few trusted aides, supposedly covered a mountaintop crosshatched with horse trails. As far as Dan was concerned, Cutler could just as well precede him and break the worst of the news to the family. The girl's first name was Barbara. She was quiet most of the way home, stirring herself to flail and curse a couple of times, then again while Dan threaded the last mile of well-kept, curving, foothill streets to the wrought-iron fence surrounding her family's five-acre estate. She started to wail when she saw the gates already open. Being surrounded by her money made Dan hate her—until he realized that it was he himself who was the instrument of her privilege.

Cutler had arrived; his own Lincoln Mark, bearing the vanity license plate, N4CMENT, was parked under the portico at the top of the drive. As Dan pulled up behind the Lincoln, the front door of the house opened. Light poured out from inside, and that was as far as Dan got. Cutler moved quickly through the door, and took Barbara by the arm. . . .

A few days later, a man called Dan at Hollywood Division to arrange a meeting for a drink in the piano bar at Alphonse's, in Toluca Lake, and when no one showed after half an hour, Dan returned to his car to find a paper bag full of money on the front seat. Hundred-dollar bills, two hundred and fifty of them . . .

It wasn't until after that, weeks after reading routine reports and bulletins, that Dan learned that the victim of the hit-and-run had not been a burglar, prowler, or peeper. He'd lived three blocks away—thirty-eight years old, married, with three children. The night he'd been killed, he'd been unable to sleep, and had gone for a walk. Dan figured the guy had left very little, because soon enough a real-estate broker's sign appeared on the lawn of the house where Dan had driven by. He'd done it more than once. . . .

Mike didn't know which Los Angeles family Dan had tangled with—Dan had not said the name, and Mike had known better than to ask. Only a few families in this city were that powerful; *old* families, which meant they dated back to the late nineteenth century, a long time in the history of this part of the world. No Jews, no Catholics. No one in show business was quite so important, with the probable exception of Gretchen's boss, Norman Birnbaum, who had turned a tacky little factory producing low-budget movies into an entertainment conglomerate of international consequence—but Birnbaum's children were bloated middle-agers, nothing more sinister than idle and whimpering neurotics.

Mike had no curiosity anyway. The lesson Dan had wanted him to learn was clear. Mike had already known that no one important in Los Angeles had ever gone to jail. There was a covenant among the controlling families of the city set down decades, even generations, ago. They who had once owned all this land where safe forever, safe behind the line their forebears had drawn, the line invisible to all those who did not need to know it existed. When you needed to know, when you had risen so high that in your ignorance you could possibly threaten them, you were not told, or shown, or had your nose rubbed in it, but somehow—somehow—you were made aware, the way Mike himself was aware. What happened to Dan *could* have happened to Mike. Mike would have done the same thing. There would have been no real choice. If Dan had crossed the line, Cutler would have come down on him like a DC-10 hitting a trailer park. A man who tried to play Ralph Straightarrow would not be able to stay in Los Angeles, probably not in the state of California, and even some other western states as well. . . .

What Dan had wanted Mike to see was the way it worked. Twenty-five thousand dollars had been nothing to the other party involved. The method of payment had been exquisite. Until he had gotten the money home, Dan had not been sure that he had not been set up for Internal Affairs Division, who would have pulled him over to the curb and searched the car on "information" that Dan had been taking bribes, shaking people down, peddling stolen property. Years had passed when Dan had told Mike the story and he hadn't dipped into the money yet, dared put it in an interest-bearing account, invest it in his children's education.

"Twenty-five thousand isn't a lot of cash," Dan had said. "Five wrapped packets of one-hundred-dollar bills. All old. No consecutive serial numbers—I checked them one day when Marge was at work." No smile. Throughout the whole long narrative, Mike remembered, Dan had not smiled once.

Dan had had to get the girl out of it. Creating a record on her would only have made a bigger mess that Cutler would have had to clean up. The money was simply Dan's signature on the contract. There was no point in contemplating what would have happened if he'd figured out a way to return the money. Under the circumstances, Dan had said, he really wasn't supposed to give much thought to the victim, dead before Dan had stepped out of his car. The money settled all moral causes, which was what the money meant: they owned him, but not as a human being, not as a slave, but as an object, like the old toolbox in his garage where the money lay hidden, inert, harmless. Dan had been given a twenty-five-thousand-dollar dose of saltpeter for his conscience. "Now I'm someone they can count on. If you're watching traffic, you can step in dog shit. If you're looking where you put your feet, you can get hit by a bus. It's what happened to the dead guy. You see?"

Mike called Gretchen at three o'clock, but she was already in another meeting. He told the secretary that Gretchen should try to reach him at Hollywood Division, adding that he would be working so much overtime that it would be pointless to try to catch him at home. The only hours she could do that was when she was at home herself, when all her calls would be traced. Mike could only hope that she was smart enough to see what he meant.

From Pendleton, the commandant's office reported that it had pulled the names of twenty men fitting Mike's requirements.

Mike needed a full set of fingerprints of each. No problem, he was told, but it would take a few days—was that all right? That was fine, Mike said.

Yolanda called again. She had a thick, singsong ghetto accent. "That dude that got offed last Friday night? He was one bad dude. He was mean!"

"How do you know, Yolanda?"

"Him and me used to run around. He was always bragging on these heavy things he used to do to these old chicks back East. You know, real old chicks."

Mike was writing. "Where back East?"

"He say he from Pittsburgh, Chicago, Detroit."

"Any one of those in particular?"

"That's it! One day it was from one, the next day one of them others! That asshole thought I wouldn't remember!"

"Do you have any information about who killed your friend the other night?"

"He wasn't no friend of mine!"

"All right, your aquaintance."

Dan came in. Mike put his hand over the mouthpiece. "Yolanda. Background on Friday night's victim."

"Yeah," Yolanda said, "that guy Mitchell done it. He a skinny black dude with a little goatee. He wear a earring."

"Mitchell." He motioned to Dan to pick up an extension. "Is that his first name or his last name?"

"His onliest name, so far as I know."

"Where is this Mitchell now?"

"Oh, he split. He left town."

"What did he tell you about the killing?"

"He say Earl was giving him some shit, so he pulled his piece and unloaded on him. Shot him right in the brains."

"Did he say that? In the brains?"

"Sure. He even show me where. He put his finger on the place. Right above my eyes."

Mike and Dan exchanged glances. "Why did Mitchell tell you this?"

"I was giving him head. He be trying to give hisself a extra thrill."

"Where can we find you if we want to talk to you again?"

"I be around."

"Give me a telephone number where you pick up messages or somebody who usually knows how to reach you."

"Oh, you can call my sister in Pasadena. She usually knows where I am."

Mike asked for the number and Yolanda gave it and Mike said he'd be in touch. The victim had been shot in the back. Still, Mike and Dan would have to try and locate this Mitchell and make inquiries of the three departments back East for any information on the dead man's pre-Los Angeles activities.

Dan turned his chair around to face Mike. "You call Cutler?"

"Spoke to a sergeant. I'm due there Thursday morning at ten o'clock. If Cutler thought he had a real problem with me, I'd be down there now."

"True enough. I got lucky with Donnie Jackson. His driver's license had to be renewed last year and he hasn't moved since. He's in a garden apartment just a few blocks from where Chambers was living, on the west side of Highland. Paula Rogers is in the same building—on the other side of the pool, in fact. I saw her. She was out by the pool with a very pretty blonde who's probably the third woman in the group down in Palm Springs. She lives with Jackson. After I found Jackson on the tenant directory, I rang the manager, identified myself, and told her I was interested in someone I thought might be living in the apartment next to Jackson's. That got me a guided tour. It turned out that the apartment next to Jackson's is occupied by a bunch of Russian immigrant cabdrivers. When we got out to the pool, I had no difficulty identifying Rogers from Grant's description and her behavior—when she caught me glancing at her, she just opened her legs. A psycho. The manager told me she sees a lot of people coming and going from the Jackson apartment. That's day and night. The last three days have been the quietest she was able to recall. His car wasn't in the lot all during that period. I asked her about that. She said that Jackson was the only person she ever saw driving the car. Six months ago, he was out in the lot showing it off to a bunch of people—some were among the crowd she sees coming and going. Jackson hardly ever goes out. Make that practically never. Occasionally he takes trips with the blonde. The manager sees them coming and going with overnight bags. The blonde always carries dresses.''

"And he hasn't been around the past three days, while the blonde has been at the apartment.''

"This is the first time that's happened," Dan said. "We ought to keep an eye on that guy.''

Novak came in, picked up a folder from his desk, and went to the file cabinet, which was behind Mike. Mike turned around. "Greg, did you get into Ruppert's office this morning?''

"Yeah, Mike.''

"You don't even discuss Laurel Canyon with your own mother, do you understand?''

"Captain Ruppert really made that clear. I ran into that guy from the *Herald-Examiner* up on Sunset. He asked me why we weren't involved in the case.''

"What guy?''

"Wills. Bob Wills—is that his name?''

"I didn't know you knew him. What did you say?''

"I told him to call Public Relations.''

"Atta kid.''

"There's an apartment available in the complex," Dan said, "but we'd have to find some budget money for rent—and we can't justify it. There's no point in going to the narcotics guys about Jackson, because we can't tell them why. The manager is going to call me if anything happens.''

"You told her you were interested in somebody in the adjoining apartment.''

"I hustled her," Dan said. "I showed her my curiosity building about Jackson. She thinks she's a good citizen. She wants Jackson out of there. He makes too much noise at night.''

Something else was bothering Mike; now it skittered out of reach.

"I've heard that before.''

"Thought so.''

Gretchen did not call, and later Mike wove his route home through Laurel Canyon, adding distance and time to his trip. At the foot of Rainbow Drive was a van from Pacific Telephone,

with no orange warning cone up the roadway from it, a violation
for which telephone company employees knew they would be
cited. Here at the end of the street, which was serviced by overhead lines, every telephone to the top of the hill could be
scanned. It was clearer than ever to Mike that something had
gone terribly wrong yesterday morning. If the arrival of the
helicopter was one clue, this was another; the investigating team
knew how the murderers had come and gone, but did not know
from where. The team had no suspects, which meant that everybody, including Gretchen, was under suspicion. When Mike got
home he decided he would erase his announcement tape from
his answering machine, then reset the beep so that people would
know they could begin talking. Answering machines got loused
up on their own in exactly this way, and no one would think
anything of it; on the other hand, his voice wasn't going to be
recorded by a police gadget that switched itself on whenever
Gretchen picked up her telephone.

At Bernie's on Ventura Boulevard, Mike picked up the day's
last editions, then stopped at the deli counter in Ralphs for some
pasta salad to eat while he went through the newspapers. In the
pool he couldn't seem to relax. Deeper into the case, he felt
safer than he had yesterday, but now something else inside him
was ringing an alarm, something not seen, left undone—he
didn't know. In the sauna he breathed deeply for relaxation, but
his mind was racing: from the caller on the talk show, to the
fact that victim Jerry Chambers had known Hollywood dope
dealer Donnie Jackson, and that Jackson's women didn't seem
distressed by his absence. Of course they didn't have to know
the truth of his whereabouts. Assholes like Jackson and that
character Mitchell told women what they wanted, strictly for
effect. The blonde and her friend Paula Rogers certainly knew
that Jackson was in the funny business, but if Jackson liked his
women two and three at a time, a steady supply of cocaine was
the way to arrange it. A steady supply was the way to lift a
Cadillac from a wimp like Jerry Chambers. Dan had seen
Chambers strung out like snot on a hurricane fence. When guys
like Chambers reached the final stages, only one thing could be
counted on: that they were focused on keeping the supply coming. At fifty, Frank Thomas had been an *old* smackhead. On

the coroner's slab, he had looked it, with legs as thin and pale as a plucked sparrow's. Add to those two Billy Lansing, who had somehow dodged a murder indictment, and the hillbilly who had said on the radio that the others were his idea of "good people," and you had a collection of people who were bound to get themselves in deep trouble.

Only the *Times* had something new, and it made Mike's skin crawl. Billy Lansing. In 1978 in El Centro, Billy Lansing had been arrested for the stabbing death of a dope smuggler, but a week before his trial, the star witness against him, another asshole with a long record in drug trafficking, had been shot and killed, resulting in a dismissal of the charge against Lansing. Who had shot the star witness? A state narcotics agent working undercover, who had said afterward that he had been attacked with an ice pick. No witnesses.

After that, according to a *Times* interview with Lansing's stepmother, Lansing had gone even more sour. Once, she remembered, he had come around to her house looking for a place to hide from a Mexican gang. Lansing had some lie to tell, but the stepmother was sure that he had double-crossed people and squealed to the police to make his escape.

Mike knew that the *Times* had a full-blown bureau in San Diego, covering that city with a complete edition just as it covered the San Fernando Valley and Orange County. The only way to check the accuracy of the *Times* story without alerting the media or law enforcement was to get the other San Diego papers, which were available on Victory Boulevard in Van Nuys and back in Hollywood, on Las Palmas. Mike thought he would go over the hill to Las Palmas. It would give him the chance to do something else at the same time.

The *San Diego Union* confirmed the *Times* story. Mike threw the San Diego papers in the backseat of his car and headed up toward Donnie Jackson's garden apartment.

A white 1978 Cad Coupe de Ville was in one of the tenants' slots of the parking lot. Mike drove around the back, looking for other signs of surveillance. Nothing. As of this afternoon, when Dan had been in there, no one had been paying attention to Donnie Jackson. Mike found a parking space and walked around to the building's entrance. The gate was ajar. Mike locked it behind him. The Jackson and Rogers apartments were on the pool level, lights on but drapes drawn. The second floor had a ring-around balcony that overlooked the pool area. Mike went upstairs. He was at the far end of the building, able to see both apartment doors, when he heard the buzzer that unlocked the gate. Mike walked quickly along Rogers' side—if the person entering was headed to Jackson's apartment, Mike wouldn't see that person's face, but he might get a look at Jackson.

It was a man, coming toward Rogers' side—in fact, to her apartment. Mike heard the door open. The man had blond hair half covering his ears, was about 150 pounds, and was shabbily dressed—or maybe his clothes were the kind of California Casual Mike had seen yesterday in Laurel Canvon.

"Bobby!" Paula Rogers squealed. "Long time no see!"

Big fucking deal, Mike thought. It was time to get out of there before someone called a cop on him for being a prowler.

Back home, the message light on his machine was blinking, but there was no message, just a hang-up. Mike was thinking that he wanted to get the San Diego papers out of his car before he parked it again in the Hollywood Division lot. Cutler's people would connect San Diego papers to the Laurel Canyon murders—the idea made Mike realize that he was going to have to watch everything he did.

6

HE AWAKENED IN THE DARK, JOLTED BY THE SOUND OF his own voice. The clock beside the bed said that it wasn't quite three A.M. The nightmare he'd been having disappeared like a letter being sealed in an envelope, but he knew what it was, anyway, his mother drunk, yelling, breaking things in a living room that existed only in Mike's own bad dream, a construction an analyst might be able to filter into its separate, meaningful elements. Mike didn't care about that shit. The dream, which came and went with the rise and fall of his emotional fortunes, was a signal to him that somewhere in his life he was on dangerous ground, possibly in ways that he couldn't see, much less understand. If he wanted more clues, his first thoughts were of Judy and that hang-up call. But Mike didn't want to think about Judy now; he had learned too well, over many nights years ago, when the marriage was over, where such thoughts always led. The dream said that this was danger time, that's all. Trouble could come from any direction.

He had had many sleepless nights years ago, and had devised a program to stave off the anger and bone-rattling dread. Now, as he got out of bed, Mike remembered that Dan had told him that *he* hadn't slept Monday night. Mike had forgotten to ask why, in spite of knowing that that man had his own demons. The thought came and went; Mike was realizing that the hang-up could have been a wrong number. A man under siege sees everything as an assault.

Mike went out to the living room and turned on the television set, fixing the volume so low that it barely reached his consciousness. Now there was "Nightwatch," the talking heads show that repeated itself every two hours. If Mike fell asleep during a segment he liked, there was a chance he would be awake later to see its conclusion. He was no longer shocked by the idea of dreaming of his mother and then waking up to think of his wife. On the surface, the women had not been at all alike. They hated each other. Now all Mike could see about the two was what they had in common. They had outsmarted themselves. Of course Mike knew that he saw them that way because Judy's actions had surfaced the rage Mike had felt for years about his mother. He had dealt with that feeling after the end of the marriage as well as he had been able. It had been at that time that he had resolved to get himself back in shape. Using his body productively had served him in his youth, and he was just that much better off for knowing that he wanted to treat himself well. The rage was still in him, he knew, not at all like a cancer in remission, more like a spot of tuberculosis so many people carried, walled off and neutralized. Only under pressure could Mike feel the walls weakening, and then—he had learned this through trial and error—he took better care of himself, slowing down, making sure his life contained those same elements he reached for naturally when he was at his best. When he couldn't sleep, that meant not bothering to try. As a child, with his mother drunk to unconsciousness, he had let television flood his mind until his escape into it turned into drowsiness. Years ago, he had fought that; now he surrendered gratefully. Tomorrow he would remember he had been given a signal about something in his life. . . .

* * *

We have to learn to be our own best friends because we fall too easily into the trap of being our worst enemies. It was clear to Mike that it had happened to Judy, that her deeply hidden insecurities had propelled her to the big, uncomprehending kid without a father, who needed molding if not direction or ambition. It was clear now that Mike had done the same thing to himself, accepting not quite without question Judy's willfulness, fights with her mother, sulking, silences. He remembered thinking that his mother had shown him that all women were like that, thinking but not believing it, because he could remember thinking, too, that he deserved better. We become the enemy, make deals with ourselves, and then don't understand why we are destroyed. When he had seen Judy do something that hurt a friend, he'd questioned her about it. The alternative had been some mild embarrassment to Judy. Now Mike could not remember the situation, only the expression on Judy's face when he'd confronted her, an expression of fear and anger—*attack*. "What else was I supposed to do?" she had asked. He could also remember deciding not to protest, as he had decided before and would do so later.

Judy had opposed Mike's decision to enter the Marines. A neighbor had been a marine and had told him that he would be better off in the long run than if he waited to be drafted. Marines, the neighbor had assured him, were members of a lifelong fraternity; everybody recognized an ex-marine as being a cut above the rest. As a football player, Mike had never been better than all-city second team; he had been offered no scholarships, only three or four invitations to attend college and try out. In those days he had thought that if his father had lived, not only would a college education have been available to him, he would have been that much better a football player and would have earned a full scholarship himself . . . madness! At that age he would have been willing to blame anybody else for everything bad that ever happened to him. . . .

He and Judy were married when he came home on leave from Vietnam. Judy issued an ultimatum, wanting to be married before he was reassigned. Mike's mother had died while he was overseas, he had no home, and now that he'd survived combat, he saw the rest of the tour as anticlimactic. He spent the next year doing paperwork at Parris Island: Judy had been hoping for an overseas embassy assignment; she hated the humidity of the South; she despised their little apartment; she complained that she was being treated as a second-class citizen because she was an enlisted man's wife. It was an awful year. Mike was glad when he was on duty, all too willing to spend their free time in roadhouses. When they returned to Los Angeles, they were telling each other that they were going to forget the past—make a new start. . . .

They went on like that for almost a decade. when he told Judy he had decided to take the police test, she objected to that, too: "I thought you had forgotten all that stuff. I don't want to be a cop's wife!" She finished college, became a teacher, more depressed and inconsolable; he blamed himself, at the same time believing he was pulling their wagon alone. A doctor told him he was developing an ulcer. Their friends, Dan and Marge Crawford, saw the end coming before Mike faced it himself, and when it came, Judy acted surprised, then martyred—and finally went on the attack against him, something he'd always feared. He had brought it on himself as surely as everything else. . . .

In that first month alone he went up to Forest Lawn, where his father and mother were buried, even back to the apartment where he and his mother had lived. The old marine neighbor recognized him right away. He seemed as disgusted as much as dismayed at Mike's divorce. The old man had sunk into sour moralizing, saying that even the apartment building wasn't what it had been while the old owner had run things. By then Mike was tired of the guy; he was asking himself what his life would have been like if he had seen him as clearly years ago as he did now.

"I don't know where you get that stuff about the apartment building," Mike said. "After my mother died while I was in the service, somebody broke in and cleaned the place out."

"Bullshit," the old man said. "We never had a robbery."

"My mother's place was broken into," Mike said.

"The hell it was. I was in there after your mother died, and I was in there again when your little girlfriend came over to throw everything out.

Mike almost grabbed him. The old man saw it. "The landlord asked me to make sure that nobody had any complaints about any of the stuff being missing,'' the old man said, backing up a step. Mike wanted to scream, and he must have looked it. "That little girl had no complaints,'' the old man murmured. "I know, because I asked her.''

Judy was calling Mike almost hourly every night, threatening to punish him by extracting as much alimony as she could. His feelings were going through terrible changes, even revulsion with himself as he remembered his acquiescence to tantrums only less intense than these to which he was being subjected now. He asked the old man what he had seen being thrown out.

"Boxes and boxes of stuff. A lot of beat-up furniture—''

The only boxes in the apartment had been his father's papers. That night Mike called Judy and told her where he had been and what he had heard. By then Mike had been listening for years to the denials of the guilty, and when he heard her response he thought that if she had been in the same room with him, he would have killed her.

"*I* didn't do it!''

In the years they had been together, she'd spoken of the "robbery'' only once, saying he was better off not torturing himself about his father. Mike remembered that, too, thinking about it, letting it feed on him. A long time passed before he woke up to the notion that no one cared about the hurts he had sustained. They were all in his mind now which meant that no one else was making him unhappy only him—and that there was nothing he could do for anyone else who could hot learn that lesson. . . .

Dick Albert swept through the door, raised his hand, and dropped his prop, a set of keys. The clapboard appeared, chalked Scene 47, Take 19, and Dick Albert swept through the door again, managed to hang onto the prop as he raised his hand, but then missed his mark and put the end of his nose in shadow. The clapboard again, Scene 47, Take 20. Gretchen had actor problems, all right, Mike thought. She had told him more than once that she was what was called a strong producer, which was supposed to mean that she got what she wanted from everyone who was working on a project. But, as she had explained to

Mike on the way over to the screening room, not only were Dick Albert's antics new to her, they had her positively dizzy.

Two weeks ago, Albert had decided that the director, who had wanted to shoot the script as written, was deliberately adding to costar Connie Lyall's close-ups. Gretchen knew that the director was doing exactly that, but not because he had become hostile to his male lead—naturally, he had—but because, as Mike could see, Albert looked too gaunt and sick to be starring in a movie at all. Mike decided against asking Gretchen about Albert's habits; she had enough on her mind. If anyone knew anything about Dick Albert and his real private life, it would be Dan Crawford. "If this movie were being shot in Germany," Gretchen had said as they walked past the sound stages a few minutes ago, "and I had to answer to the investors myself instead of Norman Birnbaum and his herd of custom-tailored asskissers, I would have fired Albert a long time ago. It would have been cheaper to reshoot his footage— really, it would have!"

She had telephoned Mike because she had received a call from Birnbaum about the murders. It had made Mike's head swim: he had just come from a Wednesday-morning command meeting, where he had heard for forty-five minutes about a uniformed officer's alleged drinking problem. Birnbaum wanted to see her, he had said; he wanted to make sure she was all right. "It's crazy!" she said excitedly only minutes later, after Mike had driven hurriedly over the hill to the studio. "I know this man. He wouldn't be bothered. I know you want to talk to me, Mike—I want to talk to you. My appointment with Birnbaum is this afternoon, so come over and have lunch with me—no, come earlier and watch the dailies with me. You'll enjoy it and we'll have more time to talk." While she hadn't discussed her business often, Gretchen had spoken of Birnbaum more than once. Mike thought she couldn't be wrong about the man by much. What Birnbaum breathed for was money. Albert was in this film because any film Albert made paid for itself in Japan alone—in fact, as Gretchen had told Mike in a fury a month ago, the profits of Albert's last film had allowed Galaxy International to buy a whole forest full of plywood in the state of Washington. Gretchen had come to Los Angeles because Norman Birnbaum had offered her a very favorable percentage of the profits her movies made, but now she knew that he had always planned to cheat her out of them. No trick was too low. Galaxy charged her rent for her office furniture, which had been there for years before her arrival, and which had been supplied by Birnbaum's own nephew. So much for the glamour of Hollywood. Looking at Albert's work, Mike could understand Gretchen's feelings of panic at the prospect of a failure here in America. She would be back to the beginning even in Germany. And success here, she had told Mike, depended less on the quality of her work than on the attitudes of marketmakers like Birnbaum, his fawning entourage, and the American theater owners, whose greatest profits came from the popcorn they sold. When she had thought Mike had found that unbelievable, she had said, "It's true! I have the statistics! I'm really in the popcorn business!

Mike had already known it: without popcorn and candy, most of the movie theaters in America wouldn't be profitable enough to survive. Now he heard the door of the screening room open behind them, but he said nothing to Gretchen. She had a clipboard in her lap, and on it, she had told him, was a memo from the director indicating that Albert's best work was on Takes 21 and 22. Out of the corner of his eye Mike caught the shadow of someone sitting down behind them. If Gretchen noticed, she gave no sign. There was a Take 23, like 22 a cover for any technical problem with Take 21. As it ran, a startlingly gay Dick Albert tossed the keys across the room and told his lesbian girlfriend that her truck had been towed away by the police who had been rude to him. Gretchen turned in her chair to speak to the projectionist and jumped at the sight of the figure sitting in the seat behind hers.

"Good morning, Mr. Birnbaum," she said as softly as Mike had ever heard her.

"Good morning, Gretchen."

Mike wanted to be careful. He moved his foot over onto Gretchen's and pressed gently as be reached around to Birnbaum. "Barney Phillips, Mr. Birnbaum. How are you?"

Birnbaum extended a limp, thin-boned hand. "Mr. Phillips." He gestured toward the small screen. "A brave role for Dick, don't you think? Imagine Humphrey Bogart camping it up like that."

"He did, in *The Big Sleep*. In Arthur Geiger's bookstore." Mike went into a lisp. "Do you have a *Ben Hur*?"

Birnbaum offered a small smile. "When I started in this business, no one knew anything about its history. Now you youngsters quote the classics scene by scene. A boy in our mailroom recites every line of *All About Eve*." He touched Gretchen's shoulder. "You're a little over budget, but it's understandable. A lot of actors wouldn't touch this part. They're not so secure about their image as Dick Albert."

Birnbaum was terrific. You *youngsters*; fair warning that your bullshit wasn't going to top his bullshit. Gretchen had told Mike that at Galaxy you learned quickly not to argue with Birnbaum. By listening carefully to his every comment, perceiving the intention of each inflection, each quick glance, you might arrive at the right place at the right time—*in the right way*, so you could flatter and praise Birnbaum without seeming to kowtow to him. With originality, surprise, art, charm, and selective repetition, you could be elevated to Birnbaum's inner circle of sycophants and acolytes. Mike believed it. For Gretchen it was a game for nitwits, working on her fear of failing, and she knew that the already-anointed at Galaxy were laughing at what was going on inside her. Through it all, she had told Mike, Birnbaum himself was always gracious, never rude. He was interested in what he could get out of her, which was this movie—and the next, if this was successful. His softspoken, seemingly gentle demeanor left her powerless. Galaxy International was a giant whorehouse and Norman Birnbaum its boss pimp, which made Gretchen Heidl one of the whores, she said—one of the *lesser* whores. The fact was that Dick Albert's role in her film was perhaps the juiciest for an established star since Dustin Hoffman's in *Tootsie*, a classic case of playing against type. But the Birnbaum-Galaxy party line—a rehearsal for the publicity campaign that would accompany the film—was that the story was unimaginably clever, the best man-woman brawl since *Adam's Rib,* and that its stars would be elevated to screen immortality.

The party line was also a certain amount of self-bullshitting craziness. Gretchen herself thought the script was, in its present form, derivative, cheap, and exploited the audience's sexual obsessions. The three fatassed, nicotine-stained writers had cranked in so many fast-paced, richly detailed bits of funny business that the audience might not see the script's fundamental weaknesses, like the characters' failure to come to terms with themselves—too serious, Birnbaum's flunkies had said. Certainly the finished product was going to have laughs, but it would have none of the poignant edge of Gretchen's last film. *Product* was the key word—Hollywood executives loved that word. It provided the clearest evidence of all that they wanted not her work, but her name to add prestige to what they were hoping would be a mass-market hit.

"I don't believe I know you, Mr. Phillips."

"I'm a writer."

"Have you written anything I might know?"

"I don't think so. I have a book coming out next year on Vietnam."

"Vietnam is a hot subject right now," Birnbaum said smoothly.

"I'm afraid my book may be too realistic," Mike said. "Gretchen has been explaining to me that you have to have somebody to root for."

"Yes, indeed." Birnbaum turned to Gretchen. "I had a few minutes and your secretary told me you were over here. I wanted you to know that what happened in your neighborhood the other day isn't really typical of America. Have the police been in touch with you?"

"No."

"Where is your place, by the way, in relation to the scene?"

"Across the street. I'm up the hill just a little."

"For God's sake! I didn't know! I was told you were close, but I didn't realize—"

Mike pressed Gretchen's foot again. Birnbaum knew where Gretchen lived. The police hadn't tried to contact Gretchen yet, but they would—they had already talked to Birnbaum. Why would somebody downtown want to do Birnbaum a favor? Contacting him couldn't be anything else. Under normal circumstances, detectives would knock on her door or simply show up at her office. That procedure wouldn't change because Mike had been seen and the police wanted to know who he was. The guy leaving with Gretchen the other morning really wouldn't have been a suspect anyway, not one guy wearing a white shirt, tie, and sports jacket. The police knew one guy couldn't have done all that killing in that manner without the help of others. This was something else. Birnbaum's interests were at stake. Gretchen's activities on Monday could make problems for Birnbaum only if those activities were publicized—and the police had almost perfect control over that. So it *was* something else. And Gretchen was caught in the middle.

"Well," Birnbaum said, "under the circumstances, I'm sure the police will be in touch with you soon. Tell them what they want to know and that will be the end of it."

Gretchen laughed, but Mike could hear her nervousness. "I don't know what they want to know."

"I'm sure it's just routine," Birnbaum said. "In this country, Gretchen, the police have very limited powers, and they interpret any sign of unwillingness to cooperate as hostility, or even guilt. Isn't that so, Mr. Phillips?"

"I guess it's something like that." Mike smiled easily. "I've never had any trouble with them, myself."

"A wise policy." He turned again to Gretchen. "I really want to see you give your full attention to this picture. The audience in Europe is waiting to see what you do with your first big-budget American picture. This can be a breakthrough for motion pictures."

Birnbaum's bullshit pushed the wrong button in Gretchen, because Mike could feel her jump. Breakthrough? Mike had heard how Birnbaum's henchmen had badgered her into removing the little that was individual or stinging in the original concept. Gretchen had said that she could barely remember that the gay man and the lesbian were to have been shown as fools whose wrecked lives were finally redeemed by the goodwill, trust, and compromise at the heart of any adult relationship, which the two had childishly evaded in their rush into homosexuality. "Why do you want to say a thing like that?" one Birnbaum princeling had asked. "All you're going to do is offend people." "Mike, having something to say has nothing to do with American movies," Gretchen had said. "These people out here believe that it is impossible for humanity to survive without moral or intellectual argument." According to Gretchen, Dick Albert was playing himself as a seducer of men instead of women, without a hint that the character had ever violated a single macho precept, much less had a dick up his ass.

Birnbaum saw Gretchen's reaction. "I'm afraid that this is really very important. In the natural course of things, Hollywood gets too much bad publicity. If William Holden had been somebody's Uncle Fred, or Natalie Wood the housewife next door, no one would have thought twice about their deaths. Everybody has problems. The police are going to ask you where you were that night and if you heard anything. Did you hear anything?"

"No."

"I don't mean to pry into your private life, but—"

"My private life is private, Mr. Birnbaum."

"Other neighbors heard things, Gretchen."

"What is the point of this? If there is something you want me to tell the police, just say what it is."

Birnbaum glanced at Mike. "Gretchen, you were seen leaving your house that morning *very* early."

"How do *you* know this?"

"Gretchen, what's important is that the police are curious about why you left your house so early. There's more to it than that—you're correct, you have a right to a private life. By the same reasoning, you can see that Galaxy International has just as much right to go about its business unencumbered by that same private life." He cleared his throat. "I'm certain there's a simple and entirely satisfactory explanation for what you were doing and it is my most sincere and thoughtful counsel that you put the police at their ease by answering all their questions quickly and completely."

"I left early that morning to be on the set, to do my job!"

"You're upset," Birnbaum said. "A mass murder is very serious business, especially in Los Angeles." Suddenly he stood up, and the inclined floor of the little theater made him tower over her. "If you consult an attorney—and perhaps you should—he might say that you would be well within your rights not divulging your private business, whatever your reason. But an attorney might also say that it would be a better course to give the police whatever they want to know, so they can go about their business—and you can go about yours."

The red light of the exit sign let them see him contract his dry cheeks in a tight, toothless, unforgiving smile; then, with the smile erased and his face hardened again, he turned to leave the room. At the door he did not look back. Mike did not believe that what Birnbaum had just said was wiped completely from his mind, but he looked it.

"I don't know if I can stand this," Gretchen said through her teeth. "I really don't give a shit about America anymore—"

The door opened again. Birnbaum stood silhouetted in the light from the hall behind him. "Gretchen? For your information, a city detective is on the lot somewhere—but not your office. I called there when I was given the word. Mr. Phillips? A pleasure to meet you." He closed the door again before she had a chance to reply. Mike couldn't help smiling. Gretchen didn't get the joke.

"He's talking about me," Mike whispered. "I flashed my badge at the gate. It's okay. Even if Birnbaum figures out that I'm the detective, he won't be able to connect me with a real name, because the guard waved me through."

"The one who reported your arrival," Gretchen said.

"If I ran a zoo like this, I'd have the same kind of standing orders." Mike remembered Dick Albert. "Does your star have a coke problem?"

"Oh, yes. He's got every kind of problem." Gretchen stood up. "He really isn't acting up there, you know. He's a bisexual who fucked his way to the top. For years he and a lesbian acted like they were wildly in love so their fans wouldn't get wise to them. On television! I thought you knew that, Mr. Detective. Don't you police know what goes on in this town?"

"The movie colony keeps itself closed to us."

"Yes, of course. Shall we forget about lunch? I'm not terribly hungry now, and I can catch up with some of my paperwork. You're an excellent actor, Mike. If I was seen, so were you—"

By the neighbors, Mike was sure; the noise of the killings must have awakened a lot of people.

"They'll want my name even though we couldn't possibly be suspects."

"What will I say?"

"Tell them the truth, up to a point. Tell them you're married, and that that's an embarrassment to the gentleman—he's a respected member of the community, blah, blah. If you want to get a lawyer, I'll pay the bill. A lawyer's probably a good idea anyway, now.''

"Because of Birnbaum? An army of lawyers wouldn't do any good if Birnbaum has already made up his mind to get me out of his life—and he's decided one way or the other already, I'm sure. He has an option on my next project. I won't know how he feels about this until I submit that. I won't know if I'm wasting my time—and *that's* depressing.''

"Suppose this picture is a big success?"

"Oh, I'm sure it will be, but if Birnbaum doesn't want me here, he'll have his goons spread the story that my contribution was zero—that it was a project no one could louse up.''

"I'm sorry.''

"It was already a bad situation. I don't belong in this country.''

He kissed her. "Call me later if you feel like taking the night off.''

She smiled. "I could use a swim in your pool. Would that be enough for you? Could you sleep with me without the sex?'' She pinched his cheek. "You should see your face—such disappointment! Well, I'll call you, and don't worry, I'll remember not to do it from home!'' Then she kissed him, moving away again with that dreamy, happy look—she would be with him tonight. There was no doubt about it.

Two blocks from the studio, Mike pulled into the parking lot of a junior market, and called Dan. Just in time, Dan said.

"That character Mitchell was arrested this morning up in King City. A guy in a gas station thought he was acting suspicious and got the drop on him. Mitchell was carrying a piece, same caliber as the one used in the motel room. Mitchell denied knowing anything about the car he had driven into the station, and when the locals ran the license through the computer, they thought they had a stolen car. They called down here to tell us, and the kid who took the call recognized the name of the car's owner as that of our victim. It looks like Mitchell really did kill the guy.''

"So we've cracked another case,'' Mike said.

"Damn right. The taxpayers should thank God we're on the job.''

7

THE CHIEF OF THE LOS ANGELES POLICE DEPARTMENT IS the highest paid official in the state of California, receiving over a hundred thousand dollars a year. By contrast, California's governor is paid approximately sixty thousand. Additionally, the chief of the LAPD is probably more powerful than any other individual answerable to the California public. The Police Commission is a rubber stamp, its meetings no more controversial or newsworthy than a class in Chinese cooking. The mayor of Los Angeles, on the other hand, cannot even effect an economy in the operation of the city without the approval of the twenty-one-member City Council. A chief has not only the income and the power, he has the *trappings:* two cars, a driver, a paneled, carpeted office. The people admitted to that office who considered Tom Cutler America's number one law enforcement officer found no fault with his taste or style; those who thought Cutler a power-mad fraud saw his mahogany desk polished with snake oil, the sheen of the blue silk drapes muted with whiffle dust.

"J. Edgar Hoover Revival," Dan called it. Dan liked to say that Cutler's office was as carefully prepared as a hairdresser's dinner party.

Behind Cutler's desk were the flags of the United States, the state of California, the city of Los Angeles, and the Los Angeles Police Department. To their left was a locked gun rack containing six rifles and shotguns from his private collection; on their right, a waist-high shelf bearing a small color television set and a multiband radio capable of receiving police transmissions from all over Southern California. Cutler kept his desk clean; the *Los Angeles Times* had reported that he was happiest when only his appointments calendar, dictating equipment, and telephone were on it. His paperwork, in neat piles, was on a side table against one well-rubbed paneled wall. On the opposite side of the room were a sofa, two chairs, and a coffee table where he met with guests. Subordinates sat on the other side of the massive desk from him, in chairs lower than his own. When his guests left and subordinates were dismissed, the last thing they saw was a photograph of Tom Cutler with the president of the United States. The picture was on the wall next to the door so people didn't notice it when they arrived. On their way out, however, it served as a reminder that they had been in the presence of a man completely comfortable with power. The picture showed the president and Tom Cutler in hunting clothes, holding shotguns. At their feet were a pair of cowed retrievers and the morning's kill, a half-dozen mallard. The president was laughing uproariously at something Tom Cutler just said. Cutler was a big, barrel-chested man, as tall as the president, with blue eyes and salt-and-pepper, crew-cut hair. It was not possible to pass the photograph without reading the President's inscription: *For Tom, Good Friend, Boon Companion, Great American and Reinventor of the Martini—Always the Best.*

And it was signed with the president's nickname.

Mike had last been in the office about six months ago, for an organizational meeting of a Hollywood street crime task force that was later delayed, then finally canceled. Cutler hadn't even sat in on that meeting, spending the hour and a half behind his desk, talking on the telephone; apparently he had only wanted it to take place where he could watch it. Now Cutler was on the telephone, the handset braced against his shoulder. He acknowledged Mike with a little wave and pointed to one of the chairs facing the desk.

"I don't give a flying fuck what the councilman wants, or thinks his district deserves," Cutler said into the telephone, while Mike took a couple of deep breaths and tried to relax. "Sure, tell him what I said. Where the hell was he last year when those witch doctor ministers were raising hell about that Aunt Jemima who got shot? Where's the fair play? She threw a knife at one of my boys. Your fucking councilman kept using the word 'alleged.' We had four eyewitnesses, and you know as well as I do that my boy was *trained* to empty his gun. That training holds—it won't change while I'm chief." Cutler hung up. "That needle-dicked bugfucker doesn't even know why he called me now. Where the hell is Hammond? Larry Hammond was supposed to be here." He picked up the telephone again and pushed a single button. "Get Hammond, will you? I've got Gallagher sitting in front of me instead of checking fingerprints and shit, which is what he's being paid for." Now Cutler winked at Mike, clasped his hands, and pursed his lips. "Ruppert says you got another one yesterday."

Mitchell. "The guy jumped into jail." Mike saw Cutler's eyes go to the door. "We have a bit more to do before the case is made."

"Hello, Gallagher," Hammond said as he sat down.

"Let's get on with this," Cutler said. "Mike, Larry tells me that you were at the Laurel Canyon crime scene the afternoon of the murders and then at the autopsies the next morning. Now I know you didn't get the word we passed down until after the autopsies that we wanted the cooperation of all concerned—"

"Actually, Chief," Hammond said, "Gallagher and I had a conversation on S level—"

"I know that," Cutler snapped. "Gallagher, it has to be as obvious as the dick on a moose that this is a Parker Center case, but for your information, it's a little more than that. If I hear word one about what I'm about to tell getting around, I'll have your balls grooved for yo-yos and strung with barbed wire, so help me Christ. This is a federal case. There has been an investigation ongoing for almost a year. How the murders of these assholes fits into the scheme of things is not your problem, has never been your problem, will not *become* your problem. Captain Ruppert assured me as recently as an hour ago that you're doing a superior job. Let's keep it that way. Do you have any question about what I've explained so far?''

"No." Cutler hadn't explained anything so far—it was all bullshit, and Mike wondered how Cutler and Hammond were able to keep their faces straight. There had been no federal people on the scene Monday afternoon, none at the coroner's building on Tuesday morning.

"There will be arrests in connection with this case very soon," Cutler said. "Perhaps as early as the weekend, certainly by the middle of next week. Do you get the fucking picture now? Stay away from this, Gallagher. Mind your own business."

Mike stood up. "I have the idea."

Cutler brought his hands down hard on his desk. "What the hell were you doing at the murder scene in the first place?"

Mike could see the corner of Hammond's mouth twisting smugly. Mike had prepared himself for the question. He said, "I was doing my job. If you were in my position, you would have been there, too."

Cutler glanced at Hammond, but from what he saw Mike couldn't be sure that Cutler knew Hammond hadn't been on Rainbow Drive that afternoon. Nothing Cutler had said about arrests forthcoming explained the electronic surveillance of the neighborhood—what were they trying to find? And what about Norman Birnbaum's insistence that Gretchen tell all to the investigating team? Cutler was bubbling confidence, but there was a lot he didn't know, and was scrambling desperately to learn. Now he waved his hand in a gesture of dismissal. The telephone rang and he grabbed the receiver. "I told you no calls." He listened. "Oh. Get his number and ask him if I can call him back." He paused. "When this man says he's home, you find out which one, San Marino or Malibu." Mike noticed Hammond looking concerned and unhappy. Cutler hung up. "Get out of here, Gallagher. We've got more important things to do than piss around with you."

* * *

When he was out of the downtown area, Mike called Hollywood Homicide's direct line and caught Marvin Burgess. Burgess had one of those deep bass voices and sang at his church, the oldest African Methodist Episcopal church in Los Angeles. Dan was out cleaning up the Mitchell case, but had said he would call before lunch. Mike remembered that Burgess had been the one to warn him about the Laurel Canyon case, which made things simpler now.

"A message for him, Marvin. Tell Dan that it's time to lay off the German dame matter. He'll know what I mean."

"I think I do, too," Burgess said. "I'm glad to hear it. I've been around a long time, and I have seen some shit."

"You're seeing some now. Just tell Dan to lay off. We have enough to do."

"You can be sure I'll tell him," Burgess said.

Next, Mike called Gretchen's office. She was out. He wanted to ask the secretary when Gretchen would be back, but he didn't want to show an anxiety the secretary would translate into something stronger when she relayed the message. He just wanted to be sure Gretchen really knew she could cooperate fully without giving his name. All she had to say was that her boyfriend was married and she wanted to protect him. When the team came up against that once or twice, the questioning would stop. No detective wanted his superiors asking if he was harassing a witness. If Gretchen waved a lawyer at the department, that's exactly what would happen.

Maybe arrests really were forthcoming, and Cutler's apparent confidence was authentic, but Mike couldn't help focusing on the massive electronic surveillance and the pressure Birnbaum was putting on Gretchen: those things told Mike to be more careful than ever. If Mike took a certain paranoiac—or simply self-protective—point of view, Cutler's instructions to Mike to mind his own business was only the first step in setting him up. All Cutler needed was one asshole claiming that Hollywood Division had knowledge of what was going on in Laurel Canyon before the murders, or that Mike Gallagher had muscled into the Rainbow Drive operation, and Mike would be suspended immediately, outside looking in, and dependent on lawyers and private detectives—whatever he could afford, which wasn't much—simply to clear his name. Of course he would fail: charges against a cop were always page one; dismissal of those charges were always in the back of the paper. Maybe Mike would be able to continue as a cop, but his command would be gone, and he would never get another one. For that matter, if Cutler wanted, he could even twist Mike's relationship with Gretchen into something criminal.

So Mike had to defy Cutler. He had to continue to pursue to protect himself down the line, if necessary. But now the penalty for taking that course was clear—had been *made* clear by Cutler. If Cutler learned that Mike or others were poking around in the Rainbow Drive case, the outcome of the confrontation that followed would have the predictability of a battle between an ant and a garbage truck. Mike wanted Dan well clear of Rainbow Drive—it was much too serious for any trading on friendship, no matter how long, abiding, or deep. Burgess having the message was almost as good as Dan having it himself: Burgess was that kind of reliable. Mike already felt lighter on his feet, he was so relieved.

He was almost amused with the other relief he felt, the relief of not having to walk away from what he heard, the murders themselves, or being saddled permanently with the memory that he had done as much on Monday morning. He knew intellectually that there was nothing he could have done at the time, but he could not help feeling something unpleasant that had seemed in just moments to become something awful, terrible—a sense of having abandoned his duty. . . .

"Flatfoot," he said aloud, as he got back in the car.

Back at his desk, he did the preliminary paperwork on the Mitchell case for the DA, and in the evening at home, when he had a load of laundry in the dryer, he worked on his backstroke. He wanted to call Judy about the dog, but didn't, afraid that pushing would cause her to react badly—or rather, give her the opportunity to react badly. Mike knew he would have only himself to blame if he wound up spending the night stewing about Judy. Gretchen had closed the apartment that morning, leaving behind a note in German—a joke: Mike couldn't read German, and didn't know anyone who could. It was altogether possible that Gretchen's German was a double-barreled joke: she had that kind of sense of humor. Mike had slept like a puppy last night and she had joked about having to wait until this morning for seconds. The note just might take the complaint one step further.

June weather had come early to Los Angeles this year, the return of skies that were overcast in the mornings, the sun breaking through by midafternoons. Mike could still remember his father talking about Southern California weather. His observations were engraved on Mike's mind: if you did not have air-conditioning, June provided the last good weather for sleeping until mid-October. Mike's father had liked the winter best. The winter light had reminded him of England, which he had seen during World War Two—he had seen Italy, France, and Germany, too. Mike could remember his father's stories, which played in Mike's mind in the grainy images of newsreels re-shown on the black-and-white television of the fifties. There were times now when live by-satellite pictures of Europe made Mike think of his father's odd, short life. Gretchen knew that Mike's father had died young. And had fought in the war. Gretchen's parents had told her stories about having had to eat cats and dogs to stay alive in the months following the Allied invasion of Germany. Every vestige of all those years had disappeared, and now their only meaning seemed to be in their meaninglessness.

Friday was busy. Mike caught a young woman in her apartment on Beachwood, dead three or four days, almost certainly of an overdose. No drugs or paraphernalia in any of the rooms. Dan was downtown presenting the Mitchell case. Yesterday he had tracked down Yolanda and had gotten the motel clerk to identify Mitchell from a mug shot as the man who had registered at the motel with the victim. Without both of those elements, the case remained only circumstantial—Mitchell could claim that he had bought the car and the gun from a stranger. Reasonable doubt. Rosenberg had taken the call on the dead woman for the coroner's office and did not look happy when

Mike told him that no probable cause of death had been turned up yet. "You're not going to get anything definite out of me for a week or ten days," Rosenberg said. "It's going to take that long to run the tests." The body was in a fetal position, nude, in the bathroom where a window had been left open. Insects had gotten at her and it was possible there wasn't enough skin left to reveal a puncture wound if one existed. With the balcony door open for air, Mike stayed in the living room leafing through her address book while Rosenberg's assistants got the corpse into a bag and down to the wagon. The fingerprint team and the photographer had yet to arrive. This case got photography; it wasn't important enough for videotape. None of the names in the address book seemed to be that of a known asshole. According to the driver's license and pay stubs in her purse, the woman had come from Kansas and had been working in the record business. At this stage, the body bore only a resemblance to the photograph of the perky young girl on the driver's license. Mike was going to need a dental chart for identification. If the young woman's Los Angeles friends knew something about her using drugs, or running with bad company, they weren't going to volunteer helpful information. Why should they? Her family was half a continent away and there was no sense of community in Los Angeles for which to put anything personal at risk. Death by misadventure was always a less satisfying professional experience for Mike than suicide or murder, which at least had the heft of intent.

Mike stepped out on the balcony, and after a moment Rosenberg found him. He told Mike the joke about the proctologist's patient who asked for the insertion of another finger because he wanted a second opinion. Mike had heard that one, but the pleasure Rosenberg got from telling his jokes was infectious. The balcony gave a view of the bank buildings downtown, lookalike rectangular high-rises that someone had described as the boxes Disneyland had come in. The air was better outside, two stories above the street. TGIF, Mike thought.

"Those people on Rainbow Drive were killed early Monday morning," Rosenberg said.

"So?"

"So the ambulance didn't take away the survivor until after

four o'clock. His Elmership, Washington, knew about the murders in the morning. Now Elmer is all excited about being the subject of a miniseries.''

Rosenberg was saying that the clearance to sell his story to television was Washington's payoff for playing along. Mike smiled. "Why are you telling me all this?"

"I thought you were interested."

"I was told not even to be curious. How is the survivor?"

Now it was Rosenberg's turn to smile. "Still comatose, but stable. She's a long way from being brain-dead, by the way."

Mike eyed him. "People were concerned?"

"According to my friend in the hospital's pathology department, people have been. There is a wall still going up around this case. Washington told me not to be curious, too. Somebody denied that woman necessary medical treatment, and Washington made himself an accessory. I'll tell anybody who asks, once he's out. I love to piss in people's soup—it's a little perversion I have."

"Watch your shoes," Mike said.

"Oh, I do. I'm not a brave man. I don't even want to be. I just wish I was a more serious person. I got into this work because I wasn't going to be good dealing with patients, and pathology interested me. I didn't think that there would be advantages I could take. Naive, that's my problem."

Mike didn't get back to Hollywood Division until almost four-thirty, but by then he had already resigned himself to working into the evening and probably Saturday, too. Someone had been in the apartment when the girl had overdosed, removing drugs or paraphernalia, which made that person at least an accessory. Waiting for the fingerprint team and the photographer this afternoon, Mike had interviewed people in the apartment building, and by telephone, the owner of the place. The girl had been a resident for a little over nine months, and no one remembered a thing about her. In the downstairs garage, her car keys had unlocked a 1976 Datsun 210, beat up and rusting through, probably a Kansas car. The California pink slip dated from '83. Mike didn't want to call her employer until he knew a little more about the girl's personal life. Chances were good that the girl had had friends where she had worked, and anyone Mike spoke to wouldn't necessarily cooperate because Mike was a nice guy. He had to have a plan. The place had been lousy with fingerprints, but that was normal. He wasn't going back to her apartment until tomorrow, when some of the stink had blown out. A young woman wouldn't have a lot of papers, and Mike hadn't seen them today in any of the obvious places. The names in the address book could be checked for everything from felonies down to traffic violations. Even at the beginning, this seemed like a very long road, but Mike wanted to go it alone. Dan had covered for him enough this week. There had been a message from Dan waiting when Mike had come in from Beachwood. The Mitchell case had been no problem. Of course, the filing deputy DA had pissed and moaned about Yolanda being from the street. Dan wanted to have a telephone conversation with Mike before the end of the day about some information that had come in on another matter. Juan Lopez was the only one to have seen Dan, but Lopez didn't know where Dan had gone next. Now Lopez was gone for the day, and Greg Novak and taciturn Bill Blair were cleaning up their own paperwork. Taking his turn, Novak picked up the next call.

"Yeah, he's here. Hang on. Mike? It's Dan."

"Hello, you old turd."

Dan waited for Novak to hang up. "I had a call from the manager of Donnie Jackson's apartment house. He's moving—"

"Hey, I thought you were going to lay off. You got the message I gave Burgess—"

"Oh, sure. This is all right. We're at a distance, and I think I'm on to something. Jackson gave the apartment manager his notice yesterday afternoon. Jackson will be out by tomorrow night."

Mike concealed his reaction. There was nothing he could say directly to Dan about disobeying instructions when he had drawn Dan into this—for personal reasons—in the first place. He was going to have to figure out another way to get the message across. "That's quick."

"Quicker than you think. Jackson told her he bought a house.

When he paid his rent at the beginning of the month, he didn't say a word about moving. How fast can you close on a house, even on a cash deal? He's already been to the PO with a forwarding address—or rather, his blond girlfriend has. I got a line on her. She used to be in the same business as Paula Rogers. After checking the county records on Jackson's new address, I ducked into a porn shop and looked at some magazines. After seeing the blonde by the pool the other day, I had a hunch. If still pictures tell us anything, that girl can suck the tiles off a space shuttle.''

''You're too old to be an astronaut.''

''That's what you think. Look, I got a lot more on this. I'm going to grab a bite downtown here and wait for the traffic to let up. You know the Clown Club on the Strip. Meet me there at nine o'clock.''

''Why so late?''

''The library's open,'' Dan said. ''I want to catch up on my reading.''

Handing over the valet parking ticket, the red-jacketed young Mexican acted as if he thought nothing of Mike, but then Mike saw the kid's eyes in motion, as if he wanted an emergency exit. The roar of the overamplified rock band inside the Clown Club assaulted Mike's ears all the way out here on the sidewalk, within feet of the rumbling bumper-to-bumper traffic on Sunset Strip. Mike had arrived feeling unpleasantly antsy and tense, and the valet's poorly veiled suspicion was not helping. Mike was wondering if the youngster was going to report Mike's arrival to Jack Skelley, the club's owner. Dan thought they had business in this dump, and having Skelley watching them was only going to make business difficult.

Jack Skelley was a hood whose record in prostitution, extortion, and arson predated by many years his arrival in Los Angeles from Detroit, where he had been connected with financing the porn racket. Skelley did not know Mike, but Mike had been aware of Skelley for years. Mike had seen an FBI crime flow chart, a kind of table of organization, that had put Skelley in the middle level of porn financing and production. Mike knew Dan too well to believe he had chosen the Clown Club for a meeting place without serious reason. Dan could always find another way to express his contempt for the punk and new wave music Skelley threw at the loony kids who came in here. Mike had grown up on rock 'n' roll, but he knew popular music had been getting progressively worse since World War Two, and so had the kids who listened to it: if there was a conclusion to be drawn from that, it went beyond music and possibly had nothing to do with it.

Dan was at the far end of the long bar, a bottle of Heineken in front of him. He looked tired as well as soured by the environment. The place smelled lousy, almost like backed-up sewage. In this crowd of emaciated twenty-year-olds, two beefy cops were as inconspicuous as a pair of pimps in a convent. As Mike approached, Dan gave the bartender a V sign for two more beers.

"You look like a cop," Dan said. It was his standard greeting.

"You're not the only one who thinks so," Mike answered. "The valet just gave me a worried look."

Dan laughed. "He probably thought you were Immigration."

Mike smiled sheepishly. "That didn't occur to me." The bartender appeared with the Heinekens. He was a big, powerfully built guy with dark curly hair and a close-cropped mustache and beard. He had a small gold hoop in his ear that made him look like a pirate. "What do you have to eat here?"

"Dead hamburgers and soggy fries," Dan said.

"Why does this place smell so bad?"

The bartender glanced at Dan and shrugged. "Maybe it's the food."

"I guess I'll pass," Mike said.

When they were alone, Dan said, "Donnie Jackson's moving into West Hollywood, which is still under the jurisdiction of the sheriff's department. I have the address, on Norma Place right behind the 9000 Sunset Building—you know, that office highrise. The view into the place on Norma ought to be terrific from the upper floors. I really think I'm on to something. I only went to the PO to get Jackson's change of address so we could keep tabs on him, but I know Norma, it's just a run-down street of old bungalows, slated for redevelopment, and the move itself seemed awful sudden. The manager of the apartment building was emphatic about him saying he'd *bought* a house, and given the way he showed off that Cadillac, I thought we ought to know more about the deal he'd made. It turns out that he didn't buy anything. The title of the house has been in the same name since the late seventies. It's never changed hands. There's a daisy chain here, if you'll bear with me. Jackson used to be a stand-up comic. In that capacity, he worked for the owner of this club, Jack Skelley—''

"I know who he is," Mike said. He told Dan about the FBI crime flow chart and how Skelley fit into the Detroit picture.

"I didn't connect the name on the deed to the Norma place to anybody right away," Dan said. "I went around to the porn shop to see if I could find the blonde, which I did. No name, unless you want to believe it's Baby Rae Bozo. Those guys have some imaginations. The magazine was a C. C. Publication, and C. C. Publishing Company has its offices in 9000 Sunset. C.C. is close enough to Clown Club. I stopped by the 9000 Building on my way here. Actually, I found a parking space down the block from there and walked here. Guess whose name I found on the directory, under C.C.?''

"Not Skelley's," Mike said. He knew how Dan's mind worked.

"No. A guy named Bernie Maxwell. Ever hear of him?''

"Nope.''

"Neither have I," Dan said. "He's the guy who has title to the house on Norma. In the same suite in the 9000 Building is Maxwell-Skelley Productions. The mortgage on the Norma house, by the way, is held by Harcourt Pryor. I've seen him in the society pages." Dan sipped his beer. "Yeah," he said after a moment, "Pryor is on the business pages, too.''

The band stopped and the crowd gave a thin, short-lived cheer. Mike said, "The only connection all this has to Laurel Canyon is that Jackson knew one of the victims, Chambers, and that according to Jackson's landlady, Jackson was off his turf for the three days overlapping the time of the murders, and the further circumstance that an asshole named Bernie Maxwell has helped him with his housing problem.''

"Or put Jackson right where he can keep an eye on him. You know, there's usually some truth behind an asshole's bullshit. Jackson was pretty proud of that Caddie that he got from Jerry Chambers. Now he's making noise about buying a house. Renting with an option to buy is the same thing, from the buyer's point of view. Skelley's no dope—figure Maxwell isn't a dope either. After five murders in Laurel Canyon, the heat is on and they have to protect one of their boys, whatever the reason. In the house on Norma, Jackson's under their thumb, whether he knows it or not."

Mike said, "You know, Chambers could have gotten back to Jackson about you talking to him about that car. It would be nice to know if Jackson has registered the car or transferred it to somebody else. Has he tried to put distance between himself and the murders?"

Dan laughed. "I thought we were going to drop it."

"I said it would be nice to know, not that we were going to work to find out. We have to talk about this—"

Dan shrugged. "It's a difficult thing to let go of. I told you I wanted to catch up on my reading—"

"Hold it," Mike said. A movement at the other end of the bar had caught his attention. Three people, a man and two women, had just entered, the three holding each other so tightly around the waists that Mike was ready to believe they were holding each other up. In the middle, the man was scanning the room as if it could be full of snipers. Dan put his hand up to his mouth.

"Surprise. The redhead is Paula Rogers. I don't know the other two." The woman in the man's left arm was a chalk-white, dark-haired, dulleyed waif who looked as if she weighed no more than ninety pounds. Rogers looked like a nasty piece of work, with dark, angry eyes slathered with mascara—all of her makeup was heavy, and it made her look tough. Under everything, Mike thought, was an attractive girl, but not bright, and without real joy. She had a chip on her shoulder, ready to tell you what to do with yourself if you criticized or even questioned her style or behavior. It was the man who really interested the cop in Mike. The man was in his late thirties, tall, relatively well-proportioned, with brown eyes, even features, and dark brown hair. He looked as if he were suffering from lack of sleep, but his interest in the women indicated that he was not upset with the prospect of another long night. In fact, he was acting as if he were more than man enough for both of them. That he was their style there could be no doubt: in a nightclub, he was wearing a sleeveless undershirt, unpressed baggy pants held up by wide suspenders, and a broad-brimmed, soiled Panama hat.

"Here comes Skelley," Dan said.

A little guy in his forties was pushing through the crowd toward the guy in the Panama hat.

"Does he know you?" Mike asked.

"No, I'm making him from what I just saw in the newspapers I was reading. I told you I was at the PO. The blonde didn't leave a change of address form for herself. I guess she doesn't get any mail. I got a good look at her the other day. At the library I was hoping I'd see her picture in one of those ads you say are near the television listings. No sale. The other thing I was looking for was a story I read last year about Skelley being questioned by a federal grand jury. No sale there either."

Skelley had slicked-back, graying hair and the pinched features of a ferret. The big guy in the Panama hat disentangled himself from the women and shook Skelley's hand. Skelley waved to the big bartender, who responded quickly. Instinctively Dan turned away and Mike hid his face behind his upraised bottle of beer. From what Mike could see, the bartender said nothing about them. Mike told Dan what Cutler had said the other morning about the Laurel Canyon murders being part of a federal case. "To tell you the truth, I didn't buy into it at the time."

"That grand jury was investigating RICO offenses," Dan said. "That's all that was ever said. If it ever got anywhere, it wasn't to arrests and indictments."

RICO was a federal statute, the Racketeer-Influenced and Corrupt Organizations Act, and had just stood up to Supreme Court challenge. Aimed at millionaire dope dealers, its strongest provision allowed for the confiscation by the government of a convicted mobster's assets—houses, yachts, cars, airplanes, even businesses. Unless the accountants could prove it came from honest labor, it was gone, sold by the government at public auction. Mike knew one guy who had made ten million dollars in a single year; now the guy was back working for hourly wages in the construction business, bolting together fast-food stores. Being without his Laguna Beach condo and Jaguars hurt him more than the three years he had spent on Terminal Island.

Now the big dark-haired guy did something that startled Mike.

"How about that?" Mike said mostly to himself.

"What?"

"He's speaking German. When Gretchen starts going, her mouth changes shape a little. You know how a Frenchman dangles a cigarette out of the corner of his mouth the way nobody else can? Same thing. The big goon's speaking German."

"He could be faking it," Dan said.

"I don't think so." As Mike watched, Skelley and the big guy stepped away from the bar, in the direction from which Skelley had come.

"Now we know what this little party is for," Dan said. "I suppose it's as good a way of doing business as any other."

"This is early in the day for a dope dealer," Mike said. "All night tonight, all night tomorrow—that's his busy season. Chambers knew Jackson, Jackson knows Skelley and Rogers, and they know this clown. If he's scoring, he's going straight home. I want to see where he lives."

"Okay," Dan said. "The five people in Laurel Canyon were scumbucket dirtballs. This is a little bigger league, pointing toward one bigger still, if it was the subject of a federal grand jury investigation. Tell me how it all ties together."

Mike didn't know. "I'd like to learn more about that Billy Lansing. Lansing beat a murder rap because a state cop shot the only witness."

"I thought we were out of this," Dan said.

"Oh, we are—believe it, Kimosabe." Another guy joined the two women. He was slight, fair-haired, and shabbily dressed. He had a four-day growth glinting on his cheeks. Mike remembered "Bobby" arriving at Paula Rogers' apartment the other night. Now she seemed less enthusiastic about seeing him. And the other girl eased away. "Do you know that character?"

"He looks familiar," Dan said. "Oh, shit. If it's the guy I'm thinking of, the mighty fall hard." Mike watched the guy smile submissively at something Rogers said. Dan said, "I know him. You were in the service. He was a television actor, ran with the biggest. He was going to be a star."

"His first name is Bobby," Mike said.

"Bobby Michaels. He worked all the series, even had one of his own. Another guy I was wondering what happened to. We can see it now. It looks like everything disgusting has him by the balls. For a while he shared a house in Malibu with your girlfriend's star, Dick Albert. The creep had a couple of hot years. The story about him was that he would do anything to any woman, no matter how ugly or foul-smelling. Now he looks like he lives in the streets."

"He probably does," Mike said. "Gretchen told me that Albert has nose problems, too, and judging by what I saw in those dailies, those problems are current. A big movie star like Dick Albert doesn't have to use a bullshit guy like this Michaels to run his errands for him, but he would if he wanted to do him a favor—or remind the guy what he's done to his life. I'm going to get out of here so I can tail the big guy when he leaves. You pay for the beer. Give Marge a kiss for me and have a nice weekend."

"Call me tomorrow," Dan said. "I'm interested in where Panama hat lives."

Mike was on his feet. "Be ready to get up early. I pulled a juicy one on Beachwood Drive and I want to get a jump on it."

"Sure you don't need me?"

"Nah. Come down to her autopsy Monday with me. You're going to fall in love."

Outside, Mike quickly maneuvered his car onto a side street facing the Strip and the entrance to the Clown Club. It took the big guy and the two women another fifteen minutes to emerge, and while they waited for the red-jacketed valet to return with their car, the guy looked over one shoulder and the other, then deftly and quickly spooned cocaine into the nostrils of his lady friends. The sidewalk under the Clown Club's glaring flood-lights was fairly crowded, but none of the passersby seemed to notice.

Now the Mexican brought up the big guy's vehicle—not a car, but a badly dented, rusted, faded red, sixties Volkswagen bus. After one of the women had settled herself in the middle seat, the big guy leaned back from behind the wheel and kissed her. The Mexican valets watched with unconcealed admiration as the bus burned rubber pulling away. The thing had a souped-up engine or, more probably, a Porsche implant.

The bus was headed east on Sunset. Because of its height, it was impossible for Mike to see into it. The guy was in the left lane. Past Casablanca Records on the north side, then Liquor Locker. On the south side of Sunset at the corner of Crescent Heights was a branch of Great Western Savings and Loan, the parking lot of which had been the site of the old Garden of Allah, where Scott Fitzgerald, Dorothy Parker, and Robert Benchley had lived. Dan had taught Mike all that. That was the Hollywood Dan cared about, the Hollywood of great, hilarious stories. Until last year, Schwab's had been on the next block, and the legend had it that Benchley once had been so drunk that he called a cab to take him to Schwab's. Fitzgerald's last apartment was around the corner, on North Laurel Avenue. Mike knew the big guy wasn't going to glide by Schwab's. No, the big guy slipped into the left-turn lane, put on his directional signal, and waited for the green arrow that would allow him to turn north.

Mike was right behind the bus at the turn, but let it scoot ahead at the next light, where Hollywood Boulevard began to wind up into the hills. Mike wasn't concerned. Ahead, Crescent Heights became Laurel Canyon Boulevard, two lanes wide, twisting upward through the steep hillside chaparral. There weren't a half-dozen turnoffs between Hollywood Boulevard and Mulholland at the top of the hill, and if necessary, Mike would go up and down every one of the Canyon's side streets to find the bus—but Mike was more sure than ever that that wouldn't be necessary.

The bus darted in and out of view up around the curves winding up the bottom of the Canyon. Higher, the air became cool and damp, and refreshing, air that made Los Angeles such a pleasant place to live, the result of the marine layer that eased in nightly from the Pacific. It reached the higher elevations first, which was why the rich had appropriated the hills all over Southern California. As Mike turned into the long straight of Rainbow Drive, he saw a set of taillights wink out far up the hill. The garage door of the murder house was still up, but now the garage was empty. Along eight feet of sidewalk was a row of plastic garbage cans, filled, their lids balanced on their contents, and on top of them were several heaps of carpet, discreetly folded with the undersides showing, lest the neighbors see the dried, brown bloodstains on the sheared broadloom. The VW bus was farther up the hill, parked, dark.

Mike's heart was pounding. He backed off the gas pedal and looked up at the canyon walls encrusted with houses. Even though the helicopter's flight records might be in the hands of the men culpable of the malfeasance after, during, and perhaps even before the murders, and therefore unavailable, the noise of the helicopter ratcheting off these stone formations must have awakened many witnesses—but that probably didn't mean much, either. People didn't want to get involved, and with the passage of time, the story would fall out of their heads. But not only was that the way L.A. worked, it was the way people who had something to hide *made* it work. They played for time, and in time their problems faded.

As his car slowly climbed Rainbow Drive past the big guy's bus, Mike kept his head straight and turned only his eyes toward the figures he could faintly see moving away in the darkness. The house was higher than street level, and the big guy and the women on either side were trying to climb the narrow stairs as a threesome. The house above looked like something out of an English horror movie, with one light on in an upper corner window, but the important thing was that it was only a few hundred feet up the hill from the murder house. Mike had already memorized the license plate of the bus, and unless the big guy was already known to Parker Center, a check on his identity could be run out of Hollywood Division without the computer electronically hollering "Rape!" Still, Mike was not certain he wanted to run a check on his own; what he knew of the heat coming out of Cutler's office made it clear that security around Laurel Canyon murders extended to people unknown to anyone except the few who had the real inside information about the case.

The thought was barely out of Mike's mind when he reached

the top of Rainbow Drive and ran out of pavement. He hadn't even thought of looking to see if Gretchen's lights were on. He had his foot on the brake pedal when he looked over his shoulder to check his maneuvering room. Far down Rainbow Drive, under a streetlight, but as if in a shadow, something moved: a car. A car traveling without headlights? *He had been followed!* There was nothing Mike could do about it now, or the tip-off lie had given the tail by stepping on the brakes. The car was pulled over to the curb, and if the driver knew his business, he'd be long gone on foot by the time Mike got back down there—but probably not so far away that he would not see Mike take down the car's license number. But there it was: somebody was on to Dan and him. It was useful to know that they could not proceed without that somebody knowing—somebody who could be *anybody*, from Cutler and Hammond to these coke-dealing cheesebrains to person or persons unknown who could be just as dangerous as the others.

Heading down the hill, Mike flipped on the high beams and let the car drift toward the left side so the front license plate of the other vehicle would show up clearly. The letters started with W—that was '78 or '79. The car seemed older than that, one of those lumpy Japanese luxocruisers from the middle seventies. The car or the plate could be stolen, or the whole package could already be logged in the Sacramento computer as a trap for Mike—or Dan—to put a foot in. Mike went slowly the rest of the way down, watching the rearview mirror, but the other car did not move. Mike turned off Laurel Canyon Boulevard and nosed the car around again to see if the other car was still following. No. He waited ten minutes. Dan was going to hear about this promptly—which meant in the morning. Dan needed at least a half hour to get to Valencia and by then he and Marge were entitled to their privacy. Mike headed home.

The light on the answering machine was blinking three times rapidly between long pauses—there had been three calls. Mike got a pencil and paper. The first message was from Gretchen. She had been invited to a barbecue in Calabasas on Sunday and wanted him to join her. Birnbaum wouldn't be there, so he could be himself. She said she was still thinking about Mike's quick improv in the screening room—it was no wonder that he had been offered so many opportunities to act. The Calabasas barbecue was being given by an old character man and his wife of thirty years who were famous for their hospitality. Gretchen wanted Mike to attend, that was clear. He'd have it figured out in the morning. Actually, it didn't sound like a bad idea.

The second message was a hang-up, the second of the week. One hang-up meant nothing, but two in four days was a matter of interest. Mike's number was unlisted, but that did not mean it was not widely circulated. The first call had come in while Mike still had had his announcement tape running. If the same person had made both calls, it was someone who wanted to talk to Mike without leaving evidence. Of course, that could mean that the caller was only someone from Mike's past, feeling shy.

Mike had other things to think about, like being followed onto Rainbow. Drive. The big guy in the goofy clothes who spoke German lived in a house that would have been a perfect staging area for the ragged band Mike had heard outside Gretchen's window. Chambers to Jackson to Skelley to the big guy. And with branches leading off to a federal grand jury, an overdose in Palm Springs—the pasty-faced little drip with Rogers and the big guy had looked a likely candidate for the overdose, but she hadn't looked or acted as if she had the clout to get her out of a jam in high style. Of course the bailout from the hospital could have come from another direction, for another reason. Somebody had *followed* Mike. That sort of thing made a cop mad—and probably clouded his judgment.

The voice on the third message was new to Mike, female, soft, musical, and gentle.

"Mr. Gallagher, my name is Laura Demming. My colleague, a friend of your ex-wife, gave me your number and asked me to call about the dog given to one of the students in my class. I'm sorry to say that she no longer has the dog, but her aunt, the little girl's guardian, brought it down to the school yesterday after school, which was after Judy called my colleague. I was able to get a look at the dog's vaccination tag and copy all the information on it. My father was a policeman, so I assumed that that was what you really wanted. I would have called last night but I left your telephone number in my desk in the classroom. There's a special situation that I have to discuss with you." She left her number for a return call, and then added that his announcement tape seemed to be out of order.

He swam, did his sit-ups, boiled out in the sauna, showered, went to bed, and then got out of it twenty minutes later to turn on Carson—a rerun, with jokes about Walter Mondale. It took Mike a few minutes to realize that he had seen the show the first time, which seemed at this moment a long time ago in his own life. Just last summer, when Mike had been between women he could be interested in. He had been out of his marriage three years when he had realized that he had never been really in love. Now he left the program on not because his memory of it made him lose interest and he could relax into drowsiness, but as a matter of curiosity, because he couldn't remember any of the program. He couldn't remember anything of his own life the day of the original broadcast either. Carson was America's nightlight—if Mike himself was any example, there were millions of Americans who needed one.

The telephone awakened him. Outside, the sky was still pitch-dark. As he picked up the handset, the digital clock on the VCR penetrated the surface of his vision: 5:14.

"Mike, it's Marge. Is Dan with you?"

"No, he isn't. Did he call you?"

"No, I haven't heard from him since he told me that he was going to meet with you. Did you see him?"

"Yes." Mike was waking up faster now. He had been followed. He should have tried to alert Dan. He should have gone back to the Clown Club—it could have taken Dan that long to finish his beer. Dan might even have ordered another. "I said good night to Dan around nine-thirty. That was in a joint on the Strip."

"He's never done this before, Mike," Marge said, her voice rising.

"I know. I'm as alarmed as you are. Let me make some calls. From where we were, he would have taken Coldwater to the Ventura Freeway, then headed up the San Diego. I'll call you back. If he comes in, call me right away. Maybe he just had car trouble.''

"He would have called me and I would have come and got him. It's the way we've always done it.''

Mike knew. "I'm sure there's a simple explanation,'' he said, but it was like hearing somebody else say the words, they were so removed from what he was thinking. He had been followed. What would have been the harm in going back to the Clown Club? Not that much time had passed. Mike hadn't thought of it. He hadn't even thought of it.

BOOK THREE

8

Aᶠᵗᵉʳ CHECKING WITH EVERY DIVISION ALONG DAN'S route, the highway patrol and two or three hospitals that seemed like logical places to have taken an accident victim, and learning nothing, Mike set out to retrace the route, driving over the hill to Sunset, then on into Beverly Hills to Coldwater Canyon, and finally onto the freeways. No sign of Dan's car. In Sylmar the San Diego Freeway merged with the I-5 and then the Interstate climbed out of the San Fernando Valley, through canyonland toward Valencia, Newhall, and the other northernmost suburbs of Los Angeles. The sky was bright now, but the Saturday traffic still light, containing a higher-than-normal percentage of motor homes and pickups with camper shells, some towing boats or rigs bearing trail bikes and three-wheelers. Mike was in the right lane, hoping now that he would see Dan's car on the shoulder, Dan asleep inside it. Mike saw the fresh, thick, black skid marks a long way off, veering sharply from the center lane to the right, where the shoulder gave way to what had to be a steep drop. He put on his directional signal, slowed, braked, and pulled onto the shoulder a little past the skid marks, which were thick enough to be felt when the tires rolled over them.

Even from the shoulder Mike could not see down the slope. He set the emergency flashers and got out of the car, leaving the motor running. Eight feet of gravel bordered the blacktop shoulder, where the skid marks ended, and the gravel was thrown up in deep waves, like the wake from a boat. Mike could see nothing in the deep little canyon below him. The brush was as tall as a man in some places, heavy enough to hide a car. Mike walked back toward the marks, his palms itching again, his mouth dry. He was wishing like a kid that he would find nothing when he saw the rear quarter of Dan's blue Cougar hardtop. There was no doubt about it. For a moment Mike stood motionless, as if he could stop time himself. He remembered that his car was running—even here, even now, the only person to stop would be an asshole seeing if there was something to steal—including a car. Dan could be alive down there, but Mike would be able to do nothing for him if he had no way to get to a hospital, or worse, an emergency telephone. He got his car keys and started down the slope.

The Cougar was near the bottom of the little canyon, maybe two hundred feet down. The slope was as steep as a stepladder, naturally barren in small spots. Lowering himself down, using the chaparral for foot- and handholds, Mike could see that the hood of the car was crumpled, angled up like half of a small tent. Dan usually cruised the freeways at sixty-five or seventy. The only broken branches Mike could see were around the car itself. The skid marks on the roadway indicated that Dan had braked and swerved simultaneously—he had seen something in front of him and reacted to it. Not a small animal. Dan had once said he had taught his kids never to brake for small animals. "Too dangerous," he had said. "It's too easy to lose control of a car and go off the road." A human being wouldn't have been in the center lane—not one sane or sober. There was no telling what a drunk or someone high on angel dust would do, but at the time Dan would have been traveling through here, the traffic had been too heavy to allow a person in that kind of condition to get out into the center lane . . . *maybe*: but at that hour, someone would have seen Dan go off the road. A lot of people would have seen him, and someone would have pulled off at the next exit and called the police.

Mike was thinking these things when he saw Dan behind the wheel, his seat belt looped snugly over his shoulder. Dan's head was forward, angled toward the right side of the car. Mike could see that the windshield was smashed, but not as if Dan had hit it with his head.

"Dan!"

Mike slid down the last ten feet, tearing his pants. His hands were raw, and he was perspiring now. "Dan!" he shouted louder, and heard an echo. The sound of the traffic up on the freeway was muted down here, Mike realized. No one was going to hear him if he yelled for help. The skin on his back was crawling in that familiar, awful way—he almost *wanted* to be sick to be rid of it. The car rocked easily when he touched it. It was resting, balanced delicately on chaparral.

Now Mike saw that the front end was completely crushed. He turned around and looked up: it was like looking up to the roof of a building. The car must have come down here on the fly, bounced, and then flopped on the brush. Mike almost wet his pants. "Dan?"

It looked as if the lower half of the steering wheel was buried in Dan's stomach. Mike saw blood on Dan's legs. The top of the steering wheel was folded flat up against Dan's chest. "Dan?" He felt for a pulse on the side of Dan's neck, then twisted Dan's head around so that it fell back against the headrest. More blood, dark, but clearly still sticky, from his nostrils and mouth. The eyes were half open, almost dry. Mike had seen enough corpses to be able to recognize another. He cried out.

"Hey! What's going on down there?"

Mike turned and looked up again. A California Highway Patrol officer stood at the top of the hill.

"My friend—!"

"Come on up here! We'll take care of him!"

Mike remembered himself—his emotions were crazy now, he realized. "LAPD!" He waggled his badge. "This is my partner!"

"Come on up anyway!" the officer yelled. "He's dead, right? We'll take proper care, I promise you!"

Mike wanted Dan's notes about Jackson, the address on Norma in West Hollywood—everything. Baby Rae Bozo, for Christ's sake. Sticky blood: Dan hadn't died last night, but within the past two hours. At the *most*. At about the time Marge had been on the telephone with Mike. Where had Dan been? What had been important enough to keep him from going home? Mike slipped the ignition key from the ring and palmed the ring with Dan's other keys. Dan wasn't that cool to the touch either. Oh, yes, within the past couple of hours. Mike cursed aloud, cursed louder and louder, until he was shouting. Something had kept Dan in town, something had made him swerve off the road. Given what Mike now knew about Elmer Washington's shenanigans, there weren't that many people in the coroner's office who could be trusted. Mike wanted to know everything a pathologist could tell him about Dan. Heart, blood, stomach. Marge didn't have to know. She had no choice about the autopsy itself, because Dan had died without a doctor in attendance. Maybe Ira Rosenberg wouldn't want to do this job, but he was going to have to—and report to Mike any attempt to interfere with him, as well.

Climbing the hill was a lot harder than getting down. When he was halfway up, the CHP guys threw him a rope. They were both young. At the top, they pulled him to his feet.

"Are you all right? You're pretty badly scraped up."

"I'm okay." Mike gave the officer one of his cards, then recited Dan's full name, home address, and telephone number. "I've got to tell his wife. She called when he didn't come home last night. I saw him at nine-thirty and he was sober."

The bigger of the two officers stepped closer to Mike.

"What did you take from his body?"

"His notebook."

"Let's have it."

"Fuck off!"

"Don't fuck with *me*! You know the rules of evidence!"

"You bet I do—and this is *my* case before anybody else's! Now I'm going to go tell his widow! If you want to do it, you're going to have to bust me—"

"All right, calm yourself," said the second officer. "I've already called it in. You have our word he'll be treated properly. We'll call you for a complete statement."

"You already have it."

It was only another five miles to Dan's—*Marge*'s now. All Mike could say was that Dan had gone off the road. All he could say was that he didn't know why Dan hadn't come straight home. Mike didn't believe it was as simple as that, and he didn't know what Marge was going to be able to accept. Dan had uncovered a real lead in the Laurel Canyon murders, which had not been their case—Marge would know that last part even if Dan had not discussed it with her. She read the newspapers and knew how the department worked. Mike owed her the truth. And maybe that included the fact that Dan had gotten involved in the Laurel Canyon case because it could become trouble for Mike, and that Cutler had told Mike to stay away from Laurel Canyon. Dan had received the message, but friendship—among other things, like his instincts as a cop—had caused him to continue anyway. There was no concrete connection yet between Laurel Canyon and Dan's death, but the circumstances were all but overwhelming—specifically, the entire scene at the Clown Club, right down to the parking valet. . . .

For all Mike knew, news agencies that monitored CHP transmissions were calling Marge at this very moment. Yet he couldn't seem to hurry—or thought he couldn't: in another moment he was at the off ramp, having been in a trance since he'd gotten in the car. It was fair warning about what he would expect for himself for the foreseeable future: not even his sense of time was functioning properly. . . .

Marge came out of the house when he pulled into the driveway, and to him it seemed as if she was about to say she hadn't heard from Dan. When she saw Mike's face, her life ended. She was a petite woman, thicker around the middle than she had been just a few years ago, her fading hair cut short in a practical style. She grimaced as Mike got out of the car. She tried to fight herself, biting her lip. He reached for her and she let out a howl. The Crawford's youngest, Lori, burst from the house.

"Where's my father?"

Mike held Marge firmly. "His car went off the highway." He jerked his head toward the purple hills behind him. "Up there. The CHP has him."

Lori stepped back, clenching her fists. "Is he dead?"

Marge reached for her. "Oh, Lori—"

"No! No!" Lori wrenched herself away from her mother, backed up, doubled over, her elbows against her waist. *"No!"*

A neighbor's door opened, and someone came running.

Mike used the neighbor's telephone to call the coroner's office for Ira Rosenberg's home telephone number, and when he was finished talking with Rosenberg, Mike dialed Hollywood Homicide's direct line. Greg Novak picked up.

"It's Mike. I was going to come in, but I didn't figure to see you today."

"Just paperwork," Novak said. "What's up?"

Mike told him. Novak cried out. "Let the others know," Mike said.

"Can you reach Dan's desk from where you are?"

There was a clatter. "Yeah." He was breathless.

"Are the drawers locked?"

"Let me try them. Yeah, all of them. Ah, *shit*, Mike!"

"Never mind that. Inventory what's on the top of the desk. Do it aloud." Mike had seen Dan's desk last night.

"Five or six case files—do you want the names?"

"No."

"His Rolodex."

"Where is it turned to? What name do you read?"

"Bunn, Moe. Do you want the number?"

"No." Moe Bunn was a television repair guy who worked out of his apartment. What Mike remembered was that Dan's Rolodex had been turned to the Ws. "Just call the other guys. Tell them I'm at Dan's and I expect to be here for the next several hours. Maybe some of the wives want to come up here with food. It's going to be a long weekend."

Mike thought of stopping for a moment and stepping outside for a breath of air, but he saw that he couldn't give himself that kind of time for thinking. That Dan was dead was still sinking in. Intellectually Mike knew he had seen the body, but now he had no true memory of it. If he wasn't careful, he would start flashing on Vietnam or his father. Mike picked up the telephone again and called Captain Ruppert.

"What do you think, Mike? Did it look like an accident?"

Mike wanted to be careful. If he said the wrong thing, Ruppert would begin worrying about him. Ruppert was nobody's hero; he was close to sixty and had trouble getting his jacket buttoned over his potbelly. Mike didn't want Ruppert thinking that his acting head of Homicide was too distraught or gripped by fantasy to be able to function in his official capacity. Mike said, "It looks like Dan saw something in the road in front of him, and when he swerved to avoid it, whatever it was, he lost control of the car and it went into one of these canyons up here. I don't think he suffered."

"He wasn't drunk, was he?"

"I doubt it. I saw him last night, and he was sober and alert."

"Well, he may have had a heart attack," Ruppert said.

"That will turn up in the autopsy."

"Right, right. Keep me informed about the arrangements and so forth. I want to be sure that we're well represented. Of course I'll be there myself. I'm sorry you lost your partner, Gallagher. We've all lost a good man."

"Yes." He couldn't say any more. Outside, Dan's son Billy and his girlfriend were arriving. Billy was twenty. Mike couldn't remember the girlfriend's name.

"Where is he?" Billy asked.

"Heading downtown by now. One of his friends is coming in to take care of him."

Billy was tall and thin and his out-of-style hair was down to his shoulders. Now he looked stricken. "Does he have to have an autopsy?"

Mike sighed. "Yes." He didn't want to discuss with Billy the question of the hours between his own departure from the Clown Club and what now seemed like the time of Dan's death. Billy was mature enough for his age, but Mike did not want to deal with the results of Billy thinking that Mike was accusing Dan of having been copping a time-out from marriage. "Let's see how your mother is doing."

There were almost a dozen people in the living room now, including Alice, the Crawfords' middle child, who was talking on the telephone. Marge looked up at Mike. "The newspapers are calling. The fellow from the *Herald-Examiner* asked if I thought the accident was suspicious. I couldn't take it."

"Do you remember the guy's name?"

She shook her head.

"How about Wills?"

"That's it. Bob Wills."

Somebody else Mike wanted to talk to. Mike didn't know him, but every time Mike turned around, there was Wills. If Wills smelled something, maybe he might be willing to say what he thought it was. "Marge, I have to see you alone for a moment."

She got up and led him toward the kitchen.

"We have to go in the garage," he said. He fished in his pocket. "I took Dan's keys, but I want only the one to his desk. He told me something a couple of years ago, and at the time he said you didn't know anything about it."

She looked alarmed. "I still don't."

When the garage door was closed behind them, Mike said, "If I waited for a better time to tell you this, you might wind up the victim of something just plain dumb. You'll understand. I swear to you, Marge, Dan never did anything wrong, or bad, or hurtful to you, in all the time I knew him—but he did get caught in something beyond his control." Mike spotted the old toolbox Dan had described. Mike told Marge the story about the hit-and-run on Tampa Avenue. "I didn't need to know, so he never told me the name of the family involved. I'm happy to let it go at that." Mike had the box open and the top tray of old, rusting tools removed to expose the thick, soiled, business-size envelope. "That's yours. You see? You might have given the toolbox away."

"When did Dan die? Could you tell?"

"I'm waiting for Ira Rosenberg to give me his authoritative opinion. You don't need to hear any speculation on my part."

"But you have your own thoughts, don't you?"

"Yes. Marge, I'll tell you everything Rosenberg tells me. As I said, in all the time I knew Dan, he never did anything to hurt or dishonor you."

"I *know* that!" She started weeping. He gave her the envelope, but she didn't move to open it. "This is his," she whispered. "If you need any money to find out what really happened to him, I'll give it to you out of this, I promise."

"Marge, let's wait—"

"*You* promise *me*! I can see what's on your mind! Don't you think I know you after all these years?"

"I promise," he murmured. For just a moment the idea seemed comfortable, but then Mike shuddered—*shuddered*: he felt as if someone had run a sword clean through him.

Normally on a Saturday morning the Hollywood Division squad room was almost empty, with as few as a half-dozen detectives curled uncomfortably over paperwork, or interviewing a tense witness or hyper suspect; but today it seemed to Mike that there were almost twenty guys in various parts of the room, their eyes on him when he came in. They wanted to offer their condolences, but he waved them off. The news was already on the radio, and the newspapers were calling for more information. After he had settled at his desk, it seemed to Mike that more guys were drifting in by the minute. Novak was gone now—on a db, according to his note. Mike wanted to be in a glass booth, unassailable. There was nothing he wanted to say to anyone—or say back: people wanted to express their regrets, but he wanted to get through these minutes, hours, days . . . he did not want to look ahead, or side to side. He wanted to work. He wanted to dig a hole in his work and pull it in after him.

The mail arrived early, including a packet from Camp Pendleton. Mike was going through twenty sets of fingerprints when Marvin Burgess appeared. His eyes were swollen.

"What happened to our man? Greg Novak was in awful shape over the telephone."

Mike told Burgess only what he had found this morning. Burgess pulled up Dan's chair and leaned over Mike's desk.

"I gave Dan your message," Burgess said.

"I know, he told me." Mike casually picked up Dan's Rolodex and put it in his own bottom drawer.

"He was on to something, wasn't he?"

"Let it go, Marvin."

"Marie went straight up there. Marie was terrible—horrible. I hate to see a woman like that—you hear?" Marie was Burgess's wife. "Even she can see that it's bullshit, Mike. There are no bends in that road. Did he have a blowout?"

"It's going to be hard to tell."

"I'll tell *you* something. When I was the only black man sitting at this desk, it was Dan Crawford who went out of his way to make things easy. He called me 'Blue Eyes.' I wish you could have seen Marie laugh at that. Marge and Marie hit it right off, you know."

Every summer Marvin and Marie had a barbecue in the back yard of their Crenshaw home; they probably lived better, more decently and stylishly, than anybody in the division. Mike said, "You've seen some shit, Marvin, remember?"

"Maybe so, but I don't recall eating any that tasted quite this bad."

Mike stared at him.

"Just think about it," Burgess said and heaved his weight erect. Mike reached for his paperwork, trying to look as if he was gathering his concentration. When Burgess was at the other end of the room, Mike stood up and fished the key to Dan's desk from his pocket. The way to hide something was to put it under people's noses. Mike remembered thinking that recently, but couldn't remember when. He opened Dan's desk and stacked the files and papers he took from it on his own blotter. As he emptied each drawer, he reached in and felt around for hidden envelopes or folders. None. Nobody was watching. He locked the desk again, and in another moment he had Dan's papers fitted into his own desk. He would go through them later, when he was more confident that he was thinking clearly.

One of the Pendleton thumbprints matched the print on the victim's headboard, and the information described its owner as a twenty-year-old redhead from Tulsa, Oklahoma. Mike called the Tulsa PD, identified himself, explained what he had, and told the listener what he wanted. He was put on hold, and while he was waiting, another line rang. Mike waved over a plain-clothesman, who picked up, then covered the mouthpiece.

"It's Chief Cutler. For you."

"Monitor my line, will you?" Mike pushed buttons. "Chief, I'm trying to get some information from Tulsa on a marine who killed a guy here ten days ago."

"Jesus fucking Christ, Gallagher, didn't I hear right about Crawford?"

"Yes, you did. I'm keeping busy."

"I was told that you found the body. What do you think happened?"

"I *know* he went off the road at speed. From what I saw, there was no way of telling why."

"You're sure it's an accident?" Cutler asked.

"There was no apparent evidence one way or the other."

"Well, we're going to go over that car with a fucking micro-scope, if we have to. I don't like my boys dying in goddamned freak one-car accidents. I'm sorry about your partner. Nobody likes to lose one. Have you talked to his widow?"

"I've already seen her." The plainclothesman signaled that the other line was open again.

"I'm going to call her now," Cutler said. "Well, you hang in there—but don't be foolish and try to work yourself into the ground. I've seen that, too. We've had words Gallagher, but they don't mean shit now."

"Thank you." Mike connected the other line and learned that his chicken hawk suspect had been arrested in Tulsa for beating up a girlfriend.

"Later she dropped the charges—but it says here that he broke her nose and knocked out a couple of teeth."

"Just your typical lovers' quarrel," Mike said.

"It's the same all over," said the guy on the other end. "We had one here the other night where the woman stabbed one of the responding officers while he was duking it out with her boyfriend. Some of them would rather take a beating and a half than face the fact that the guys they pick for a little nooky are crazier than shithouse rats."

Mike smiled for the first time today. After Tom Cutler, the guy sounded more clean-cut than Pat Boone at a prayer meeting.

"Nice talking to you," Mike said as a good-bye. He called Pendleton and left a message for the commandant to call back. After a moment's thought, Mike gave his home number, too. Before he left the office, he gave Marvin Burgess the telephone number of the apartment on Beachwood Drive, in case Ira Rosenberg called.

There was no point in telling anyone that he planned to be in the Clown Club after six o'clock.

Only the smell of death brought Mike around to a realization of how much time had passed since he had been in the Beachwood apartment—only a day, not the year it seemed to be. Mike was thinking of Dan now, thinking of the moment of Dan's death. It must have been quick. Mike hoped Marge understood that from what he had told her. There must have been a moment of confusion, terror, hopelessness, but that was probably the case with every death. Looking at a corpse, Dan had liked to say, "Well, his troubles are over." Mike only hoped that was true for all. Mike knew any death made him afraid, afraid deep into his bones sometimes—only the aging process seemed to numb the pain. He could not help wondering if this was the one that numbed him forever. Alone now, he wanted to cry, but couldn't. He knew that what had happened hadn't been an accident. It had been too convenient. Maybe all by himself Dan had blown open the Laurel Canyon case better than anybody knew. He had linked one of the victims to a gang of human monsters, including one whose residence was only a few yards up from the murder scene. Mike had heard the killers coming from that direction. It had been Dan who remembered his contact with Jerry Chambers, tracking down a car involved in an incident in Palm Springs. Don Grant. Mike wouldn't need Dan's Rolodex to find that guy. Mike was going to call Grant. He was going to talk to anyone who made the trip to Dan's funeral — and that would be a lot of people, including some from San Diego, Mike hoped. Dan had enjoyed going to the 187 meetings. Now all that time spent might have an ultimate meaning.

The dead young woman's legal name had been Ethel Moreland, but no one in California was named Ethel, so she had

changed it—on her own, which was legally okay—to Valerie. In
her closet Mike found oversized drawing pads with sketches of
women's clothing, as well as a folder full of pages torn from
several fashion magazines. There was a photo album, all the
prints affixed therein apparently from Kansas, faces and loca-
tions interconnected in various ways. Parents and other older
people, group shots of the victim and her friends, two showing
her leaning into the arms of slack-jawed young men. Moreland
had been a widehipped but otherwise slender blonde with blue
eyes and a thin nose with the kind of bumpy bridge women
considered a disfigurement. By the look of the early pictures
and those still in the yellow envelopes of the developers, Moreland had spent a lot of money on her hair as well as her clothes.
She had had a fantasy not much different in its hopefulness from
Dan's dream of San Luis Obispo, and only a judgmental fool
would say that the heart's desire of one was more worthy than
that of the other. Her life was complete now, too—as if he had
known her, Mike wanted to console himself with the notion that
her life had had meaning which he would see if he had the
wisdom to clear his eyes. Mike could not even say that her needs
had been more desperate than his own. Dan would be alive if
Mike had not drawn him into the Laurel Canyon case. Now
Mike wept. He worked, but he wept. Under Moreland's telephone he found pieces of paper bearing numbers in the Los
Angeles area. Mike would want to know to whom they belonged
before calling any of them. In the bottom of the hamper in the
bathroom he found a pair of men's socks, as large as his own,
a set of yellow-stained briefs, size 42-44, and a T-shirt from
Hussong's Cantina in Ensenada, the most famous saloon just
south of the border. The T-shirt was an X-L, stretched and limp,
more than big enough now to fit the guy who had worn the shorts
and socks. A guy with BO that smelled like cat shit, Mike noted
carefully. The telephone rang.

"Yes?"

"Mike? Ira Rosenberg. Our good friend died at about five
this morning of massive trauma to the pleural cavity. In English,
the steering wheel crushed his heart and lungs. Death was instantaneous. So was loss of consciousness, I'm sure. He was
sober. We have to wait for the tests on that, but I'm sure of that,

too. There was a lot of coffee in his stomach. And fresh lettuce.''

"How fresh?"

"A couple of hours. Not really more than that."

"If he'd gotten hungry at three in the morning and stopped at some all-night place for a dinner salad to keep his stomach from growling, that would be consistent with what you saw?"

"Exactly."

Dan's car hadn't burned. Whatever was in the gas tank would confirm or refute the last charge on Dan's gas account. Dan always used Mobil, always kept the receipts. Mike was thinking that a little arithmetic would give him a fair idea of how many miles Dan had traveled last night after Mike had said good-bye to him. Had Dan been talking to somebody afterward? Whatever that person had had to say had been too interesting for Dan to excuse himself and call Marge to tell her he would be late. Or maybe Dan's hold on the person had been too tenuous—that was common with informants. If Mike could satisfy himself that Dan had not traveled far from the Clown Club last night, it wouldn't be that much of a job to canvass the all-night joints that served salads for a description of the individual in Dan's company. It was a last-resort kind of move, but it would have to be done soon, before people's memories faded. Mike was going to need a picture of Dan. Hell, he realized, there would be one in tomorrow's papers, which would be in the racks tonight.

"There's no chance that Dan had a heart attack?"

"No. A myocardial infarction is easier to see than a black eye. He didn't shoot a clot, either—a coronary thrombosis. Dan didn't have the cleanest arteries I've ever seen, but he was at least ten years from trouble. Fifteen."

"Has anybody called you about this?"

"You mean officially? Cutler's office, but that's standard. He always wants to know everything when an officer died in the line of duty."

"This wasn't in the line of duty Ira."

"How are *you* treating it? The newspapers are calling, too. They're wasting their time. My findings are a matter of public record—or will be, when I finish the paperwork. I've never had anything to say to those media characters. I'm afraid of Elmer-itis. Old Elmer has done all the talking anyway, for as long as he's been the big cheese."

"Then you haven't heard from him yet?" Mike said.

"No, he's in New York seeing network execs. That's the way he put it when he sailed out yesterday. One of the guys here said that he's comparison shopping for blow jobs. That's Elmer's speed. He likes to kick back and relax under any circumstances."

"Do you have anything on the Beachwood Drive case? I'm in her apartment now."

"Oh, yeah. It's a good thing you asked. She was murdered. Maybe the tests will show that she's full of junk, but she was strangled. It wasn't easy to see, given the condition she was in, but her larynx was crushed by an object of some kind, like the handle of a baseball bat. About that diameter. Her tongue was pushed back in her mouth to fool us."

"If the killing was done here, she wasn't conscious when it happened. There's no sign of a struggle. The tests will show if she was unconscious, won't they?"

"If the dose was massive enough, if there was a dose at all. It could be in the gray area. Remember that some of these kids have built drug tolerances that were unimaginable a few years ago. Of course it's possible that we'll find no drugs in her at all."

"I know. We're only thinking drugs because of the position of her body."

"And the room it was in," Rosenberg said.

"So now I'm looking for one very smart son of a bitch," Mike said. "I really don't need this, Ira. What I'd like is two weeks at camp, making wallets. Enjoy what's left of your weekend."

"I've got to sign Dan out first. His family wants arrangements. I want to be at the funeral, Mike. I'll be welcome there, won't I?"

It wasn't the saddest thing Mike had ever heard, just the saddest he could think of right now. "Sure. Dan would want you to be there."

"It's an awful thing, Mike. I'm sorry."

"Yeah. I'll tell Marge what you said about it being instantaneous. Let me have a dental chart on this dame, too. I don't want the guy who did her getting away because I have other problems. When can I have the chart?"

"This afternoon, if you want—but you won't be able to do anything with it until Monday. Pick it up then. You have to be here anyway."

Mike had forgotten Moreland's autopsy. Now he knew he was getting tired. "I'll tell you about Dan's arrangements, too."

He called Marge. She had been waiting. "Tom Cutler says he wants to take the car apart. Is there something going on, Mike? I want to know."

"We're going to have to wait and see, Marge. Rosenberg says Cutler's interest is routine."

"This is difficult for me, Mike. I'm not used to it."

"I'm not either. I'd be up there this evening, but I can't be in two places at the same time. From here on, if I have anything to tell you, it will be when I see you."

He heard her sigh. "I guess so."

There was no point now in running Moreland's little stash of numbers past the telephone company—as with the dental charts, Mike wouldn't be able to make use of them until Monday. If Moreland's murderer was in flight, so much time had passed since her death and the discovery of her body that time was no longer of the essence. Mike scooped up her Los Angeles photographs. He would study them, then show them to her friends—at the rate he was going, he didn't think he would be able to talk to the first of them until Tuesday. Unless he worked on the Pendleton case tomorrow. Figuring all of next week—a half-day when Dan was buried—Mike would be going twelve straight-days without one for himself. Pendleton was in Oceanside, almost two hours south of Los Angeles —and only a half hour from San Diego, less than an hour from Chula Vista and National City. Mike was going to talk to everybody at Dan's funeral. He needed a new partner, a matter he would have to discuss with Ruppert. Mike needed someone who already knew the job; there was no time to train a kid. Before he could see the bartender at the Clown Club, he had to go home and clean up. And call Gretchen from a pay telephone to cancel the barbecue tomorrow. Without explanation. An explanation would surely identify him to any wiretappers. And he wanted to call that teacher with the little-girl voice and the big-girl brain. Maybe all of them had big-girl brains . . . a thought like that was all the proof he needed that he was really very tired. . . .

At six-thirty the Clown Club had more waitresses than customers, and at the bar there were only three or four emaciated types with English accents, whom Mike took to be rock 'n' roll musicians. They were loud, laughing heartily about one of their own who smoked marijuana onstage during other musicians' solos. The big guy behind the bar recognized Mike, but didn't offer a smile. Mike headed down to the end where he had been sitting with Dan less than twenty-four hours ago. It might as well have happened on a different planet.

"I was in here last night with my buddy."

"Sure, I remember. The two cops."

"Next time I'll wear a Santa Claus suit. I left first. What time did my friend leave?"

"Right after you. He finished his beer, settled the tab, and split. That's it. Tipped me a buck."

"You're sure of that?"

"Absolutely. I've been doing this work a long time. When something unusual happens, I make note of it."

"What was unusual?"

"You. And your friend. This ain't Disneyland. You two meant trouble. I wasn't sure about him, but when you walked in, I figured the place was surrounded."

"Not Disneyland," Mike said.

"I'm only the bartender."

Mike was looking at the size of the guy. Mike took out what he had judged was the most recent picture of Ethel-and-Valerie Moreland. "Ever run around with her?"

The bartender squinted. "Kind of like an aircraft carrier?"

"What do you mean?"

"Skinny on the top, fat on the bottom."

"Yeah, that's her."

"Her name is Val. A skuzzball. She stopped coming in here

last winter. They come and go, but this was her second home for a while. She had the hots for me, but I never went for it.''

''Why not?''

''She could never make it to closing time. When they stagger out of here with another guy, they're off my A list. The first night I thought I was home free, but she got drunk, and left with another guy, and that was the end of it. She pitched me a couple of more times afterward, but she never copped to me not being really interested. I'm the bartender and I'm supposed to be polite, you know?''

''Ever go to Hussong's Cantina?''

''In Ensenada? I got to Tijuana one time, but it was everything I dreamed it would be, so I turned around and came back. I'm not a big fan of the Third World. I don't need a discount on anything that bad.''

''Did you ever see Valerie in here with a guy about your size?''

''Do I need a lawyer?'' He was grinning. Mike smiled back.

''As long as you mention it, where were you last Monday night?''

''Here.''

''Sunday?''

''Here. I'm off Tuesdays and Wednesdays.''

''Did you ever see her with a big guy?''

''She liked big guys. They were *all* big guys. Some dames like the motion, some like the pressure, and the best like both. What can I tell you?''

''How many guys?''

''Three or four. I called her a skuzzball only because she couldn't handle the booze. Three or four in three months' time isn't bad in today's market. I've been behind the bar a long time.''

And you've seen some shit, Mike thought. ''My buddy left here last night right after me.''

''Just as I told you the first time.''

''Tell me about the parking valets outside.''

''The valets? Wetbacks. No Engleesh. They don't get minimum wage—but don't quote me.''

"Now if any of those big guys you saw her with come in, I want you to give me a call."

The bartender glanced over his shoulder. "Put your card on the bar when you leave. I don't want to be seen taking anything from you. But I'll tell you right now, I don't think I can remember any of the big guys with her. It was awhile ago, and we get a lot of big guys in here. I wouldn't want to make that kind of mistake." He looked at Mike. "You had a Heineken last night. I take pride in remembering what my customers order."

"I take pride too, pal." Mike patted the bartender's meaty fist and let the business card he had palmed settle on the bar.

"I got to tell you, I've been thinking about getting out of L.A."

"So was my buddy."

"Was? Oh, shit. A *cop*?" He straightened up and filled his lungs. "Let me hear that you *burned* the motherfucker. Hear me? *Burn* the fuck!"

Easy for you to say, Mike thought as he got up. "How do I find you when you're off the campus?"

"I've got a place in Panorama City. Last name's Azzolini. I'm the only one in the book."

Outside the Clown Club, the traffic was bumper to bumper in both directions. The sky was beginning to darken, and the streetlights and neon signs were coming on. The air was still warm, thick with the exhaust fumes of the traffic. Mike walked down to the 9000 Building to get his own look at the place. Bernie Maxwell. What Dan hadn't done was ascertain that the offices in the 9000 Building had a clear view of the new Jackson place down on Norma. An infrared beam focused on a window of the Jackson place would carry every sound in the house up to the 9000 Building. Infrared eavesdropping was so advanced that Mike wasn't even sure it was illegal. Anybody could buy the equipment: all he had to do was find a dealer in surveillance and countermeasures equipment.

The underground garage of the 9000 Building was open even though the building itself was closed to the public for the weekend. The tenant after-hours sign-in was probably down in the garage, too, where the garage attendants could oversee it—saving the building management the cost of a uniformed guard on the ground floor. Two cars turned into the garage entrance and Mike followed them on foot down the ramp. He timed his pace so that he passed the cars' returning occupants as they reached the foot of the ramp. Their cars were rolling off in the distance. Mike stepped quickly toward the attendants' desk, where only one man remained on duty.

"There's a hippie up at the top of the ramp taking a leak. He's stoned out of his mind."

"Oh, Christ." The attendant looked around.

"Go ahead," Mike said. "I'll wait for the next guy to get my car."

The attendant took off. When he turned the corner, Mike followed the arrow on the wall to the elevator bank. The directory said that C. C. Publishing and Maxwell-Skelley Productions were in Suite 905.

There was only the red fire exit light in the corridor on the ninth floor. In the quiet Mike heard another elevator start up from below. The parking attendants were wise to him. Unless they stopped on the ground floor to read the indicators over the elevators, they wouldn't know which floor he was on. Either way, he only had a few moments. When his eyes adjusted, he moved rapidly down the corridor to 905. No light showed from under the door, but that didn't mean anything. The kind of equipment Mike had in mind could be voice actuated, fully automatic. Mike went on to the fire stairs. On the eighth floor he found a door under 905 with a nice, loose fit and kicked it in. The windows beyond revealed a view to the south, toward Wilshire Boulevard. Norma Place was directly below. Mike grabbed a two-foot shard of the doorjamb and returned to the fire stairs. He hurried down to the second floor, made his way to the elevator bank, and pressed the up button. When the car stopped, Mike was back against the wall, his fist cocked. And remembering what Dan had said about pulling punches. The car was empty. Mike pressed the alarm button, wedged it down with his oversized splinter, and sent the car upward, its bell ringing furiously. Heading back to the fire stairs, he pulled the fire alarm—more bells, even louder. Coming out of the stairwell on the garage level, he flashed his badge.

"The front door is wide open," he yelled. "What the fuck is going on here?"

The two other attendants gaped. "The boss is upstairs looking for a guy who broke in. He's raising hell."

"Well, you two go up to the street and flag down a sheriff's car. Hustle!"

When they were out of sight, Mike picked up the tenants' sign-in book and tucked it inside his jacket. He ran after the attendants. "Hey! On second thought, you guys stay down here! I'll hail the sheriff!" As they passed, he called, "You want to give your buddy a hand!"

There were a half-dozen sushi bars within walking distance on Sunset, and Mike was thinking that he would go from one to the next until he found some decent-looking Spanish mackerel, really fresh fish with clear, firm eyes. Dan had hated sushi, and most of all he couldn't bear watching Mike wolfing down Spanish mackerel sashimi, the head, spine, and tail arranged artfully around its minced flesh, but still looking like a cartoonist's idea of what cats do to fish. Mike would go through the tenants' sign-in book over dinner; maybe there was something to be learned from the signatures of the people who had been in and out of 905 after hours in the past week or two. He'd already planned to kill the hours before the lobster shift down on Norma Place, logging the traffic in and out of Donnie Jackson's. Looking for the place that had served Dan his salad, Mike could toss out all the places with liquor licenses; they would have been closed after two A.M. At home he'd had his own photograph of Dan, taken last Christmas. Mike had been at the Crawfords' last year, and Marge had sent him prints of the pictures that had been taken. Now Mike realized that he hadn't eaten all day today. His thoughts were beyond Spanish mackerel. He was thinking of crab roe, topped by a raw quail egg. The first time Mike had eaten crab roe in front of Dan, Dan had to leave the restaurant and wait for Mike out on the street. He'd told Mike not to look in the gutter.

* * *

Maybe Jackson had made a lot of noise at night in his old apartment in Hollywood, but now that he had his own home, or thought he did, he was being a good deal more discreet. Mike could hear the crickets chirping. The Cadillac was in the driveway—Jackson had not sold it. Oh, there was traffic in and out of the house, all right. Between nine o'clock and midnight, Mike logged eighteen short-term visitors, and six people who had arrived and not left. A real smorgasbord of slobs, goons, creeps, wackos, and geeks. By contrast, none of the dozen other houses on the street had had even a single visitor. Mike thought he saw Paula Rogers, but from his angle he could see too little of the faces of people arriving for positive identifications. Not that Paula Rogers was the only woman in and out of there. Of the twenty-four people entering the house, eleven were women, young women, too many of them yummy. And the blonde — Baby Rae Bozo: she was the one who always answered the door. Dan had indicated that she was pretty, but not seriously gorgeous, but she was. A wrecker. Even half a block away, Mike could see that she had one of those sweet smiles. Mike wasn't sure he needed the girl's real name, but it was through the magazine Dan had found—or others—that Mike would be able to learn it. In a telephone call to C. C. Publications he would identify himself as a producer or photographer interested in hiring the girl, and if that didn't get someone to cough up her name right away, it would lead to someone who would.

At dinner Mike had gone over every page of the tenants' sign-in book. Jack Skelley's name didn't appear in it at all. Maxwell's could be found on almost every other page. Up until last week, he had worked late two or three nights every week. The boss, last week, the week before the murders, had not worked late at all, but he had signed himself in on Saturday afternoon at four o'clock, and had not left the building until almost midnight. Arriving at five o'clock to visit Suite 905 had been a man named Hans Roehrig, who had given his address as East Victory Boulevard, Reseda. Reseda was in the west San Fernando Valley, so Roehrig, if that was his real name, was having a little joke. At six-thirty another visitor to 905 had signed in. The handwriting was a scrawl, but Mike thought he could read the word "Barranquilla," which was a city in Colombia, South America.

Bogotá, Colombia's capital, was the market maker for South America's biggest export, cocaine. The address "Barranquilla" had put down was 9345 Sunset, which Mike had checked before rolling down to Norma Place. The number 9345 did not exist, and Mike now assumed that the numbers had popped into the gentleman's head because he had been standing in the garage of the 9000 Building. Both men had signed out at eleven-fifteen, more than a half hour before their host, Maxwell.

Mike left Norma Place at twelve-fifteen, even though there was no sign at Jackson's that the action was slowing down. Mike worked his way east on Santa Monica Boulevard to Crescent Heights, looking for the place where Dan had stopped to eat last night. Dan had liked Canter's, the Jewish deli on Fairfax, but if he had gone there early Saturday morning, he would not have ordered a salad. On Sunset Mike wheeled into Norm's, part of a chain with outlets all over the city. At the register was the manager, a fat young man with plastered-down blond hair and an incongruously bushy mustache. Mike guessed that the mustache was supposed to make the kid look older, but it just made him look like a puzzled walrus. His eyes popped a little at Mike's badge. Mike showed him the Christmas photograph.

"Did you see this guy in here early Saturday morning?"

"Oh, yes. He came in with grease on his hands and asked for some cleaner. He said he's had some car trouble. He was pretty annoyed about it. He was really angry with the Triple-A."

"Was anybody with him?"

"No, he was alone."

"You're sure?"

"Oh, yes. He told me the Triple-A had told his friend it would be where his car had broken down in an hour, but after two hours when the truck didn't show up, he called back and they said they had no record of the first call."

It didn't make sense. "The guy in this picture said *he* called back?"

"No, wait a minute. He said *they. They* called back."

"You mean he used the word *we*?"

The young man nodded.

"So you have no way of knowing if the man in the picture actually made the second call or not."

He swallowed. "I guess I don't."

Mike tapped the photograph again. "Did he say anything about this friend?"

"This man was really annoyed. He sat here at the counter after he cleaned up and thanked me for letting him have the soap powder from the kitchen. There was a newspaper on one of the stools, so he read that. But he talked a little bit, you know, calming down, and he said he was glad he'd bumped into his friend, or he would have been stooging around by himself all night. He used that phrase, 'stooging around.' He said he'd drunk enough coffee to float a battleship."

"Did he say where he drank the coffee?"

"In his car. Now that you're asking, I'm remembering better. He said, 'stooging around in the car drinking coffee all night.' That's when he said he'd had enough to float the battleship."

"Did he say anything else?"

"He said he was going to quit the Triple-A."

"Did he tell you what was wrong with the car?"

"Oh, I asked. Coil. He said he had a dead coil, and that he walked up to a gas station on Sunset and bought a new one."

"He walked?"

"He said, 'So I walked up to Sunset.' *I*."

"Did he say anything else? Anything at all?"

The manager pulled at hairs of his mustache. "No. He had a salad, paid his check, and picked up a couple of extra napkins to wipe off his steering wheel. He said that's what he wanted them for, that the wheel probably had grease on it."

"Did he mention his wife?"

"Wife? No."

Mike gave him a card and told him to call if he remembered anything else. *Friend!* Someone had followed Mike up into Laurel Canyon. Someone had been waiting for Dan. On Monday Mike would call the automobile club and see if it had a record of anyone calling on Dan's card. Marge's card had the same number; Mike wouldn't have to wait for Dan's wallet. Dan had known something about cars. He would have spotted obvious sabotage. If someone had broken a fuel line, or taken the wire running from the coil to the distributor, Dan would have known right away that he was being set up. Alone, without evidence of sabotage, he would have called the automobile club himself. He would have had his car towed to a gas station and then he would have called Marge to come and get him. The *friend* had volunteered to call the automobile club's road service. Mike had never heard of the club not responding, not having a record of an earlier call. In the company of someone he knew, someone he *trusted*, Dan had thought only that he had run into a patch of inconsequential bad luck. It happened to everybody. When the bartender at the Clown Club had told Mike to ''burn'' the guy responsible for Dan's death, Mike had recoiled from the idea. He was a cop. He had been a marine. He had never been a murderer. When the bartender had run his mouth, Mike hadn't believed he had evidence conclusive of anything but an accident. But now he had more. A *friend*! Mike had to think the unthinkable. What was he being shown? That someone had kept Dan in town until the only time of day the stretch of the Interstate on which Dan had died would be deserted. Someone Dan had known and trusted. Almost certainly Mike knew that individual, too. Oh, yes, Mike knew him. An individual who had made himself part of a conspiracy, because killing Dan had required someone to set him up—a *friend*—and someone else to knock him over. For what other reason had Mike been followed last night? No one had been following him today. He had been watching his back almost from the time he had gotten into his own car in the predawn darkness this morning. No one— nothing suspicious all day long. No one had tried to kill him. He had been an easy mark until he picked up the tail last night on Rainbow Drive. No one had tried to kill him *yet*. You couldn't kill two cops—partners—in the same time frame without raising suspicions. What Mike had learned tonight still fell short of the rules of evidence. Even if the automobile club had no record of calls on Dan's card last night, the series of events could be seen as no more than *very* consequential bad luck. But Cutler wanted to tear Dan's car apart. Ira Rosenberg had said that Cutler always paid careful attention to the death of an officer in the line of duty. *In the line of duty.* Mike had seen the thick tire marks on the pavement up in the canyonlands. There had been nothing wrong with Dan's brakes. Steering gears rarely failed, and even more rarely on a straight, level road. It was impossible to accidentally damage any of a car's safety systems by replacing the coil. Dan had known what he was doing. And would not have been able to solve the problem of a dead coil without the help of the *friend*. Once you knew you had fuel and it was getting to the engine, you traced the electrical system from the spark plugs back through the points to the coil. All that required was someone in the car cranking the engine and someone else with his head under the hood—Dan, because his hands had been greasy. And how did you make a coil fail? Maybe there were hard ways to do it, but the easiest way was to open the hood and replace the functional coil with one already dead. Someone had followed Dan from downtown to West Hollywood, someone who must have known that he was being presented with an opportunity to get Dan. Mike hadn't known until the afternoon that he would be meeting Dan in the Clown Club. If the person who had followed Mike up into Laurel Canyon was part of the same conspiracy, a lot of people were involved. Why? Why Dan? Why Dan *first*?

In the parking lot of Norm's, Mike checked his service revolver and shifted his belt holster around so the pistol was more accessible. He was underarmed, he decided. One gun was not enough. Maybe he didn't have enough firepower either. Fired with accuracy, a .38 Police Special could kill any living thing smaller than an elephant or maybe a bear.

Mike wanted more than accuracy. There was no way of telling what might be necessary. Well, yes, one thing: what Mike would have to do when he found out what had happened to Dan. The people responsible were too clever for the criminal justice system, perhaps because they knew it so well. Yes, there was that. *Wheels within wheels*, Dan had taught him long ago. He had said it again the other day. Once he had said it frequently, pounding it into Mike's skull. They had just become partners when a downtown plainclothesman was shot in his car en route to the pistol range to qualify. The plainclothesman accused Cutler, saying Cutler wanted to get rid of him. When Mike wanted to know what Dan thought, Dan produced a newspaper clipping with an account of the nighttime shooting of a burglar in one of the suburban communities: three bullets behind the ear from a distance, the police report said, of fifty feet. Dan had asked, "Have you ever heard of anyone shooting a one-inch group with a thirty-eight at a distance of fifty feet, even in the daytime?" It was impossible, Mike knew. "You'd have to know more about both situations to make a judgment of them," Dan said. He'd heard stories about "executioners" working for departments all across the country, guys who liked to kill who reported to the chiefs or intermediaries. "Nobody has ever found a shred of evidence," Dan had said. "We mind our own business. I don't worry about the wheels within wheels."

This was Saturday. Less than six days after the worst murder case in Los Angeles since the Manson killings, the story was drying up, off the front page of the *Times*, reduced to a few hundred words in the *Herald Examiner* and the *Daily News*. According to all the stories, the police were looking for Billy Lansing's partner in crime, Dale Freeman, originally of El Centro, but lately of San Diego. In the early seventies, Freeman had spent three years in Soledad. According to San Diego authorities, he had been involved with Lansing recently in a series of drug hijackings and rip-offs. The whole story was too pat, the timing of its release too orchestrated. It was news managing at its best, and of course Cutler was completely responsible for it. All that astounded Mike was the shoddiness of the work of the press, which printed or read over the air exactly what it was given. Nobody did any digging, asked any questions. If the investigating team really was looking for Freeman, allegedly in flight, why hadn't Hollywood Division received any official notification? None of the newspapers had pictures of Freeman. Didn't that ring anybody's bell? There was a certain logic to what was happening, but only if Freeman was the caller who had described himself on the talk show as "marked" and there had been nothing in the papers about Freeman being someone who should have been in the murder house—or, for that matter, on the radio. All three papers reported that Lansing and Freeman had been in Los Angeles for two months, which was exactly what the talk show caller—and the police—had said.

We *worry about the wheels within wheels now*, Mike thought. What had happened to the witness against Lansing, the serendipitous arrival of the helicopter over Rainbow Drive, the conspiracy to allow the survivor to die, and Dan's okay-car "accident," were all too much like the sniper shooting of a police officer on his way to pistol qualifying, or the assassination of a burglar. What Mike was going to have to do was beyond choice, beyond all other considerations. The people responsible for Dan had thought they were safe—and they were, except from Mike. So Mike was going to have to kill them all.

But right now, he had to figure out a safe route home, and a place where he could hide the 9000 Building's after-hours visitors' register.

9

HE DIDN'T SLEEP—HE HADN'T EXPECTED TO. THE AN-swering machine light was blinking like an emergency warn-ing, but he didn't bother with his messages. With the television set showing the original *What Price Glory?* and the door double-locked, Mike spread index cards and notebook paper out on the coffee table and made a chronology of events, cross-referenced by the names known to him so far. The 9000 Building register was in the glove compartment of his car. Dan had tracked Jackson to Norma Place just hours before the meeting in the Clown Club, but it was possible that the juxtaposition of events was entirely coincidental. For one thing, it had taken the conspirators time to get themselves and their scheme together. Mike had known Gretchen Heidl since sometime in December of last year. At that time, she had already met Dick Albert. Albert had known Bobby Mi-chaels since the sixties. Mike had seen Michaels twice last week in the company of Paula Rogers, who was connected

151

in various ways—like the Palm Springs incident—to Donnie Jackson, who had bought his car from Jerry Chambers, whose body had been found across the street from Gretchen's place, and who apparently had been murdered while Mike and Gretchen had been making love. It was some circle, and it was only one of many.

There were the other victims, the female survivor of the attack, Elmer Washington, and Bernie Maxwell. That schoolteacher wanted Mike to have the information on the dog's collar—the daughter of a cop, she had used her head. But there was a special situation, she had said in her message.

And Mike had two other active cases, fresh cases. One, involving the Pendleton marine, was winding down. The other, on Beachwood Drive, which had started so deceptively quietly, was beginning to wind up.

Mike swam at dawn, his short-barreled .22 wrapped in his towel by the side of the pool. In the garage, both doors of his car had bits of transparent tape affixed down low on their leading edges. It was not possible to open the doors without peeling the tape from the front fenders. The tape could be put back in place, but it would be clouded with what it had lifted from the dirty surface of the paint. A professional would go under the car to install a bomb to the speedometer cable or driveshaft, setting it to trigger when Mike reached a certain speed, or had gone a number of miles. If Mike died that way, soon after Dan's death, people would be suspicious, but they should have been suspicious about the departure of the ambulance so many hours after the arrival of the police in Laurel Canyon—and their suspicions would do Mike no good even a split second after his death.

He set his alarm for eight-thirty, but was awake before it went off. He was a little stiff and raw from sliding down the hill beside the I-5 yesterday. In the shower, he saw that he had a strawberry the diameter of a baseball on his right hip, a skinned elbow, and scraped ribs. The firearms man he wanted to see, Chino Gomez, was in West Covina in the San Gabriel Valley. Gomez worked out of his house, but it was still too early to disturb him. The first message recorded last night on the answering machine was from Cutler's office.

Dan's car would be dismantled in Van Nuys, on Monday, eight A.M. sharp. Mike was invited to attend if he wanted to be there. The car was in a sealed garage, and the officer calling for Cutler said that the chief personally guaranteed the security of the seal. It seemed to Mike that Cutler was going to extremes to see that Mike and other interested parties were satisfied . . . about *something*. Mike could only allow the little drama to be played out to see what that was. He could arrive early in Van Nuys, but that wouldn't prevent anything. They, whoever *they* were, could be anticipating him at every step now. Mike had to be careful—he had to *think*! He had habits of all kinds, from swimming and sitting in the sauna to his dietary habits and the hours he worked. If he didn't think and make himself aware of what he was doing, he was wide open to anything anybody wanted to do to him. He had to be careful about everything he said on all the telephones he used regularly. He had to vary his route back and forth to work, shop at different stores, become unpredictable. It would be a long time before he would be able to take anything for granted again.

Marge had called last night, too. The funeral would be Wednesday. Now Mike knew where to send flowers—he wanted his flowers as close to Dan's coffin as possible. Marge was calling everyone listed in their address book, but she was sure Dan had kept more telephone numbers in his desk at work. Another of the newspapers and two of the television stations had asked Marge pointed questions about the circumstances of Dan's death. "One asked if I thought it was suspicious. What do they expect me to *say* to that?"

The third message was from Gretchen, returning his call in the late afternoon: "I had the radio on today and heard the news. I'm sorry. Maybe you've forgotten that you mentioned your partner to me. Several times, actually. I'm calling from a pay telephone. At last I've had a pair of visitors, and I see now that they were inevitable. It's a good idea for you to wait until Monday to call me at my office. Even then we may have to be circumspect. So you'll call me from a pay telephone, and I will call you back. I am very sorry about your partner. Please take good care of yourself, my friend."

Next was Marvin Burgess: "I'm calling from home, Mike. We had a call at the shop from Larry Hammond. He wanted to talk to you and got quiet when I told him that you were out of the office. Because it was Hammond, I didn't volunteer that you were out on a case. He expressed his regret about Dan. After the silence, I thought I smelled something. Then he said he wanted me to give you a message. He wanted me to ask you to stay available next week after midnight. He didn't say which night and he didn't say why. The man is colder than a scuba diver's dick, Mike, so I can't give you a reading on whether what he has in mind is positive or negative. After midnight, it's certainly no office meeting. Whatever, he knows what I know about it. I'll be home tonight if you want to call."

Then there was a hang-up, the third of the week. Burgess hadn't given the time of his call, but he would remember. The next caller gave the time. She said her name, but Mike didn't place it until he heard a few more words, soft and girlish. "This is Laura Demming again, Mr. Gallagher." He had called her, too, but she didn't have an answering machine. "I'm calling at a quarter to ten. On this evening's news on TV was a story about the death of a Hollywood Division detective, whom I assume you knew quite well. I'm sorry about your pain and loss. In any event, I should be home all day tomorrow if you have the time and the inclination to call."

Mike met Chino Gomez at a shooting range in Arcadia. Gomez was almost sixty years old, white-haired and heavy. He had been trading guns with cops for as long as Mike had known him. Mike had bought the little .22 from him five years ago. All Mike had said this time was that he needed something with more stopping power, so Gomez had come up to the foothills from West Covina with a trunkful of revolvers, remembering that Mike was one of those guys who didn't like automatic weapons. Shooting a human being was something that had to be kept simple if you did it only when necessary and under stressful conditions. You pointed and pulled the trigger, and the last thing you wanted to have on your mind was the technology involved. Gomez had brought a black five-shot .357 Magnum that was uncomfortable to Mike because of its greater heft than his .38.

"I set the sights myself," Gomez said. "If you can shoot, you can do pretty good with this. I hit one of those old Bakelite telephones at a hundred feet with it. Terrible mess. I know it will knock down a little airplane. The guy who sold it to me said it gets hot during practice—but that's an awful lot of steady shooting. You'd have to be in a real war for it to jam. I think it will shoot through five or six lath-and-plaster walls. They can run from this, but they can't hide. Maybe behind brick, but I wouldn't count on cinder block, especially the thin kind. Put this in the hands of a fellow who can't hit water if he fell out of a boat, he'll still kill you with it. If it hits you in the arm, you're dead, because it will tear your arm clean off."

"How much?"

"Three fifty."

"You brought some rounds?" Mike asked.

"Oh, sure."

Gomez had brought cotton, too, and after the first shot, Mike wadded his ears. Movies never had the sound of a Magnum right. It would knock people out of the theaters. A Magnum went BANG! the way they used to do it in comic books. Mike was shooting at a standard paper target no more than fifty feet away. Down the range were three or four other guys, one of them quick-firing an automatic. From that end of the range was a steady popping, then *pop-pop-pop!* Mike was shooting slowly, two-handed, trying to get a sense of this heavy, seemingly seamless chunk of steel. Even through the cotton the sound was spine-rattling. After five shots, Gomez reeled in the target. Four holes.

"You missed the first time. I saw that."

"The kick surprised me."

"Try a little more distance. That will surprise you, too. Shoot for the bull."

At one hundred feet Mike shot a wavy line across the center of the target.

"I'll get the papers for you to sign," Gomez said. "You can have the ammunition."

"I want a shoulder holster," Mike said, reloading.

"Are you going to keep the thirty-eight?"

"Oh, yeah."

"If you want a backup, I've got a cute little gadget. A ball-point pen that fires a single .22 long. Accurate across a dinner table. Good for one firing—it self-destructs. You just click the button as if you're accessing the pen point. It might hurt your hand, but it might save your life, too."

"Who makes a thing like that?"

"I do. I have to build them loaded. I've sold dozens of them to undercover guys."

"No papers for it," Mike said. Gomez shook his head no. Mike reloaded the Magnum, ran a target out to a hundred feet, set himself, took a breath, and quick-fired. Three hits, one out of the target, and he thought he knew when he had missed the paper completely. He wrote Gomez a check for four seventy-five. Gomez brought two pens from his car; he was wearing a thick leather glove on his right hand. While Mike signed the papers on the Magnum, Gomez hung up a new target. He moved it just beyond arm's length.

"Maybe you ought to stand behind me," he said.

Mike took the cotton out of his ears, but even so, he barely heard the little round go off. The end of the pen peeled back like a miniature banana. There was a tiny hole in the paper target.

"Stings like a bitch," Gomez said. "But if you get shaken down, they won't take your pens. Carry more than one, it looks better. And remember the fucking thing, will you? You forget you have it, you'll wind up shooting yourself in the balls."

On the way back to the city, Mike felt around under the dashboard for a place that would hold the .38 without causing a rattle. The Magnum was under his left arm. He would carry his little .22 revolver for a backup, and the trick pen. If he ran into someone smart enough to look for a backup, he might still have the pen, and if he didn't have that, the .38 that was standard police equipment would not be far away.

He was back in his apartment by noon. The light was blinking. Pendleton—they wanted him to return the call as soon as possible. The commandant's office had been left instructions to give Mike the commandant's home number. The commandant's wife answered and Mike identified himself.

"Oh, yes," she said. "Please hold on."

"I'm glad you caught us," the commandant said after a moment. "We were on our way down to Mission Valley to see the Padres. I'm afraid I have bad news. I received your message yesterday too late to prevent your suspect from leaving the base on a routine pass, and this morning he was AWOL. Because of the seriousness of the situation, we felt obliged to take some steps. They may not be good police procedure, but the Corps has its own responsibilities to the community. We questioned the men who know him, and they report that your suspect said he was going up to Los Angeles."

"That doesn't create a problem between us, General," Mike said. "You've already furnished us with his photograph, and if he's wandering around up here, we'll have a better chance of picking him up. I ought to be able to have copies distributed in the division by the four o'clock shift. Ah, did you ask these men who knew him about last weekend?"

"One of them said he accompanied the suspect to Los Angeles on the bus, and that they said good-bye at the Hollywood station."

"That helps our case, if in fact your man actually killed our citizen last week. The physical evidence puts him in the murder room, but doesn't fix the time he was there. You and I have worked Saturday and Sunday on this, so I don't think anyone can fault us for not moving quickly enough to prevent whatever he may have done last night. What I'd like you to do, if you don't mind, sir, is have someone gather up his personal gear and secure it under lock and key. A witness to take inventory would be helpful. Since you can do this without a warrant and I can't, you're going to have to be willing to testify, if necessary, that this idea was your own. But I don't think a defense attorney would want to call you in a trial. The man who actually does the work will be called, so maybe you want to involve the people who have already helped. You can see that if the truth comes out, the attorney will claim that I used the Corps as an instrument to violate his client's civil rights. All we're doing is applying my expertise to the common sense of the matter. If the suspect took something from the victim, we'd be betraying the public trust if we stooged around only to give him the chance to get rid of it.''

"I understand completely, Mr. Gallagher, and I couldn't agree with you more. In fact, I admire your thoroughness.''

Mike had to swallow before he could speak again. "We'll be in touch. Enjoy the ball game.'' When he hung up he wept aloud. *Stooged around.* Dan had loved to talk like that. He had loved to tease Marge. When he'd learned that the town's foremost bodybuilder had won a sweepstakes at his local gym for the most money offered to a muscleman by a homosexual—Marge's dreamboat had been offered five thousand dollars by an Englishman for the chance to perform fellatio on him—Dan hadn't been able to wait to get home to tell her. He'd told her over the telephone, with Mike sitting at his own desk helpless with laughter. "What do you mean, 'Is nothing sacred'? He took the five grand! *Money* is sacred!''

Now Mike wondered if the twenty-five thousand would make Marge remember that moment. There had to be other moments—maybe many thousands of moments. When he felt better, Mike called her. She said she was doing all right. She was on Valium, she admitted, but she was all right.

"I'm going in to Hollywood now,'' Mike said. "Dan had a Rolodex and I'd like to drop it off later. Probably this evening.''

"I've been keeping a list of the people who called,'' she said. "I don't know most of them. Don't eat today, Mike. The house is full of food. I'll want you to take some home.''

There was no point in telling her now that most of the food

he had taken away from the Crawfords' house in the past had eventually turned into Technicolor special effects in his own refrigerator.

On his way over the hill to Wilcox, Mike stopped at a florist's. No FTD on Sundays. Tomorrow was fine, Mike said, looking out the window as the florist took down the Valencia address. Mike didn't think anyone was following him, but he was still going to keep his eyes open.

The big squad room was almost empty today. Mike checked last night's crime reports—no murders, no assaults on homosexuals. Juan Lopez called in. He was on duty, out on a db call, an old man in his bed, surrounded by Polaroids of a tall redhead forty years his junior. "A real redhead, man," Lopez said. "Her pussy hair is so orange it's almost pink. The old man's son is on the way over. Wait until he finds out what a lusty old fart his father was."

"It's probably no news to him," Mike said. "I want you to keep your eye out for another redhead." He told Lopez about the AWOL marine. "I'm preparing some paper on him now. Everybody should know that if we catch another dead fairy, we might have a serial killer on our hands."

"Okay. How are you doing, Mike?"

"I'm coming around. Dan's funeral is Wednesday. Somebody has to mind the store. What do you think?"

"Oh, I want to go, man. I loved him. Please don't make me work."

"I'll do the best I can." Mike thought of something else. "Were you working Friday night?"

"Not after six o'clock. I went home to beat my kids." He laughed at his own joke. "Actually, I wanted to beat my wife. Every time *Miami Vice* comes on, she gives me shit. I love that show, and she thinks I'm whipping around Hollywood like that."

"Aren't you?" Mike asked. "*I* am."

"That's good," Lopez said. "I'm glad to hear you joking. But please don't make me work on Wednesday."

Mike went into a Mexican accent. "Don't take de old mon's dorty peectures," he said, and hung up.

He was at the copying machine when someone bellowed his name. "Pendleton on the phone!"

The voice on the other end identified himself. "The commandant isn't available now. He told me to call you if a Private McCallum returns to the base. McCallum is in custody. His gear is sequestered. McCallum is sporting a pretty good mouse under his left eye, also a fat lip."

"Would you please photograph McCallum to establish that he returned to base in that condition?"

"I'm not aware of any orders to that effect, sir."

Mike's entire military career flashed before his eyes. "You're aware of such orders now, youngster. We're trying to build a chain of evidence. If you don't want to remember today for the rest of your life, take the pictures. Close-ups of every bruise and scratch. Strip McCallum nude and make a list of every mark on his body, no matter how old, and take a picture of it."

"May I ask what this is about, sir?"

"It's about your commandant being at Jack Murphy Stadium watching a ball game in the innocent belief that the intent of his orders will be followed when he's off the base. If you want to fuck around, I'll call the commandant at home tonight—at midnight—to make sure that the bruises are photographed before they heal." Mike had the commandant's home telephone number in hand, and read it off. "All right?"

"They tell you only what they think you need to know down here," the young officer said. "The pictures will be taken, sir. I guarantee it."

Mike said good-bye and returned to the copying machine and threw out the copies he had made. On the original he typed the new information that McCallum was in custody at Pendleton with facial bruises he might have sustained in a fight with a Hollywood homosexual, who may or may not have been murdered. If alive, the victim might be blabbing about a fight he'd had last night with a redheaded marine. There were few enough uniformed officers and plainclothesmen working the streets on a Sunday evening, but there was usually less for them to do, too. Mike couldn't ask the duty sergeant to make this a priority item; on the other hand, someone who was on the streets regularly might have some insight into the problem. Now Mike called Laura Demming. The telephone rang five times before she picked up.

"This is Mike Gallagher, the cop. Do you have a moment for a conversation about a dog? You said there was a special situation."

"Well, yes. Can you hang on a second? I want to turn off the stereo."

He couldn't hear anything, and when she came back to the telephone, he told her so.

"It's a meditation tape," she said. "It had run out of things to say. You caught me in a trance. Don't laugh."

"I didn't laugh, I smiled."

"Well, I heard you." Now he heard something from her, a little gasp. "Oh, I'm sorry. I read in this morning's *Times* how close you were to Mr. Crawford, and that you were the one who found his body. I am sorry. You don't have to do this if you don't want to. It will keep."

"I'm trying to stay busy," he said. "You said there was a special situation."

"I don't think I could do what you're doing. It's the girl's aunt. She doesn't want to be involved with the police. Let me just say that she's a very tense person. The afternoon she came down to the schoolyard with the dog could have been a disaster. Do you know what I mean? You work with the public."

"And you're making progress with the niece and don't want to jeopardize it."

"You're very perceptive, Mr. Gallagher."

"Not really. You forget that my ex-wife was in your line of work."

"Oh, yes. I didn't know her. That was before my time at the school. She talked to another teacher who knows me, and your telephone number was passed along. Are you really all right after what you've been through?"

"Two hours ago I was a blubbering mess. It will catch up

with me again. I've been through this sort of thing before. It's a matter of knowing how to manage yourself.''

"That's why I meditate. Can you promise me that you'll keep the little girl and her aunt out of this from now on? I think I told you, they've already passed the dog onto other people. The little girl wanted to keep the dog, but her aunt said no, and the dog is better off out of that household, I'm sorry to say, even though the dog would have been good for the girl.''

"I can promise you that *I* will keep the little girl and her aunt out of it. I don't know what else will happen.''

"Then you're not in charge? Today's paper said you were in charge of Hollywood Homicide. Laurel Canyon is Hollywood Division. My father was a policeman.''

"I didn't know him.'' Mike could have chosen his words more carefully. Now he wasn't sure she was going to give him information he wanted.

"Oh, he wasn't a policeman here. In Chicago. My father and mother retired here. You didn't answer my question.''

"I don't want to discuss police business, Miss Demming. I said I was speaking for myself. Neither of us knows if you have pertinent information.''

She was silent a moment. Then: "Do you know anything about Chicago, Mr. Gallagher?''

"No, I can't say I do.''

"Los Angeles was not a good place to retire from Chicago. It wasn't the change my father thought it would be. Am I clear yet? I'm not sure I am.''

He didn't want to antagonize her. "I think I want the information you have now more than ever, Miss Demming.''

She sighed. "My father didn't like what he saw happening—''

"We understand each other,'' Mike said quickly.

"Actually, I know that the information I have is pertinent,'' she said. "I'm a policeman's daughter. I couldn't resist the opportunity and my own curiosity. I learned something.''

Mike recognized the shock he felt. Maybe she would perceive it as a silence, but if she had been able to hear him smile, there was no telling how sensitive she was. "You probably shouldn't have done that, Miss Demming."

"I think you should understand how *I* feel about Los Angeles, Mr. Gallagher. I think it makes Chicago look like day care."

He liked that. "How long have you been here?"

"Eighteen years."

"How old are you?"

"Thirty-three."

"Where do you live?"

"On Shadyglade, in Studio City. I inherited my parents' house. The mortgage is two hundred and fifty dollars a month. I put my father's mortgage insurance in the bank."

He grinned. "Did I ask all that?"

"Well, you're seeing if you want to pick me up. You're pretty amazing."

"All right, then, what I was thinking was that we could discuss what you know in a more private context. I have to go up to Valencia this evening. There's a Thai restaurant on Ventura Boulevard in Sherman Oaks, Anajak Thai. Why don't we meet there?"

"That's more private? Oh, I see what you mean. No, just come here. I have yard work to do. I'd made up my mind not to go out today."

He called Marge and told her that he would be at her place by seven o'clock. Judy had called, Marge said; she had seen the story in the *Times* and wanted to come to the funeral. It took Mike a moment to realize that there might be a call from Judy on his machine when he got home. He had thought he would have the energy to stop at the apartment building of the victim of last week's murder to show people the picture of McCallum, the redheaded marine. No. Things were catching up with him. Of course he was thinking about Laura Demming. *You're seeing if you want to pick me up*. She was pretty amazing herself. He had just begun to think about it. And she'd been playing detective. He'd caught her in a trance. Some of these people in L.A. who meditated thought they traveled to Mars, changed red traffic lights to green, and employed The Force to find them parking spaces. They read magazines devoted to their former lives on the lost continent of Atlantis and imagined they flew around the city at night. If Dan were alive, he'd be rolling on the floor laughing. "Wait until you find out she lives on roots and berries and won't show you her tits until she consults the stars. If you get a disease that hasn't been seen since the conquest of Peru, don't come running to me."

Finally Mike called Don Grant, in Palm Springs. He wasn't on duty, but Mike had expected that. He told the voice on the other end that Grant had worked with Dan Crawford, the L.A. detective killed yesterday.

"Give me your number up there. If Don doesn't call you back right away, I will."

Juan Lopez came in. "Do you know how many redheaded muscleboys are peddling their buns on Santa Monica Boulevard?"

"Forget it, they already got him down at Pendleton."

The telephone rang. "Is this Gallagher? This is Larry Goldfarb, plainclothes. I think I got the fairy who pounded that marine last night. A dancer, solid as a rock. He overheard me asking a bartender, and spoke right up."

"Hang on," Mike said. "Juan, will you take this, please? Goldfarb is bringing in a guy who might be able to tie the marine to last week's killing. See if the marine said anything to the guy. I'm trying to get out of here."

Lopez picked up and another line rang. "Gallagher? It's Don Grant in Palm Springs. I'm calling from home—Cathedral City. If we talk for long, I'm going to have to ask you to call me back. I've got a teenager and her phone bills look like exacta payoffs. What happened to Dan?"

"I'd like to tell you Wednesday, at the funeral. He was on to something up here that he developed out of information arising from one of your cases. I think you know which one. I'm going to need your help. Confidentially."

"We'll talk," Grant said. "Give me the when and where on the funeral. I'll be there two hours early."

10

MIKE OVERSHOT THE CROSS STREET AND THEN HAD TO come back down from the north on Shadyglade, looking at the hill on the other side of Ventura Boulevard that rose to Mulholland and Laurel Canyon beyond. Shadyglade was what Los Angeles was supposed to be about, tree-lined, quiet, the lawns manicured, shrubs trimmed. A lot of the city had looked like this when Mike and his parents had arrived back in the fifties. From almost any high ground, all you had been able to see were the trees. There had been a limit to the height of buildings, a street railway called the Red Cars—phasing out then, but enough of it left to take you all over town. Down at the beach had been amusement piers, the big movie houses had been on Hollywood Boulevard, and Westwood Village had been reserved to college students and the old ladies running their boardinghouses. The city had been declining ever since—growing larger, but declining. Mike and Dan had discussed the city's changing, Mike's memory of his father never far away. What they were seeing, Dan had said, was not so much the commercialization of Southern California as its brutalization by people who cared about nothing but money. It wasn't an accident that the richest escapees of the worldwide Communist tidal wave were settling in Southern California. They knew their money was safe here. And they expected to be served by the millions of Americans who had come out West from all over the country ever since World War II in the hope of finding the values their predecessors, the pioneers, had been searching for a hundred years ago. Dan had called it a prescription for disaster.

Not that a hundred years ago had been such a moral bargain either, Dan had said. After the buffalo had been killed to make the continent safe for the railroads, people had paid as little as a dollar to ride from Kansas city to Los Angeles—of course, it had cost a lot more to go back. No jobs, and the city had gone boom and bust three or four times before the advent of oil, the aircraft industry, and the movies, the latter two having been lured here by the kind of cheap labor and favorable taxes states of the Deep South now used to suck industry out of the industrial Northeast. Out of all that not only had fortunes been made, but decent livings, too, the kind that had created the Shadyglades of the city. Now the Shadyglades were vestigial, these pretty streets, and Mike wondered if Laura Demming knew that builders planned a high-rise office building on Ventura that would block the street's view of the hill to the south. She probably did; Studio City had a homeowners' group—there were homeowners' groups in every section of the city, famous for losing their battles.

The address Laura Demming had given him was painted on the curb in front of the creamy beige, brown-trimmed ranch-style bungalow, well hidden behind its border plantings. Mike parked in the driveway behind a moderately clobbered old Toyota station wagon. A dog barked, and as Mike approached the house, the animal jumped at the other side of a wooden fence next to the garage. The dog's paws scratched at the wood. The front door opened and a petite, sandy-haired woman wearing glasses stepped out. Her hair was

straight and pulled back in an unkempt ponytail. The glasses
looked as big as pie plates. Laura Demming wasn't pretty,
but she was cute, with a button nose. No lipstick. She had a
splash of large freckles across her nose. She was wearing
blue jeans and a plaid shirt—or rather, they were covering a
curvy figure. She was narrow-waisted, with a full bosom and
rounded hips.

"Hi. Pay no attention to Agnes. She wants to love you to
death."

"Hiya. Can I use your telephone? On the way over I realized I'm booked for a conflict tomorrow."

Laura Demming laughed. "In the kitchen. I just roasted
some chickens. Would you like chicken with a glass of
wine?"

"I'd love some chicken, but wine would knock me out
now."

In the kitchen there were two chickens in a pan on the
stove, an ancient white enamel Gaffers and Sattler with a
folding top. The whole kitchen was a near-antique, maybe
not even postwar, perfectly spotless. "Are you cooking for
the week?" Mike asked.

"I don't do it all the time. Von's had a chicken sale. I
never waste money. It drives some people crazy." From a
drawer she extracted a huge Sabatier carving knife and easily
split one of the chickens in half. Mike was looking around
while dialing Ira Rosenberg. It was a pretty place, old-fashioned. Laura Demming said, "By the end of the week I'll
have chicken salad and stock to cook rice in. I don't eat red
meat anymore."

"Except for bacon, neither do I." Ira Rosenberg said hello.
"Ira, it's Mike. Can you keep Moreland on ice until noon
tomorrow? Cutler invited me to watch them taking Dan's car
apart, and I want to see what the old turd is up to." Laura
Demming laughed before he could signify an apology for his
language. Rosenberg asked if Mike had learned anything new
about Dan. "I'll tell you tomorrow. Look, do you want me
to bring in lunch? Tell me what you want to eat." He had
caught Rosenberg by surprise. Now Mike bit into a drum-

stick. The meat was moist and the skin crisp, rubbed with garlic and cilantro.

"What are you eating?" Rosenberg asked. Mike told him. "Bring that, smartass," Rosenberg said. "I want to see if you can eat it over Moreland's dead body. Do you know what color she is?"

"Gray," Mike said, and hung up.

"My chicken isn't gray!" Laura Demming cried.

"I wasn't talking about your chicken. Did you like being a cop's kid?"

"Yes. My father never made homicide. I think he always wanted to. He drove my mother crazy with his stories. I loved them all. Tell me what's gray. Come on!"

"Ethel Moreland. Her friends knew her as Valerie." He bit into the chicken again. "She gets her going-away party tomorrow."

Her eyebrows were up—she looked like a little kid. "Murdered?"

"Strangled. For a minute I was hoping you knew her. I've already been lucky once with her. Twice was too much to expect."

"Why did you ask Ira what he wanted to eat?"

He told her about Rosenberg's wife calling about dinner.

She laughed, then became serious. "What about Mr. Crawford?"

"We don't know each other, Miss Demming. I'm sorry."

"I'm sorry, too. Call me Laura. I already have an idea. I've been following this since I heard the police helicopter Monday morning while I was at school, and then saw the ambulance pulling away on the afternoon news. Funny, but nobody said a word about the time gap. I know you're not going to comment on that. I didn't see the name Gallagher in any of the newspaper accounts—I've read them all—and I was confused when I received your ex-wife's message that you were looking for the dog. Who's this guy Gallagher? I asked myself. My colleague, who knows your ex, said that you're head of Hollywood Homicide . . . and I didn't see your name in the paper. Well. My colleague doesn't think much of you, as I hope you understand, but she didn't say anything I couldn't understand myself, because I fell out of love with a man before he fell out of love with me, and he thinks I'm a terrible person. So anyway, a little intrigued, I called you. I liked your voice."

"I liked yours, too. It made me wonder about you. You're really into police work, aren't you?"

"I told you, I loved my father's stories." She grinned teasingly. "Am I under suspicion?"

"Not of anything criminal." He was enjoying this—he wanted to push it a little, but she spoke first.

"What I want to say is, let's understand each other. Do you want to take off your jacket? I knew before your message was passed along that something was screwy about the murders on Rainbow Drive. Your presence, or interest, doesn't change or enhance my opinion. Just don't bullshit me." Now he put his jacket over the back of a chair. "My father carried a backup," she said. "Ankle holster. He taught me to shoot."

"You're an only child," Mike said.

"And set in my ways. You're fast."

"How about telling me what you learned about the dog?"

"I have it all written down inside. The dog was wearing a collar with a vaccination tag from a veterinarian over here on Burbank Boulevard. I called the vet and told him I'd found the dog and wanted to return it to the owner. This was Thursday. From the number on the tag, the vet told me that the dog belonged to Howard Green up on Mulholland Drive. The next morning on my way to school I checked the address. It doesn't exist. There's a Howard Green in the new telephone book, *not* the old one, with no address. I called the number. It's already disconnected. The newspapers said that Daisy Nunn was the owner of the house on Rainbow Drive and that her boyfriend was with her since last fall. Jerry Chambers lived in Hollywood—"

"Franklin Avenue."

"Right. The young girl and Billy Lansing came from the San Diego area, along with the one who's in the hospital. She was supposed to be up here seeing Lansing about a reconciliation. According to the papers, Lansing arrived here two months ago, with a partner, up to no good. That leaves the

young girl, Marylou Brown. Why would she use the name
Howard Green to get her dog vaccinated, and give a phony
address? Women don't do that with dogs. I know. Young
women love their animals too much for that shit."

"When was the dog vaccinated?"

"Last December. That's months before Lansing and partner were supposed to have come to Los Angeles."

"Doesn't prove anything," Mike said. "The dog could
have belonged to somebody else last December. We already
know he's a peripatetic dog."

Laura Demming giggled. "Peripatetic?"

"I'm trying to tell you not to play cop."

"Okay, but there's more. I called the veterinarian again
and asked if he was sure of the address. I played dumb. The
vet told me that the patient's human fills out the card himself.
The vet couldn't imagine why there would be a mistake, because the card shows that the party paid cash, not by check.
Only people who want to *bounce* checks screw around like
that. The vet didn't remember a thing about the dog or the
people."

"More than one?"

"I asked," she said. "He was using a figure of speech. I
thought he was getting on to me by then."

"What was the dog's name? That was on the card, too."

"You *are* a tough cop. My father would have loved you.
The dog's name is Jones. That's street argot for addiction."

"Argot?"

"I can do it, too."

He hadn't meant to come down hard on her for playing
cop. "Look, you already know, or have figured out, more
than you should. You really don't want to find yourself in the
middle of a mess like this. Even if your father taught you to
shoot, and this place is an armed camp—"

"How did you figure that out?"

"It goes with the territory of a woman like you, good with
money and all that. You don't smoke—no ashtrays—and drink
very little, or I'd see it on your face. You're conservative in
your life-style, if not your politics. Your father brought his
guns out from Chicago and they're still here. Keep them

clean, go out to a range often enough to stay comfortable with what you're doing, and renew the ammunition every year.''

"You even sound like him. My mother would have thought you were a big goon, but that's besides the point. She thought any guy over five-ten was a big goon."

"That description fit me when I was a kid."

"I got carried away. You're right, we don't know each other. I think I wanted you to like me."

"I think I do. You've saved me a lot of legwork, but as I say, do yourself a favor and eschew your curiosity about the Laurel Canyon murders."

"Eschew? Gallagher, two, Demming, one."

She was staring at him. She wanted eye contact. So did he. He said, "The trouble with keeping score is that the difference between fantasy and reality has to do with control. I'm an only child, too. Maybe selfishness is part of the territory but so is fantasy." He tapped his temple. "Vaudeville ain't dead here."

"My colleague said you were a lady-killer."

"Your colleague knows a time of my life when I felt like a prisoner. Delicious chicken. Can I have a thigh?"

"Can I tell you the story of my life first?"

He stepped in and took off her glasses and put them on the counter and kissed her. Her lips were smooth, soft, parting— she knew what she was doing. Her hand was on the back of his neck. Now her mouth opened. They took their time, exploring. Her body was firm, her belly rounded. She felt light and small in his arms. He drew her closer against him, almost into the air. She was breathing harder, letting go. He brushed her glasses back across the counter and lifted her up and kissed her neck. She held his head with both hands, trying to turn it to kiss him. He opened her legs and wrapped them around him and she thrust herself against him. His mouth on hers muffled her squeals as she held him even more tightly, shuddering. She broke away and buried her head in his shoulder.

"You're under arrest," she whispered. He tried to kiss her

neck again, but she pulled away. "You said *wine* would knock you out."

"I have another appointment this evening."

"Not for more chicken, I trust. I hope."

"No, with my partner's widow. Actually, she said she was going to load me down with food."

"Bring it here." When he didn't answer right away, she said, "I don't always know what's good for me."

"I don't have any commitments, Laura."

"Obviously I don't either. Maybe you ought to leave now."

"The only thing that keeps me from being all over you like a cheap suit is this situation I'm in. My partner may have been killed because of me. Until this morning, I carried one gun."

She gave him a sheepish half-smile, a little sad. "I'm trying to say that I don't want you all over me like a cheap suit. It would be nice to go to the movies and up to Mulholland to neck."

"Before I got here, I offered you dinner."

"Okay, I outsmarted myself. I really was doing yard work. I haven't showered. And it's been so long for me in the kissyface department that I can't remember the last time I shaved my legs."

"I won't tell you about this case."

"I don't want you to just come and go. Pun intended. I'm scared, and I'm not trying to bullshit you."

"You're not the only one who's scared. This was the last thing in the world that I was looking for. But now I wouldn't leave if I didn't have to. One of the things I have to see Marge—Dan's widow—about is money to cover the cost of a wireman. Do you know what a wireman is?"

"Electronics."

"Don't call me at my home anymore until I know it's safe. It's possible that you're at risk already. If you change your mind about later, just leave the front light off and I'll drive on by."

"Jesus, I hope the bulb doesn't blow out."

He kissed her again.

"Do you think I'm at risk?" she asked.

"Only if things are completely crazy. I want to be sure my line is clear. If I'm followed tonight I won't come here. I'll call you from a phone booth. But don't think you've shaved your legs for nothing, because I'll be back."

"I usually wear slacks or jeans, so it might be awhile before you see anything."

"You said you were meditating when I called earlier."

"So you think I'm all earthed out? What an asshole. The one has nothing to do with the other." She pinched his ribs. "God, you're solid. Maybe I'll take a nap while I'm waiting for you. I think I'll need it."

"Why do you meditate?"

"Give me a little room. Step back. Relax, I'm not going to weird you out." She brought her hands out in front of her, fingers spread. She held her hands an inch or two apart and seemed to concentrate a moment. "All right, slide your hand down between them."

He did. There was a current between her hands, not air, but like the current underwater near the nozzle on the side of a hot tub, and mildly tingling. He'd never felt anything like it before. "All right," he said, "what's the gag?"

"No gag. No batteries either. It's done through the imagination—and really quite beside the point of meditating."

"What is the point?"

She smiled. "I think it's God. Don't be afraid. One of the most important things I get out of this is that I get back to my center faster than I used to."

"I can appreciate the value of that."

"You said on the telephone that you manage yourself."

"I try," he said. He kissed her neck. "If I'm going to get back here at a reasonable hour, I have to go now."

"What did you mean when you said you've been through this before?" He had been thinking of his father. "Not now. Please. We really don't have time for life stories. I don't care anyway. We all have our fantasies." He turned over her collar and kissed her shoulder.

"You're getting me excited again."

"Then we've found a perfect place to leave it until later."

* * *

No one followed him to Valencia, and no one followed him back down to the Valley either. Lack of sleep was catching up with him and he was trying to be extra careful. Marge had given him two thousand dollars, twenty of the hundred-dollar bills Dan had told him about, to cover all the work Mike wanted done by the wireman. In addition to his own line, he wanted to know about Donnie Jackson's and Paula Rogers'. He already knew about Gretchen, who was back in his thoughts again. He had seen the telephone truck at the foot of Rainbow Drive. Gretchen had had a pair of visitors, the police. From her tone on the tape this morning, Mike had concluded that he still had nothing to worry about from that end—but the operative word was *still*. The more time that passed, the more often the investigating team would go back to close every gap in what it knew, no matter how small. Mike was too enraged about Dan to worry anymore about the consequences of having been with Gretchen. Maybe his rage was a way of covering what he thought was his responsibility, or complicity, in Dan's death—but he didn't care about that either. He didn't care about his feelings, or guilt, or even his pain. Dan had told him that something would come along to make him care about the work again. Oh, yes. Mike wanted to do this work and get away from the job forever, because the thought of the job made him sick. Lansing and Freeman were supposed to have come up here two months ago, but a guy named Howard Green had taken the dog to a vet last December. Not a woman—Laura Demming had had that right. The bumpkin on the radio had said two months, too. According to the week's newspaper stories, that bullshit was also the official police line—the same police who had choreographed an elaborate and still disgusting cover-up on the day of the murders. The whole thing was a dance performed for the public by one and all to a tune the public could not hear.

To get the meaning of it, you had to go up to Valencia and sit in the living room where not even the air wanted to move without excusing itself. Widow and children looked like they were taking a break from beatings that would begin again tomorrow, and continue until they simply learned how to forget the pain. Mike had been younger at his father's death than Dan's kids were now, yet he felt sorrier for them than he ever had for himself because the Gallaghers had never been a happy family the way the Crawfords had been. The Crawfords had had a future filled with real joy. Mike didn't know what he meant by that, although he had an idea that he was saying something about himself that wasn't very good. He hadn't solved his father's killing as he had promised himself, which made him a failure like his parents. Both of them. His father had been up to something. He had been involved with the wrong guys. Dan had thought he had been corrupt for having involved himself in something that had turned into twenty-five thousand dollars, but that had been nothing compared to what Mike felt in his own blood and bones, something *in* him, part of him. He had been a madman today with Laura Demming. If she had not said no to him when she had, he would have arrived at the Crawford's reeking of sex. Looking it. Marge knew him. She would have seen.

Now he couldn't figure out what he had found appealing about Demming. He had felt it, he knew, because he felt it still. For all of that, the whole episode seemed like proof he was cracking under the strain. Didn't he owe Gretchen something for covering for him? There were no commitments between them, he had not lied to Laura about that. Gretchen wasn't available every time he wanted to see her, and they had devised a way of talking to each other that had no importance, but there was friendship, laughter, and sex that was pretty good even if it was without love, and not that much lust anymore. Sure, he was cracking up. He would feel relieved if he found Demming's light out because it might mean she was doing herself a favor, sparing herself the pain of what would happen after he came to his senses. Freckles, for Christ's sake, full lips, and eyes as big as doorknobs. She wasn't a player. She wanted him to believe she knew more than she showed, but he *didn't* believe it, not about the person he had met today, a lonely young woman who talked too much when she was nervous, who had somehow become intrigued with what she had heard about him. Dan had chastised him for dumb stunts like this, and if Mike couldn't think of a specific instance now, it was only more evidence of the true state of his mind. . . .

He had told Marge practically nothing of what he had learned so far, nothing about Dan's car trouble, the *friend*, what Dan had been developing. "I need a wireman," he'd said to Marge. "It's illegal to tap people, but it's not illegal to see if they're being tapped." He hadn't mentioned that he wanted to check his own line. "There are other avenues I want to explore that won't cost money. No matter what I do, no matter where it leads, I'll tell you everything just as soon as the smoke clears. You may realize that that time has come before I do. So be it, that's when you'll hear."

He didn't think he needed the whole two thousand for what he wanted done. The money was in her purse—what safer place? They were in the kitchen, the door closed, having left instructions that they were not to be disturbed. While she counted out the money, he reached for her credit and identification cards and copied the number on her automobile club card. She saw, but she had no questions.

In the living room, Billy said that he would walk Mike out to his car. They were barely outside when Billy asked what was going on.

"Maybe nothing," Mike said.

"My dad told me about what happened to your dad," Billy said. "I'm sorry, Mike, but I don't want to be in the same position as you."

"You won't be."

"You don't have the right to keep anything about this to yourself, away from the family—"

"You won't be in the position I'm in because you're getting the best professional shot I can give it!" Mike stepped closer, trying to intimidate the boy. "Now that's a hell of a better deal than I got! I was twelve fucking years old, and it was the first time I ever had a suit on my back! What the fuck are you going to do about it anyway? Are *you* a detective? You wouldn't know what to do first! If you can't trust me, then stand here and tell me you can't trust your mother!"

"I'm sorry, Mike—"

"I know you're suffering." He put his hand on Billy's shoulder. "Nobody will get away with anything, I promise. I've promised your mother. If you tried to get involved, you'd be spinning your wheels. You know it's true. Right now the family should be together and not worried about itself. I feel *I* should be with you, but I'm not for only one reason. You'll hear everything—but as I say, it may be nothing."

Billy nodded, said he was sorry again, and went into the house.

A block from his apartment building, Mike parked his car, and walked the rest of the way, his jacket open. The heaviness of his stride told him how tired he was. There was no one on the street, no one inside the lobby of the building. He stood back from the elevator as the door rolled open, and inside, he kept his back to the farthest wall, his hand on the Magnum, as the car rumbled upward. The upstairs hall was empty, as still as a freeze-frame. And his apartment was empty.

He played the message tape while he gathered the things he needed for tomorrow. Of course he was crazy: he was exhausted and he was looking forward again to Laura Demming. Not even Gretchen calling from her Calabasas barbecue intruded on his goofy little reverie. Gretchen had to be called tomorrow. He'd have to call Juan Lopez from Van Nuys, too. Lopez's message followed Gretchen's; the dancer who had beat up McCallum seemed to be not only a good citizen, but a fine witness, too. The dancer had thought McCallum had seemed nervous, and had concluded that McCallum hadn't had much experience with men. McCallum had assured the dancer that he'd been with a man the previous Saturday, and had named the street on which last week's victim had lived. Later, when the trouble had started, McCallum had yelled repeatedly, "I'll kill you! I'll kill you!" Lopez had reviewed the entire file, and he thought there was enough to present to the DA. Mike wanted a little more, like a witness who could place McCallum at the crime scene at the time, or one who could put McCallum with the victim on the murder night. Mike took McCallum to be a very bad boy, one who should be out of circulation for as long as the law allowed, and the only thing Mike could do to accomplish that was build as strong a case as possible. McCallum was still too young for a prison sentence long enough to allow him to outgrow his violence; the best that could be hoped for was the kind of stiff jolt that would give him a permanent fear of prison. If necessary, Mike would drop a dime on McCallum, letting it be known at the prison to which he was sentenced that he was there because a fairy had beaten him up. That would unleash the animals—they wouldn't quit no matter how hard he fought. But seven or eight years of sexual degradation for McCallum might be better for society than having him swagger around the yard representing himself to be an ex-marine killer who had gotten off lightly. To the best of Mike's knowledge, no one he had ever put away for murder had come out to kill again. It was a record made to be broken, but it was also one to work to preserve.

Lopez had another piece of information. A guy had called, asking to speak to Mike Gallagher. He hadn't wanted to give his name, but had said he had something he was sure Gallagher wanted. He wouldn't say what the information was about. When Lopez had tried to press him, the guy had hung up.

There was a hang-up on Mike's tape, too, which brought the total to four.

And just as interesting, no call from Judy. She knew how deeply Mike would be feeling Dan's death. It had passed through Mike's mind sometime this week that these hang-ups were from Judy, but he hadn't believed it and he didn't believe it now. His call to her at the beginning of the week hadn't been enough to provoke her to a pattern she had abandoned five or more years ago. But Judy *was* expressing her feelings about him with her silence. She had talked to Marge. In Judy's view, Mike was some kind of subhuman, and in Mike's view, her behavior only made him that much happier to have gotten away from her. The hang-ups were something else. If they were an attempt to induce a little paranoia in Mike, they were going to cost the caller a lot more in time and money. Right now the calls were only a pain in the ass.

Laura had left the light on—Mike's heart was thumping like a kid's, and made him smile. The light was on, the garage door was open, and the Toyota was parked on the street. He pulled into the driveway and his headlights showed the garage to be empty. He rolled on in. Some cop's daughter. She didn't want his car on the street where it could be seen. The garage door rumbled down noisily, but there was no movement inside the house that he could hear. Juggling tomorrow's clothing and his toilet kit, Mike rang the bell.

"Who is it?"

"Mike."

Two locks turned. Laura peered out at him, then swung the door open wide. In her left hand, pointed safely away, was a fourteen-shot nine-millimeter automatic. She was wearing a gray sweatshirt and white cotton shorts, and she was barefoot. "Let me put this away. I want you to kiss me hello, but after what happened to me this afternoon, I might wind up shooting the dog." In the kitchen doorway, waving her tail, was an Irish setter. Agnes, Mike remembered. Agnes regarded Mike with curiosity and a little trepidation.

"She didn't sound off when I closed the garage door."

Laura was putting the gun in the drawer of a corner table. Mike realized that the furniture in the house had been Laura's parents', from the fifties, and in beautiful condition. "I told her not to," Laura said. "Agnes, come say hello to Mike." To Mike, Laura said, "She won't jump up." The dog walked over slowly and sniffed Mike's shoes, cuffs, and knees, in that order, then looked up at him expectantly. "Just scratch her at the back of the head, near her ear." He did, and the dog smiled. She looked to Laura, whose head gesture told the dog to scram. With another unhappy glance at Mike, the dog turned and padded out toward the kitchen. Laura put her finger to her lips. In another moment, there was a series of thumps and scratching sounds. "Her doggy door. She always sleeps outside." Laura raised herself on her toes and kissed him lightly. "Except in the rainy season." She kissed him again. "Then she sleeps in the kitchen." She took his suit and toilet kit. "Come on, let's put this stuff inside." She led him toward the side of the house. "The last thing you said was something about each of us having our fantasies." The bedroom, too, was filled with the heavy, dark furniture of thirty or forty years ago. "The mattress and innerspring are new," she said.

Mike smiled. "After that stunt with your hands this afternoon and what I just saw with the dog, I'm wondering if you're reading my mind."

"No. I could see you looking things over, and after what I said today about being careful with money, it was a logical thing for you to have on your mind. The dog is only well-trained. I did it myself. I decided in the winter that I was going to have a dog, but I waited until the start of the summer break before getting her. We spent the summer learning who was boss." She eyed him. "Why are you grinning like that?"

"You're terrific."

"Atta guy."

"Why a nine-millimeter?"

"I was wondering when you'd get to that. It's my favorite. I'm a good shot, Mike. Better than my father."

"Do you think you could shoot a human being?"

"In this house? When I'm in fear of my life? Absolutely. That's what my father trained me to do. I was always his little girl. He outlived my mother, but not by much. Old men are at risk when their wives die. I don't want to talk about that now. You left me all excited this afternoon and thinking about my fantasies, and I just went haywire about what I was going to do to you tonight. I must have overdosed or something, because now I'm absolutely flat. I have no interest—is that okay? Would you be terribly upset if we just had a cuddle?" Laura stepped back, giggling blushing. "You should see the expression on your face!" she cried.

Gretchen had played the same trick on him only last week, which said something about how sex-crazed he was. Now he was blushing, too. He had to think about it, that much was clear. "There are no guarantees about anything, kid. I didn't sleep last night and I'm really beat. A cuddle is probably what it's going to be."

He could see she wasn't taking him too seriously. "I did prepare a little surprise," she said. "Come into the bathroom.'' In the hall the door to another bedroom was closed. ''That's my old room. I have it done up as a study.''

''You do read minds.''

''I guess I know how cops think, that's all.'' The bathroom sink was filled with ice, almost burying a bottle of champagne and two glasses. ''You'll let me get in the shower with you, won't you?''

''I guess we can go that far,'' he said.

''You didn't bring any food.''

''She forgot. I forgot. Food never got mentioned.''

''That's understandable. Are you hungry?''

Mike grinned again, but did not know what to say.

''That's right, forget everything. This is as wild as I've ever gotten, and I want it to work.'' Laura took his jacket from him and draped it over the hamper. ''I've been alone for longer than was good for me, I think. I just didn't realize it.''

''You don't have to tell me that stuff. It's not my business. And it's working fine.'' He tilted her head up. She was crying. He kissed her eyes. ''What happened to the glasses?''

''Contacts. I'm really embarrassing myself. I'm not a dizzy dame, Mike. I just started acting like one the moment I saw you.''

''You only think so. But why do you think you're doing it?''

''Open the champagne first, then I'll tell you.'' Laura stopped unbuttoning his shirt and handed him a towel that he wrapped around the bottle. ''It goes back to the kind of meditation I do,'' she said. ''Maybe you don't want to hear this.''

The cork was moving. ''Laura, you're as sane as anyone I've ever known in my life.''

''I asked for you. That's the easiest way to say it. Months ago. Very specifically. Oh, I didn't say, 'Send me Mike Gallagher.' I said, 'Please send me a man who's big and smart and sensitive and tough and who loves to laugh.' Then I sat back and waited.''

He got the cork out without making a sound. ''Do you always get what you ask for?''

''Yes.''

"And this has to do with God?"

"Yes."

"How does He feel about this?"

"How do *you* feel when someone you love is happy?"

"I don't know if I ever really loved anybody." He gave her a glass of champagne.

"Well, you're capable of it. The question is, do you want to?"

"Only a dope would say no."

"Can you say yes? *Yes* is an important word in this context, and I promise you'll feel better if you say it."

He knew he wasn't enjoying what he was feeling now. He felt terribly uncomfortable and pressured, but not by her: by himself—his reaction to what she was saying. "I'll feel better?" he said.

"Instantly."

"Yes, I do want to." He felt better—*instantly*: he felt so flushed, emptied of the hurtful blockage that had been building inside him, that the feeling of relief was perfect—beautiful. He was smiling like a child on Christmas morning. She put her fingers to her lips and raised her glass to touch his. Now it was her turn to smile radiantly—he wasn't sure he understood why. He knew he didn't understand any of the rest of it, how she knew what was going on inside him so well, or what she meant by having "asked" for him—*that* was nuts—or why she wanted him quiet now, when he had so many questions. He knew that he would hurt their situation if he tried to take control of it. That wouldn't be difficult, but he did not want to do it. He did not want control . . . and now that he thought of it, he could see that he would not want it in the future either. This woman was showing him that he had learned something about himself, or women, or what he needed in a relationship with a woman, from every woman he had ever known. She seemed fearless, as if in possession of a secret he could not even imagine—and of course that was it exactly: she had put her finger to her lips to keep him from asking, and not because she did not want to tell, but because he really did not know how to ask. *What's the gag?* He felt foolish, and when he found himself wishing that Dan had lived to meet her, he began to weep again. Laura saw what was happening to him, took his glass and set it on the counter, and led him into the living room. On the couch he held both hands to his face and *wailed*—worse than this afternoon, worse than anything he could have imagined. Laura brought him tissues. He wiped his eyes.

"I don't know if I'm responsible for what happened to him."

She was sitting beside him, her hands on her knees. "Probably not."

"My father died when I was twelve. Hit by a truck. I knew even then that there was something funny about it, but I never really learned anything else. I've got to do better this time. I don't think I could live with less."

"If you were home, how would you wind down so you could sleep?"

"Swim. Sweat it out in the sauna. Shower. If I can't sleep in the bed, I sleep on the couch with the television set on."

"I don't have a pool or a sauna. A very hot shower would help, when you're ready. I can give you a massage."

His first stop tomorrow was going to be in Van Nuys. He wanted to call Juan Lopez—about what? He couldn't remember, and hoped it would come back to him. He wanted to call the automobile club about Dan. Mike had let all of the day go by without pushing the Ethel Moreland case forward so much as an inch. Now he flashed on Dan, dead in his car at the bottom of the canyon, blood on his face. Laura stood up and reached for his hand.

"You're cooked," she said. "Come on before you fall on your goddamned chin."

He was dreaming—he knew it, which was curious enough, but even more curious was that he knew too, that he was having a dream within a dream. He was in an interior room of an old wooden building, and somehow he knew that the building was in a city of wood, ramshackle structures leaning against each other at crazy angles, divided here and there by barren yards and dilapidated fences. He was with an older man who was a teacher or psychologist, not big physically, but of exalted and obscure position. The odd little man was holding Mike's hand palm up and examining it, and when he pulled back his head Mike could see what interested him: in the pad at the tip of Mike's middle finger was a small, fully formed iris of an eye, perfectly round. It did not see, or Mike could not see with it, but Mike had no doubt about its identity or purpose. He was growing another eye, small as a pearl, spanking new. The doctor, if that's what he was, was explaining the phenomenon, but his words weren't registering. . . .

Now Mike was awake, or risen up from the dream within the dream, out of the interior room into the rest of the building, rooms of unfinished, weathered wood run together railroad-style and crowded with boys and young men. Mike was their caretaker or guardian, and the whole enterprise was under threat from without: beyond the windows, on the bright, litterstrewn sidewalk, were watching, menacing uniformed officers in helmets, bearing nightsticks. This building was some sort of haven and Mike was in charge of it. Something was wrong with his left arm, but he couldn't get his attention on it. The young men were former drug users or dealers, Mike's assistants now, guarding the doors and windows, watching the watchers. Was an attack imminent? Mike did not know, and the young people were counting on his judgment. A couple of them were standing on chairs looking out a high window across a sunlit backyard to a nearby low roof, where a large telescope was focused down on them. It was both zany and threatening, but Mike wanted to move on, holding his left shoulder. He didn't know why.

Farther along inside the rough building a young woman stood over a stove. The woman did not look like Laura Demming, but Mike wanted to believe it was her. She turned to Mike and began to talk, reaching for his shoulder. Mike couldn't hear her in the noise of all the voices around them. The bizarre little doctor appeared to examine her hand. Now Mike saw her hand as his own, turned around as if attached to his body. The middle finger had an eye. Mike began talking about it, explaining it, he thought, even if he couldn't understand the words coming out of his mouth. The little man was

*glaring at Mike as the sound of his own voice awakened him
again, even more. . . .*

Mike sat up with a shout, terrified, holding his shoulder.
In the moment he realized where he was, Laura was up beside him, swinging her hair out of her face. She touched his
back tentatively, as if in the semiconsciousness in which she
imagined him to be he could lash out like a gaffed and gasping shark and break her ribs.

"What is it, Mike? A dream?"

He could remember the eyes, but as he had burst upward
toward the real world he had become aware of something
else. As hideous as it was, he wanted to tell her. He knew
he was still not fully awake; when he was, he was always
more self-protective—but now he shuddered in the most awful fear, growled like a dog lying in the street, crushed by a
car just disappearing around the corner stop sign. He cursed
now, the words tumbling over each other incoherently. "My
arm. It wasn't there. You were trying to put it back on. It
wouldn't work right, all twisted up like a half-dead claw."

She rubbed it. "It's there. Can you lie beside me? Come
on, let me put my arms around you."

"Yeah, that's what I want." He was thinking of Dan and
knew why: Dan was the arm, lost forever. But if he knew
what the arm meant in the dream, who were the boys and
young men? His first thought was that they were Hollywood:
murder rarely concerned women, except when they were victims (now, dancing through his mind like a nymph, Ethel
Valerie Moreland, hippy and small-shouldered, her throat
crushed by something as slender as the handle of a baseball
bat, or a lead pipe or police baton: Mike knew enough psy-
chology to understand that everything passing through his
mind now was meaningful, to be excavated as carefully as
the mother lode dream itself) and so finally the eyes, the
surreal eyes in the fingertips: now he believed that the second
hand *was* Laura's, believed it enough to tell her.

He did. She had no comment, just pulled him closer to
her, so that he was nestled in the sweet, soapy smell in the

crook of her neck. Her body excited him, wonderfully curvy and graceful. They were not lovers yet. He was feeling for her what he saw in her eyes for him, this lovely young woman, smiling, all smiles, as his fingers found their way into her swollen wetness, the bed smelling soapy and sweet, the cool air of the marine layer coming in off the Pacific washing across his back as he mounted and entered her, her short legs trying to wrap around him. They grunted together, embarrassed for having surrendered so much so easily. Laura giggled and buried her face in his chest and whispered things he could not hear. He wanted to be gentle, easy, slow, but he was too excited. She knew it. She guided him onward. She was filled with him, and then flooded: he cried out loud. If such a thing were possible, he would have poured all of himself into her. She needed him to continue, using her legs to drive him on through sensation almost unendurably intense as her strength took over and then she gasped, gasped again, louder, until a cry poured out of her, her legs seizing him tightly, her back arched, before she subsided and curled herself into a ball underneath him. Mike kissed her forehead while she continued shuddering. He said thank you.

"You're welcome." She looked up and smiled. "I'm wide awake."

"I think I have a cure for that."

"Don't administer it right away. How do *you* feel?"

"Like I'd be better off if I paid attention to you. Please."

"Praise me. Tell me what you like about me."

He did, and soon enough he was lost again.

BOOK FOUR

11

THERE WAS NOTHING THE MATTER WITH THE MECHANICALS of Dan's car even now, after a two-hundred-foot plunge into a canyon. Mike had wondered if the inspection would be some kind of charade, but no: Tom Cutler, cursing with every other sentence, wanted the door torn off so he could step on the brakes himself. Cutler asked the mechanic questions about the possibility of the brakes locking, the steering gear failing, bolts having been loosened. He was thorough. The more systems that checked out, the angrier Cutler became.

"So we're back to square one," Cutler seethed. "Now what the fuck would make him step on the brakes and swerve like that?"

"A horse," the mechanic said. "You hit a horse, you're dead."

"I checked on that," Cutler said. "The CHP reports there were no horses missing or stolen that night. Besides, interstate highways are fenced everywhere in the country. Up there, the fence is on the other side of the canyon from the roadway, but the fence is there, six feet high. Gallagher, you say he wouldn't have braked for a smaller animal?"

"Absolutely not. He thought it was dumb and dangerous."

Cutler cursed again. "I want to talk to you alone. Let's walk out to your car." In the sunshine, Cutler gestured toward the airport. "On top of everything else, we had a burglary at our helicopter facility over there last week. We still don't know what's been taken. We're keeping it quiet because we don't want the assholes to know how vulnerable we are. I just want to be sure of a few things. You saw him last in The Cat and Fiddle on Sunset at around nine-thirty?"

"Yeah." For all Mike knew, Cutler fully understood the connection between the Laurel Canyon murders and the Clown Club, its owners, and customers, and he wouldn't need more evidence than Mike and Dan's presence in the joint that they had been disobeying his own direct orders about the Laurel Canyon case. Today Mike didn't give a damn about Cutler, his discipline, and his power over Mike's career and pension—but Mike did care about the leverage his position at Hollywood gave him in unraveling what had happened to Dan.

"And he was sober?" Cutler asked.

"While I was there, he had two beers to my one. He didn't act like he was going to order more after I left. He was sober."

"And you checked out the lettuce in his stomach?"

"Yeah, Norm's on the Strip. I told you what the manager remembered." There had been no coffee containers in the car— Dan must have dumped them—and so Mike had not had to mention the *friend* who had kept Dan company while waiting for the automobile club. There had been no coil in the car either—but most places that sold auto parts gave a break on the price if you brought in an exchange unit. Dan would have done that. Alone—alone by then. And all set up for whatever happened up on the I-5. Maybe Cutler was wondering if he was getting everything out of Mike, but Mike was wondering the same thing about Cutler. If Cutler knew something, he was giving a great performance concealing it.

"Shit," Cutler said. "I was hoping that we'd come up with some answers. I've already sent flowers, and I'm going up to the funeral parlor tonight. I can't be there Wednesday. He had kids, didn't he?''

"The youngest will finish high school next year. It could have been worse.''

"Bullshit,'' Cutler snapped, and walked away.

Captain Ruppert was having a container of yogurt at his desk. Mike had not gotten back to Hollywood Division until after eleven, but Ruppert's message to see him, Marvin Burgess had said, had been on Mike's desk since Burgess's own arrival before eight o'clock. Burgess had looked concerned, but Mike didn't have time to explain why he thought there was nothing to worry about. When Tom Cutler snapped his fingers, Ruppert jumped; but Cutler never pushed unpleasant personnel problems onto subordinates when he could attend to them himself— and he'd just had that chance with Mike in Van Nuys. Ruppert was so overweight that he wasn't comfortable with his collar buttoned, and the only thing whiter on Ruppert than his expanse of hairless chest was the hair on his head, which billowed upward in a very good impression of a cumulous cloud in the midday sun.

"We've got to replace Dan,'' Ruppert said between mouthfuls of yogurt. "I know this is rough for you, but we have to get on with things.''

"Actually, I've been thinking about it,'' Mike said. "I don't think it would be a good idea for me to take on the responsibility of breaking in someone new on top of the responsibilities I already have—not at this time, anyway. When Pete Rose isn't hitting, he benches himself.''

"I see your point. All right, we'll shift Greg Novak over to you tomorrow—that is, if he's not still sick—and Marvin can start training somebody else. Do you have anybody in mind? I'd like to keep it in the division. It's good for morale when people see somebody moving up.''

Burgess hadn't told Mike that Novak had called in sick. There was no point in letting Ruppert see that even as busy as he was today, Mike was not up on the business of his squad. "I want to do it another way," Mike said. "I want to move Novak over to Blair, Marvin to me, and have Lopez train the new guy."

Ruppert's expression turned sour. "I don't like the idea of busting up good partnerships. Blair and Lopez are a good team. Besides, Lopez has never taught anybody. We don't know if he can. Of course for his sake I hope otherwise—"

Mike was ready for Ruppert's arguments. "I was going to discuss this with you anyway—before last Saturday, I mean. I want to rotate new people among the experienced guys because having only one teacher increases the risk of not learning one fine little point that can save time and money. I cleared a db last week because I guessed that she kept her medicine in the kitchen. The kid from the coroner's office was all set to start cutting because there was no evidence of a preexisting condition. Dan was with me that day, and *he* learned something. Besides, the question you raise about Lopez's ability to teach ought to be answered now. You need at least a year in Homicide before you can be considered seasoned—maybe *blooded* is a better word. Novak doesn't have that year yet, and Marvin deserves a break from teaching. Especially now. He was close to Dan, too."

"Let me think about it. Who do you want to move up to Homicide?"

"Larry Goldfarb."

"Nah. That was luck yesterday."

"Goldfarb was alert. He had the facts of the chicken hawk case at his fingertips and asked the dancer the right questions."

"I think he's a troublemaker," Ruppert said.

"I think he's too smart for the job he has now and knows it," Mike countered. "He speaks Spanish and understands Yiddish. He's got a college education and when he had to kill that guy in Rampart Division, he didn't hesitate. He's overdue for this. He makes things happen, and I think he'll be good for the squad."

"Well, I'll think about it," Ruppert said.

Mike stood up. "I've got to get down to S level. I'm late as it is. When do you think you'll get back to me? We both want to get the squad settled again."

Ruppert hesitated. "Tomorrow. Ask me tomorrow."

Before leaving the building, Mike detoured back to the six desks. Marvin Burgess looked up.

"What's the matter with Novak?"

"Bad clams, he said. I should have told you. I'm sorry. It didn't cause a problem for you with Ruppert, did it?"

"Walk out to the parking lot with me." On the sidewalk Mike waited for people to pass by before speaking. "I asked Ruppert for Goldfarb. He didn't go for it—"

"I could have told you that," Burgess said. "Ruppert doesn't like Jews any more than black people."

Mike was looking up toward the lunch-hour crowd on Sunset. "I'm sorry I mentioned it, Marvin. Am I stupid or something? I thought I knew who all the bigots were."

"Ruppert doesn't say anything because of the position he's in. It's his eyes that give him away. He doesn't look at you the way he looks at me, like he's hiding something. I'm sure he doesn't think he's doing it, but round about the age of eight or nine you develop a sensitivity if you're on the receiving end of that shit. I've never seen it in you, and neither has Bill Blair or Juan. You're one of us, if you want to look at it that way." Burgess smiled, but then the smile faded abruptly. "Dan was, too. There have been a lot of tears shed for that man already."

Mike had wept quietly this morning in Laura's backyard, watching Agnes eat her breakfast. "Tell me about it. While we're on the other subject, what about Novak? What do you see in Greg's eyes?"

"He thinks he's a Yuppie. I never see anything in the eyes of those little pricks. All they think about is themselves, and it makes them look like zombies."

"Interesting. With me he's always the good kid. He hasn't proved himself to be the world's greatest detective, but it's early in the game yet."

"Oh, he's all right," Burgess said. "I don't mean there's anything bad about him, it's just that whole generation. They're *cold*."

Mike grinned. "I'm part of the Yuppie generation, Marvin. I'm in the thick of it."

"You're a throwback. Marie calls you The Animal. She means it in a nice way. She asked about you this weekend. How is The Animal taking it? I feel so sorry for him."

"Tell her I was thinking of her, too. The other thing I wanted to do—and Ruppert didn't like this either—was shuffle us up, Novak to Blair, you to me, and Goldfarb, if I get him, to Lopez.''

Burgess stepped around in front of Mike, almost angry. He'd picked up on Mike's real intent. "What do you know about Dan that you haven't told me?''

"Do you still have that regular poker game?''

"Every Friday night—'' Burgess's chest heaved. "All right, I played last Friday night. Bill Blair was with me, by the way. Tell me why you're asking. Tell me what you know.''

"At three-thirty on Saturday morning Dan told the manager of Norm's on the Strip that a friend kept him company while the Triple-A didn't respond to the calls the friend made for Dan. Dan wound up fixing the car himself with the help of the friend. They replaced the coil. Dan died at five-thirty on the emptiest stretch of the road he had to drive—''

"Did you check Triple-A?''

"This afternoon. I'm not looking forward to it.''

"And if you find out that no calls were received by Triple-A?''

"I want to take it one step at a time. If Ruppert approves what I've asked for, all I want from you is a little jive. I want that now, about what I've just told you.''

"You didn't tell me anything. If it turns out that I know the guy who set up Dan Crawford, I want a piece of him. I want to see him wishing he was dead.''

"I've lived with this a little longer than you have, Marvin. I just hope we can put a cap on it without having to debase ourselves. But I'll do what needs doing.''

"And you'll come to me for help if you need it.''

"I already have.''

From the coroner's building Mike went up to Beachwood Drive to have another look at Valerie Moreland's car. On her forearms Ira Rosenberg had found the kind of bruises that indicated that she had struggled for her life, flailing at her assailant. In the absence of signs of a struggle in her apartment, it seemed reasonable to conclude that her death had occurred elsewhere; and since practically nobody went anywhere in Los Angeles except by car, Mike hoped that Moreland had driven herself to the place of her death, and her killer had driven her body in her car back to her apartment. The car's doors, trunk lid, and interior surfaces were still covered with the fingerprint team's powder, and Mike remembered that good prints had been lifted from the trunk lid. The trunk's interior looked like that of any other middle-aged car, a repository of everyday detritus—female-style, in this case: an unopened but badly bashed box of tissues, more of Moreland's fashion magazines, a small heap of too dainty, automotively impractical rags, a pair of battered sandals, gritty from the beach, and a plastic bag full of soiled underwear in the size and style Mike had found in her dresser upstairs. Moreland had been a girl who had spent enough nights away from home to have figured out a way of dealing with the need for clean underwear on the following days.

She hadn't been pregnant, and Ira had said that the scarred condition of her Fallopian tubes might have even made her sterile. Repeated bouts of pelvic inflammatory disease would have been the cause of the scarring, and the PID may or may not have been the result of what Ira had called, "long-term, very active promiscuity."

There was a dried brown stain the size of a dime on the edges of the pages of two magazines, and to Mike it looked a little fresher than the fine dust that had settled around it. Ira had said there had been dried blood in her mouth from the broken bones in the base of her throat. Blood from last Monday, when Valerie Moreland had died, would have covered dust underneath it, and to Mike's eye, the stain looked like a fluid that had commingled with underlying dust. Mike had missed this the other day, but he had taken a picture and the fingerprint guys would confirm that the magazines had been in the trunk when it had been opened the first time. Mike still did not have the clothes she had been wearing at the time of her death. Ira had said that in her death throes Moreland's bladder had relaxed, but there was nothing that smelled of urine in her laundry bag. Her killer had been clever, but not so cute as to put the clothes she had been wearing with the rest. You couldn't show such stuff on television because, the television people liked to argue, Americans wanted their little fantasies. Mike had to call the lab downtown about the stain he believed to be blood. He had to make a lot of calls on this case. And he had to call the Triple-A. And Marvin about the license number of the car that had followed him up onto Rainbow Drive Friday night. Mike wanted to have the energy left to get up to Valencia tonight, even though he expected to be there tomorrow night as well. But what Mike really wanted to do, what he wanted to do most of all, was curl up like a puppy and sleep. He had not slept since he had awakened in the middle of the night from that dream of eyes growing out of fingertips and Laura trying to attach his missing arm. He and Laura had made love again and still had found themselves so alert that there was nothing left to do but get out of bed and make breakfast. Then he had gone out to the yard alone with the dog's food. . . .

Now it was only five to two, still lunchtime in Los Angeles, but it was five to four in Kansas. Mike called the dentist listed in Moreland's address book and asked him to get her chart to compare with the one Ira Rosenberg had made. A match. Mike asked the dentist if he knew anything about the Moreland family. No, he had only one other Moreland in his file and didn't even know if Ethel and Jack, who was in his thirties, were related. Jack hadn't been into the office in five years. Ethel had come in for a checkup and cleaning two years ago, and the dentist hadn't known that she had moved to California.

Mike called the number Moreland had written under the words "Mom and Dad." Four rings. He was thinking of Dan, not only because he was dead, too, and Mike had just played this scene with *his* family, but because Dan's presence had always been helpful when it had been Mike's turn to make these calls.

"Hello?"

Mike identified himself. "I'd like to speak to the mother of Ethel Moreland, of Beachwood Drive, Hollywood, California."

"This is she. What is it? What do you want?"

Mike took a breath. "I'm sorry to have to tell you that your daughter is dead, Mrs. Moreland. We have a positive identification—"

A scream. The telephone clattered. Mike had heard it all before. He waited, telling himself that this had nothing to do with him. Joe Friday just doing his job. Joe Friday did everything but the hard parts, dealing with corpses and the grief of the living. He wasn't much on the paperwork either, making note of every call and conversation. The telephone was picked up.

"Are you sure it was her?"

"Dental records." Mike named the dentist to whom he had just spoken. He rattled off Ira's statistics, height, weight, eye color, observable birthmarks and scars. The woman wanted to know how her daughter died. Mike told her.

"Oh, my God! Do you know who did it?"

"We're hoping that you can help us with the letters she wrote to you and what you recall she told you over the telephone about her life here. Everything you have, Mrs. Moreland, especially about her friends and associates. I want you to take down some telephone numbers. The first is my office number." He gave it. "The second is the Los Angeles County coroner. I suggest that you simply pass it along to the funeral director you choose. They're experienced in these matters." It was the nice way of telling her to clean up the garbage. When she had written down the coroner's number, he asked, "Is there anything that comes to your mind right now about your daughter's life here, Mrs. Moreland? Time is important in a business like this."

"No—no, I can't think of anything."

Mike decided to try another tack. "Can you tell me why she changed her name from Ethel to Valerie?"

"Oh, I argued with her about that. I didn't like that at all. She always had these big dreams, and now look where they've gotten her."

Mike waited for a pause in her bitter weeping. "Well, you just give me a call if you think of something, Mrs. Moreland. I'm sorry for your troubles." He was, too—as sorry as he was for her dead daughter, who had spent the last months of her life drinking too much and going home with gorillas. Mike wasn't sure that he was seeing it right, because Valerie Moreland may not have been a girl with a lot of hidden anger unconsciously engineering herself toward destruction. Getting loaded and banging big guys may have been only her youthful, first-taste-of-freedom idea of a good time. Mike had only one direction to go in this case, and that was the girl herself, who she had been. Finding out was going to be a lot of work, and if at the end of it he came up empty on the question of who had offed her, he was not going to be consoled by the idea that he knew her better and deeper than any of the vegetables who had surrounded her in life.

Now he called Marvin Burgess and gave him the license plate number. "I just want to know who owns the car," he said, to avert Burgess's questions. "Sign my code."

"You know, the car may be owned by somebody involved in another case," Burgess said. "If people on it have the computer flagging every access, you'll have to explain what you're doing."

"I'll tell them most of the truth. As long as the other side of the story is on the other side of the law, there isn't much anybody can do about my wanting to know who followed me. I don't think they'll want to, considering that Dan's death is probably mixed up in it—or will be, if I have to go public. I really want to know why he died, Marvin."

"So do I, kid."

"Has Lopez done anything on the chicken hawk killing? He may have forgotten."

"He told me he was going to go up to the apartment building tonight to canvass for an eyewitness.

"Thank you."

"Yeah, well, don't worry about things here."

The automobile club needed an hour to go back through its Saturday-night records, and Mike used the time to call the telephone company for a backtrace on the toll calls listed on the bills he had found in a shoebox in her bedroom. He didn't bother with the Kansas numbers. Ethel/Valerie had called Mom every Sunday, a faithfulness that sort of scotched Mike's hidden anger notion. The bartender had said that she'd stopped going to the Clown Club last fall, but the telephone bills didn't seem to show that she had found a steady guy—unless, of course, he lived inside this central office area, in which case there would be no record of them gabbing. None of the names given by the telephone company woman rang any bells—but one address did:

Rainbow Drive. The address wasn't Gretchen's, the murder house, or the spooky old joint where the big goon had taken his two bimbos on Friday night, but it was in the ballpark.

Mike called Gretchen. For a change, she was in her office. But she couldn't talk long. "Something's brewing here, Mike. I don't know what it is yet, but Birnbaum has called a meeting with the director and me at four o'clock. Nobody's saying anything, but I know that Birnbaum met last night with Dick Albert, and just a little while ago I had a call from that little shit who has the gossip column in the *Daily News*. He wanted to know if Albert has AIDS, for God's sake. Dick has lost weight lately, but that's because he's had his nose glued to a mirror. My visitors Saturday knew that I had had an overnight guest last Monday, so somebody on the block must have seen us—whatever. I told the two gentlemen that I wouldn't give them my guest's name without his permission, which I doubted would be forthcoming. They didn't like it, but apparently there isn't very much they can do about it. They said they would get back to me. What does that mean?"

"To you, not a thing. To them, you're a waste of time. Did they leave their cards?"

"Oh, yes. I'm supposed to call them if I remember anything about Monday morning that I do feel like telling them. They were quite snide."

"I just told a woman the same thing, and maybe I was snide, too, but I was trying not to show it. I want to ask you something else." He was looking at his notes. "Do you know a guy named Ben Hollister? He lives on your block, I guess a couple of houses down the hill."

"Odd or even?"

"Even. The south side. Across the street from you."

"He may be the man who makes the pornographic movies. There's a man across the street, down the hill a little, who uses his house for a location for dirty movies—the real ones they show in those smelly theaters."

"I never stuck my nose in one."

"Women get curious, Mike. I have to be quick, but please tell me, how are you doing? I should have asked earlier."

"I'm all right. He just went off the road. It was one of those things."

"Would you like to see me?"

Actually, no, but he had never figured out how to say that to a woman. "His funeral is on Wednesday." He had told Laura that he would call her this evening. "Let me settle down."

"Of course. Is there anything I can do?"

"No, I don't think so." Now he wanted to get back to the automobile club. "Let me know what's going on." He thought of something else. "This guy down the block who makes the dirty movies. Is he a big guy? Have you ever seen him?"

"Oh, I've seen him—figured out who he is, you know? He's average. Why do you want to know about him?"

"Another case. We'll be talking."

He called Chino Gomez in West Covina.

"No refunds, no exchanges," Gomez laughed.

"I need a wireman," Mike said.

Gomez gave Mike the telephone number of Frank Kennedy, a private detective with an office on Wilshire Boulevard. Gomez said Kennedy was a retired Justice Department agent who had all kinds of connections. Kennedy picked up on the third ring and said his name.

"Mike Gallagher, Hollywood Homicide. Chino Gomez says you have a wireman."

"Oh, yeah. How are you doing? I'm sorry you lost your partner."

"I didn't lose him. I know just where he is."

"I've been following it. I'll give you the name of the wireman, but I'd rather see you for a drink. I know some people who've been watching this."

"Don't fuck with me. If you know something, I want to hear it."

"I know what they're saying, clear? I live in the Valley. Do you know The Tail of the Cock on Ventura Boulevard?"

"Sure. But I'm not much of a drinker."

"I know," Kennedy said. "You're some kind of free-lance health nut."

Mike was stung as well as momentarily surprised that Kennedy knew so much about him—but Gomez had said that Kennedy had connections. "I keep in shape, Kennedy. I figure in this job, I need all the edge I can get."

Kennedy laughed. "The story is that you make up for that edge off-duty, too—but you're a good cop, Gallagher. Everybody knows that. There are people who are afraid of you."

"What time?"

"Five-thirty. I'm wearing a herringbone sports jacket with those leather shooting patches."

Mike pressed the disconnect button. The automobile club had gone through its Saturday-night road-service calls. None had been made on Dan's card. Mike thought he had prepared himself, but now he found that he really hadn't. He felt ill, trapped. Violated. There was no question anymore: somebody had murdered his friend. Mike could not tell if this was worse than what he had felt at his father's grave, because he knew from this distance in time how much that event had changed and shaped his life—and he did not know yet what his responsibility was in the death of his friend. Mike did not know what he could do but continue in the direction he had taken already. He could not tell himself that the people watching him did not matter or could not influence his behavior, when among them were Dan's widow and children. He knew he did not want to face their condemnation and rage, and he could see too clearly that he might have to. As if in flight from himself and his thoughts, he quickly pushed the telephone buttons that would connect him with Marvin Burgess.

"That car was last registered in California to a Moishe Liebowitz, in the Fairfax district. He sent in a transfer of ownership last March. New owner, Felix Gutierrez, who never reregistered—in this state, anyway. I called Liebowitz, an old guy, who remembered Gutierrez as a weird little guy in a white suit. There are over thirty Felix Gutierrezes licensed to drive in California, and probably a lot more without licenses. For your information, that car is a white 1978 Toyota Cressida. Do you know what the fuck that car looks like?"

"I saw it, Marvin, and I didn't know what it was."

"Well, it was easier in the old days when cars came in only three or four flavors," Burgess grumbled. "I had a thought today, and you're going to have to take it seriously: suppose somebody turns you into flank steaks? How do we pick up the trail? It could be a deal like that, you know.''

Mike sighed. ''Were you planning on going up to Valencia tonight? This is the first night in the funeral parlor.''

''I thought tomorrow. That's what Marie wants to do. What do you have in mind?''

Mike told him about the meeting with Kennedy in Sherman Oaks. ''The Triple-A had no record of anybody calling on Dan's card Friday night. We'll take your car up to Valencia—that will give us the opportunity to talk. I'm coming back in now, but I don't want to take a chance of Lopez being in and out before I get there. He should call in a report on my home answering machine on what he's done tonight on the chicken hawk case. Pendleton has our suspect on ice, and while I intend to tell them this afternoon that we're presenting tomorrow, I'll want to know in advance what the paperwork is going to look like.'' Mike was thinking that he wanted to gather up all of Moreland's photographs and take them back to the office. He was thinking something else about her, too, about her car. ''I have to call that guy Kennedy and tell him you're coming. He didn't sound like the type that likes surprises.'' If he did nothing else with the photographs, Mike would keep them in his desk to take out and go through every once in a while, just to get familiar with the faces. In the next days, more likely, weeks, he would be interviewing everyone in Moreland's address book, everyone she'd called in the last six months. Some narcotics guys in a raid scooped up a suspect's photo albums as a matter of course; it was hard to believe, but some dealers just loved to take pictures at their parties, and so they were often found together, blitzed out of their brains, laughing hysterically, and squeezing every tit in sight. That sort of thing was probably going on in the bungalow on Norma Place right now. In this case, what Mike wanted to do was catch somebody in a lie. *How well did you know Valerie? Did you ever party and picnic with her?* The pictures would tell the truth, and Mike would know where he was going. Right now the case was a total blank. And what he was thinking was no help: he wanted to run a check on Hans Roehrig, the name on the register from the 9000 Building. Mike was thinking he would reach all the way to Washington, if he had to. In fact, there was no point in waiting. Mike called the telephone company and gave the guy on the other end the address of the spooky old house on Rainbow Drive. The guy rattled off the telephone number before Mike could turn to a clean page in his notebook to write it down.

"Tell me the name of the person responsible for the bills," Mike said.

"Ernst Röhm."

"Thanks." If Roehrig with the funny address and the big goon were the same guy, he had some sense of humor. The real Ernst Röhm had been head of the S.A., Hitler's strong-arm squad, whom Hitler had had murdered when his power in Germany was secure. Röhm had also been a homosexual, and maybe Hitler's girlfriend. Terrific. Mike would have no trouble dealing with Roehrig, if that's who he was, if he had anything to do with Dan's death.

On the way down in the elevator, Mike remembered what he had thought in Moreland's apartment about her car. If the rust on it meant that it had not been a California car at the start, chances were good that Moreland had owned it for years. What Laura Demming had said about young women's feelings for their dogs was just as true about their feelings for horses—and cars. Not knowing what he was looking for, Mike had searched her apartment carefully and thoroughly. He hadn't done as much with her car, which had been hers longer than the apartment. The laundry and magazines indicated she was as comfortable in the car as anywhere—Moreland had probably had as much faith in the car as anything she had ever owned, and Mike had not really searched it—not the way Tom Cutler had searched Dan Crawford's car.

Mike started in the trunk, peeling the floor mats back to the bare metal, pulling the spare tire from its well, then moving forward to the passenger compartment and pulling up the seat cushions. It was all dirty work, and he was finding only coins, matchbooks from Kansas, a swizzle stick from the Pow-Wow Lounge in Tucumcari, New Mexico—and a confirmation that Moreland had owned the car a long time, a 1979 airline ticket receipt in her name, the faded markings showing a round-trip tourist trip from Kansas City to Fort Lauderdale. Spring. Six years ago, she would have been young enough to be interested in the college spring break scene in Florida. . . .

Pieces of a life.

Next, the dashboard. Mike's old Cutlass wasn't the only car with hiding places under the dash. Mike learned years ago that the Jaguar E-type had a space between the dashboard and the fire wall that could hold two hundred pounds of marijuana. But these spaces were as dirty as any other part of a car, and Mike could see that he was going to need a half hour to clean up when he was done. He had an extra shirt in his locker at the division. . . .

In the space above the radio, his fingers touched something that moved, then slid back and forth when he pushed. Rectangular, about the size of a book. Not metal, he thought. He was on the floor of the car now, on his back, his legs draped over the reclined seat. He could get his head under the dashboard if he wanted, but he was afraid of getting falling dust in his eyes. Finally he wrapped both hands around the radio and pulled it down. The dashboard bent with a crunch, and the loose object clattered down onto the transmission console. It was a videotape cassette, VHS format. Mike reacted aloud.

"What the fuck?"

12

FRANK KENNEDY TURNED OUT TO BE A BIG, BLACK-HAIRED-but-balding guy in his late fifties with coarse features and meaty hands with arthritic knuckles the size of walnuts. He had taken a table in the far corner of the bar, away from the television set tuned to the Monday-night baseball game. Kennedy was drinking a double Scotch on the rocks. Mike and Marvin Burgess ordered light beer. Kennedy still had all his cop's instincts intact: he was sitting with his back to the wall, positioned on the banquette so the other two didn't have him in the middle. The first thing he did was slip Mike a piece of paper with the name of the wireman written on it. "I called him already. He'll give you a break on his fee. If you don't think so, call me. This afternoon's papers say the car was in perfect condition and that your partner was sober. Your boss, Cutler, was at a meeting this afternoon with friends of mine and couldn't stop talking about it. I called a guy downtown before I came over here. Federal guy. He said that Cutler couldn't sit still, he was so angry. He thought he was talking to people in confidence or that word wouldn't get around the way it is right now. There's no such thing in our business, especially in a matter like this. Cutler assumes foul play—at least, that was the drift of his remarks today. 'How do you kill a guy without touching him or the car he's driving?' was one of the questions he asked—you know, thinking out loud. It could have been a show, of course. There's been a lot of fucking around lately. The federal guy I talked to today goes through Laurel Canyon every morning. He saw the helicopter over Rainbow Drive early the morning those people were killed—don't worry, I know it's not your case. That night on the news, he heard one of those reporter clowns say that the survivor had just gone off to the hospital. My friend called me the next morning, and I called a gal I know in administration there—I work for the supermarket tabloids now, and they pay plenty for information on VIPs in and out of the hospital and what for. Anyway, the gal accessed the hospital computer about information about the survivor. They only had one 'Jane Doe' the day of the killings, and Pathology didn't do the work on the tissues removed in the emergency room until the next day. My contact says that the printout proves that the sample didn't get to Pathology until after they'd closed the department for the day at five o'clock. I asked what tissues. She said, 'Her brain.' I asked her to get me a printout because, what the hell, five people get murdered in a celebrity playground like Laurel Canyon and you figure it might blow up into something big, but it hasn't. In fact, I've never seen anything fall out of the newspapers so fast in all my life. Of course, the feed from LAPD dried up.''

Mike was sitting straight up, almost on the edge of his chair. ''Do you have the printout?''

Kennedy reached with his fingertips into his jacket inside pocket. ''This is a copy. After we talked, I made a few. Anyway, I was talking about the fucking around that's been going on lately.'' He sipped his drink. ''You know, Cutler isn't as popular in Washington as he thinks he is. A couple of years ago he blew the cover on a CIA operation when those people came home from Iran. Cutler wasn't directly responsible, but he was careless in how he instructed his people who were involved. Anyway, Cutler's career stops here. That's the background on what started a year ago. This administration enjoys the appearance of pounding on organized crime. Rounding up a busload of goombahs is good PR and takes America's mind off the fact that those who are supposed to be running things aren't smart enough to chew gum and fart at the same time, which is what Lyndon Johnson really said about Jerry Ford. Anyway, based on information from Washington, the local *federales* started developing a case to present to the grand jury against several individuals, including one Bernie Maxwell. Ever hear of him?''

Burgess shook his head no, and Kennedy noticed Mike wasn't answering.

"That's okay," Kennedy said to Mike. "I'd be goddamned careful if I were you in this."

"What do you know about me being in this?"

"Only what you know, or should be able to figure out. You punched a guy on the chin so hard that you fractured his skull, and you're so honest that nobody's ever let you in on something crooked in your entire career. Now your partner's dead and you want to know why. I'm with you on this, believe me, but given what to expect from you, if I were the guy responsible for the death of your partner, I'd shoot you right now because my chances of getting out of here are better than they would be if I had to deal with you later."

Burgess's eyebrows were up. "That tells it like it is."

"Cutler asked a very good question," Kennedy said, "I would be *very* careful."

"Maxwell," Mike said. He was thinking that somebody had put him in a position where he couldn't trust anybody anymore. He had to keep telling himself that, over and over.

"Maxwell's been in L.A. since the seventies. He comes from New Jersey—there's a German enclave there. He speaks German fluently, but he's been connected to the Italians for years."

"Describe him."

"In his forties, dark, thinning hair, mostly scalp now, five-nine, skinny as a rail, probably because he's his own best customer. He's probably the biggest longtime cocaine dealer in the city. For years he's had the West Side all sewed up, if that's possible. Bev Hills, Bel Air, Hollywood. He cranked up here with a string of porn and marital aid shops. Now he is a very,

very heavy hitter. All the cops in Washington, if not the world, really want this guy, but nobody here or back there—I still have those connections, too—is willing to say any more than they've had enough of Mr. Maxwell. My own feeling is that he got himself into something very dirty, *very* evil. Drugs are here to stay, as long as nobody wants to punish the users, so there's no percentage in knocking off Maxwell as a dope dealer because his replacement will set up shop next week, so it's something else, that's what *I* think. But when the agents here started to work on Maxwell, the going got heavier and heavier. Postponements, delays, resistance, lost files and papers. This was supposed to be a task force operation, but it was more like negotiating with the Russians. There were always excuses.''

''How does this tie in to the murders on Rainbow Drive?''

''Well, I couldn't help but notice that you Hollywood guys weren't in on the Rainbow Drive killings, and I've been told by my guy downtown that the LAPD people who were so full of shit on the Bernie Maxwell case were the same who were all shook up—*and* involved—with what happened on Rainbow Drive. The guy downtown got the idea months ago that something was being cooked up to take the federal pressure about Maxwell off the local cops. Exactly what that has to do with the Rainbow Drive murders is something I don't know. That guy P. Vik who was supplying Daisy Nunn a year ago disappeared right after those arrests, but I figured he would.''

''Why?''

''P. Vik is the name of a horse that used to run at Santa Anita. I won a lot of money on him, so I should know.''

Burgess snorted. Mike couldn't help smiling.

''Cops get high on arresting people. Jesus, I know that as well as anybody alive,'' Kennedy said. ''I just loved it when a guy would wet his pants when he saw the gun and the badge. But Daisy Nunn stayed in the business, by all accounts, and somebody was supplying her. That guy Lansing and his partner moved in with her and her boyfriend two months ago, and if you read between the lines of the newspapers, Lansing was a guy who seemed to be playing both sides of the street.''

''Do you have any proof of that?''

''No, but it looks pretty obvious. For all anybody knows, that witness to the murder Lansing committed in El Centro never existed in the first place. In Florida one time, I got an undercover guy out of the area with the heat off him by reporting to the newspapers that his body had been found in a swamp with no head or hands. You never see that on the TV news, or pictures of it in the newspapers. So he was away free. The guy is in law school in Spokane. Gonzaga, where Bing Crosby went.''

Mike said, ''So you figure that Lansing and Freeman were run up here from the San Diego area and something went wrong?'' He was thinking of what Laura had learned about the dog, and the connection between Rainbow Drive and Maxwell—Jerry Chambers, who had known Maxwell's partner's former employee Donnie Jackson and had been found dead in Daisy Nunn's house.

Kennedy shrugged. He turned to Marvin Burgess. ''Your kid used to fight at the Olympic, didn't he?''

''That's my older brother's boy. He's with the sheriff's department now.''

Kennedy nodded. ''The family resemblance is very strong. I was there one night when he had a war with a kid named Ramirez.''

''I was there that night, too. Marlon had three ribs broken in that fight. That's when he started thinking of quitting.''

''The Mexicans love to work the body, but your nephew threw the best left hook I've ever seen. I thought he'd killed Ramirez. What was that, welterweights?''

''Middle. I'll tell Marlon you remember. He'll like that. He wanted boxing an awful lot.''

Kennedy saw that Mike was staring at him. ''What's on your mind?''

''The federal case against this guy Maxwell. Do you think you can learn more about why Washington wants to get him?''

Kennedy shook his head no. ''I've tried. My best friends turn into zombies when I ask questions.''

''I'm not fucking around with anybody, including you,'' Mike said. ''I loved Dan Crawford. He was better to me than my own father. I want anything and everything you can get for me about Maxwell. No shit.''

''I hear you,'' Kennedy said. ''I'll do the best I can. A thing like this just bugs the hell out of me. I told you, I'm with you on this.''

"Thank you." Mike reached for the check, but Kennedy beat him to it.

"Go on, get out of here," Kennedy said. "The way you guys drink, I thought I was in West Hollywood.''

Mike told Kennedy to go fuck himself.

"It's the only way to avoid AIDS. I'll be in touch."

Mike thought of something else about which a Hollywood-wise character like Kennedy might have some information, what Gretchen had told Mike this afternoon, but then decided to let it go and get on up to Valencia and Dan's coffin. Marge had said that the coffin would be closed. She had forgotten that Mike had already seen her husband dead.

It was ten o'clock when Marvin Burgess let Mike off at The Tail of the Cock where Mike's car was still parked, and ten-thirty before Mike stepped into his own apartment for the first time in more than twenty-four hours. Mike had been careful all the way home, and he didn't relax until he'd looked in the closet and behind the shower doors. The answering machine was blinking rapidly without stopping—five or more messages. Burgess had the whole story now. On the way back from the funeral home, he'd said that he thought he could understand why Dan had gone forward with the Rainbow Drive case in spite of being warned away. "Dan found a can of worms," Burgess had said. "I think I would have wanted to go fishing, too. What the hell, man, they turn us into bloodhounds and then expect us to behave ourselves after they wave meat under our noses? The more I think about it, the madder I get. I don't want to get involved— I don't want to think about it. Man, I want to *run* from this! If I had the years, I'd be gone—really. Out of here. At least, that's what I'd like to think. But I don't know. I don't really know, because I don't want to *not* think about it. I don't mean that I feel like a little kid getting a first look at pussy under a window shade. I mean the opposite of that. All my sense of duty and training says, go *get* the motherfuckers. That's what's good and worthwhile about me, and *that*'s what I want to do. But I have a wife whom I love, and kids whom I love, and my whole life as it exists now says, You're *not* a kid, you *know* the ways of the world, and you shouldn't want to risk your life and the happiness of the people who love you because you want to waste a guy who sells dog shit to teenagers and the people who are protecting him and making fortunes off of him. But waste him is what I want to do. Dan didn't know anything about all that Washington shit, he was just being one of the good guys—and somebody figured out a way to kill him and some kind of fucking *friend* was in on it so he never saw it coming? Fuck that shit! Every bone in my body cries out, *Fuck that shit, let's waste the goddamned town!* Yet what's sane in me says go home and have a drink, turn on the TV and be grateful if that wonderful lady sees that I'm really looking for a little curb service to forget what's on my motherfucking mind." Then Burgess looked up at the night sky passing over the windshield. "Tell me, God—tell me now! You want me to be crazy for you? You want me to be crazy so the rest of the world can get a little saner without even *knowing it*? Why is it you can't seem to have any fun unless you're whipping around your loving son Marvin? Is this how we're going to have it out? Because I'll tell you right now, I'm not opening my heart to love some dope-dealing pimp!"

Hearing him talk to God made Mike think of Laura Demming. "Do you believe God hears you, Marvin?"

"He answers back, man! All I have to do is say something wrong out loud, and He makes me feel so lousy! He *whips* me!" He was in tears. "Of course I believe, Mike. What do you think I'm doing in church every Sunday? Niggers are crazy, Mike, but we ain't stupid!"

Mike had never heard Marvin Burgess use that word before. Now, as a helicopter roared over the building, Mike took paper and pencil to the answering machine. He had to wait another minute for silence.

The first call was another hang-up. Number five. Mike had left here last night at ten o'clock. He was beginning to think that the next generation of answering machines should be equipped with clocks that would record the time of a call—although knowing exactly when these calls were being made would get him no closer to knowing who was making them. The second call offered only a slight clue. It was from Laura. "Hi, it's your friend with the Renaissance body, if you remember saying that, and as long as it doesn't mean that I look four hundred years old. I'm calling from work before my clients arrive. Thank you for a beautiful night. I know you're busy and I probably won't hear from you at all, but I'll be home tonight if you have a minute, or better yet, an hour or two." The third call was another hang-up. The fourth caller gave the time of her call, one o'clock, which put the hang-up before that hour and the time Laura's kids arrived at school. The fourth caller was Gretchen, and since one o'clock had been before the call he had made from Beachwood Drive, he could ignore her request to call him back. Mike was still thinking about the morning hang-up. If someone was checking to see when Mike was home and out, if that someone knew Mike, or knew what Mike did for a living, he would have known that Mike would have been at work. Lopez had reported someone calling the office for Mike yesterday but not giving his name—but that wasn't the same thing.

The next call was from Lopez. "I just spent the night up to my armpits in faggots. One at the apartment house who says he was in New York for the past month says he knew the victim and the bars he cruised, so I took the victim's picture down to the bars and a couple of guys in one of them recall the victim being with a young redheaded guy the night of the murder. I asked what kind of haircut and they both said crew. They both said they think they would be able to identify the guy, so if the deputy DA wants to go for a lineup, I think we'll get over that hurdle. The next time my wife mentions 'Miami Vice' to me, I'm going to hit her in the mouth. Now I'm going home and fuck her brains out. I'm no good for deals like this, Mike, it just makes more Mexicans. Signing off."

Gretchen again—given all the work Lopez had done, Gretchen's call must have come in within the last hour. Her voice was up half an octave, thirty decibels above normal, and she was distraught, to say the least. "Call me as soon as you can, Mike! That little bastard Birnbaum has suspended production— stopped everything! He said that AIDS has taken the comedy out of homosexuality! It's bullshit, Dick Albert wasn't at the meeting, my agent is walking away, Birnbaum says he'll settle my contract—sure! He'll offer five or ten thousand, enough for me to get back to Germany! It has something to do with these murders, I know it. Birnbaum said I didn't cooperate with the police—he *knew*! How did he know? My agent is in on it—he must be. I'll read tomorrow in the trades that Birnbaum has given him a three-picture deal—oh, call me, Mike! I'm so angry and frightened!''

After he thought about what he could tell her. If Birnbaum was being fed information on how Gretchen was responding to police questions, he certainly knew about the connection between Dick Albert and Bobby Michaels. Did that make Michaels a suspect? Who was feeding Birnbaum? There was still another call.

"This is Larry Hammond, with special instructions—shit, I'll put my assistant on. Pay close attention.''

Dickhead, Mike thought. He could even make being interrupted sound important. Another voice came on: "Gallagher, keep your schedule free tomorrow night. The chief wants you in on a task force operation in your territory. I'll call Hollywood Division late tomorrow to tell you where to be and when. You understand I can't give you more details at this time. Let this office know in the morning that you received this message.''

Now the telephone rang. Mike switched the tape back to record and let the telephone ring a second time, which activated the answering machine. If this was his mystery caller, perpetrator of the hang-ups, anything Mike could get him to say would be recorded. Mike picked up the handset as his announcement tape beeped. "I'm here.''

The handset on the other end was slammed down and the line went dead. Almost as if the guy was scared. Mike wanted to compose himself before calling Gretchen or playing the tape he had found in Moreland's car. On television the eleven o'clock news was just getting started. Before Mike adjusted the volume, something in the montage of clips previewing the night's stories caught his attention: a familiar face. Mike saw it for just a second, but he had no doubt about whose face it was: Azzolini, the bartender at the Clown Club, being led away in handcuffs by sheriff's deputies. Mike had the volume too loud when the station cut to the news that Alpha Beta was having a sale on Penn-zoil. He turned the volume down again and stood in front of the set. The energy generated by the hang-up was churning into an ugly anger. Waiting for the commercials to clear the screen, Mike began to see all the things that needed doing tomorrow and the day after. He had to present the case against McCallum and see that McCallum was brought up from Pendleton—he didn't want to have to do that himself. He had to nail Ruppert down on the changes he wanted, or figure out a way to live with the changes Ruppert dictated. The wireman. He wanted to check out Roehrig.

Mike was going to talk to Don Grant early Wednesday morning. And he wouldn't be back to Hollywood that day until after one o'clock. After the most God-awful morning—Mike still didn't want to think about it. He was supposed to be the big tough guy, the human water buffalo, the flesh-and-blood tank. It was all shit. He'd live the rest of his life wishing he could talk to his friend Dan just once. Nobody understood the world. All the songs were about love, but none were about friendship. More and more Mike wished Dan had met Laura. Laura had held Mike in her arms on her couch last night while, impotent in all ways, he had propelled himself, weeping, into the death throes of his best friend. Women knew the truth about men, and only a few women—like Laura—assigned it any value. An honest man knew at once when he was in the presence of a real woman, as obvious as a sunrise. All day today, all day long, Mike had been filled with her even more than he had filled her, finally, in the wonder of the darkness of last night.

And now the news: tonight sheriff's deputies descended on the Clown Club on Sunset Boulevard in West Hollywood to seize seventeen pounds of cocaine, four thousand Quaaludes, a pound of China white heroin, and four bags of sensemilla mar-ijuana from the office safe of the youth-oriented club, while at the same time deputies arrested Jack Skelley, owner of the club, and Bernie Maxwell, in Skelley's office at the club. Lawyers were already on their way downtown to post bond. The picture went to the female anchor, who started talking about a hotel fire in the Wilshire District.

Mike turned it off. Not Disneyland. He wanted to go out to

call Gretchen, but before that he wanted to talk to Laura, which he thought he could do from here. Outside, a car slowed, then sped up again. With the handset wedged between his head and shoulder and the phone on the other end ringing, Mike pushed back the drape to look down into the street. Moving away, gaining speed, a white sedan he had learned today was a 1978 Toyota Cressida. Laura picked up. "Hi, are ya naked?"

"Not yet," Mike said. "This will be brief. Until further notice, keep Agnes in the house on red alert and your windows and doors locked."

"Call before you come over," she said. "I don't want any accidents."

He hung up and turned out the lights. It would take the Cressida awhile to get around the long block. Mike unlocked the door, stepped out into the hall and across to the stairwell. He had to wedge open the metal fire door to the stairs to hear what was going on in the hall. His digital watch had one of those soft, black plastic bands. It tore off the watch easily, and Mike put it between the door and the jamb. Then he went up to the next floor landing to wait.

With his apartment lights out and his car in the garage, it would seem as if he had gone to bed. The driver of the Cressida would not have slowed unless he had something on his mind. While Mike waited, he played with his watch, timed his pulse—66—and wondered again about liquid crystal and how it worked. He had no idea. Nobody knew how to explain these things to laymen. He had the watch on twenty-four-hour time, reading 23:56, when the door on the garage level opened. Mike slipped the watch into his pocket and wrapped his hand around the .357.

The man was quiet, but not silent. Mike could hear the rubber of the guy's sneakers chirping lightly on the concrete of the stairwell. Then there came the hiss of the pneumatic check on the fire door. Mike had the gun out in case the guy saw the watchband wedged in the jamb. No—or apparently not: Mike heard the knob on his apartment door turn. Mike started down the stairs slowly, listening, careful.

At the fire door he had the .357 going through into the hall before him, but the hall was empty. Mike stepped to his apartment. Silence inside. Mike took a breath and flung the door open.

The guy was still in the darkened living room, and instinctively he ducked down, pulled his head into the shoulders of his white suit. He had a wiry gray Afro and medium brown skin. Mike recognized him—he had seen him before. A little guy. Mike had seen him in the light of the front door of the bungalow on Norma Place, one of the many assorted nuts who had been admitted inside by the blonde, the beautiful Baby Rae Bozo. Now the guy wheeled. Mike saw weapons, but Mike didn't want to shoot him, not here, not now.

"Barranquilla, right?"

The guy lunged, his mouth open in a silent scream, knocking an end table aside. Mike saw a tire iron or crowbar before he saw the knife, a long-bladed pigsticker of some kind. Mike's hand went up to block the crowbar when the knife flashed outward—this was how it had been done on Rainbow Drive, how all those people had died so easily—and Mike felt the flesh on the pad at the base of his thumb open up, pour blood, but he kept reaching for the crowbar at the same time he swung the .357 around against Barranquilla's jawbone. Mike was sure it was him, the guy who had done the killings. The MO was perfect—he was a killing machine. His eyes glazed momentarily from the glancing blow. Mike kicked the apartment door closed and now they were in the dark, but at least they might not alert the neighbors. Mike was already clubbing the guy again as he struggled against Mike's weight. Mike's blood was everywhere—he could feel it flying. Mike hit him a third time, on the neck now, and the crowbar slipped backward out of his hand. Mike felt the blade in the meat of his upper arm. With the wound on his hand raining blood, wide open, Mike grabbed the little man by the throat and turned him around against the wall and with all his strength brought the gun butt down and smashed a hole that felt as if it could cradle a gold ball in the side of the guy's forehead. Barranquilla slid down the wall and fell forward on his face. He was on his knees, like a Muslim praying. Mike kicked the corpse in the head five times, cursing and growling furiously, before his rage was spent.

Hand. Arm. Mike had to make the bleeding stop. He'd worry

about cleaning up the apartment after he knew he'd live. This didn't solve the mystery of what was behind the Laurel Canyon murders, or the coverup. Mike doubted that this little piece of human shit had killed Dan. Mike had hoped to get the guy to talk—he had thought he was tough, the creep. The arm didn't feel so bad, more like a puncture wound, although Mike could feel it bleeding freely. In the kitchen light he could see that the classic defensive wound on his hand was more than two inches long, and almost a half-inch deep in one place. Pressure—he squeezed his hands together over the sink, flipping the tap lever upward with his elbow. The hole in his shirtsleeve was just a quarter-inch slit—that wound might stop bleeding on its own. Neither would kill him. He opened his hands and the bleeding started again. Mike almost smiled, because the pressure was working. He was thinking of how he was going to get rid of the body. It wasn't going to do him any good to call the cops. He'd made a computer inquiry on this guy today and he'd been told earlier to stay out of the Laurel Canyon case. He'd have a little more room to move if it took a couple of days to find the little bastard's body, and maybe they'd have trouble figuring out what happened to him. The guy had been something special. None of the people in the house on Rainbow Drive would have been willing to go up against that knife. While they'd been staring at the knife, he'd bashed their skulls in. There had been one body with a couple of fingers missing, Mike remembered. In Nam Mike had shot at guys and seen them fall, but he'd never known he'd really killed anybody. Now he knew. No big fucking deal, man—his adrenaline was talking, but that was all right. It had bragging rights, too. The guy had died at once, easily, as if having his skull dented had made him lose interest. He'd gone not limp, but dead, like a duck hanging in a window of a Chinese restaurant. Mike was going to have to remember to call the cleaning woman and tell her not to come this week, or as long as it took him to rent do-it-yourself rug cleaning equipment. He hated housework. He was probably going to have to paint a wall, too. Maybe that guy Kennedy was right about him. Maybe people should be scared. Now Mike wanted to howl like Tarzan.

Asshole.

He was still bleeding, but not so profusely. He wanted to

think clearly. Somebody had sent the little guy, Gutierrez, or, more accurately, Barranquilla. That was the name by which his friends had known him. Colombian criminals changed their names more often than their underwear, one narcotics officer had told Mike. Barranquilla had been one of those guys who'd kill anybody, even God, for the fun and the money. Mike had seen Barranquilla at the Jackson bungalow on Norma Place the night after Dan's death. That tied Barranquilla through Jackson to Skelley, the big goon who might or might not be Roehrig, and Bernie Maxwell. In the coke business, no matter where you started in it, the connections would lead you eventually to everybody. Daisy Nunn had been in the coke business. Her fellow victim, Jerry Chambers, had sold Donnie Jackson a Cadillac, probably to settle a coke debt. Connections. A ball of maggots. But none of these people had killed Dan, and none of them explained the motive for the Laurel Canyon murders or the cover-up.

Twelve-twenty. The bleeding from his hand was much slower, and it had stopped on his upper arm. Now he had a plan. He just wasn't so sure he could execute it. He turned on a light in the living room and sat down to give his hand another five minutes.

Barranquilla was a real mess. His head disappeared in a puddle of blood—under the carpet and padding was a five-eighths-inch-thick sheet of plywood. The blood would be dry before it dripped down through the ceiling below. Mike wanted to search the body, but he had to wait for his own bleeding to stop. Now he could see that there was blood on two walls, the apartment door, and his own ceiling. It didn't take much. He remembered Gretchen. He had to hope that putting her off until tomorrow would not anger her more—and he had to hope, too, that he would remember her at all tomorrow. It was going to be another full day. He called Laura.

"You can put the dog outside again. Do you remember where you wanted to neck?"

"I sure do."

"Meet me there in an hour. Take the shortest route from your house, then turn right. Use your bright lights."

"I understand."

Now Mike searched the body. A gram of coke, seven hundred dollars in cash, keys, no ID. Mike decided to put the seven hundred in Marge's account. He went back to the bathroom for a gauze pad and adhesive tape, then to the bedroom for a jacket and a pair of black leather gloves Judy had given him one Christmas—he couldn't remember ever having worn them before. In the kitchen, over the sink, he taped the hand wound, then pulled on the gloves. He carried the jacket and a dish towel to the living room. From the window he could see the white car parked in a red zone. Mike was putting things together quickly now. He would go out to the street and bring the car into the garage and then come back up for Barranquilla. Barranquilla had taken the stairs up to the apartment? He would take the stairs down again. The gloves solved the problem of fingerprints, and if he started bleeding again, there was less of a chance of the stuff getting on the inside of the car. The kitchen towel would keep Barranquilla from messing the hall, stairwell, and garage. Mike would take the tire iron and the knife with him when he went down to get the car, and throw them in a storm drain along the way. Yes. He had to get another towel. . . .

With the car key and the towel in his left hand, the jacket turned inside out and folded over his left arm, with his right hand Mike lifted the corpse by the back of the collar while blood rained thickly onto the carpet. When the bleeding had almost stopped, Mike wrapped the towel around its head, then hefted the corpse comfortably onto his shoulder. At this hour all the odds were with him, Mike knew. He wasn't going to get any sleep again tonight, but that was better than what Barranquilla —and the people behind him—had had in mind. Mike was still feeling the adrenaline in his bloodstream. He wished he could kill the little son of a bitch all over again.

He took Laurel Canyon Boulevard up to Mulholland and then turned right at the top of the hill, following the route he had given to Laura. Even with the automatic transmission of the big Japanese sedan, he was going very slowly. Barranquilla was propped up beside him—it would do no good for blood to be found anywhere else in the car. Mike was wearing the jacket now to cover the mess on his shirt. His hand felt as if it was bleeding again, and the tight curves of the old scenic route over the crest of the Santa Monica Mountains made for a lot of wheel winding. Just beyond the Laurel Hills tract the road swung out to a vista point over the Valley, then back in two tight left turns to a spot the kids who raced up here called Charley's Curve, or Curley's Curve—it was not the kind of thing an adult could ever remember—but named at all because the fellow could never negotiate the spot at racing speed, and had sent several cars into the canyon below. He had been only the first, for there was a pile of decomposing wrecks at the bottom of the steep wash, and nobody was ever surprised when another was added to the collection. Sometimes days passed before anyone noticed a new trophy down there. Mike was hoping for such a break. But on the other hand there were people waiting for Barranquilla to report, and they probably knew enough about Mike to figure out what had happened to their little killing machine.

Nearing the curve, Mike doused the lights and eased the car close to the edge, then stopped. He stepped out, pulled the body over to the driver's side and cut the wheel hard over. The car rolled forward, up over the curb, and down the other side, going faster and faster through the brush. Then Mike saw a flash of white paint as the car pitchpoled forward, pirouetting a full turn on its trunk in midair, and crashed down on the heap of debris and then continued to roll another three times. The damage to the car might explain Barranquilla's crushed skull to investigating officers and the coroner's office, if not the people who knew him. No matter: the death of one scumbag wasn't enough for Mike to roll his readiness back to Defcon One. No, definitely: now they would be sending someone else.

He was walking back toward Laurel Canyon on the side of the oncoming traffic when a pair of bright headlights approached. The vehicle stopped and the passenger door opened. Laura's old station wagon. Holding his left hand up, Mike slid into the car and closed the door.

"Jesus! What happened to you?"

"I cut myself shaving."

"You haven't had hair on your palms since you graduated high school." She put the car in gear. "I've got a good first aid kit. Let me clean that up, and then I'll take you home. If you want me to say I was with you tonight, I will."

He looked at her. "You'd do that?"

"You were worried about me."

"Well, he—I was calling to say good night, and I saw something."

"That's what I thought," she said.

"You don't need more explanation than that?" Now he started to shake. The pain flared out of the wound and up his arm.

"When you've got something to say you'll say it," she said. "I already know that about you."

BOOK FIVE

13

MIKE WAS AT HIS DESK AT SIX-FIFTEEN AND READY FOR Ruppert when the captain arrived at seven-thirty. Ruppert okayed Mike's reorganization, but not without the grudging reservation of the world-class bureaucrat: "If this doesn't work out, it's going to wind up on your record, not mine."

Ruppert was the first to ask about the bright white bandage on Mike's hand. Mike said he'd cut it while trying to make a salad.

Over breakfast up on Sunset Mike told Marvin Burgess to play dumb if anyone asked about the computer inquiry on the Toyota Cressida. Burgess pointed to Mike's hand.

"You don't have a problem, do you?"

"No more than I had before—but if I have another car to check, I'll do it myself. For all I know, they're going to start dusting the computer for fingerprints."

"That close?"

"Dan had a *friend*. We're all breathing the same air. Now

you keep your eyes open too." Mike stood up, the McCallum file under his arm. His hand throbbed so badly he could barely feel the soreness in his arm. "He and I used to take turns picking up tabs. I'll get the one tomorrow up in Valencia. I'm meeting Don Grant from Palm Springs at Dan's favorite Burger King at eight o'clock. We'll find someplace else to eat, where they custom-tailor the bacon and eggs."

"When do you figure you'll be back to the division?"

"I'll keep you posted," Mike said. Burgess was going to tell the others of the reassignments. "I'm hoping I can spend some time today on the Beachwood case."

Down near the freeway, Mike pulled into Denny's and got a buck's worth of change from the cashier so he could make some calls. His first was to the wireman, Maurice Constantine. Constantine was ready for him. He'd just got off the telephone with Frank Kennedy, who'd wanted to know if Mike had called him yet. "I've got to talk to Kennedy, too," Mike said. "I'm due at the DA's office at ten o'clock. Can you meet me before I go in?"

"How about The Pantry?"

The Pantry had been serving enormous portions of properly cooked, premium-quality American food at reasonable prices twenty-four hours a day since 1924, and logically enough, some people saw no point in ever eating anywhere else.

"It's going to be crowded," Mike said.

"It's always crowded. We'll talk on the line outside if we have to. I'll see you there in forty-five minutes. I'm a fat guy with black hair."

Mike called Kennedy. "I think I need your help now. You said you work for the supermarket tabloids. How well do you know your way around Galaxy International?"

"I got the chief of security his job."

"Yesterday Norman Birnbaum abruptly canceled shooting of the new Dick Albert picture. The columnist of the *Daily News* in the Valley wanted to know if it was because Albert has AIDS. The producer is a friend of mine and she says while Albert looks lousy, it's only because he's doing too much cola. I also know that Albert was or is friends with the ex-television actor, Bobby Michaels—"

"That turd," Kennedy said. "I know him."

"Well? Do you know him well?"

"I've seen him around for years. He used to come in to Musso's and The Cock and Bull. Now he can't get a job parking cars at either one."

"That's the guy. Michaels is running with a bad crowd now—"

"He *is* a bad crowd."

"What I want to know is, is there still a connection between Michaels and Albert, and if so, how strong? I want to know, too, why that picture was canceled. Birnbaum seems to know an awful lot about the Laurel Canyon murder investigation."

"All this may be a little heavy for my sources. I got a gal in the office there, but she's not that close to Birnbaum."

"Can you tell me what she is close to?"

"Oh, sure. The legal department."

"Well, that might help. The producer expects that Birnbaum will offer to settle her contract. She has no power. Dick Albert does—and most of these big guys have a play-or-pay deal. Albert wasn't at the meeting that scrubbed the picture. Is he getting paid anyway?"

"It may take a bribe to find out," Kennedy said.

"How much?"

"Roughly three hundred dollars."

"That sounds like the price of an eighth of an ounce of toot," Mike said.

"Ask me no questions," Kennedy said.

"What about your fee?"

"Under the circumstances, pay me for my results. What is Constantine charging you?"

"We haven't discussed it yet. We're meeting at The Pantry."

Kennedy laughed. "You'll like Constantine, he's a nice guy."

Now Mike was quiet.

"What is it?" Kennedy asked.

"I wanted to ask you something, but I changed my mind." Mike had already decided that the condition of his apartment made it impossible for him to allow anyone inside it. If his own line was being tapped, he was just going to have to live with it.

Or more accurately, around it. "It's all right, Kennedy. I'll get back to you later."

Mike had something else on his mind this morning, something new: the videocassette he had pulled out of Valerie Moreland's dashboard. He had played it this morning while gingerly getting into his clothes—tying one's tie with a hand and a half had not been as easy as he had thought. According to the label, the cassette was number 74. Just about twenty minutes of material had been recorded on it, so clear in Mike's memory that he could play it in his mind on the Hollywood Freeway as the traffic rolled smoothly but slowly downtown. Smog today—you couldn't see the windows of the high-rises, and the mountains north of Glendale and Pasadena had all but disappeared.

There had been so much lead on the tape that Mike had had his thumb on the search button for what seemed like two minutes. Then, without titles or other introduction, the image, what directors and cameramen called a full frame, a head-to-toe view. The subject was a young woman standing in front of a pale gold drop—no set or props. She was roughly twenty years old, with shoulder-length light brown hair, bangs, hazel eyes, and fair skin. Even features. Medium figure. She was wearing a navy blue flight attendant's uniform complete with hat, white blouse, and black high-heeled shoes. Her eyes were directed away from the camera, and she looked a little nervous.

There was a sound track that at first Mike thought was simply poor, because it was full of noise, coughs, and muffled thumps. Then a man spoke. He was off camera, apparently where the young woman was looking. "Take off your jacket," he said. As she did, he said, "No, more slowly. Don't look at me, look at the camera." Then he added, "Look at the birdie," and laughed a little at his remark.

His tone was imperious, as if he thought he was dealing with a lower order of animal. She removed her blouse next, responding to his instructions to turn from side to side. She had no presence or grace—an amateur. The man told her to turn around before removing her skirt, and when she glanced over her shoulder at him—without obvious intention of disobeying—he grew angry with her: "*Forget* about me! You're distracting from yourself!"

On the freeway Mike remembered thinking at that moment that the sound track itself was what was distracting. Without sound, the girl's nervousness and off-camera glances could have taken on an erotic character, and might have been enough of a hook for the imagination to hang a narrative. The guy was so obnoxious that Mike was still wondering what kind of monkey the girl really was, obeying him perfectly like that. She did not seem to be high on anything. Slip, white bra, panties, and garter belt. Beige stockings. Her back to the camera, she removed them all, still graceless, not so much innocent as untrained or even stupid about herself. When she was nude, the man told her to turn around again, his voice almost a derisive laugh. She stood still for no more than five seconds when the man said, like Porky Pig, "Th-that's all, folks!" and the screen turned to snow. Mike was still thinking what he had thought yesterday afternoon, when the cassette had fallen out from behind Moreland's dashboard.

What the fuck?

Mike was already seated at a table in The Pantry, sipping a cup of decaffeinated coffee, when a shadow the size of a small cloud fell across him.

"Mr. Gallagher?" the big man mumbled. "Maurice Constantine." He extended a surprisingly small hand. Mike took it as he rose and gestured to the other chair. Constantine's lips had barely moved. He was about five feet ten and weighed more than three hundred pounds. He had a potato nose and the happy eyes of a man whose good Christmases had come late in his life.

"I already had breakfast," Mike said. "But you order up."

The man shook his head negatively. "I'm trying to lose weight. I had my jaw wired shut." He peeled down his lower lip; his teeth were hidden by a mass of wires that looked like a prop out of a horror movie. "I saw you on the late show last night. You played a rancher in a pickup truck." He smiled eerily. "You had three lines. Stupid movie. I don't remember the title, but it starred what's his name, the skinny guy with the straight blond hair. I didn't know it was you until I just saw you. What happened to your hand?''

"I don't know how to cut a tomato.'' Mike knew the picture he meant. A week's work in the Imperial Valley, with Judy out of her mind because they were separated for six days. That was the week that convinced him that movies were a waste of time. Now the waiter came up and Constantine ordered coffee.

"What?''

Mike repeated it for him. The waiter looked stunned. "Are you two going to tie up this table? All these people want to *eat* here.''

Mike didn't want to show his badge. "I thought he was going to. We'll be out in a minute.''

"I'll cover it,'' Constantine murmured, throwing a five-dollar bill on the table. The waiter backed off.

"The job changed a little,'' Mike explained quietly. He told Constantine about the Maxwell-Skelley offices in the 9000 Building on Sunset, and what he suspected about the bungalow on Norma Place. "They've got a straight shot, line of sight. The bungalow is a busy retail dope operation. It may be wired another way, other ways, I don't know. You can't get in there, but I want to know if people are listening and your professional opinion about the sources of the tapes or whatever—who's doing it. The other thing is, can you find out what's being said in there?''

"The reason that I'm not in jail,'' Constantine mumbled, "is that I never do anything illegal.''

"Can you do it legally?''

Now Constantine gave that strange smile again. "Oh, sure. I can tell you how they eat their eggs in the morning.''

"You mean boiled or fried?''

"I mean sunny-side up or over easy.''

"What does that cost?''

"I canceled a day's work today expecting you to call. I have seventy thousand dollars' worth of equipment outside in my van. Frank Kennedy told me what this means to you, but I'm in an expanding field and have to go all over the world to buy my stuff. You should see the reading I have to do. My van is probably the only vehicle with a toilet on this continent besides an airplane that can break a hundred miles an hour. I got to have the toilet for stakeouts. My daily break-even point is three hundred dollars, my accountant says. Can you handle that?''

Mike nodded. "Let's get out of here. I don't want to give you money in front of people.''

"You can pay me later.''

"I might not see you. And don't call me anywhere. I'll call you and leave a message and meet you later.''

"Oh, I have a cellular phone in the van,'' Constantine said through his teeth. "You can get me anytime.''

"There's no privacy on those things, is there?''

"There's no privacy anywhere anymore,'' Constantine mumbled. "Privacy is a thing of the past.''

The deputy DA complained about Mike's paperwork but accepted the case anyway, and an hour later Mike had a warrant for McCallum the marine and was on his way back to Hollywood Division. He was trying to remember to call Gretchen, and he wasn't sure he was going to be able to do it there. It was only Tuesday, or *already* Tuesday. *Shit.* Last night Laura had cleaned up his hand and arm without question and had torn his shirt into shreds and burned the shreds in her fireplace. Then she had driven him home.

"Do you want me to walk upstairs with you?''

"No, I was entertaining in the living room and it isn't fit for more company yet.''

"You can't handle the keys and your gun at the same time.''

"If I have to handle the gun at all, I don't want you around.''

"Will you call me?''

"Hell, I don't want to say good night.''

He had told her the truth, but he still had to call Gretchen today, and she deserved his best attention. At the division, Mike learned that Bill Blair and Greg Novak were up in the Hills tending to a messy murder-suicide, a woman and man in that order, clearly the end of a very unhappy marriage. There were two messages for Mike, one from a deputy DA who was going to trial with a case that Mike and Dan had handled last winter, and the other from somebody named Hollister—he wanted to see Mike, too. Mike couldn't place the name.

Burgess said, "That trial starts Thursday. The deputy wants to see you ASAP."

"As always." *Hollister?* "We have to have people on tomorrow, while the rest of the world is at Dan's funeral."

"I already dealt with that," Burgess said. "It's going to be Novak and Goldfarb. Goldfarb wants to thank you personally. I think you made a good choice. He's dressed for the street today, but he won't be tomorrow. He just came right out and said it. Jacket and tie."

"Right on." Mike was on to the Beachwood case, Valerie Moreland. *Now* he remembered Hollister, *Ben* Hollister. "How did Novak take the idea of being on duty tomorrow?"

"Well, there was some bullshit about it, and finally he volunteered."

Mike was still remembering Hollister: he lived up on Rainbow Drive and *could* be that pornographer. Maybe that was the way to see Gretchen, if she was home. Two birds, et cetera. "Fucking DAs," Mike thought out loud. "Maybe I can put him off until tomorrow. I've got to review that case before I can talk to him about it. Six months after the experience, they want us to hotfoot it down there and then they wonder why we can't remember anything. Where are Lopez and Goldfarb now?"

"A db, a guy in his fifties—sixties. Whatever."

"Well, they can go down to Oceanside to get *this* turkey." He waved the warrant for McCallum. Gretchen's answering machine came on, and Mike looked for the DA's extension number while he waited to record his message. He was thinking that he would have to be careful, talking to Hollister. He had no idea what Hollister had to offer. Now the beep: "It's me. I've been very busy since you called last night, and I'm sorry about your troubles. Maybe we can catch each other later today." The telephone rang and Burgess picked up as Mike compared the Hollister number he had found at Valerie Moreland's yesterday with the one Hollister had left when he'd called here today. Not the same, but the new one was in Hollywood. Burgess pointed to the telephone and Mike grabbed the handset.

"Mike, it's Marge."

Hammond—Mike had forgotten to call Hammond's office. "Marge? How are you?"

"I'll be glad when tomorrow is over. There was a telephone call for you here two nights ago after you'd left. I meant to tell you last night and forgot. A young man—young enough. I could hear youth in his voice. Am I making sense to you?"

"Perfectly." He remembered two nights ago: he'd gone home from Marge's and then back to Laura's. Champagne in the bathroom sink.

"Anyway, I told him you weren't here, and he hung up. I was about to ask his name, but he was gone."

"All right, thanks for telling me. Don't concern yourself about it, it could have been anybody."

"Are you going to be here tonight?"

"I don't know. I've got to call downtown."

"Please be here tomorrow."

"Absolutely."

They said good-bye, and Mike dialed Hammond's office. It couldn't have been *anybody* trying to reach him at Dan's house. He couldn't imagine who could have known that he would be there. Someone with youth in his voice. Who? Why? A guy at Hammond's office picked up and Mike said that he was calling in as instructed. The guy on the other end told him to hold on. Now another line rang, and Marvin Burgess took it.

"Frank Kennedy for you, Mike."

"Ask him to hold on if he can, Marvin."

This was the way the world was going to end, Mike thought, with everybody on hold. In another moment the line opened and the guy in Hammond's office said, "Call back here at eight o'clock. Don't make any other plans for the rest of the night."

Mike said he understood, and opened the line to Kennedy.

"Yes, Frank."

"Did you see Constantine?"

"Yeah, his jaw is wired shut so he can lose weight."

"And he wanted to meet at *The Pantry*?" Kennedy howled. "He's a good man, but he does things like that to himself. Were you able to work something out? What kind of a number did he give you?"

"Three hundred. He'll do what I asked."

"That's the best number I've heard out of him. But listen: I called because that gal in the legal department I mentioned overheard something yesterday about the big contract. The position the studio is taking is that the star can go fuck himself. The boss started to turn sour on the picture some time ago because of the AIDS thing and has been looking for a way out and apparently the star has given it to him. I don't know how that works, because my friend in Security says that the connection between the star and his old friend was well known to the boss years ago. A still active connection. The other guy, the one who can't get a job parking cars, is used by the star as an errand boy, or has been over the years, ever since that other guy's career went on the skids."

"Did you hear anything about the producer's contract?"

"She doesn't count. Birnbaum has walked from the whole situation. It's too bad, because the picture was coming along fine, as far as anybody knew. Funny as hell."

"Now suppose the star decides to sue. What then?"

"Apparently he won't. On that score, the people in the contract department are saying that the studio is in fat city."

"That means the studio has something on the star," Mike said.

"That's the way I read it."

"And the only thing you've been able to pick up is the association with the other guy."

"And all the bad habits that go with it," Kennedy said.

"Can you stay with this? What do I owe you so far?"

"You don't owe me anything so far, but that may change. I'm on my way down to the commissary now for a free lunch. And sure, I'll stay with it."

Lunch. Mike still had his watch in his jacket pocket. He got it out and looked at the time while he was saying good-bye to Kennedy: twelve-fifteen. Mike dialed Hollister's number. A girl said Hollister was out. To lunch.

While Marvin Burgess covered Homicide's telephones, Mike signed himself in at the computer. He typed, *Roehrig, Hans.* The machine blinked. *Last known address?* Mike had the Rainbow Drive address ready. The machine chewed on it like a hippopotamus snacking on an orange crate. It burbed, *nope, sorry*. So much for Sacramento, which was as far as the LAPD could program video game tattletales to report that someone was making inquiries of interest to the department. So on to El Paso and DEA's electronic guru. This geek was in a suburban industrial park, but you couldn't get in the building that housed it without an appointment with a clown in a smock to walk you around, yakking about the wonder of it all. Mike said hello and it said hello and Mike gave Roehrig's name and the address on Rainbow Drive where he'd seen Panama Hat and the two cock-suckers clamber up the steps the other night. After a few seconds, the video screen waved the law enforcement equivalent of Maggie's Drawers. *Hello, Washington. Hello, Hollywood.* It was the FBI's turn to come up empty. Mike was not surprised. Hans Roehrig was a stupid alias, even for someone who spoke German, but maybe the big goon knew more than he showed. Mike had one last shot at the guy, the Defense Department.

Of the Defense Department, Mike could ask two questions.

Had Hans Roehrig ever been in the armed services?

USAF, 1968-72, *Captain. Vietnam, two tours.* Dates, skills, and decorations filled another three lines. Mike decided to ask the second question:

Had Hans Roehrig ever been given a security clearance?

Jackpot!

Hans Roehrig—*Mike's* Hans Roehrig—was a certified failed genius.

Munich-born, a naturalized citizen who saw combat as a hel-icopter pilot in Vietnam, with advanced degrees in chemistry and chemical engineering earned in the early seventies from MIT and Berkeley, Roehrig had had his Top Secret security clearance revoked at Huntsville, Alabama, in 1979, for reasons of moral turpitude.

Nineteen seventy-nine wasn't that long ago. Mike went back to his desk and called the Redstone Arsenal in Huntsville, Al-abama, and asked to speak to the security officer. Mike said that he was inquiring about Roehrig in connection with a murder investigation.

"It's murder now," said the voice on the other end. "Well, I'm not surprised."

"You had another inquiry about Roehrig recently?"

"About a year ago," came the reply. "Federal. I don't know what it was about. They were much more interested in what I had to tell them. I had to mail them copies of the stuff I had, not that I had much. Most of what I have is in my memory of the bastard. Very arrogant. He beat a rap here, knew it, and didn't hesitate to rub our noses in it. The federals weren't surprised by that or the rap itself."

Mike's head was throbbing again. "What was that?"

"He was shacked up with a couple of teenagers," the voice said. "Fourteen—fifteen years old. He had them doped up. We had to keep it out of the papers. There are some eccentrics working here, and we don't need to have the locals stirred up about perversion. That's how Roehrig slipped the hook. He signed a paper admitting to the charges. If he hadn't had such a distinguished service record, he would have been deported."

"He won a Silver Star," Mike said.

"Legitimate," the security officer said. "I hope you can gas the bastard, though. Even after six years, I still get sick just thinking about him. He laughed at us, and *argued*. The girls liked it, so that made it okay, he said."

Mike said, "The law protects children precisely because they don't have the intellectual equipment to differentiate what feels good and what *is* good. We have a whole city full of guys advancing Roehrig's horseshit argument for the sake of their own pleasure. But I think you can forget about us gassing anybody out here. That hasn't happened in over a dozen years, and our state Supreme Court spends most of its time looking for excuses to keep from sitting in judgment of people." Mike wanted to do something about his hand, but there was nothing he could do short of taking a painkiller, which would leave him groggy. Last night Laura had talked about meditative techniques easing and even eradicating pain, but he was in no mood even to think about that stuff. "In any event, this guy Roehrig isn't a chief suspect in my case. But I've seen enough of him to share your sentiments." He said good-bye, and hung up. Marvin Burgess was staring at him.

"Why don't you go home?" he asked. "All this shit will keep. You look like you're ready to fall over." Burgess pointed to Mike's hand. "You're in agony, too. Don't bullshit yourself, because you're sure not bullshitting me."

Mike dialed information, eyeing Burgess as the operator asked, "What city, please?"

"The Valley," Mike said.

"Sir, that's in the eight one eight area code."

Mike disconnected and dialed the 818 Information number. Burgess was right. This time, to the operator's question, he said, "Panorama City. The last name is Azzolini. I don't know the first. He says it's the only one—"

The operator didn't need to hear a story. The computer voice came on and gave Mike a telephone number, which he committed to memory. If he forgot it later, he could call Information again. He was not going to write anything down that connected him to the Clown Club. The line was busy. If Azzolini was only a bartender, as he had said, he might be upset enough to talk a little about what he knew about his bosses.

It was a little after one o'clock. Mike gave Marvin Burgess the name of the DA who wanted to see him. "I'm taking your advice," he said while dialing again. "If I can't reach this guy now, call him back when he's back from court or whatever and tell him I wasn't well—" The telephone on the other end was picked up and Mike identified himself. "Look, I'm not well and I'm going to my partner's funeral tomorrow. I'll be free in the afternoon—"

"Oh, that's not soon enough," the guy on the other end said. "I want to go through your testimony step by step. We have an exhibit that's only going to make sense if the jury understands what you and your partner found when you arrived on the scene."

"I don't think you heard what I said—"

"You didn't hear what *I* said! I want to call you to the *stand* tomorrow afternoon! I want to make sure the jury understands this complicated business! This is not a popular prosecution! We have a sixty-two-year-old female defendant who bursts into tears every time her husband's name is mentioned!"

Mike pulled himself up as his hand stabbed with a very sharp pain. He was bleeding again: he didn't have to see the bright red spot blossoming on the white bandage to know it. Now the spot appeared, widened. "Listen to me, you son of a bitch! Your female defendant—"

"What did you call me?"

"An asskisser and motherfucker! Shut up! *Shut up!* Your female defendant in your unpopular prosecution stuck a knife in her husband seven times because he was packing his bags to leave her! If you can't get the old cunt time for that, maybe you ought to be in another line of work, like taking fly shit out of pepper! I told you my partner's dead and I'm going to his funeral! You should have called us last week! You can get the fucking case adjourned until Thursday, but you couldn't hear what I had to say in the first place! I'm going to my partner's funeral, I said, and if you don't like it, you can eat shit and bay at the moon!"

The DA hung up before Mike did. Mike looked around. Burgess was staring at him. Other guys around the room were on their feet, looking. Mike reached for the handset again but Burgess's black hand, as large as his own, folded over his wrist. "Time to go home, Mike," he said. "You're done for the day."

Mike turned his palm up so that Burgess could see the blood. "Look at this hand!"

"It isn't your hand, Mike. It's Dan Crawford."

Mike could see Dan—as if Dan had not suffered a moment, as if he were alive and whole. Mike started to cry all over again, proof that all the mourning he had done already hadn't meant a thing. "Fuckers!" Mike cried, not knowing who he meant.

"It's all right," Marvin Burgess said. "We'll get them all."

"*Kill* them all!"

"You get first dibs."

"His kids. His wife."

Burgess had him by the arm. "Come on, my friend, don't worry about the DA. I'll square him away. Do you want a doctor? How about somebody to drive you home?"

"Fuck it." He pulled free. "I can take it." He had meant to say, *I can handle it.* A lot of people were on their feet now. Mike knew what was happening to him. He turned back to his desk and grabbed the Hollister number. He'd have to call Information again about Azzolini. "Take care of the DA for me. Please."

"Don't worry about it. It's the first thing. Anybody tries to make trouble, they'll have to answer to me."

"Me, too," a guy nearby called.

"And me," said somebody else.

Mike started out, holding his left hand up close to his chest. Somebody called, "You're all right, Gallagher!" and started to clap, slowly. Another guy joined him, then a third. Assholes, Mike thought, trying to muster his anger. All they were doing was making him cry. They were still clapping when he reached the door and paused, thinking of turning around and acknowledging them, but then he sailed on through into the tiled, secure foyer and the sunny, smoggy freedom of Wilcox Avenue beyond.

He awakened not knowing what time it was. The telephone was ringing. The answering machine was set to intercept on the fourth ring, but Mike was still too full of cobwebs to know how many rings he had heard when the machine clicked in. He was setting his feet on the floor when he ran into Dan's death like a wall—he had been through this experience before, perhaps too many times. *Altogether* too many times: he never wanted to go through it again. The clock said it was a quarter to five. Afternoon, he remembered, as he saw the daylight outside the windows. His hand hurt. And he was still remembering: he was supposed to call Hammond's office at eight o'clock. Mike let the answering machine click again before he picked up and heard Laura Demming's voice. He did Bogart.

"I thought I told you never to call me here."

"Tell me what you're wearing," she said.

"My underwear."

"Take it off. How's your hand? I called your office and they said you were gone for the day."

"The hand kicked up," he said, remembering his outburst at the DA. "You have it right." Dan, he thought. He looked over at the mess in the corner of the room by the door. "I still haven't cleaned this place, otherwise I'd ask you to come by."

"That's why I called. Two plus two. With that hand, you probably need a housekeeper."

Mike was quiet, thinking about it. They had been talking almost two minutes. If his line was tapped, whoever was doing it had her. Now he knew how he felt about her, but he had cried enough today. "Come on. Bring some dinner."

"I wish you weren't hurt," she said.

He was thinking of the calls he had not made at the office, and whether he should attempt to make them from here. What the hell, he thought, if someone wanted to know his business, there really was no defense. Maurice Constantine was right: privacy was a thing of the past. Mike said, "I take you very seriously, Laura."

"I know. You're a good guy and you deserve better from life."

In the kitchen, while he was making tea, he thought about that, and what he had told her that made her think such a thing. She knew very little about the death of his father, and nothing about his mother having drunk herself to death. If Laura saw something in the way he carried himself, there was not much he could do about it. He wanted to tell her again what he suspected about being tapped. He couldn't bear to think of anyone trying to hurt her.

He got Azzolini's number from the new Northwest book and tried it, but it was busy, so Mike called the operator and asked her to check it. Azzolini was listed with no address, which didn't mean much. His phone was off the hook, which was an acceptable way of dealing with the pestering of the media fools. Now Mike tried Ben Hollister's business number. The girl asked who was calling, and Mike gave only his name. "Mr. Hollister has been trying to reach me."

Hollister sounded nervous. "I'm glad you got back to me, but this isn't really a place I can talk. Can we meet somewhere? Maybe I can call you back."

"I'm at home, Mr. Hollister, and I don't like to give out my number. I'm booked for the rest of the evening and all day tomorrow. Let me ask you some yes-or-no questions right now. Do you know Valerie Moreland well?"

"Valerie Moreland? I didn't call you about her. How do you know her?"

"Me first, I'm bigger than you. How well do you know Moreland?"

"She's done some costuming for me a couple of times. She wants to break into theatrical costume design, but she doesn't have any credits."

"When was the last time you saw her?"

"Last month sometime. My other calender is at home. It will have the exact day."

"What do you mean, she did some costuming for you? What kind of work do you do?"

"I make nonunion films, Mr. Gallagher. There's nothing illegal about them."

"I didn't say there was. Tell me what you know about Valerie Moreland."

"I guess I don't really know anything. What's this about?"

"Keep talking, Mr. Hollister, you're doing fine. How did you meet Valerie Moreland?"

"Next—wait a minute. I don't know if I can answer that, or should, without an attorney."

"Really? Maybe you ought to talk to an attorney. Valerie Moreland was murdered last week and yours was one of the telephone numbers we found in her apartment."

"Oh, my God!"

"I didn't think you'd be trying to reach me if you had killed her, Mr. Hollister," Mike said smoothly. "But now it sounds to me that you do have some information that would be of value in the investigation. Why don't you want to talk about how you met her?"

"It's not important. Look, I don't want to get dragged into anything. I thought—"

"What did you think?" Mike asked.

"Look, I live on Rainbow Drive."

Mike waited, but Hollister stayed silent. "What about Rainbow Drive?" Mike asked.

"Oh, Christ. Look, I made a mistake. I shouldn't have called you."

"I think you can see that you would have been talking to me

anyway. Now if you don't want to tell me how you met Valerie Moreland, I'm going to start having all kinds of crazy thoughts about illegal activities that you're involved in, including nonunion movies. You know as well as I do that you can make movies of any kind of sexual act, but you can't pay people to perform those acts, even for a movie.''

"Let me think about this.''

"What did you want to tell me about Rainbow Drive?''

"I thought I knew something. It's heavy. I didn't know Valerie was dead. Now nothing makes sense. Everything's screwy.''

Mike was ahead of him—his mind was racing. He had to be near the phone at eight o'clock—he dared not make a false step. "Just let me be the cop. You wouldn't like the pay anyway. Calm down. You have nothing to worry about. I've got things to do, then I'll get back to you. Do you think you'll be all right?''

"Yeah, sure.'' Annoyed.

"If anything happens, call the number you've been using. But tell whoever answers that your name is Bob. Got that? *Bob*.''

"I understand.''

"We'll be talking.'' Mike disconnected and, with his finger on the button, said, "Shit!'' He dialed Hollywood Homicide. Novak answered. "Greg, it's Mike. If anybody named Bob calls me, I'm to be told right away, no matter where I am, even in court. Make sure everybody knows. As a matter of fact, call people at home and let them know. If Bob calls, I'm to be told.''

"Is there anything else they need to know, Mike?''

"No. That's it. If you can't find people, leave messages and have them call back to confirm. I've got other calls to make.'' Mike hung up and sat back. He was *in*! Maybe he should have known more about Ben Hollister before calling him, but Hollister thought that Valerie Moreland's murder was tied into the Rainbow Drive killings, and Mike was required by law to proceed accordingly. Tom Cutler, Larry Hammond, and anybody else at Parker Center could make life difficult for him, even ship him down to Pedro for the remainder of his career, but they dared not take public action against him. He *belonged* on Rainbow Drive, following every lead from Lansing to Freeman to the postmurder cover-up. He had to be careful—know in advance what he was doing. He wished he could talk to Dan—he wanted to tell Dan the news. Instead, he pushed himself off the couch and turned on the television set. Fritz Coleman was in front of the weather map. Mike picked up the telephone again and called Maurice Constantine. Constantine had it on the first ring, or chirp, or whatever cellular telephones did. Mike identified himself and asked if Constantine had anything to report.

Constantine answered through his teeth.

"A lot, Mr. Gallagher, if you want to hear it now."

"Call me Mike. Do you think you ought to stay on it?"

"Oh, sure."

"I'll call you back in an hour. In spite of what you said today about privacy, I think I want to call you from outside."

Constantine chortled. "Some of this is pretty funny. These people are lunatics."

It was a quarter after five. Mike had to call Hammond's office at eight o'clock. There was Laura to consider. She knew about cops, thanks to her father. Hell, she liked the action. From the television set came a name Mike knew.

"Hold on." Automatically, Mike put his hand over the mouthpiece, then took it away again. Kelly Lange was reading from a piece of paper that was handed to her. There was urgency in her voice. "In a surprise development, Jack Skelley, owner of the Clown Club, was picked up just an hour ago at Los Angeles International Airport in what police say was an attempt to flee the country."

"I'll call you within the hour."

"That's okay, Mr. Gallagher."

Kelly Lange continued: "Jack Skelley was taken into custody at four-twenty-five this afternoon while trying to board a Quantas flight bound for Fiji, New Zealand, and Australia. Skelley was already on the seven forty-seven when authorities boarded and led him off. They say he offered no resistance."

Mike smiled and dialed Azzolini's number again. Still off the hook. He called Laura to tell her to stay home. Too late, she was already gone. Mike dressed. Ten minutes later he was in the kitchen washing his teacup when the buzzer from downstairs sounded. Mike pressed the talk button.

"Are ya naked?"

"No," Laura said, "and I'm not alone either. Thanks a lot. It's going to be an interesting ride in the elevator."

"I live on the first floor, lady," a man said sourly.

Mike pressed the button to admit her and went out to the hall. When the elevator opened, Laura was holding a bag of groceries up in front of her face.

"I'm sorry."

"You're an asshole" she said, marching by him. "And I went down to Ventura Boulevard to get you sushi."

"You're walking the wrong way."

She wheeled around, her nose still in the air. "The good news is I'm not wearing a bra."

"What's the bad news?"

"Guess."

He opened the door and she stepped in and looked as if she wanted to be kissed until she saw the corner. He had to catch the grocery bag. Laura looked at the spatters on the wall and ceiling, her hand coming up as if, involuntarily, she had to touch them. Her lip quivered. She turned away.

"Are you all right?"

She shook her head no. "I should stop this—break it off right now. I should teach myself to hate you or something. Or something." She wept, shaking. "Where's the bathroom in this dump?"

"Past the kitchen."

"I'm sorry, it's not a dump. It's very nice, except for the—" Laura waved vaguely toward the corner as she passed out of the room.

Mike unpacked the grocery bag, the sushi take-out trays on top, a couple of bottles of Kirin beer, a spray can of carpet cleaner, then a bottle of ammonia and a large box of commercial meat tenderizer. Laura reappeared, her face blotched, sniffing, wiping her nose. "You may need a rug cleaning machine or even a new carpet. I think I underestimated the size of the mess."

"Meat tenderizer?"

"I'm glad I brought that. It's an enzyme that will change the chemistry of the stain."

"I'm glad you're not leaving."

She looked down. "I didn't like what I felt, Mike. Don't remind me."

"I have to pass on the beer. I've been on the phone since we talked, and I have to go out. To make a call, but it may lead to something else. I'm concerned about the length of time the line here was open to yours—long enough to be traced, I think. Please be very careful. Maybe you ought to stay away from me for a while—"

"No."

Mike put his finger to his lips and motioned to her to follow him back to the living room, where he had pencils and paper. He wrote, *A certain kind of tap can listen to our conversation when the telephone is on the hook. When I come back, I'll knock three times, then twice, then once.*

She took the paper from him. *Why would anyone want to hurt me?*

He pointed to the corner and wrote, *You know some shit.*

"Maurice, it's Mike Gallagher. What do you have for me?"

"There's something going down right now. This guy Jackson is a crazy bastard. He's beating up his girlfriend. Her name is Jennie. Jackson has the television set on all the time, dialing from one news show to another. He's very interested in the Laurel Canyon murders. He got upset when he heard just now that Jack Skelley tried to jump bail. Do you know about that?"

"Yeah. Let's go back to the beginning. What have you been able to find out about that whole scene down there?"

Constantine giggled. "That's the word for it, a scene. Jackson's under surveillance from the 9000 Building, all right, but it's not from that room you said, nine oh five. The surveillance is from the tenth floor. Infrared, almost certainly law enforcement. It's a good thing I checked that out first, or somebody overseeing that setup would have seen my beam too, if he had bothered to look. I was going to use infrared on Jackson myself. But when I saw the beam already on the place, I figured I was done and would have to pack it in."

Mike was in El Torito on Riverside Drive, and he had to move out of the way of a guy coming out of the bathroom to get back to the bar, which was crowded and noisy.

"But you're listening to what's going on in there now."

"Yeah, I'm telling you. Just because there was infrared on the place didn't mean that there wasn't something else, too. I figured I could take a chance and set up my own infrared for a little while on the 9000 Building."

"On the window you saw the beam coming from?"

"That was the safe thing. I was a mile away. If anybody up there was looking through the lens and saw it, he'd say something that would tip me off, and I'd be long gone. From what I could make out, there're two guys up there listening to everything being said in the Jackson bungalow on Norma. They have a speaker arrangement because I could hear stuff that doesn't come from an office, like water running and dishes rattling in a sink. That's what I wanted, because I figured if there was a transmitter in the Jackson place, too, all I had to do was match up the sound I was getting on my infrared with what I could pull in on my receiver. I have an all-band that pulls in everything but the secret government channels. There's a transmitter in the Jackson house, too, way up on the UHF band. It took awhile to find it. I figure it's television. I don't have a television receiver that will pull in the picture, but I can build one if you give me a day to do it."

Constantine had been listening to the UHF audio all afternoon. The telephone was wired in so Constantine could hear both sides of the conversation. It was good work, Constantine said—there could even be a microwave transmitter in the telephone. Jackson was a dope dealer, no question about it. He'd had thirty-four calls since Constantine started listening at twelve-thirty. People asked Jackson if they could come over, wanting to know if he had cassettes, groceries, tapes, books. It was always something like that, preceding the request for the permission to come over. They wanted to know if he had the stuff. Constantine had spent an hour actually on the block, logging people in and out, matching them to the voices he'd heard. Most of the people had been no more than fifteen or twenty minutes away. Constantine had logged all the names and times. A few people had used both names, but most only their first.

"Read them off," Mike said.

Constantine did. The next-to-last was Ben Hollister.

"What time was that?"

"A quarter after five."

Hollister hadn't wasted a moment. "What did he want? Do you remember?"

"Oh, I have everything on tape, don't worry about that. But I remember. He wanted to go over, too. And he asked if Paula Rogers was there. She wasn't. Isn't. The girl in the house, Jennie, has been trying to reach Paula Rogers all day, all over town, but can't locate her."

"What kind of a television camera can you hide in a guy's house?"

"One the size of a Zippo lighter, Mr. Gallagher. With non-reflective glass masking a wide-angle lens, even a good housekeeper wouldn't see the thing behind the grate of a heating duct. And these people are stoned—wired. They're doing every kind of drug you can name. Apparently that's all they do."

"What kind of places has Jennie been calling for Paula Rogers?"

"Offices, friends. An agent named Bill North. She called him twice. A couple of girls she called three times."

"Did she call a guy named Hans Roehrig?"

"Yeah, but he said that Rogers knows better than to show up around his place. He definitely doesn't like her. He called Rogers a douche bag."

"Has Jackson mentioned a guy named Barranquilla?"

"Jackson and Roehrig talked about him. Barranquilla's on the wind. They figure he took off. They talked about Skelley and Bernie Maxwell. This is when Jackson got upset. Roehrig thinks Skelley made a mistake in the sense that he didn't have to do it because Bernie Maxwell is too well connected. Nobody can touch him. That's almost the exact language, but I have it all on tape."

"Bernie Maxwell is so well-connected that Skelley made a mistake trying to get out of the country," Mike repeated. "And after Roehrig said that to Jackson, Jackson started to beat up the girlfriend."

"Well, they're stoned. They're into some crazy perverted sex stuff that I don't have figured out yet. Jackson is a sly, sneaky guy. When a few people came to the house, he hid in the bed-

room while she tended to business, telling the people that he
was asleep. He was listening at the bedroom door like he was
trying to catch his customers and friends in lies. She's some
kind of a coke slave. I heard her in the bathroom sneaking snorts
while he was in the kitchen getting a beer.''

"Build the television set. If you can hear all that, the camera
is in there for a reason.'' With Barranquilla's money, Mike was
still running a profit for Marge, but it wasn't going to last long—
unless Mike got lucky again. That was guilt running away with
him, Mike knew. "Start on the television set right away. I have
a feeling things are going to be happening fast.'' Mike was
thinking of Azzolini again and that maybe he hadn't simply left
the phone off the hook. And now Mike knew what Hammond
had in mind for after midnight. "When we talked earlier, you
said some of this was pretty funny.''

"A couple of musicians were in for about half an hour in the
middle of the afternoon, and Jackson was telling them why farm
boys fuck chickens. Explained exactly. He said he never did it,
but I don't believe him. Do you want to hear it?''

"No.''

Mike made two more calls from El Torito and then walked
back to his car quickly. At this time of night the traffic was heavy
and he wanted to be back in the apartment by eight o'clock,
when he was supposed to call Hammond's office. If Hammond
said he wanted to call Mike back, Panorama City was almost
the last place Mike wanted to locate him, especially if Mike's
thoughts about Azzolini were correct. Ben Hollister was nervous enough to want to dose himself with coke because a cop
had tied him to the people who had died in a house near his own
on Rainbow Drive. Moreland had gone to the Clown Club,
where she may have met Jackson or his girlfriend Jennie or
Paula Rogers or Hans Roehrig or any of the people in the murder
house, which was where Hollister had met her. *Next*, he had
said before stopping himself. Next *door*. What Gretchen had
said put Hollister on the same side of the street as the murder
house; maybe she just hadn't resolved that Hollister was next
door to it. It seemed to Mike that Hollister was less afraid of
the police than he was of others. That wasn't true of Jackson,
who had been moved to a little girlfriend thumping because Jack

Skelley had tried to jump bail. Jackson wasn't necessarily a dumber guy than Hans Roehrig, but Roehrig's intelligence had been certified, and *he* wasn't disturbed. Maxwell was too well-connected. How well-connected do you have to be to get away with a massacre? *And* the murder of Valerie Moreland?

Her death made no sense at all to Mike. If Billy Lansing and Dale Freeman had been brought up from the San Diego area to infiltrate the Maxwell organization and had somehow exposed themselves, what was the point of taking out Moreland? She'd died at about the same time as the others, and not in her apartment. And certainly not in the house on Rainbow Drive where the others had died. But maybe, just maybe, in Roehrig's place. But why?

Azzolini's garden apartment complex wasn't difficult to find, a half-block off Osborne Street. Most of this part of town had been farmland when Mike had arrived in Los Angeles. As of ten minutes ago, Azzolini's telephone was still returning a busy signal. The second call Mike had made from El Torito had been to the telephone company: he'd identified himself by badge number and said he needed the address that went with Azzolini's telephone number. It would be more difficult for Mike to show Azzolini's connection to the Moreland murder without revealing his own continuing interest in the Rainbow Drive murders, but Mike was more distant inside himself from Tom Cutler's wrath then ever, now. He didn't think Cutler would have much to say anyway. Things were popping now, like Jack Skelley trying to leave town. Hans Roehrig's opinions on that subject were not conclusive, but they were informative. All that Mike did not know about Hammond's after-midnight business tonight were the details—and Hammond's after-midnight business would be additional confirmation of what Mike already suspected about Azzolini. The first confirmation was in Azzolini's apartment, waiting for Mike to discover it.

The building reminded Mike of Donnie Jackson's old place in Hollywood, two stories of apartments facing a central swimming pool. This was a little bigger than the other, with a patch of lawn and a couple of palm trees. The glass doors to the street were locked, and Azzolini did not answer to his bell. Of course. Mike rang for the manager. She responded over the intercom.

"Police. Open up."

The buzzer sounded, almost lost in the noise of a helicopter passing over.

The manager's door opened and a woman in her sixties stepped out. She was in a housedress and slippers. Her white hair was a mess, and she smelled of cigarettes and gin. Mike showed her the badge.

"You have a guy named Azzolini living here," he said. "Do you have a pass key to his apartment?"

"I have it right here," she said. "Follow me. The owner called me today about this fellow. Normally the owner wants me to follow a rule, that you have to show me a paper first. But the owner saw Mr. Azzolini s name and this address in the paper today, and the owner doesn't want dope dealers on the property if he can help it. He had a dope dealer in another one of his properties, and that turned into an awful lot of trouble."

"Tell me about Mr. Azzolini," Mike said.

"Oh, I never saw him."

"He was a bartender who worked nights. You never saw him around here during the day?"

"That's what I just said."

"Did you see him today?"

"I didn't see him today either. I thought he was in jail."

"He's out on bail."

"That's a terrible thing," she said as she stopped in front of one of the apartments. "What's wrong with the courts these days?"

Mike waited for her to unlock the door. "Step out of the way." The air smelled terribly stale. Mike felt for a light switch.

"It's on the other wall."

Mike found it. A small table lamp positioned on the floor four feet inside the apartment came on. There were no other furnishings in view, just the carpet and drapes that were the standard issue for Los Angeles apartments.

"For God's sake!" the manager said.

"Stay outside," Mike said. Mike walked through to the bedroom. One of the bulbs in the ceiling fixture blew out when he flipped the switch. The room was bare. Nothing in the closet. In the bathroom, the medicine chest was empty. No toilet paper on the roller. The kitchen cupboards and drawers were empty. Where was the telephone? Mike went around the kitchen counter into the living room, where he found the thin, new-style telephone wire attached to a wall jack. The wire ran back around the base of the counter and into the refrigerator. Mike put his ear up to the door. He could hear the telephone company's off-the-hook howler faint inside. Mike went back to the living room, removed the wire from the wall, and pulled. The refrigerator door flew open and the telephone skittered across the kitchen floor. Mike really hadn't thought the refrigerator was booby-trapped, but there was no point in taking an unnecessary chance. The refrigerator was empty and smelled awful.

"Can I come in now? I don't know when he moved his stuff out. I'm here all day long, day in and day out, and I haven't seen a mover in three months."

"Do you remember him ever bringing anything in?" Mike asked.

"No, come to think of it, but that was awhile ago."

"When?"

"Last September."

"How did he pay his rent? Was he on time?

"Oh, they mail their checks to the owner. I just take care of the building. You'll have to talk to him. Do you want the owner's phone number?"

"Nah. Thanks for your help."

"What should I do about this?"

"Not a thing." Mike gave her a card and started away. "If you or your boss hear anything from Azzolini, let me know."

Maybe they'd get a note from him, with his door key taped to it. Some Azzolini. *Only the bartender*. Jack Skelley gets pulled out of his seat on an airplane and Azzolini is gone easier than checking out of a Holiday Inn, which was what the busy signal had finally pounded into Mike's thick Irish skull. Under-cover guys usually disappeared like that. Gone—just gone, like that P. Vik who had originally greased the skids of Daisy Nunn. Azzolini wasn't LAPD. Tom Cutler didn't throw money around on apartments only to discover he had no use for them. But now Mike was more sure than ever that Azzolini had not lied to him in the things he'd said about Moreland *or* Dan. What Mike had to do was remember what those things were. Azzolini put Roehrig's opinions in proper perspective, too. People were pulling the chain on Jack Skelley and Bernie Maxwell. They were big-budget, high-priority federal customers. Frank Kennedy had told Mike that his *friends* weren't talking about Bernie Maxwell. *Not Disneyland*, Azzolini had said. As soon as Dan was in the ground, Ben Hollister was going to tell everything he knew or Mike was going to tear the lungs right out of his chest. The same was going to happen to a lot of people, when Mike got his hands on them. The more he learned, the angrier he was getting, and he wasn't sure he understood why—or didn't care. Whatever the problem was, it had cost a lot of people their lives, including Dan Crawford, who was the biggest *Why?* of all.

14

HE AND LAURA WERE MAKING LOVE WHEN THE TELE-
phone rang and the machine answered and then began to
recycle at once—another hangup. Before Barranquilla's arrival last night, the caller had heard Mike's voice and hung
up in a panic. Mike was sure that that was the way it really
had happened, that Barranquilla's white sedan cruising outside had been only a coincidence. The caller was somebody
checking on Mike, keeping tabs. Still, the door to the hall
was double-locked. . . .

Laura sensed his distraction and sat up with a sad half-
smile, "You owe me." She cocked her head in the direction
of the telephone. "Is that what made you tell me last night
to put Agnes on alert?"

"Last night I got to the telephone before the machine. He's
been calling every night. Last night was the first time I was
home."

"Let me stay here tonight," she said. "Don't make me go home by myself in the dark."

"Okay." Hammond's office had told him to be ready for picking up at two-thirty, which was still five hours off. Mike had hoped to get some sleep. Laura had done such a good job of altering the color of the stain on the living-room carpet that Mike had told Maurice Constantine to come by at six A.M. He'd called Marvin Burgess, too. Burgess had straightened out the DA: the precious exhibit would be covered by an assistant coroner; and Mike was not due in court until two. Valencia at eight. The sleep Mike had been going to get tonight had to be now, if at all—but he was awake with his mind on other things. He told Laura he was sorry.

"I understand. Do you have a gun here for me after you leave?"

"If a twenty-two is enough firepower for you."

"That knocks you out, I know. Are you falling for me, even a little?"

"I think so."

"I did ask for you. I've wanted to change my life for so long. Please don't ever forget that, will you?

"Do you think I'm going to hurt you?"

"Think twice. That's all I ask."

He reached for her and as soon as they touched they were making love again.

He was downstairs at two-thirty and five minutes later Larry Hammond's unmarked black sedan turned the corner and a rear door opened. Two plainclothes guys were in the front seat and Hammond was alone in the back. When the car was rolling again, Hammond said, "We'll have a few minutes when we get where we're going, Gallagher. You and I will talk then. What happened to your hand?"

"I was cutting a tomato and the knife slipped."

They took Riverside to Laurel Canyon Boulevard and turned toward the hills. At the Mulholland light the driver turned left and then immediately right into Woodrow Wilson Drive. A quarter of a mile along, the driver pulled over and killed the engine and he and the other guy got out. Another sedan came along and they got into it and it pulled away.

"You're carrying, aren't you, Gallagher?"

"Always."

"Well, you'll need it, but only for show, I hope. We want to take everybody alive and with as little fuss as possible. The house we're going to hit is just around the bend. You and I will go by my watch. At six minutes to three we're going to get out of the car and walk around the bend. At five minutes to three we'll join the rest of the detail and move on Bernie Maxwell's house. The chief wanted you in on this because of your concern about the murders on Rainbow Drive occurring on your turf and you being shut out of that investigation—*this* investigation. This case has been in the works for over a year."

"Maxwell killed those people, eh?"

"He ordered it," Hammond said. "This has been a task force operation. City, county, state, and federal. Maxwell has been very big league for much too long, and now—at last—he's overstepped himself."

Hammond shifted position, as if uncomfortable with the role he was having to play. Mike wasn't going to argue or otherwise lengthen the conversation. There was nothing new here. Mike had heard it from Cutler or read it in the papers or learned it from Frank Kennedy. As for Cutler wanting him in on this bust, Mike doubted that he would have been the beneficiary of such thoughtfulness if Dan were still alive. All Mike wanted now was to get as far from Hammond as the circumstances were going to allow. Hammond said, "After Daisy Nunn's arrest a year ago, she had to find a new supplier. She turned to Bernie Maxwell. At the same time, she took on a new boyfriend who had a very expensive habit of his own. Two months ago, she added some friends she would have been better off without. A month ago, because the gang in the house on Rainbow Drive had partied their way through all the cash reserves they had, Daisy Nunn came up here—not alone—and asked Maxwell to front her some product. He did. Payment—thirty thousand dollars—was due in a week. It was not made. Maxwell demanded payment. The truth was, the money was not available because the men in the Rainbow Drive house had partied their way through that, too. Frank Thomas, Daisy's boyfriend, the man who accompanied her up here to Maxwell's house, had a *very* expensive heroin habit. If you read the newspapers, you know that the other two men in the house were bad boys from the San Diego area—''

"You mean Lansing and that guy Dale Freeman."

"Yeah. Jerry Chambers just happened to be in the wrong place at the wrong time."

"Freeman got away," Mike said. "Do you know where he is?"

"We're focusing our activities on El Centro. He knows that area. Let me go on, we're going to run out of time. There was another man involved, a failed actor named Bobby Michaels. Do you know who he is?"

Mike saw an opportunity to make Hammond squirm and think Mike was stupid at the same time. "Dan Crawford pointed him out to me once."

"When was that?"

"Last year. It was a while ago." Hammond could chew on that for a while. He had just given something away in a cheap hidden brag on the order of explaining why farm boys fuck chickens instead of saying you had done it yourself, or telling a street girl that you had shot somebody in the head when you had shot him in the back. Mike had another clue, and he was going to run with it. Hammond twisted his lip in that way of his and then looked out the window as he began speaking again.

"The Rainbow Drive group broke into Maxwell's house two weeks ago after Bobby Michaels dropped by and made sure the pickings would be easy. There was nobody here but Maxwell's young male cousin from Germany. The gang terrorized him and made off with cash and drugs. When Maxwell returned later, he didn't have much trouble figuring out who had done the crime, or who had set it up. Maxwell kidnapped Bobby Michaels and convinced him to do to the Rainbow Drive people what he had helped them do to Maxwell. We're looking for Michaels now; we'll be going public with it in the next day or two. What we're doing tonight is the same thing the sheriff did last night. We'll be seizing drugs, but this time we'll be doing what the sheriff couldn't do, which is to arrest Maxwell's Japanese bodyguard, Kiku, who we think actually killed the people on Rainbow Drive. That's the whole story. Let's go.''

Mike walked a step behind Hammond. Some whole story. If they were serious about Kiku, they were simply floundering. Mike had heard a small squad of guys, and his experience and the sign-in register of the 9000 Building said that a little geek named Barranquilla had been one of them. Maxwell had been under investigation by a task force for a year and only now he was being taken into custody, not once but twice, for possession of drugs with intent to sell, which was not a schoolyard crime only because of the amounts of the drugs seized. The Rainbow Drive group was supposed to have been so stupid or drug-crazed to compound the damage done by not paying its bills with a petty break-in that wouldn't have passed muster as a script for "Miami Vice." No, "The A Team": it was *that* bad. Maybe they had done a break-in, but the motivation could not have been anywhere near so simple. Even morons like the victims would have known that thirty thousand dollars was nothing to a Bernie Maxwell, less than a week's take from his legitimate enterprises. If Daisy Nunn had owed him thirty grand, Maxwell would have cut off Nunn's supply, spread the word that she was a deadbeat. They would not have compounded their problem with a break-in unless compounding the problem had been part of someone else's secret agenda. Lansing and Freeman and the complex of lies told about them were the key. Daisy Nunn had been pushed toward Maxwell and then infiltrated by guys alleged to be working both ends of the street. Wheels within wheels. If Mike was going to unravel Dan's death and square that account, he was going to have to do it alone, without recourse to authority. There wasn't any authority. The whole game was being played on a field where there was no law; and power, which was always more potent than the law, had given way to savage violence. Cutting and slashing. In the dark. So be it. Whatever it took.

Hammond checked his service revolver and reholstered it. Behind him and out of sight, Mike did the same with the Magnum. This was a heavily wooded area, and now four plainclothesmen stepped out of the darkness. One of them had a walkie-talkie.

"Everybody set?" Hammond asked.

"Oh, yeah."

Hammond turned to Mike. "You'd better put your badge on your lapel now. This is supposed to be a clockwork operation, but the chief scared the piss out of everybody telling them how much he didn't want a fuckup." The others smiled, and Mike concealed his reaction by doing what Hammond said. Mike couldn't figure if Hammond was playing to the crowd or making an implied threat.

"I'm going to stick with you," Mike said. Hammond waved the others forward and headed toward the front of the house. Now he drew his gun again, and Mike did the same. From across the road came more plainclothesmen and some uniformed officers. Mike got closer to Hammond, just a little nervous about the way the picture was unfolding. He didn't really think he was being set up, not with Dan's body still in the funeral parlor in Valencia; but if an accident was going to happen, it was going to be an accident that involved Hammond taking a .357 in the liver.

As they stepped onto Maxwell's lawn, Mike heard muffled sounds from all around the house. This was steep country, and it wasn't going to be easy for people inside the house to escape out the back. The terrain behind the house was the worst wilderness in any city in the Western world. From the side of the house came a shout, the sound of breaking glass, and three sharp reports, the flat *pop! pop! pop*! of pistol fire. Everybody crouched, two guys to the right of the house went down on their bellies, and a shotgun boomed.

"Don't kill anybody!" Hammond yelled.

Now the front door opened and a young man in his underwear came sprinting out, straight at them. He put a fake on Hammond, windmilling his arms, his eyes wide with panic, as he hoped to get past the rest of them, but Mike put another move on him, stepped in and clubbed at his ear with the barrel of the Magnum. The guy's momentum continued to carry him forward while the blow propelled him sideways, and he went down, skidding on the bare skin of his elbows on the concrete of the walk. Mike winced as he pulled the guy to his feet. Others grabbed him. From the back of the house came three more pistol shots, more glass breaking, and the heavy explosions of shotguns firing. It was beginning to sound like a fucking war, Mike thought.

"Don't kill anybody, for Christ's sake!" Hammond screamed. "We want everybody alive!"

A plainclothesman went through the front door, with Hammond and Mike right behind. In the back of the house men were shouting that they gave up, while more glass shattered and what seemed like a dozen voices yelled "*Freeze!*"

Mike put his gun away again and allowed himself a deep breath. His hands were shaking and wet with sweat. Two uniformed officers hustled in the man in his underwear, his hands cuffed behind him. He was dirty, his deep abrasions beginning to bead with blood. The officers looked to Hammond for instructions.

"Hold him here while we get the others together," Hammond said. "There should be four of them. Come on," he said to Mike as he marched toward the back of the house.

The place was bigger inside and more luxurious than Mike had thought when he was out on the lawn. The floor in the foyer was marble, and the carpet in the living room seemed to be two inches thick. The furniture was European, ultramodern, overstuffed, fanciful in its soft shapes and vivid colors, red, blue, and yellow. The dining room off to the right looked like something out of a science fiction movie, furnished entirely in stainless steel, glass, and silver wallpaper. A plainclothesman stepped from a doorway to the rear.

"We have three of them."

"The fourth's by the front door," Hammond said almost gleefully. "Some place, eh?"

"Wait until you see the playroom."

"I don't want anybody taking any souvenirs," Hammond said. "All we need is this prick saying we ripped off the candlesticks."

"There's some coke on the table back there."

Hammond eyed him. "Get the cameras in. I want to get some pictures while Maxwell's still here."

They stepped into the playroom. What would have had a couple of sofas, a television set, and perhaps a pool table if the house had had a more conventional occupant was obviously supposed to be an orgy pit, the floor covered from wall to wall with a thick mattress upholstered in crushed red velour. Mike felt as though he were clomping around on the moon. The walls were red, and the pieces of furniture that weren't soft to the point of framelessness were devices that looked like gym equipment. A couple had leather bondage straps, but Mike couldn't figure out exactly how a person or persons made use of some of the other devices. A chairlike gadget in the center of the room seemed to be designed to facilitate butt fucking, and it revolved, like a Ferris wheel.

"Nobody talks to the press but Whatley downtown!" Hammond announced. "The papers start printing that we saw this crap here, this guy's lawyer is going to say his client can't get a fair trial."

Mike picked out Maxwell, but kept his eyes away from the gaunt, balding, smallish, well-tailored man. One of the others was Kiku, the huge Japanese bodyguard—he had to be six-five. He was sweating and gasping for air. The fourth Mike took for a coke dealer, a roly-poly little man in a blue suit, red sports shirt, neck chains, and a very precisely trimmed graying beard. Maxwell's eyes were darting from one face to another. He looked smug, as if he had powerful and wonderful secrets.

"Has anybody read these goons their rights?" Hammond asked. Somebody said yes.

"What are the charges?" Maxwell demanded.

"Possession of cocaine and other controlled substances with intent to sell. This is a real gotcha, Maxwell. We have lots of charges. You're cooked."

"And you're a fool."

The guy with the camera came in. This was Mike's chance. He stepped assertively toward Maxwell. "Did you know Dan Crawford?"

"Gallagher!" Hammond yelled.

Mike was watching Maxwell's eyes. Maxwell didn't even read the newspapers. Mike stepped back.

"Stay out of this," Hammond said. "You're here to observe." He turned to the cameraman while Mike continued to study Maxwell, whose attention was focused on Hammond again. Natural—not acting. Hammond said, "Stand them over there by the table and take a few pictures so that the dope is shown, then get them out of here."

"You have no idea what you're dealing with," Maxwell said.

"We're dealing with a dope dealer, Maxwell," Hammond said. "That's it, that's all."

The pictures were taken. Mike watched Hammond looking at the walls and ceiling. Out beyond a pair of sliding glass doors was a hot tub big enough for a Buick. Maxwell and the other two were shaken down, cuffed, and led out. Hammond waited a little longer before he spoke, his mouth twisting.

"Who was supposed to handle the bodyguard?"

After a pause, one big, fair-haired man raised his hand. "We fucked up."

"You were supposed to make that big bastard bleed!"

"I know, I know. We tried, but it just didn't work out."

"What *happened*?"

"He saw us outside and started shooting. We returned the fire. The information was right, he was scared shitless. A little too much so. When we came through the windows, he threw down his gun and covered up. The guy is all blubber. We pounded on him, but there was a limit, with the other two assholes witnessing it."

"We wanted a sample of his *blood*, for Christ's sake! Didn't anybody have the sense to pistol-whip him?"

"We were carrying shotguns," the detective said sheepishly. "If we'd clobbered him with a shotgun barrel, we'd have killed him. Heat of the moment. You said you didn't want anybody killed. He turned out to be such a girl that it scared us. We reacted without thinking."

"All right." Hammond was obviously controlling himself.

If they had wanted blood, Mike was thinking, it was to send to the lab for comparison with fingernail scrapings of the Laurel Canyon victims. They didn't have enough of a case to get court orders—they were floundering, all right. Hammond looked as if he were contemplating having to go through a session with Cutler, explaining what happened. Hammond blinked and drew his breath, and Mike almost smiled. "Let's get the job done," he said in a near whisper. "Let the fingerprint people do their thing *first*. We have a warrant that lets us take this place down to the concrete slab, if necessary. It should look like the Manson gang went through here. Start at the perimeters of the house and work in. Gallagher, stay close. You with the camera—you, too." He nodded to a couple of others and then waited again while the rest cleared the room.

"The chief wanted to be sure that you saw this, Gallagher," Hammond said, and gestured to the table on which the pile of cocaine looked like a miniature mountaintop. Two plainclothesmen got on either side, tested the table's weight—it was heavy—then lifted it aside. As the base moved, a round floor safe the size of a manhole cover was revealed. "The surveillance equipment available to us today is unbelievable," Hammond said as if to himself but really for Mike's benefit, Mike thought. He decided to play along.

"Do you have the combination?"

"Oh, sure," Hammond said. "Whenever they opened the thing, they made sure the drapes were closed—there's another street on the top of the hill across the canyon, about a mile away. We got the combination through sound amplification. *You* won't even hear the tumblers turning. Maxwell isn't supposed to know that we knew the location of the safe, much less had the combination. That's why we're trashing his house." Hammond smiled. "Crime doesn't pay."

Working from a slip of paper, one of the plainclothesmen spun the dial on the safe. He looked around at Hammond. "Ready."

"You won't need help opening it. According to the information, it's counterbalanced and ought to float up with the touch of a finger."

Mike leaned forward, acting amazed. He was supposed to
see what was inside? That was exactly what he was going to
do. The polished steel door swung upward, but slowly, like
a 747 lifting off a runway. The hole in the floor had the diameter of a garbage can. In the movies these things were
always neat. This looked like a kid's toy box, only the toys
were in plastic bags—white powder, white pills, green cash.
The cash was loose, in slathered heaps. And on one side, a
medium-sized paper bag, about five by eight by twelve, filled
with an object or objects that conformed almost exactly to
the dimensions of the bag. Black plastic. At the top of the
bag was a five-by-eight surface of black plastic. Mike assumed he wasn't supposed to touch anything. What the hell
in the bag could be as valuable as all the money and drugs?
Maybe it wasn't.

"Want to count it, Gallagher?"

Mike shook his head. "I'd make a mistake." The bills
were hundreds, *all* hundreds, and it looked as if there could
be thousands upon thousands of them. Seventy, eighty pounds
of big money.

"You can go home now, if you want. Charlie, would you
run Mike Gallagher down to Toluca Lake? Wait a minute,
I'll walk with you. Commander Whatley is waiting downtown to get this story out to the media. I don't want him
bellyaching that I kept him from making the late editions."

What did he know? What did he really know?

Mike was back in the apartment at four-thirty, exactly one
hundred thirty-five minutes after the evening's festivities had
begun. Not that it had been exactly, or completely, "Show-
time." Mike expected that everything he had seen and
heard—or more accurately, had been *told*—would become
part of the public record.

(One thing he did know now: Laura was a light sleeper
and one very sharp little cookie. She had heard him unlock-
ing the door, and had asked, "Who is it?" This was the
second time he had to come to a door she was on the other
side of, and the second time she had asked, *Who is it?* All

the other women he had ever put in that situation had said
his name in the form of a question. *Mike?* If it had ever been
anyone else, all that guy would have to do was grunt. Laura
always made him say his name in a voice she could recognize.)

She had gone back to sleep. Too much sex, she had said,
but more truthfully, she had put too much into the sex between them tonight. Mike had never known a woman who
enjoyed lovemaking so much, or so openly and freely. She
loved it all, a major leaguer. It had made him remember that
she had said she had gone a long time without sex before
meeting him, but his instincts as a man and a cop told him
that her behavior was not contradicting her words. Mike had
met a thousand different kinds of crazy women—men, too,
but humanity at large wasn't the issue here—but there was
only one kind of honest person, one kind of sincere expression. Mike was not trying to tell himself that he had not been
fooled before, or that he was not being fooled this time: only
that he did not think so. She was telling him to believe in
her, and he did.

But that did not mean he was not going to check her story
about the dog that the uniformed officer had given the little
girl outside the murder house. Mike was going to check and
double-check everything. He was going to go back to the
beginning—*his* beginning: the footsteps outside Gretchen's
window. He had seen the coroner's van arrive hours before
receiving the call from the *Herald-Examiner* guy. Bob Wills.
Hans Roehrig and Barranquilla had had a long meeting with
Bernie Maxwell on the Saturday night before the killings.
The guy Mike thought was Roehrig had been in the Clown
Club the following Friday. Roehrig knew Paula Rogers, and
Maurice Constantine had reported that Roehrig and Jackson
had talked about Jack Skelley jumping bail. Never mind that
Azzolini had vanished—they probably didn't know that. Larry
Hammond—and presumably, Tom Cutler—wanted Mike to
believe on the one hand that Maxwell had been the subject
of a task force investigation for a year, and on the other that
there had been no task force action until, *under its nose*,
Maxwell planned and carried out a massacre. Frank Kennedy

had said that the task force had run into heavy traffic. But nothing explained the delay in getting the survivor to the hospital, or Dan's death the following Friday, or Valerie Moreland's death at approximately the time of the massacre. It seemed clear to Mike that Dale Freeman was in police custody, and had been since the morning of the day following the killings. Freeman had told the radio-talk-show host the same story about the arrival of Lansing and him in Los Angeles as that given out by police investigators. In his own way, Hammond had repeated it tonight. Freeman was *cooperating*: he was afraid of—what? Death. He didn't want to be grass food.

For all of that, Mike really believed that Washington authorities wanted Maxwell. Federal agents and investigators had run into trouble securing cooperation from the same people who had swarmed all over Rainbow Drive the day of the murders. The "official" story about Freeman and Maxwell was refuted by the information on the tags on the dog. Kennedy's informant downtown was under the impression that something was being "cooked up" to take the Maxwell pressure off the locals. Lansing and Freeman? Mike was going to go through everything, all night, and then he was going to go through it again. Lansing. Freeman. Roehrig. Jackson. Azzolini. Barranquilla. And who the fuck was calling Mike at night. And Gretchen. Birnbaum. Dick Albert. Bobby Michaels. And all the dead.

Maurice Constantine arrived promptly at six and Laura peeked around the bedroom door at six-thirty. "Oh, yeah, I remember," she said sleepily. "I'd better get dressed and get out of here. I'll take my shower at home." She closed the door and Mike went into the bedroom after her, Constantine's clenched teeth making his laughter sound like something in a jungle movie. Mike closed the door behind him and stayed silent, watching her. There was nothing more beautiful than a naked woman in the bright light of morning. Watching Laura cover herself made Mike feel the kind of pang that accompanied watching a doe dance into the woods. Gone, as if it had never been. She stretched.

"Do you want to hear that I took a chance last night, that I'll be taking a chance tonight, or that you have to honeymoon in Acapulco?"

"San Francisco," Mike said. "Let me take you to San Francisco."

"I'm serious, Mike."

"So am I. You're a nice girl."

"That's good to hear, but—"

"But nothing." He extended his hand. She looked confused. "My gun," he said. "I want my gun back."

With a smile Laura went to the bed and turned over the pillow that was indented. The gun was pointed toward the headboard, as black and ugly on the sheet as a cockroach on a wedding cake. Apparently she didn't see having a gun under the pillow as a calamity, as he did, so he said nothing. As he bent over to slip the gun into his ankle holster, she put her arms around his neck. "Just think about it, okay? I don't want anything bad between us, and the one time I tried to take the pill I had trouble. It wouldn't work this month anyway."

He stood up. "Don't bullshit me. You want to get married and have kids."

"That's what I've been saying. But I think we owe it to ourselves to find out which way the toilet paper is supposed to go on the roller."

"Yeah. Okay." He was thinking of Azzolini's apartment, hoping the guy had never actually lived there. No, nobody was *that* bad.

When Mike was ready to leave, Constantine told him that he thought the telephone was clean but that he wouldn't be sure for another couple of hours. He had already built the television set that would receive the Donnie Jackson Television Network. Mike gave him the seven hundred dollars he had taken from Barranquilla. Constantine seemed pleased. Mike was thinking about Laura, who wanted to get married but didn't want to get pregnant now. Mike felt like a hooked fish. He could hear the reel turning. She had told him to think twice, whatever that meant. He wasn't going to think twice about stopping at a drugstore. It had been a long time since he had entertained the idea of having children, but not now—he wasn't going to think about it even once.

Rolling into Valencia, Mike was thinking about Gretchen. He was early for his meeting with Burgess and Don Grant; so early, in fact, that he had time to stop off and see Marge Crawford. He did not want to do that: it would accomplish nothing he could not do as well at the funeral, and would give them an unnecessary added opportunity to open their emotional floodgates. This was the day for both of them to take it easy. He wanted to talk to Gretchen not so much for what she could tell him about Birnbaum and Dick Albert, but to show his concern for her situation. He owed her that. How she had dealt with the police who had questioned her hadn't shut down her movie, but it was affecting how she was being treated in the aftermath. Birnbaum had his excuse. Mike made the call from an open half-booth outside Dan's old Burger King. Gretchen's phone was ringing when Mike suddenly realized that Dan had talked to him from *here*, out-of-doors. There had been times when Mike had walked to Riverside Drive in the rain. Dan had *stood* in it. Gretchen's voice was sleepy when she said hello. Mike had to clear his throat before he could talk. Marvin Burgess's car rolled into the lot and Mike waved.

"Hi, it's me," Mike said to Gretchen. "I wanted to see how you're doing."

"What time is it?" When Mike told her, she said, "I was out late at Spago last night. It was good of you to call, but ah, can we talk later?"

"Sure." What he felt wasn't supposed to make him smile, but he did it anyway. "Sure."

When Burgess stepped up, Mike was laughing quietly. "You look like a cop," Burgess said. "What's so funny?"

Marvin's tribute to Dan. "You look like a cop, too. What's funny is that I spent last night with a little schoolteacher I just met, and I'm bugged because the German movie producer I was seeing and wanted to go away spent last night with another guy. He's in bed with her right now. I could hear it in her voice."

"Serves you right," Burgess said. "I sent you home to *sleep.*"

"I'm glad you're early," Mike said. "You said you wanted a piece of this. Do you still feel that way?"

"I think I have a piece already. You said that Dan was with a friend. You'd just left him, Lopez was working, Bill Blair was playing cards with me. That left Greg Novak."

Mike's eyes narrowed.

"Relax," Burgess said. "He told me some time ago that he was taking a course at Valley College. Friday nights. He couldn't cut the class, he told me at the time, because Professor Popejoy made people sign a roll sheet. Popejoy is right—I remembered the name, so I called Popejoy and asked him to check last Friday night's roll. Greg's signature is on it."

"That's a relief," Mike said. "I'm glad it wasn't one of us. But I'm still on square one. That's not what I had in mind when I asked if you wanted in." He told Burgess the entire story Laura had told him about the dog, and that he wanted Burgess to check it out.

"Don't you trust her?" Burgess asked.

"I want to make sure of everything," Mike said. He couldn't tell his new partner that he intended to verify the story on Novak.

Ten minutes later, when they were sitting in a booth sipping coffee, a dark-suited man in his fifties, with thinning white hair, put two big meaty hands flat on the table. "You two birds are sitting at my table. I sit at this table every morning. Now get the fuck out of here before I call a cop."

"We *are* cops," Marvin Burgess said sternly.

"Don Grant," Mike said.

"Funny, that's my name, too." Don Grant offered his hand. He was wearing his small, gold-plated 187 pin on the buttonhole of his lapel. "Which one of you is the Irishman?"

Mike moved over to give him room and introduced him to Burgess. He told Burgess how Dan had loved the Christmas card with the handcuffs. *Ho-ho-ho.* Burgess nodded, finally smiled, and extended his hand. Mike put his hand over the other two. He started to cry, and thought of Dan standing in the rain to talk to him on the telephone.

"Dan said you were a good cop," Grant said.

"He *is* a good cop," Burgess said.

"And he's my partner," Mike said, gesturing to Burgess.

"I want to do whatever I can to help," Grant said. He was an old country boy. Mike remembered that he had punched Paula Rogers in the stomach. Grant said, "Mrs. Crawford, Marge, is a great lady, and she and my Susan just loved seeing each other. Susan told me that Marge was very proud of their children and that they were looking forward to retirement. Susan cried about this. She wanted to come today, but she's a teacher."

"My wife will be here later," Burgess said. "She cried, too. She's going to be crying again, I know."

"I'm divorced," Mike said, to change the mood: it was developing all the insanity of a wake, not a funeral.

Don Grant smiled. "Dan told me you fucked everything that moves." Burgess laughed. "One night he and Marge were over for dinner and we were talking about The Animal here, as my wife calls him, and Dan was a little oiled and said that, and my wife said, 'Oh, no! Everything that *really* moves!' The women couldn't breathe right for ten minutes."

"I'm paying for breakfast," Mike said. "If you want to keep this up, you'll eat here."

Don Grant eased out of the booth. "You're not only paying, you're driving."

In the car Grant wanted to get down to business. Even at this early stage, Mike said, he couldn't tell them everything he knew. He had to have their trust. No one was going to be drawn into an indefensible position, he promised. Grant said he was comfortable with that.

"Let's get on with it," Burgess said. "There's Denny's. Good enough."

Mike waited until they had ordered. He wanted to work backward, starting with Hammond's raid on Bernie Maxwell last night. Almost immediately Grant interrupted him.

"After you called the other day, I got out the file on Paula

Rogers.'' He had to tell Marvin Burgess the story of the girl overdosing at the Palm Springs motel. ''Rogers made a couple of calls to L.A. One of them was to Bernie Maxwell. She said she was connected. I didn't recognize the name. She's due in court this Friday.''

''Don't be surprised if she's a no-show,'' Mike said. ''Her friend Jennie was trying to reach her by telephone all day yesterday.''

Burgess chuckled. ''You've been busy.''

''I'm very busy,'' Mike said.

''That Jennie might be Jennie Wagner,'' Grant said. ''The woman who registered at the motel where the girl OD'd signed herself as Paula Wagner.''

''That's an asshole's trick,'' Burgess said.

Mike stopped the story of raid-and-counterraid that Hammond had told him when the waitress brought their orders. After she was gone, Grant spoke again. ''I might have known this Billy Lansing from years ago. The name seemed familiar when I saw it in the papers last week, but I didn't give it any thought. Of course, when you called about Dan, I didn't connect anything because you didn't give me anything to connect to. The fella I'm thinking of ran with a big country boy. Lansing, if that's who he was, was a real problem. He pulled a gun on one of our people. If I remember the story right, our man had to jump out a window to keep from getting shot. We thought we were making a dope buy; it turned out to be a rip.''

''The disposition of that case might be helpful,'' Mike said. ''There's circumstantial evidence suggesting strongly that Lansing and his partner, Dale Freeman, were working both sides of the street.'' Mike told him of the killing of a witness against Lansing by a state cop in San Diego County.

''Same fella?'' Grant asked. ''I can find out about that for you. I have good connections in San Diego.''

''Without tipping our hand,'' Mike said. ''As for Freeman, Hammond gave the game away. Freeman's in custody, and Hammond said that they were concentrating their efforts in the El Centro area. Freeman was active there, but the way Hammond spoke makes me think that they're actually hiding

Freeman down there. If LAPD is operating a safe house in that area, I don't know of it."

"Riverside and Palm Springs both have access to a place near El Centro," Grant said, "and to the best of my knowledge, San Diego city and county have use of it, too. Jacumba."

"Is that a place?" Burgess asked.

"Only hardly," Grant said. "It's a wide spot in the road on this side of the border halfway between San Diego and El Centro. You fart there, the whole town smells it. But there's an old hotel that some retired cops have put money into, and those guys have tried to help them out when they could. It's perfect."

"Do you know the people involved?"

"No, but I know people who do."

Mike said, "Hammond told me that they're looking for Bobby Michaels as the fingerman in the murders."

The other two laughed aloud.

"He's a hopeless drug addict," Burgess said.

Mike turned to Don Grant. "How do you know Bobby Michaels?"

Grant's old country boy eyes glowed with mirth. "In this company, maybe I shouldn't say it. Oh, what the hell. Down in the Springs years ago, Michaels used to be known as a guy who'd fuck anything that moves."

Burgess was helpless. He pointed his finger at Grant. "I *like* you! I wasn't sure at first, but I *like* you!"

Mike was thinking that Dan would have loved the crack.

15

MARIE BURGESS HAD ALREADY ARRIVED AT THE CRAWfords' by the time Mike and the other men rolled up. The house was crowded with neighbors, and friends of the children, Marge's mother, Dan's cousin from Modesto, Captain Ruppert, Bill Blair and his wife, Darlene, Juan and Linda Lopez. In his mounting dread of the coming hours Mike completely forgot the presence of the others besides Marge and the Crawford children. He wanted to talk to Marge before making some calls, and Billy Crawford wanted in on the conversation. Marge saw Mike tighten up.

"Billy, please."

"Mom, I want to know what's going on!"

"Billy, please don't make this day more difficult than it's going to be!"

Mike extended his left hand, bandaged, palm up. "If I told you about this hand, Bill, would you be able to guarantee that nobody else would ever hear about it?"

267

Billy stared at Mike, sheepish, stricken.

"You see, your mother doesn't need to know, and she knows it. The rest of our conversation either isn't your business as your mother defines it, or isn't going to help you a bit, believe me."

Billy nodded and backed out. Marge closed the door. Mike said, "I'm on to something." He flashed the hand again. "Something was almost onto me. But thanks to that, I haven't spent any of your money yet."

"I don't want you hurt."

"Too late. Some of this is in the newspapers. The guy busted last night is supposed to be at the bottom of the Laurel Canyon murders. I was there. The way he reacted to me was zero. I was just another bull." Mike waggled his hand. "So he didn't order this—or rather, what it was supposed to be. It came from some-place else. If it was supposed to happen before Dan's death, it would have. I wasn't being careful. But the little geek who did this to me did it because somebody's gotten afraid of me since Dan's death. And I think the little geek is the guy who killed all those people on Rainbow Drive. Not to worry about him any-more, obviously. But he didn't kill Dan. To quote Tom Cutler, how do you kill a guy in his car without touching him *or* the car? The little geek wasn't that kind of sophisticated. But I'm still at square one about Dan—I need all the help I can get. Carry a notebook. If you remember anything—anything at all—write it down. I'll be out of town for a couple of days. I hope I can start tomorrow. When I get back, we'll talk."

"There's something you're not telling me."

"Somebody set Dan up. That's why he stayed in town so long."

Marge's lips trembled. "You knew this the other day when I gave you the money."

"I wanted to check some things."

"You mean people."

"All right, people. And now I'm double-checking. So far, so good, Marge, I swear to you."

"You'll tell me the truth," she said.

"Absolutely."

"I don't want you to get in trouble, Mike!" she cried.

Dan's troubles are over. He almost said it aloud, but no one knew it better than Marge. "Do you want to listen to these calls? It will give you a better idea—"

She shook her head. "I'm sorry I started this."

"You didn't start this."

"I don't care, I'm still sorry."

She went out, pulling the door shut behind her. Mike called Frank Kennedy.

"I've been trying to reach you," Kennedy said. "I have information about Dick Albert."

"That's exactly what I was going to ask you to get," Mike said.

"Albert blew town. Yesterday. I guess he was given advance word that his friend Bobby Michaels was going to be arrested for murder."

"Have they done that yet?"

"No, and I figure that if Dick Albert heard in advance, so did Michaels. The radio says there's a warrant out for Michaels' arrest."

"Do you have any information about Albert's whereabouts?" Mike asked.

"Oh, sure," Kennedy said. "I told you, I work for the supermarket tabloids. A guy at Burbank Airport told me that Albert flew out of there in a private jet at four o'clock yesterday afternoon. The flight plan filed said that the destination was Mazatlán, but that doesn't mean anything. It could have rerouted anywhere. The important thing is that the plane got where it was headed, or we'd know it was down. People would be looking for the plane. My guess is that Albert went to a place where there are no telephones. People are going to remember his connection to Michaels, and right now Albert doesn't want to *know*. I could go around to his house and see if I can find out where he went, if you want—"

"Don't bother," Mike said. "What I'd rather know is how he got word, although I have a suspicion. I think it came through Norman Birnbaum. The producer of the movie that was shut down was out celebrating last night. Somebody wants everybody happy."

"It seems as if they are," Kennedy said. "I'll ask. How is Constantine working out for you?"

"First rate. He really loves his toys."

"Tell him that I said that if he was bugging the end of the world, he'd be worried about getting it down on tape."

Mike said good-bye and called Constantine.

"Your telephone is clean as of this morning, Mr. Gallagher," Constantine mumbled. "I'm at the location now, and there's a new development. The infrared from the tenth floor of the 9000 Building has been turned off. The transmission from the bungalow is television, all right. The camera is in a grate high in the wall in the bedroom opposite the bed. I can see that and the closet door—I think it's the closet, but it has two Yale locks on it like a front door. The picture is in black and white and pretty furry, but I can see everything."

Swell, Mike thought. "Are you taping it?"

"They're asleep right now, even though their television set is on. I just heard a woman win a freezer. These people are something, Mr. Gallagher. The drugs are right there on a tray on the bed, while they're sleeping."

And somebody had arranged to watch this. "I'll get back to you later," Mike said. "I'm very interested in who calls them today."

"Well, the phone has been ringing, but the answering machine is on with the volume off, so I'm not hearing anything."

"The ringing telephone doesn't wake them," Mike said.

"I don't think they're going to come around until one or two this afternoon, Mr. Gallagher," Constantine said. "When the phone rings, they don't even flinch. I'd guess they were partying until only a little while ago."

"Some people are going to a funeral." Mike could hear his own bitterness.

"I'd like to get some breakfast, Mr. Gallagher."

"How are you going to eat?"

"Shit, I forgot."

Mike wanted to laugh, and decided not to tell Constantine what Kennedy had said. He liked Constantine. Constantine was just easy to pick on, and Mike wasn't comfortable doing that to people who didn't know how to defend themselves. "Take the time off to find some place that will throw a bowl of soup in a blender for you. We'll talk later."

When he stepped out of the bedroom, Mike could see that
some people had already left the house for the funeral parlor.
Mike could feel himself entering a mood, a distance, with-
drawal—he had known it was going to happen to him, and had
held it off, he had thought, as long as possible. He *hated* it.
Marge was going to make the ride with the kids. Don Grant had
left his car at the Burger King. In Mike's car Grant tried to ease
the tension by saying he would get the information he had promised as quickly as possible, but Mike didn't answer. He didn't
know what was on his mind. He hadn't been able to attend his
mother's funeral—Judy's letters telling of his mother's death had
arrived in Vietnam weeks after the fact. The plaque in the turf
at Forest Lawn said his mother was buried next to his father. So
did some papers Mike had in a box in the back of the bottom of
his bedroom closet. Those were the papers Judy had saved for
his return from Nam. The world was filled with closets containing boxes containing papers waiting for their owners' survivors
to throw out. The woman manager at Azzolini's apartment
building made Mike think of his mother. Gin and cigarettes.
Azzolini the cop. *Burn him*, he had said about the man who had
killed Dan. Now Mike wondered how much or little or even
how tauntingly Azzolini had meant it. LAPD had used infrared
on Maxwell's house—Hammond had said as much. Now the
infrared on the tenth floor of the 9000 Building was shut down.
Mike guessed it was permanent. To turn off the television transmitter in Jackson's place, someone would have to enter the
premises. Mike was guessing there, too—the transmitter could
have remote control. There had been no announcement of a raid
on the Skelley-Maxwell offices on the ninth floor, but that didn't
mean a raid hadn't taken place. It had been Maxwell who had
moved Jackson from Hollywood to the Norma Place bungalow.
Maxwell would have been able to install the television equipment before Jackson's arrival. So he had wanted to watch Jackson. It was one way to be safe. According to what Constantine
had heard yesterday, Roehrig had thought Maxwell was too well-
connected to be vulnerable to the police. Mike wondered what
Roehrig thought this morning. Maxwell had bragged about his
power. Who had that kind of power? Even Tom Cutler answered
to others—*jumped* when their interests were affected. Mike still

had to go through the papers from Dan's desk. Why had his Rolodex been turned to Moe Bunn? A television repairman, not incidentally. But if Dan had known something about the television equipment in the Jackson bungalow, he would have said something to Mike in the Clown Club—on the last night of his life.

The funeral parlor was jammed, and just as well: the room might get warm enough for the Episcopal priest Marge had hired to keep the ceremony brief. Marge had gone through the motions of asking Mike if he wanted to deliver a eulogy. She had sounded so negative in her asking that Mike hadn't bothered to explain why he didn't want to do it. This was Mike's first sight of Dan's coffin, which was covered with a blanket of white roses. There were a lot of flowers. They filled the front of the room. Now Mike wanted to go through the guest book. Twenty-six signatures per page, with eight of them filled. Other people waited their turns to sign as he ran his eyes down the names, thinking that his father's book had been thrown out with his papers, the only papers of Mike's life that shouldn't have been thrown out. Mike wanted to focus on the signatures. Tom Cutler. Other cops. People Mike had met when the Crawfords had been living off Tampa Avenue in the Valley. Ruppert. From Monday night, Lopez, Blair, Burgess—and Mike Gallagher. More cops. Judy Gallagher, in the section bearing today's date, meaning Mike's ex-wife was somewhere in the room. He struggled to focus. Valencia neighbors. A deputy mayor and a couple of guys from the DA's office. Still more cops, and Ira Rosenberg, MD, the only person to have put his title or rank. In a crazy way it was Ira's attempt to show respect.

Turning around, Mike saw Ira before he found Judy. She was looking straight ahead. She was becoming jowly. Mike remembered Dan's comment on aging: "I've got more chins than a Chinese phone book." Some people were afraid of death, some of illness, some of aging, but Dan laughed at it all. Now Ira saw Mike and raised his hand in a timid salute. There were no seats near him. Ira pointed toward the front of the room. There was an empty chair next to Marge. Now she looked around, and beckoned to Mike.

When he sat down, she whispered, "I was upset before."

"I know."

"I think you'll find the answer to this."

"I know I will," he answered.

The priest appeared, paused, and invoked the Trinity.

Marge needed assistance getting out of there. Mike knew he was in a daze, thinking that he was getting to ride in a limo again. The last time had been with Dan—and Marge, and Judy. Vegas. Perhaps the best weekend the four of them had had together. An hour off the plane, Marge hit a dollar slot for five thousand dollars. The other three got five hundred apiece and Marge put three thou in the hotel safe. After Buddy Hackett's late show they chased around a casino until they were ready to drop. Judy won money, Mike remembered. Now as he looked around for her, she was not to be seen. She had gotten out in a hurry. Ira Rosenberg made his way through the crowd. "I have some tranquilizers, Mike, if anyone needs one.

Marge looked confused. Mike had to introduce them. She nodded. "Thank you for coming."

"I considered him my friend. He was always very kind to me. It's a terrible loss."

They were in the limo with the kids when Marge turned to Mike. "Dr. Rosenberg?"

"From the coroner's office."

"He's the one you called—?" She looked out the window after Ira. "What an awful life to choose."

Mike thought of Constantine looking at a furry picture of degenerates sleeping off an orgy. "It all fits together."

"That's what's terrifying."

Mike hadn't been told where Marge had chosen to bury Dan, but the location became clear quickly enough as the procession led by the hearse got on the southbound side of the I-5 to head through the same canyon country where Dan had lost his life. There were several cemeteries on the south side of the hill, overlooking the San Fernando Valley. At the southern end of the Valley, if the air wasn't smogged over, they would be able to see the eastern end of the Santa Monica Mountains, from Tarzana past Encino and Sherman Oaks and Studio City to Forest Lawn where Mike's parents were buried. Maybe that place would be twenty miles from Dan's location. Mike closed his eyes. *I don't need this, Ira,* he had said a few days ago. He knew where he had said it, in Valerie Moreland's apartment. He knew what he had been thinking, what he had thought on an earlier visit, in the presence of a body odor that would have made a pig kill itself. What Mike was realizing made him almost bolt out of the leather seat. Marge noticed, but she could wait, he hoped. Why did the mind work in such bizarre, inappropriate, *perverse* twists and turns? You never knew when God was going to hit you in the face with a pie.

"What is it?" Marge asked.

He didn't even feel *grief* anymore. "Azzolini didn't know why Valerie Moreland had stopped going to the Clown Club, or he wouldn't have told me as much about her as he did."

"You're just like him," Marge said, starting to weep, and Mike joined her as he struggled to hold himself together, thinking of what he had to do, what he had to retain in his memory, that he was flirting with a nervous breakdown or worse, a long vacation at Restful Ranch. He was going to stop in the office before going downtown; he was going to call Laura and then see if Dan *had* called Moe Bunn. He had to talk to Grant again, too. Dale Freeman! *Dale Fucking Freeman!*

The plot was on a hillside and the air was clear. Somebody from the funeral parlor gave each member of the immediate family a single longstemmed rose. Mike could remember himself at his father's funeral, not being able to pay attention, gazing off in this direction. Forest Lawn was down to the southeast. The Valley was dotted with high-rises now, and if Mike could find one he recognized, he could work his way to where his parents were. Dan had hated what was happening to the city. Money—it was all money. Nothing else ever mattered. According to Larry Hammond, the Laurel Canyon murders had been committed over the loss of thirty thousand dollars and the take from a burglary. Mike had seen over a million dollars in that safe last night. Maxwell had had power: now he didn't. Given the footsteps Mike had heard, the murderers had probably met at Roehrig's house on Rainbow Drive, but it had been Donnie Jackson whom Maxwell had elected to watch. Jack Skelley had been as insulated from the murders as it was possible to get, yet he had tried to run for it. What did *that* mean? Mike had to zero in on Hollister. Hollister had only to start to fuck around, and Mike would squeeze him like a car in a crushing machine.

The priest started again and Mike realized that he was drifting. Even with his hand still bandaged, a long way from healed, he thought so little of how he had sustained the wound that he had to remind himself that he had killed a man by smashing his skull. It had happened in the line of duty as Mike had seen it. No one would argue with that, he knew; but he knew, too, that he had left himself vulnerable when he had hidden the body so he could go on being a cop. If he had reported the killing of Barranquilla, Cutler would have his badge and the rest of his cop's tools, even if only temporarily—Mike could have gotten them back, in court, if necessary—but if ever there was a case that was going to evaporate with the passage of time, this was it. Mike had to be on this now, not later. . . .

Good-bye, Dan.

He could not allow his emotions to go further. He looked up and around at the crowd—a *crowd*, not a group, over a hundred people—until his eyes fell on a woman staring intently at him. Judy: for a moment he hadn't recognized her. And whatever she was thinking so absorbed her that she didn't see that he had caught her staring. Why? He looked away, disturbed. What was on her mind? Had she heard he was seeing Laura, who had been warned against him? A lot of cops here, a lot of cops' wives. A lot of *people*. The priest was winding down. There would be no interment now; that would occur after the crowd had gone. The coffin rested on a carpet of Astroturf, garnished with flowers from the wreaths that had lined the wall on both sides of the coffin when it had been in the funeral parlor. The priest closed his book and nodded to Marge.

After a moment, Marge stepped to the coffin and put her rose on it. She was followed by the girls, and then Billy, whose face was contorted in anguish. Mike wanted to put his arm around the boy, hesitated, and the moment was lost: his older sister had him. For some reason Mike wanted to know if Judy had seen. She looked away from him quickly, as if she would deny she had been staring. *Again*, staring. Something was on her mind. Mike turned to Marge.

"Does he have his badge?"

"Yes. I brought it down the first night, and they put it in with him. I asked Billy, and that's what he wanted, too. Oh, Mike, there were so many nights when I was afraid. I stopped—gave it up. I thought we were out the back door, I really did."

Mike nodded. "He told me all of that."

"He knew you loved him. He loved you, too."

"I know." Other people wanted to see her. Over their heads, Mike glimpsed Judy hurrying away.

"Are you coming back to the house?"

He shook his head no. "I have to testify this afternoon."

"It's merciless!"

That seemed too ironic for Mike to comment on. Ira Rosenberg had heard. He stepped closer to Mike as Mike moved away from Marge. "My first Christian funeral," Rosenberg said. "It's pretty much the same as Reform."

"The Orthodox have the right idea," Mike said as Don Grant joined them. "Everybody takes a turn with the shovels."

Grant's eyebrows went up. "I know I missed something, not living in the big city. What's that, Orthodox Jewish? It sure makes a lot of sense."

Mike introduced him to Rosenberg.

"Cut anybody good lately?"

It was a thing cops said to pathologists. "Our friend," Mike said. "*His* friend. I asked him to."

"That took guts," Grant said. "I put my foot in it. I'm sorry."

"It's all right," Rosenberg said. They started up the hill, quiet in the effort of the climb. The other guys from Hollywood Homicide were waiting on the road, so Mike spoke quickly, softly, to Grant about his need to find Dale Freeman. Rosenberg, sensing the confidentiality of the conversation, fell behind. Grant said he would push every button, turn every dial.

"Then I'll scream," Grant said.

"You got it," Mike said. They were up on the road, joining the others. A Niles Eberhart and Son hearse rolled by and somebody behind Mike said something about having come full circle, and Mike thought yes, more than you know, and answered Bill Blair's question about the Crawfords' finances. Lopez said that he hadn't known Episcopal was so Catholic.

"It's more Catholic than the Catholic these days," Lopez said.

"Come on," Mike said to Grant, "I'll take you back to your car."

He wanted to do some business at Hollywood Division before heading downtown, but before that he had to stop at his apartment for something he needed: a briefcase. He called Laura at her school. It took two women in the office to figure out that she was on yard duty and would have to call him back. He gave his name and the number at his desk on Wilcox. "She'll be able to reach me there in half an hour, and then for an hour more." They seemed as smugly dumb as the school administrators of his childhood, living proof that post office officials and the women of the Department of Motor Vehicles met secretly, bred, and raised young. They had wasted another ten minutes of his life.

On impulse he called Constantine. Less than three hours had passed since their last conversation, but Mike was getting antsy. He had better things to do than sit in a courtroom all afternoon waiting to give twenty minutes' testimony.

"I was about to call your answering machine, Mr. Gallagher. Paula Rogers just called her friend Jennie. Rogers spent all day yesterday with Bobby Michaels. She says he took the bus down to San Ysidro, where he walked across the border to T.J."

Tijuana. "That's terrific," Mike said. "You're doing a wonderful job. I'm very interested in that guy Hollister. If he calls Jackson, make sure it gets on my machine right away."

"I understand," Constantine said. "There's another side to the Rogers-Jennie thing. His nibs, Jackson, was in the bathroom when the two women were talking. Physically, this guy is a wreck. Anyway, he wanted Jennie to tell him everything that Rogers told her. He pushed her up against the wall and held her by the throat until she passed out, or faked it. I was getting scared. What should I do if it gets bad, Mr. Gallagher?"

"Call the cops. Say you're a neighbor. You can't use 911 for that. It will kick out your real telephone number."

Constantine giggled. "Mr. Gallagher, I wrote the original paper that said what equipment and alterations were necessary to do that job."

"You're a real prick, Constantine. People don't call the cops because of that feature. Did she tell Jackson what Rogers said?"

"No, she lied. He didn't believe her, but she stuck to her story. They're both poison. She's got some pair of tits, Mr. Gallagher."

Mike laughed. "Your jaw is wired shut, Constantine." He disconnected and dialed Kennedy. Kennedy was out, but he had an answering machine. "Mike Gallagher, Frank. I'm going to take that offer you made to find the real destination of the plane. Maybe the guy has some kind of a hideaway. His old friend might be trying to get there the hard way."

From the Department of Life Goes On: the day was turning into a sparkler. Driving up Barham Boulevard toward Cahuenga Pass, Mike remembered that the area used to be called Dark Canyon, and was the location for many of the Westerns of the thirties. Where there were now apartments and condos, the Range Busters and Crash Corrigan used to ride. It had been a Western that had drawn Mike into his brief, fitful movie career. The gay makeup man had said that Mike's face was "weathering beautifully." Mike had been cast as one of the hero's lesser gunslinger pals, but the star hadn't wanted to be seen in the same frame with someone so much bigger, younger, better built, and more interesting to look at. Mike had been the first good guy to die, shot in the chest and falling out of his chair nine times before all the equipment was working properly, his killer spoke his line as written, and the director was satisfied. Perhaps the mind-numbing fakery of moviemaking was the best symbol of the city the movies had made famous, because one rolled out of the greenery and expanding view of Cahuenga Pass past the Hollywood Bowl down through the unswept, crud-strewn slum streets of Hollyweird: the closer you got and the better you knew it, the less you wanted to know and the more you wanted to run as far as possible. Still, the air today was unusually crystalline, and a nice day could put a smile on the face of anyone—almost: anyone but the dead.

Even without a smile, Mike felt propelled forward. Before he went downtown, he wanted to put in for vacation time for the rest of the week. He had it coming and under the circumstances, Ruppert couldn't object. Late this afternoon or this evening, Mike wanted to run down Hollister. Tomorrow Mike would drive down to San Diego, Chula Vista, and National City. And maybe Jacumba. Mike was thinking about what Dale Freeman had said on the radio about Marylou Brown. Like a song, he had said. Mike wanted Freeman to set it to music.

Greg Novak was telling Mike about a db—a ballbuster, a teenager with her throat slit, in Griffith Park—when Laura called.

"You rang, sire?"

"I sure did," Mike said. "I want to talk to you about those wonderful, filthy things we're doing together."

"No, you don't," she said. "You want me to do something for you and you can t talk now."

He smiled for Novak's benefit. "You're not supposed to be that smart."

"Bullshit," she said. "You knock me out, Gallagher. You talk as if you don't have a brain of your own, but then you're insulted when somebody else does something smart."

"Smarter than me, you mean," he said. Novak indicated that he was going to the filing cabinet. Mike waited. "Look, this isn't the situation here for me to talk about what I want. Can I see you around dinnertime? You get a chance to play cop again."

"Now I know you care for me," Laura said. "Something else. My student told me that detectives came around to her house looking for the dog. When the aunt balked, they told her it was for the woman in the hospital."

"When was this?"

She laughed at him. "How interested you are! Last night. It happened last night."

The woman in the hospital was getting better enough to talk—and listen. If the police in charge of the case didn't need her later, they wouldn't be chasing after the damned dog now. There was the record at the veterinarian's establishing that the dog was here last winter, she was here, and Billy Lansing was here. Rainbow Drive was part of a police operation that went haywire and she probably knew it. Or at least, believed it. The police needed her, all right. She wasn't in custody. The police had to say please.

"Well?" Laura asked.

"Well, what?"

"Are you going to tell me what it *means*?"

He'd thought she wanted a thank you—which she deserved. "Thank you."

Laura said, "You're going to play cop on me now, huh? *And* you want me to play cop *for* you later! Some nerve. You know an awful lot registers on the brain even when a person's unconscious."

"Don't get spooky on me," he said. Novak looked as if he didn't know if he was allowed to return to his desk. Mike motioned to him to sit down.

"Where do you want to meet?"

"Shadyglade," Mike said. "I have to get off now."

"One more question," Laura said. "Do you want to feel humiliated and abused?"

"Not particularly."

"Too bad," she said, and slammed down the receiver. He laughed aloud.

Mike scooped Dan's papers out of his desk and stuffed them into his briefcase. Maybe he had to hang around a courthouse all afternoon, but he was going to try to make good use of the time. He called Ben Hollister, who was at lunch. Mike left a message, and then called Moe Bunn.

"Mike, you could have knocked me over with a feather," Moe Bunn said. "I hadn't talked to Dan in over a year, and then there it was in Saturday's paper. One of the best guys in the world. He wasn't drunk, was he?"

"No, he was okay."

"Why are you calling me?"

"Just closing up loose ends, Moe, that's all. We'll be talking."

"Anytime, Mike. I'm sorry about your loss."

Mike stood up. "Greg, tell Marvin that I'll probably be calling him at home this evening."

"Okay, Mike. You're gone for the day?"

"For the week, I hope."

"You've got it coming."

Ruppert's door was closed. Mike knocked.

"Not now!" Ruppert called.

"It's Mike Gallagher, Captain. It's important."

"Come on."

Mike entered. Ruppert had the lights off so that the windowless room was nighttime dark. He was lying on the couch, his jacket off. "Are you all right?" Mike asked.

"No, I'm not. I just got a call from that Bob Wills of the *Herald-Examiner*. He wanted to know if I had any comment on Cutler's investigation of alleged improprieties in Hollywood Division."

"What investigation?"

"That's what I asked Wills. After I heard his answer, I called Cutler's office. Cutler wasn't available to speak to me, but wants me in his office tomorrow afternoon at two o'clock."

"What did Wills tell you?"

"Wills said that his sources have told him that there's going to be a major shake-up in Hollywood Division because of officers sleeping in their cars when they're supposed to be on duty, officers shaking down traffic violators, officers taking samples from the street girls. And boys. What Wills was looking for was verification. I think he's going to get it from downtown. I heard that in the tone of Cutler's man when he told me what time I was due for my audience. Now what did you want?"

Mike drew a breath. "I'm taking tomorrow and Friday off. Vacation days. I could use them."

Ruppert sat up. "You must be crazy. Didn't you hear what I just said? Cutler is looking for blood, and if he gets the idea that you're out lah-di-dahing it somewhere—"

"That's all he'd have on me, vacation days after my partner's funeral. Now, do you think there's any truth to this stuff that Wills wants to print, but can't yet?"

"No more than usual. Cutler's trying to get the heat off the Laurel Canyon mess."

"I don't know what to tell you," Mike said, and started out.

"Don't you make trouble for me!" Ruppert raged suddenly. "I'm going to take my retirement with full honors! I could have done it years ago! I should have got better than I got from this department! If you fuck me up now, Gallagher, I'm warning you, it's you who will never recover from it!"

"You're just feeling sorry for yourself," Mike said, and closed the door behind him.

Mike didn't get to look over Dan's papers until almost three-thirty. Sitting up to a scarred mahogany table in a gloomy conference room, Mike arranged the papers in a pile and used his briefcase as a trash basket. What Mike recognized and understood went into the briefcase. What he didn't know, what looked substantive, went into another pile. That was the plan. After twenty minutes, every paper Mike had looked at was in the briefcase. There was nothing he had not already seen or heard about, nothing he could not tell Marge. With Dan Crawford, what you saw was what there was. An honest man. The last items were Dan's spiral notebooks, six of them, perhaps half a year's worth. A detective carried a little notebook because it was impossible to remember exactly what people said. Your notes were an accepted part of the chain of evidence. Mike would be referring to his notes when he testified as to what he knew in the husband-stabbing trial in the courtroom across the hall. Some of Dan's writing triggered instant recognition in Mike, and when he came across a passage he couldn't remember, he paged back and forth until it made sense. No surprises, just concentration fitting together the sequence of events. Heart attack. Overdose. Shootings in gas stations and 7-Elevens, one by a storekeeper who had shotgunned at least three stickup guys by waiting until they arrived at the door on their way out, then blasting away while they were distracted reaching for the door-knob. This was how Dan Crawford had spent his working life.

After the last page of the third notebook was a card from Dan's Rolodex, facedown. Mike turned it over.

Brandon, Randall. And two telephone numbers.

Randall Brandon. Mike knew the name, but didn't know why. And why was the card facedown in one of Dan's old notebooks?

Br. The next card on the Rolodex could have been Bu. Moe Bunn. Dan had taken the card out of the Rolodex sometime before his death—and someone had come looking for it sometime after. Greg Novak had found the Rolodex turned to Moe Bunn. Mike remembered that it had been turned to another name when he had left the office last Friday night. Somebody had been sniffing around Dan's desk for this Rolodex card sometime between early Friday evening and early Saturday morning. Somebody who knew or thought Dan was dead. And Dan had thought the card important enough to keep, to move into his desk under lock and key—when? The last entry in the notebook was dated January 27. Dan wouldn't have put the card in an active notebook, where it could have been found. Dan had put the card in the notebook sometime in the last three and a half months. What had made him do it? Mike could not remember Dan saying or doing anything in the last three-plus months that suggested that he was under pressure or feeling fear. Now Randall Brandon clicked, or rather Brandon: The Brandon Museum of Contemporary Art. There was a Brandon Hall at one of the colleges. Another door opened: *Mrs.* Randall Brandon often appeared in those pictures on the society pages of the newspapers. Three dames over forty and the mayor. Five dames over fifty and Cary Grant. Receptions. Charity dinners. Debutantes' balls. Mrs. Brandon was usually in there somewhere, on committees, receiving honors, giving checks. Dan had never mentioned the Brandon family, but Mike thought he knew how Dan was connected to them. If what else Mike was thinking was true, why had Dan moved the card?

The bailiff stuck his head in the room and told Mike it was time. Mike closed the rest of the stuff in the briefcase and lugged it across the hall with him, and then spent the next half hour doing his damnedest trying to get a sobbing old woman sent to prison for the rest of her life. There had been too much blood in the apartment for her to have done anything but chase her husband from room to room with the carving knife Mike and Dan had found washed, but not clean, of hubby's blood, in the kitchen drawer. The murderess and her victim had driven each other crazy for decades, and when he had tried to opt for a few last years of sanity, she had killed him. She had told Mike and Dan that she was stubborn and not easy to live with. "That's my nature," she had said. "He knew that when he married me." When was that, Dan had asked. "Nineteen fifty," she had said firmly. "I told him then, but he didn't believe me. He kept picking, picking, picking. Now what am I going to do? How am I going to support myself at my age?"

The DA didn't ask Mike the right questions, and the defense attorney made no mistakes of his own. Mike was heading up the aisle for the door at four-thirty, briefcase in hand.

He went straight to the telephone booths next to the elevators. He wanted a phone book—any phone book. *Local, nearby areas, and rates, p. A 18.* Mike kept turning pages, looking for the exchanges of the numbers on Dan's Rolodex card. The first was in the 818 area code, which was the Valley, Glendale, Pasadena, and points east. The second was in 213, L.A. itself, and Mike thought he recognized it. He had once dated a woman who had scored her husband's house in their divorce. The house had been in Topanga Canyon, less than a mile from the ocean. Mike called the 818 number. It rang three times.

"The Brandon residence."

"May I speak to Mr. Brandon, please?"

A pause, "I'm sorry, Mr. Brandon is out at the beach house. Do you have that number?"

Mike read it off the card. "From the way you answered me, I've made a mistake I don't want to make again. Let me label my Rolodex card properly. Where is the residence I've called located?"

"San Marino."

"And if I need to speak to Mrs. Brandon, I'll find her there, eh?"

"Who is calling?"

"My name is Hayes, George Hayes. I'm with the United Way." George Hayes was the real name of Gabby Hayes, the bearded, toothless sidekick of Hopalong Cassidy and Roy Rogers.

"I see. Yes, you'll be able to reach Mrs. Brandon here. But she's out right now."

Mike wanted to say, *What's your name, sugar?* But he wasn't going to get any gossip out of her. "Well, thanks for your help, and I'm sorry I inconvenienced you."

"It was no trouble."

He decided to take a chance, and dialed the beach house. A young woman with an accent answered. Mike said, "This is George Hayes, of *People* magazine. We're checking on a story that Mr. and Mrs. Brandon are separated and headed for divorce—"

"Oh, fuck you," the young woman said, and hung up.

What Mike was thinking was that he had sensed that the other house was in San Marino before the maid had said it. He didn't know why he'd had that feeling. This whole business had him talking to himself. Every time he answered a question, two more popped up. Mike called Ben Hollister's office and—surprise!—was put through.

"Mike Gallagher, Hollister. I want to talk to you tonight at nine o'clock at your house."

"Wait a minute, Gallagher—"

"I'm going to be there at nine. If you're not, there'll be a warrant out for your arrest." Now it was Mike's turn to hang up. He was going to be at Hollister's at eight.

BOOK SIX

16

IN THE RUSH HOUR, THE FASTEST ROUTE FROM DOWNTOWN north to Toluca Lake was up the I-5 around Griffith Park and then west on the Ventura Freeway. The sun still hadn't set on Dan's grave. Mike couldn't bear to think of Dan in a grave. Awful—it was just awful. Mike wanted to talk with Marge, but on the freeway he talked to Dan instead, asking him why he had pulled the Brandon card, and when: Mike was almost certain that Brandon was the heavy hitter whose daughter had killed the guy on Tampa Avenue. The way Dan had explained the whole episode, he understood it too well to think that he could have gone back to Brandon for a second helping. Maybe Dan's guilt-driven curiosity had caused him to obtain and record Brandon's numbers, but that didn't explain his most recent action, hiding the card. What Mike hoped was that Dan had babbled one night to Marge in a way that still didn't make sense to her.

They had been married almost twenty-two years, lovers

longer than that. Soul mates. Their continuing conversation had been the center of their lives, and there was no telling what she might have forgotten—misfiled in her memory. Mike wondered how she was going to live the rest of her life, perhaps more years than she had lived already.

Mike's answering machine was blinking rapidly, but he wanted to take a shower before he returned any calls. It was five-thirty now, and he was already running out of time. He played the message tape. Frank Kennedy wanted to talk to him. Kennedy had left his home number. Laura wanted to be sure she hadn't offended him with her telephone prank this afternoon. She was home waiting for him. Don Grant had some information. Maurice Constantine could be reached at the usual location. No hangups. Somebody checking on him? There was no point to it if that somebody knew where Mike was. Mike double-locked the door before he got in the shower.

The first person he called was Marge. He gave her the Brandon telephone numbers without identifying them and asked her to check her telephone bills for calls to those numbers. Then he reminded her of how he and Dan talked by telephone when they wanted privacy: had Dan gone up to the Burger King more frequently in the last six months, even a year? Had he ever seemed troubled or agitated afterward? No and no, she said; she was scanning the bills as she spoke. Had Dan received any mysterious or disturbing calls at home in the recent past? She was slow answering, and Mike asked why.

"I've been working my way backward through the bills," she said. "Here's one to the San Marino number on April eighth, in the evening, for one hundred and two minutes. That was Easter week. He told me he had to stay in town and work. I was up in San Luis, Mike. What's this about?"

"He did work," Mike said. "I was with him most of the week. We had dinner together three times."

"You wouldn't lie to me?"

"Never. Keep going through the bills and make note of every one of the calls to either number. Then call me back and, if I'm not home, leave the information on my machine."

Now the telephone signaled that there was a call waiting. Mike said good-bye to Marge and pushed the disconnect button.

"Mr. Gallagher? Maurice Constantine. You told me you were interested in this guy Hollister. He's in Jackson's bedroom now. You can listen for yourself if you want to."

"Sure, let's hear it."

The sound was fuzzy, like an old movie, but Mike could understand what was being said. The speaker wasn't Hollister, and the accent was pure country boy cruel.

"You stupid son of a bitch. You didn't do anything, you don't know anything, and you sure as shit don't have to say anything to this jiveass."

"I didn't know that Valerie was dead," Hollister said. "This cop knows I knew Valerie. He's going to connect me with the people across the street. I don't want that. I *told* you, the cops are in this up to their necks. I think one of them did it. All that shit about a lot of people is just that— shit."

"Jackson's grinning," Constantine said. "He's lying on the bed. Hollister is standing."

"Where's the girl?" Mike asked, not knowing if Constantine could hear him.

"She's on the floor in front of the closet, with the locks on the door, weighing out Hollister's cocaine. The closet is where they keep their stuff. It's a regular Price Club. Hollister's spent two hundred dollars in the past two days. Listen."

"—so what makes you think a *cop* did it?"

"I *saw* him! At least, I think so. I've got him on tape."

"What do you mean, you've got him on tape?"

"Just as soon as the cops showed up, I set the video camera in the window. I haven't got everything, because I had to keep changing tapes, but I've got hours and hours of them being there, including the guy I'm talking about."

"Jennie," Jackson barked, "get out of the room."

"She's leaving," Constantine said. "All she's wearing is a T-shirt, by the way, and that's only to cover the bruises."

Jackson spoke again, but now his tone was low and menacing. "You better not have any fucking shit in your house, man."

"I don't."

"Get rid of that goddamned cop tape, too. If the cops knew you were interested in them, they'd get damned interested in you, let me tell you. Don't let people start thinking that you're getting dangerous."

"You don't have to come on strong with me."

"Maurice," Mike called.

"Yes, Mr. Gallagher."

"Just make sure that you have this. Why did you call me earlier?"

"Well, Jackson was beating on the girl something fierce, and suddenly there were cops at the door. I didn't call them. So that answers the question about who else is tuned to Jackson TV."

"What happened?"

"Jackson and the girl threw everything in the closet real quick, and then they let the cops in. The cops had some story about a prowler in the backyard. Not even Jackson believed that, although he didn't say anything until after the cops had gone. He stayed in an ugly mood for a while, and he made some cracks about nosy neighbors, but then some show biz guys came by, and he started talking about fucking chickens again."

"They're selling more chickens than ever, Maurice—"

"You have to have a live one."

"I told you, I don't want to hear it. How long do you think Hollister is going to be there?"

"He's already said that he has to see this girl he was supposed to have a date with before you called him this afternoon. He doesn't want to get her pissed at him. I think most of this coke is for her."

"Did he say her name?"

"Yeah, I recognized it. She's in those porn movies. You see her name in the ads all the time."

"Okay, keep me posted." It was after six. Mike called Don Grant at home.

"I have more information, Mike," Grant said. "I'm willing to bet that they have that guy Freeman at the hotel in Jacumba. My pals in San Diego say that something's going on there, but while they always used to know what it was, they don't now. The one I'm real close to said he'd be willing to talk to you about Freeman and Lansing. I had to promise that you'd keep him out of it no matter what."

"That's right. Let me get back to you in the morning. You can give me his name then."

Next was Kennedy.

"Dick Albert has a rancho in Oaxaca," Kennedy said. "That's where the good Mexican dope comes from. Albert's that kind of an asshole. It's an awful long ride for Bobby Michaels on a Mexican bus, over a thousand miles."

"But it makes sense," Mike said. "While Albert's willing to hide Michaels, he certainly couldn't take the chance of being seen with him up here, especially leaving the country. Down there, he can claim he didn't know anything. All Michaels has to do is get there. Something else: Bob Wills of the *Herald-Examiner*—"

"I know Bob."

"You know a lot of people," Mike said.

"Bob and I stood the death watch over Henry Fonda at the hospital last year. I've known Bob a long time."

"Is he any good?"

"He thinks he is."

Mike told Kennedy the story Ruppert had told him about an investigation of Hollywood Division.

"I'll check it out. I'm going to have to bill you, by the way, if that's all right. You're on to something, I can tell. I'm glad. You'll get the same break from me that you're getting from Constantine. Oh, yeah, I heard something on KFWB that will hand you a laugh. Harcourt Pryor appointed your friend Norman Birnbaum to the board of directors of the Brandon Museum today."

"What was that name again?"

"Harcourt Pryor," Kennedy said.

Mike had heard it before, he just couldn't place where. "Pryor is what to Randall Brandon?"

"Oh, he's been running things for the Brandon family for

the past ten years, maybe longer. Lately Randall Brandon has been spending most of his time out at the beach screwing a Swede he met last year.''

"He's living there with her now."

"You know more about it than I do," Kennedy said. "If Brandon was more famous than rich, I'd be able to peddle that information."

"How rich is he?"

"The family fortune comes to three or four billion. It was supposed to have come from shipping and railroads, but it really came from real estate right here in Southern California. It still does. The Brandon interests are very powerful."

"I'd like to know about the family."

"Now that could be *very* difficult," Kennedy said. "This is old money. It protects its privacy."

"I know about that," Mike said. "I have reason not to tell you now. I'd like you to get me what you can about Mom, Dad, Junior, and Sis."

"Two kids?"

"I don't know. I'm starting absolutely cold. I don't read the society pages." Now Mike remembered where he had heard Harcourt Pryor's name: in the Clown Club. Dan had mentioned it. Now Mike struggled to remember the context. "I'll call you tomorrow night and you can tell me what you have. It's probably a good idea to be discreet. In fact, be very discreet."

"Okay, but I can tell you right now that the word is that Randall is not the brightest guy in the world. And a bigot. Doesn't like blacks, Jews, Italians, Japanese. Mexicans are okay. You figure it out."

"No, thanks. But that's the idea—I want the gossip."

After he said good-bye, Mike blanked. Harcourt Pryor was stuck in his mind like a chicken bone in his throat. What was it that Dan had said about Pryor? There were others he was supposed to call, but he couldn't remember who they were. He rewound the message tape and switched it to play. Larry Hammond. Mike had gone too far. He let it play. "This is Larry Hammond, with special instructions—shit, I'll put on my assistant. Pay close attention."

Mike played it again. The telephone rang and he picked it up.

"Maurice Constantine, Mr. Gallagher. It looks like Jackson is winding up to some kind of party. What I wanted to ask you, how long do you want me to stay this evening?"

"I want you to be here at six A.M. tomorrow," Mike said.

"That's okay. That Hollister guy hasn't left yet. Jackson is giving away samples. From the conversation, the girl gives away samples, too. It's okay with Jackson. It looks like he sets it up."

"I'd rather have you tell me about the chickens," Mike said. "Don't be late tomorrow." He called Marvin Burgess.

"Everything the girl told you about the dog is true, Mike," Burgess said. "I called my nephew Marlon down at the county jail. He's in on something involving that bodyguard of Maxwell's, Kiku, but he wouldn't tell me what it was. He says he heard some scuttlebutt about people at Parker Center being in an uproar over the dog. It belongs to that girl in the hospital."

"Stay close to Marlon," Mike said. "I'd like to know what happens." Now he remembered the exchange between Hammond and the other men about drawing Kiku's blood. "Can you reach Marlon now?"

"Probably not. I was figuring I'd get him tomorrow during the day, when he's home. What's up?"

"Can you be here tomorrow at six o'clock?"

"In the morning?"

"I'm sorry, yes."

"I've got to go to bed now to do it. But if you say it's important."

"It's important." The telephone signaled a call waiting. "I'll see you tomorrow." He disconnected.

"Mike?" It was Marge. "I went back to the beginning of last year, and there are only three calls altogether to those two numbers, all three in the last six months, the one that was so long, another that was twenty minutes, and the first one, which was about ten minutes. Are you going to tell me what this is about now?"

"I think I'll know exactly tomorrow. Give me the dates

and times of the calls." When he had taken them down, he wrote, *Marvin to match up Brandon bills*. He put the note on top of the answering machine, where he wouldn't miss it tomorrow. "As I said already, Marge, this is nothing to be upset about. I have an idea, but I want to have proof, or as close as I can get to it. Don't *do* anything—you might push the wrong buttons. Do you understand me?"

"Yes." Her voice was as heavy as a gravestone.

"We'll talk tomorrow night." Six-thirty. He called Laura and told her he was on the way over.

Her Toyota was in the driveway. He wanted to use that heap later, so he parked his own car at the curb. Popejoy—there might be time now to find him. Agnes was silent as Mike walked up to the house, but the door opened before he knocked. Laura was smiling, but blushing, too.

"No getting even for this afternoon?"

He laughed and kissed her. "It won't work a second time." He told her what he wanted to do immediately. While he called Valley College, she found three Popejoys in the Northwestern Area book. There was no telling how many more would be in the Basin, up in Valencia, or out in Ventura—all reasonable commuting distance to Valley College. But the college operator put Mike through to the right office, and after he identified himself, the clerk gave him Popejoy's home telephone number—in Orange County. Figured. As Mike dialed, he could feel Laura's eyes on him. "You're making me self-conscious," he said.

"Well, you're good. I just love it."

Popejoy got on the line and Mike identified himself as the partner of Marvin Burgess, the detective who had spoken to him about their colleague. Popejoy remembered. Mike said, "We'd like to have a copy of that attendance sheet, if you don't mind."

"Of course. I'll mail it to you tomorrow. I'll be on campus to pick up my paycheck."

Mike didn't want an envelope with the Valley College return address sitting on his desk where it could be seen by

Greg Novak, or, for that matter, Marvin Burgess. Mike was really checking on both of them, and it wouldn't do his position with them any good if they knew it. "Why don't you mail it to my home—"

Laura tugged on his sleeve. "I'll get it."

"Hold on," he said to Popejoy.

"Tell him I'll pick up the attendance sheet at the college, wherever he wants to leave it."

To Popejoy, Mike said, "Professor, if you don't mind, could you copy all the sheets from that class and leave them in an envelope at the department office so they can be picked up? Put my name on the envelope and the woman coming for them will ask for the envelope for Mike Gallagher."

Popejoy said that would be fine, and Mike said good-bye. To Laura, he said, "You can compare the signatures from week to week. When I call you tomorrow, you can tell me if they match up."

She stared at him a moment before answering—to him, she looked very unhappy. It made him realize what a terrible thing it was, checking on people who worked next to him. "Sure," she said quietly, "I'll do that for you." Then she winked. "Oh, yeah, I stopped at the drugstore today. I'll bet you forgot all about it."

He had: birth control.

An hour later, when it had begun to grow dark, they set out for Laurel Canyon, leaving his car where he had parked it in front of Laura's house. They were going to the top of Rainbow Drive and then back down again. Laura was going to park the Toyota up the hill from Ben Hollister's place, but not so far as Roehrig's—Mike had told her a bit about Roehrig, and that he considered Roehrig extremely dangerous. She needed to know everything that put her at risk. If something happened to Mike while she was in the car alone—she'd know it—she was to take off. If she was questioned by police on patrol, or police called by a nervous neighbor, Laura was to tell that part of the truth that would get her free of them. *I'm waiting for my boyfriend, who's with Ben Hollister, the pho-*

tographer. She had Hollister's address memorized. If everything went smoothly, when Mike appeared on the street and waved to her, she was supposed to roll down the hill and pick him up. Mike didn't know what kind of car Hollister was driving, so she had to watch for anyone entering the Hollister house while Mike was inside. Two taps on the horn. Mike wasn't sure he would be able to hear the horn, but he really didn't think he needed any warning about Hollister. Gretchen had told him that Hollister was a medium-sized guy. And what Mike had heard from Hollister at Jackson's made it clear that he was a pussy. And not the kind to carry a gun to compensate for it.

Hollister's house was dark as they headed up the hill—and so, for that matter, was Gretchen's. But not Roehrig's place. Mike pointed it out to Laura.

"How long do you think you're going to be?" she asked.

"It depends on Hollister. I told you, don't hang around."

"You know I'm going to try to do my best."

"Yes, I do know that."

At the top of the hill, she U-turned and left the wagon in neutral so it would roll down the hill quietly. Mike wasn't sure he would have thought of doing that—bothering with it. Laura pointed the car toward a spot under an overhanging tree.

"What are you going to do while you're waiting?"

"Meditate."

"What do you do when you meditate?"

She smiled. "The question is impossible. Meditation is the opposite of doing."

"You're not going to be vulnerable, are you?"

"To every sight and sound. But don't worry. That character up there won't be able to put his hand on the knob of his front door without my knowing it."

Mike kissed her and got out of the car and walked straight toward Hollister's place, past Gretchen's across the street, past the murder house. A wooden gate five feet high screened Hollister's front door from the street. A pair of double-hung windows were to the left of the door. Mike slipped a credit card in the crack between the upper and lower sashes in the near window and turned the little pivoting lock. The lower window was warped and sticky, but opened quietly enough. Mike stepped in—the interior flooring was a few inches higher than the concrete slab outside. Mike closed the window again and locked it and turned to the gloomy interior. He was in a living room, with mismatched furniture, bookcases cluttered mostly with videocassette boxes, and a corner dominated by a wide-screen-projection television set. On the projector box was a videocassette recorder.

Now Mike's eyes were adjusted. He walked through to the rear and a filthy kitchen, a double sink jammed with dishes, and a table covered with the kind of food that belonged in the refrigerator. Under the sink were four or five bags stuffed with garbage. He looked in the refrigerator: mostly empty. The vegetable bins were empty. In the freezer were five packaged pizzas and a bottle of Polish vodka. Mike headed upstairs.

Two bedrooms, the one in the rear the kind of room one expected to find inhabited by the prisoner of a pervert. The bed was stripped to the mattress. Clothing was strewn on the floor, and where the floor was bare, it was covered with dust. In the closet was a lot of stuff still in the plastic wrappers— if he sent all his clothing out for cleaning, people who never set foot in here had no idea how disgustingly he really lived.

The front bedroom was like no other in the house. For starters, it looked clean. The walls were covered with red flocked paper. The furniture was Victorian, bright, expensive. And in the corner was a video camera on a tripod, and under it, another recorder and a small television set. On a cabinet was a Polaroid camera. Mike laughed at himself. The room was a studio—a set.

But Hollister had recorded the police in the street the day of the murders. If Mike had gotten an accurate sense of Hollister from what he had heard so far, those tapes were hidden. The closet in this room was filled with cardboard boxes and shopping bags, the bags filled with papers. In the dim light entering from the street Mike could see that the papers were mostly personal and household bills, bills for videotape and video equipment, the rental of lights, equipment repair. Other bags contained releases signed by women, releases agreeing to the sale of videotape and still pictures anywhere in the world—that phrase appeared on almost every document. Mike kept digging.

The boxes contained photographic equipment, cameras, lights, cans of thirty-five millimeter film. Another box held a set of electric trains, lengths of track, a transformer, and miniature trees. Even that didn't quite make Mike feel sympathetic toward Ben Hollister. The trains could be a prop, like the room itself.

Beep-beep.

Mike cursed. At least he had heard the horn. Meditating or otherwise, Laura had not missed Hollister's arrival. Mike stood still and listened to a car door slam directly below. The gate opened and closed. A key went into the lock of the front door. Now the door opened and closed. A lamp was lit, spreading light up the stairs. The television set came on. Hollister changed channels and Mike heard ''Family Feud.'' Hollister started up the stairs, ''Good answer! Good answer!'' sounding behind him.

Mike was ready, holding his breath. Hollister reached the landing and turned his back to Mike, heading for the rear bedroom. He was carrying a paper bag, a smallish one, and it looked full. Laura would have seen if Hollister had taken it from the car. There was only one way to find out if the bag was important to him.

''I'll take that,'' Mike said.

Hollister yelled in terror. Mike reached out and wrapped his left arm around Hollister's neck. Hollister clung to the bag, but Mike could see into it. More videotapes. Hollister was limp as Mike tightened his grip and leaned Hollister back like a drawn bow.

''I decided to come early,'' Mike snarled. ''You can't stand a frisk, can you? You were at Jackson's, dusting your nose with Peruvian marching powder. I'll bet you have more snow on you now than an Eskimo wifeswapping party.''

''Ease up,'' Hollister gasped. ''I pissed my pants.''

''Don't piss on me, that's all. Now what's on those tapes,

what you told Jackson you had, or what Jackson told you not to have?''

Hollister was silent. Mike tightened his grip more. Too much, he knew, and he would crush Hollister's larynx. Mike drew the Magnum and let Hollister see it. "Nobody around here cares about the noise this thing makes. The way your neighbors will know something's wrong in here is the smell a week from now. Say something that will encourage me not to break your neck.''

"These tapes are of the cops," Hollister said.

Mike pushed him forward against the wall, held him up with his forearm against Hollister's neck, and shoved the Magnum against his temple. Hollister still couldn't see him. "Now tell me about the stuff Jackson warned you against?''

"I can't believe he turned me in!''

"You're as stupid as he is.'' Mike kneed him hard on the back of the thigh, in the middle of the hamstring. Hollister cried out. If given the chance to run, he'd be able to take only two steps before he fell on his face. "Tell me about that shit!''

Hollister cried, "I can't, man! They'll kill me!''

"*If* you don't tell me, *I'll* kill you!''

Hollister whimpered. "Please. You don't understand.''

Mike kneed the other thigh. Hollister howled and cried. Mike knew he had overdone it. The guy was pathetic. Mike didn't really want to hurt him. Mike pulled him back from the wall, the tapes falling out of the bag and onto the floor. Mike let go of the collar and Hollister slumped to the floor on top of the tapes. Now he looked up.

"*You!*''

"*What?*''

"*Help!*'' Hollister bawled loudly. "*Help! Help!*''

"Shut up, for Christ's sake. What's wrong with you?''

Hollister crawled to the stairs, Mike watching him in astonishment. The man was sobbing, wailing. He fell down the stairs and scrambled toward the front door, his rubber legs going out under him. Mike was after him, but not fast enough. At the door Hollister suddenly turned and punched Mike squarely in the mouth. Mike staggered back, landed on his butt, and Hollister was through the door. Outside, Hollister stumbled into his car and locked the door before Mike could get to the outside handle. Wild-eyed, Hollister fumbled for his keys, got the car started, and pulled away with the tires burning. All Mike could do was get clear. Up the hill, a pair of headlights came on and began moving in Mike's direction. Laura stopped the wagon in front of Mike and opened the passenger door. "You're bleeding," she said calmly.

"As soon as he saw me, he got hysterical."

"Shouldn't we get out of here?"

"In this neighborhood? Nah." He pulled his handkerchief and patted his lip. It wasn't cut. The blood was in Mike's mouth. A tooth—the little shit had loosened one of Mike's teeth. No, *two*. "Jesus. I belong here anyway. I'm a cop investigating a murder. Open the tailgate of the wagon. There's a great load of shit I want to throw in. I scared the hell out of the guy. '*You!*' he said. He knew who I was, or thought I was some other guy, like Attila the Hun."

"Hey, say 'Please' to me!" she yelled.

He looked at her. "Please forgive me. Did he take that bag out of his trunk?"

Laura nodded grimly as she got out of the car. Now she saw that he was motionless. She said, "If cops do come, say I'm the landlady here or something. That's a lot more legitimate reason for me being here than being your girlfriend, if that's what I am."

"You wanna?" *Landlady* was a bit of fast thinking.

"We'll discuss it later. Don't you think you ought to get moving?"

"You're pissed about something."

"Well, if you're going to keep getting into these brawls, I'd like to see you win one." Now she laughed at him. "The look on your face is wonderful."

He went back up to the second floor, gathering the tapes that had been in Hollister's paper bag. They fitted in the bag almost perfectly, reminding Mike of something else he had seen recently. It came back easier than the first time he had heard Harcourt Pryor's name. Mike had seen a bag like this in Bernie Maxwell's safe. Why had Bernie Maxwell stored videotapes in a safe? Mike had no time to think about it now. The tapes on the bookcases in Hollister's living room were labeled, but there was no way of knowing that the labels were up-to-date, or in some kind of code. When he had all the cassettes, he disconnected one of the recorders and tucked it under his arm. Hollister had taken off as if he had no intention of coming back; and if he did, who was he going to call to report what had just happened, someone at Hollywood Division? Finally, Mike looked around the place one more time. There was no basement, and the backyard was only a vine-covered, sixty-degree slope, unclimbable.

Driving away, Laura asked if he had any idea about what had happened. He told her that Hollister had said that he had taped the police investigation the day of the murders. *Now* it dawned. "Holy Jesus!"

"What is it?" she asked.

"I'm not sure," he lied. Badly. Maybe Hollister had seen Mike leave in the morning with Gretchen! Something Hollister hadn't taped because he hadn't started taping "until the cops showed up"—that's what he had told Jackson. Then Mike had been back in the afternoon, as if returning to the scene of the crime. Hollister had recognized Mike and thought he had done the killing, thought it more than ever now. "What I'm going to have to do is take a look at every one of these damned cassettes."

"Let me," she said.

"A lot of it is just going to be porn."

"I'm going to be lonely, Mike. And worried. The next guy who throws a punch at you might be a midget."

In Laura's bathroom mirror his teeth—two lowers in the front—looked normal, and their movement was really very small. There wasn't much pain either. They might be all right if he left them alone. He moved her television set into her bedroom, connected the VCR, and pulled the tape labeled #1 from the paper bag. Laura had put on a light flannel nightgown, and now she entered the bedroom with a large bowl of popcorn. Mike started the tape and sat at the foot of the bed. On the left side of the screen was the corner of the murder house. In the center was an unmarked car facing up the hill. Gretchen's house was one part of the top of the picture, the house downhill from hers the rest. Within a minute a black and white nosed up behind the unmarked car, two officers got out, and headed into the house. The VCR had a Fast Forward, which scrambled the picture, but no Seek or Scan that would allow the picture to be seen if he sped up the tape.

Mike was timing the tape. Five minutes more passed before one of the officers returned to the car . . . Twenty minutes in, Hollister's arm crossed the lower part of the picture, and then he moved the camera down and focused it on a digital clock, which showed the time to be 8:42 A.M. Another black and white arrived and parked opposite the unmarked car, narrowing the passage between the vehicles. Cops got out and sprinted toward the murder house. Two minutes later, the nose of a car appeared at the top of the screen. A cop came out of the house and moved the black and white.

"I like the way it builds," Laura said. Agnes barked, got louder, then quieted down. "I'd been about to say, 'The absence of sound adds suspense.' Why do you think Hollister did this?"

"Maybe he hoped there would be something he could sell," Mike said. "He's got a regular job, shoots porn, was into something else that his pal was afraid of today—"

"How do you know? You were at a funeral and in court."

He reached for the popcorn. "I'm doing more than just taking punches. Let's leave it at that."

"Let's leave it at that," she mimicked. "Have I asked? Have I been curious?"

"A moment ago. 'How do you know?' " he mimicked back. When he looked around, she was grinning. "All right, tell me about that."

"I'm thinking that you're going to crack the case. You really are."

"I'm sorry I forgot my manners up on the hill. Dan and I never bothered with the niceties."

"I'm glad you think of me as a friend, I guess." The dog barked again. "What *is* her problem?"

Mike got up and headed to the kitchen. At the back door, he drew the Magnum, then stepped outside. Agnes came running over from the fence and got up on her hind legs. She wanted to kiss him. *Boy, am I glad to see you!* Mike scratched her head and walked slowly over to the fence, Agnes knocking against his knees. A helicopter passed overhead. Nothing out on the street—if Agnes had seen anything, it had been through a crack in the fence, and there were none more than an eighth of an inch wide. He waited, but heard and saw nothing. He patted the dog again and went back inside. He heard Laura talking, but not her words. When he reached the bedroom, she hung up the telephone.

"One of my kids' parents," she said. "I may be contending with an outbreak of mumps. You've had mumps, haven't you?"

"When I was five." He hadn't heard the telephone ring, but there had been a helicopter, he remembered. "What's happened?"

"Two cars came down the hill, and one went up," Laura said.

"Did one have a lot of guys in it? Four—five guys?"

"Uh-uh, drivers only."

"I have to go home tonight," he said. "Company's coming at six tomorrow. Will you be all right? I don't know what's bothering the dog."

Laura filled her mouth with a handful of popcorn. "If she wakes me, I know what to do. I didn't get up just now because you're here. I don't know yet if I want to be your girl, but I do know that I don't want to be your partner."

Nothing was happening on the screen. "What's the matter with being my girl?"

"For one thing, you don't take me anywhere. You've been busy, I know, but I want to see that you have the habit. Buy me presents, too. I like that stuff, I deserve it, and the process will be good for you. And I want to see if you can be faithful."

"One at a time," he said.

"We'll see." Another mouthful of popcorn. "You do me wrong, I won't hire a midget."

"You're not kidding—you know exactly what you're doing."

"I like the way you take a joke. A lot of men can't."

Now Laura pointed to the television set. Arriving was an upscale black sedan. Mike recognized it and wasn't really surprised. Larry Hammond got out from the passenger side. "A big wheel?" Laura asked.

"What do you think?" Hammond went around the back of the car and into the house. Mike turned around and noted the time on Laura's alarm clock. She winked at him, extended her hand, and Mike used it to pull her toward him and kiss her. She struggled free. "We're going to miss something! I don't want to sit through this shit again!"

He couldn't help laughing. He turned back to the screen.

"I'm still not your girl yet, Mike. We have a lot more to learn about each other."

He wondered what Dan would think of this conversation. The notion was a trick he was playing on himself, Mike knew, one that could draw him into emotions that had no place here. Dan would probably have laughed like hell at all of it. . . . Hammond came out again and backed down the hill. After a moment Mike remembered that he had been timing Hammond's stay inside. Fifteen minutes. Laura was staring at him. "I heard you," he said.

"That's good." She patted his hand, as if that hadn't been on her mind at all. "Did you see what you wanted to see?"

He laughed. "Why, do you want to watch 'St. Elsewhere'?"

She shook her head. "I'll wait for you. You have to do this first, before anything else. I know that."

"If you want me out of here, I'll have to take the equipment. I have to watch this stuff, and the sooner the better. I'm concerned about you after I leave. Agnes wasn't sounding off for nothing."

"She's coming in here when you go—later. Leave your stuff here. I want to watch the porn while you're gone. You want a report, right? Do I have to report if it excites me?"

He turned back to the screen. "I guess I asked for this." He was still watching when Laura crawled across the bed and put her arms around his neck and kissed him tenderly on the ear. She made a project of it before she withdrew.

The tape ran out. Mike inserted the cassette labeled # 2, which began with a pan down to the clock on the windowsill: 10:15. "I was in the Canyon fifteen minutes after this," Mike said. "Dan and I went up to the other side of the bowl and watched the arrival of the coroner's van. That should be at about ten-forty."

"Why were you there?"

He didn't answer. Hammond's car returned. This time one of the rear doors opened as Hammond emerged from the front. The backseat passenger was a big man, around fifty, with dark, wavy hair. He seemed to be in superb condition, but out there on Rainbow Drive, in extreme emotional distress. He looked up and down the street as he buttoned his jacket—*expensive* jacket. The guy had bucks as well as breeding. "Another big wheel?" Laura asked.

"Your guess is as good as mine. I have no idea who he is." The man glanced up, and Mike remembered that a helicopter had been overhead all during this time. The man followed Hammond into the house. Mike remembered the coroner's van making its way up the street: Hammond's car hadn't been in front of the house at that time. "He won't be in there long."

"I have a bad feeling about this," Laura said.

Mike was quiet again.

This tape and the first were solid evidence that Larry Hammond had known as early as nine o'clock the morning of the murders, that there had been a survivor. A few minutes passed before Hammond and the big guy came out, the big guy walking around the back of the car by himself.

"Turn around!" Laura shouted. "We want to see your face!"

At the car door the man straightened up and looked at the house, his face red, contorted, grimacing. His eyes were filled with tears—but he was enraged, like a child.

"That's bad news," Laura said.

"The motherfucker," Mike muttered.

"Who is he?"

"All I have is an idea," Mike said. He stood up. "I don't think I have to see any more of this. Hollister had the right idea, keeping the tapes in his car. I'll take them with me."

"Wherever you'll be. I don't know, but that's okay. Will you stay around long enough now for a good cuddle? I could use it."

"I'm not usually this bad."

She crawled over to him again and started to unbutton his shirt. "No, you're usually pretty wonderful. You have a lovely, even disposition."

"I didn't when I was married."

"Wrong woman." She pulled the shirt out of his pants.

"She was at the funeral today—pretty weird, too. This is going to be some cuddle." He pulled her nightgown up over her head. "Where did you get this rag?"

"K-mart. They had a sale. Get used to my idea of cuddling."

"You got cuddled earlier this evening," he said.

"When I have somebody to cuddle, I like to cuddle as frequently as possible. How was she weird?"

"Talking about her has a negative effect on me."

"I can solve that problem." They lay down together, face-to-face. "I'm glad you like me."

"There are times when I think you're afraid that I'm going to take off on you."

"Well, I am."

"Why?"

"Talk about negative effects!"

"That one works both ways," he said. "Lay off being afraid. Excuse me. *Please* lay off."

She laughed in his face.

He didn't go straight home. He drove around the block, parked in a red zone at the corner, and walked halfway down to Laura's house. The street was quiet, her lights out. There was no way he could guarantee her safety, and it maddened him. She had said the dog was good, and that she herself was good with firearms, but it could be all talk, in spite of his increasing belief to the contrary. The only time he had seen her rattled was on the day they'd met. He was afraid of her, he knew. Maybe God's timing was lousy: Dan had died because he had trusted someone. She was glad he felt something for her—she made sure he was getting that message. Why, if she did not feel it herself? His real fear was that he felt something for her, something that made him nervous inside and protective of her. The truth, and he knew it, was that he had never been in love—maybe he really didn't know how to behave, never mind *Please* and *Thank you.* Talking serious *How to Live* here. Or maybe, he thought sourly as he turned back toward his car, he simply wasn't getting enough sleep.

At home, more messages. The first was from Marge. She had checked all the numbers on the Crawford bills and had turned up another number she could not identify. Dan had called it only once, two days after the very long call to San Marino in April. She had not called the number, but had located the area of its exchange: West Los Angeles. The conversation had lasted fourteen minutes. She read off the number, and Mike took it down.

The next message was from Kennedy. Bob Wills of the *Herald-Examiner* was upset because the story of the investigation of Hollywood Division was getting around. Wills had thought he was ahead of his competition. There was so little to Wills's story, Kennedy said, that he didn't want to use up Mike's tape to tell it. One thing Mike needed to know: Cutler would neither confirm nor deny to Wills the presence of Internal Affairs undercover operatives working regular duty in Hollywood Division. Wills had taken Cutler's conduct to mean that there were shooflies working Hollywood, and Kennedy thought so, too. "What the hell," Kennedy said in what Mike thought was his conclusion, "in a big city department, you have to expect them. Oh, yeah. Wills told me to read tomorrow's *Herald.* He says he's got a big article on Bernie Maxwell's real-estate holdings in North Hollywood. Apparently Maxwell has been buying everything in sight for the last six or seven years. Wills had a couple of people try to estimate how much Maxwell had to be earning to be able to buy the things he's been picking up. One guy said ten million a year. Can you imagine that?"

In his whole career as a police officer, Mike wouldn't make one million.

The next call was a hang-up, and the next. Two. The somebody keeping tabs on Mike, maybe the same somebody who had triggered Agnes over on Shadyglade. Mike couldn't call Laura; she'd been falling asleep when he had let the dog in. What he wanted to do was drive over there, but he didn't have the energy—or time. He needed sleep: what he was still planning for tomorrow would keep him busy for as long as eighteen straight hours, and Friday might be worse.

But he was out of bed again less than twenty minutes after getting into it, jolted awake by what he remembered of Judy's behavior at the graveside ceremony. She had been staring at him, but not absently. Something had been on her mind, and not the past: the last time he had seen her, that accidental meeting, she hadn't wanted to look at him at all. This was something else. She had run because she hadn't wanted him talking to her—actually, vice-versa. He made another note, stuck it in the answering machine with the other, turned on the television set, and stretched out on the couch. David Letterman was laughing at a dog in a tutu. In this mood, Mike wanted to squeeze Letterman's front teeth together. But after a moment, Mike hardly noticed: he was trying to relive every moment of the past ten days—no, *longer*. . . .

He sat up. Of course!

Much longer—much, *much* longer!

17

MAURICE CONSTANTINE WAS FIVE MINUTES EARLY, AND
Marvin Burgess arrived on time. Mike had been awake for almost an hour. His hand was freshly bandaged and feeling better.
His bag was packed, parked by the door. Burgess had no difficulty with the jobs Mike wanted him to do alone, and Mike had
been correct in assuming that Constantine could make a voice
that had come through a telephone line sound like the person to
whom it belonged was standing right in the room. Mike gave
Burgess the spare key to the apartment. Burgess wasn't comfortable with the rest of the plan. There was no risk to him, he
knew; he was just not sure he could do the job properly. He
would *try*, he said.

When Burgess and Constantine had worked out their logistics, they left to go separate ways, Constantine with the answering machine tape, Burgess with the notes Mike had written for
him last night and the notes he had just made for himself. Mike
spent another minute in the apartment making sure he had

everything, and then he rode down to the garage. There had been no way for him to push Burgess, or change the situation. Mike had the wrong man for the job, and there was nothing he could do about it now except hope for the best. He felt as if he were leaving a kid alone with a loaded gun—that's the way it could work out, almost exactly.

Half an hour later, Mike was on I-5 downtown, passing County-USC hospital, the one shown from different angles at the start of the television doctor shows, and a half hour after that he was crawling past the Egyptian facade of the abandoned Firestone tire factory in the middle of the industrial corridor only a few miles south of the hospital. If there was a freeway in Los Angeles that was not a rolling traffic jam all through the daylight hours, Mike did not know of it. Except for a few enclaves like Bev Hills, Bel Air, Brentwood, and San Marino, the whole nest was fouled. Twenty years ago, people had started running to Orange County, where they had gone once to smell the orange blossoms; now Orange County was just another part of the traffic reports, and its smell was often a cause for a Stage One Smog Alert. There were high-rises there, too, glass boxes surrounded by asphalt garnished with cars. Dan and Marge had been heading to San Luis Obispo to surround themselves with the dream of their youth, nothing more.

Mike pulled off the freeway at San Juan Capistrano, close to the mission, where he could choose from a dozen places for breakfast. The city of San Juan Capistrano was still mostly in the floor of its valley surrounded by golden hillsides, under a dome of clear blue sky. There was a wait at the restaurant, so Mike left his name and stepped back outside. He thought he could see one wall of the mission, two blocks away and veiled in old trees. He and Judy had toured it years ago, stopping on one of those trips to Mexico with Dan and Marge—and the thought that Dan was dead, a thought still as fresh and new as the moment Mike had found his body, snapped Mike from his daydream.

He picked up a *Herald-Examiner*, then bought a roll of quarters from the restaurant cashier, and told her if his name was called, he'd be in a phone booth. First was Don Grant, who had been waiting for his call. Grant gave him the name of the San

Diego detective who would meet him for lunch at one o'clock at Casa Rosarita in Old Town. "You don't have to confirm, it's all set. I had a call yesterday afternoon from Paula Rogers' attorney. He's ready to go to trial tomorrow morning. I asked him if he expected his client to show, and he told me he collected his fee in advance—he knows what he's got there—and if she's on the wind, she's going to have to get another boy—*and* pay him. That's in Riverside, ten A.M."

"It's hard to figure what she can tell me that will add to what I already know."

"Well, that's up to you. Keep me posted."

Mike glanced quickly at Bob Wills's story on Bernie Maxwell's real-estate empire. Much of the piece was a recap of Hammond's raid on Maxwell's house two nights before, noting the drugs and the huge amount of cash taken from the safe. As much as he'd spent, the income from the properties was so low that Maxwell was still overextended: he needed a continued vast income to cover his overhead. It was a dumb situation even for a crook to get into—unless Maxwell was expecting a considerable capital appreciation in the near future. Mike tried Marvin Burgess.

"I'm glad you called, Mike." He sounded awful. "My sister was on the phone with Marie for almost an hour this morning, and I just got off the phone with her. Marlon is in Queen of Angels Hospital. My sister's been with him since midnight. He's in fair condition, and he'll be all right, but he's pretty busted up."

It had taken Mike a moment to remember who Marlon was, and now something else clicked in: Marlon had been part of something involving Kiku, the bodyguard. Two nights ago, Hammond's men had been supposed to draw blood; and before he'd joined the sheriff's department, Marlon had been a boxer.

"It's all hush-hush, but I can talk," Burgess said. "There's nobody around right now. Marlon told his mother what happened. They dressed him up like a prisoner and put him in a cell upstairs, away from the rest of the population, and then brought Kiku around. The rap on him was that he couldn't defend himself—if that was the case, why did they suspect *him* of being the one who'd killed these people in the Canyon? They wanted to check his blood without tipping their hand. Anyway, Marlon was supposed to pick a fight with this guy and throw a couple of short punches, the kind that cut. So Marlon was ready for it. He figured all he had to do was feint, throw a right, and the guy's nose was broken. And that's what happened. He broke the guy's nose, and the guy just stood there, staring at him. Marlon swears that the guy had him made for a cop by the look in his eyes. Marlon went to hit him again and Kiku grabbed Marlon's wrist and threw him up against the bars. Karate— something like that. Marlon knew he was in real trouble. There was no one anywhere near the cell to help him. The big guy got Marlon up against the bars and just squeezed him in a flash, grabbed the bars on either side of Marlon and just squeezed. Marlon thought he was going to die. He passed out. The guy Kiku never said a word. Marlon woke up when they were carrying him out of the cell and the other guys were beating on Kiku with sticks, but my nephew has six broken ribs and a punctured lung. Can you believe it? Where do they get that shit? They thought they had the straight dope on this big goof, and all he was doing was playing possum, hoping to slide through.''

"Maxwell's out on bail again, of course.''

"Since yesterday. I tell you, Mike, I've *had* it! What do these people think they're doing? This was just carelessness! Tell me it isn't carelessness! You know, a thing like this can wreck that boy's health!''

"Don't think about it, Marvin. Time will tell.''

"We're a close family, Mike.''

"I know. And it's nice. Leave a trail of telephone numbers so I can find you.

"I can always call that Morris What's his name.''

"It's *Maurice*, Marvin. Maurice Constantine. You're right, let's use him.''

"What's the matter with his mouth?''

"I'll tell you when I see you. This costs too much.''

Over waffles topped with fresh strawberries and a dollop of whipped cream, Mike carefully read the Wills article. Maxwell had been trying to piece together small parcels, single-family dwellings, independent gas stations, taxpayers, all in run-down condition, none of them profitable at current-market rentals.

North Hollywood had seen its worst, there was a slow-moving development agency, but it was a long way from urban renaissance. The entire area would become immensely more valuable, Wills wrote, if the subway from downtown through Cahuenga Pass was ever approved and funded, but the subway seemed to grow more and more remote every year. The recent natural gas explosion in the Fairfax district and the discovery of prehistoric remains under Wilshire Boulevard, where the subway was supposed to run before it hooked north toward the Valley, had only swelled the ranks of the subway's enemies. Mike knew all that stuff, and wasn't surprised that insiders were lining up in hopes of making a killing from increasing real-estate values along the subway's route—but Bernie Maxwell?

Until recently, Maxwell had been well-connected. Now he was disconnected, but Mike still didn't know why.

The disconnection had been a long time coming, a year or more, and the process had been started in Washington. Washington had been saying yes to the subway, and now it was saying no. Mike had been a civil servant too long to believe that government ever did anything except for reasons that served itself. In the seventies, Washington had served itself by responding to the environmentalists; in the eighties, it responded to the military-industrial complex. Like a great shapeless beast, it shuddered and shook when it was made to feel pain, grunting and moving only to make itself comfortable again.

So if Mike's thinking had any value, what it meant was that a very big L.A. dope dealer and pornographer had operated for years without disturbing the beast—but now the beast *was* disturbed, determined to purge itself of Maxwell. Maxwell was fighting back, which was understandable —and people were dying—but none of that told Mike anything about why the beast was disturbed now, after so many years of tolerating Maxwell, of respecting his connections: *they* didn't matter anymore, or they had elected to save themselves at Maxwell's expense. . . .

The second half of the 135 miles to San Diego was far more pleasant than the first, out to the sea at San Clemente, then south again through the only open country between the two cities, the ocean dark and frothing in the morning light, past Camp Pendleton and resort towns like Carlsbad, Cardiff-by-the-Sea, and Del Mar. It had been a while since Mike had been down here, and the evidence of development was everywhere, subdivisions with sales banners and pennants, freshly landscaped little shopping centers. The traffic thickened, too: Mike was sliding into the tail end of San Diego's morning rush hour. His hand was healing. He could wrap his fingers around the steering wheel without causing the wound to ache or even twinge, and for that he had to be grateful. He had not decided where he would spend the night—that depended on events.

Rolling on the freeway around San Diego's downtown, coming within sight of the Coronado Bridge, Mike realized that he'd forgotten to do something up north in San Juan Capistrano. It would keep for a little longer, but he was concerned about the meaning of his forgetfulness. His exhaustion was now two-staged: he had not slept well last night, after slogging through a brain-scrambling weariness for most of a week. Passing the bridge, Mike stole a glance across the bay to the red roofs and bright white walls of the Hotel del Coronado, perhaps the last great wooden structure on the West Coast, and a certified national monument. The main dining room with its great vaulted ceiling, all polished wood, was the size of a small sports arena. The dining room and the other public areas, the interior garden and the massive turrets, presented an opportunity to self-congratulating twentieth-century types to step back in time and see the dignity and elegance of the way things were done a hundred years ago. Mike had already thought this week that at last he had met a woman he wanted to take there—the place was famous for being one of the most romantic resorts on the West Coast. On the other hand, the Hotel Del, as the locals called it, was almost as famous for being a movie location: Joe E. Brown had chased Jack Lemmon around the place in *Some Like It Hot*, and Peter O'Toole had ranted and raved in the turrets playing the director in *The Stunt Man*. Perhaps the Hotel Del was the last twitch of the famous California imagination all the way to the Mexican border. National City rolled up next, then Chula Vista, dreary flatlands cluttered with mobile-home parks, cramped apartment complexes, bolt-together-metal factory buildings, and the kind of little stores that specialized in the items people forgot to buy elsewhere. Even the greenery looked lame, as if somebody had discovered palm tree abuse. Mike had never met anyone who said he had come from National City or Chula Vista; people wound up here. Some had children in tow, but children didn't matter to such beaten drifters, who wanted to be left alone with their booze or television or the company of their fellow failures: they created monsters, these people, dumb to their acts, and society was helpless until blood was drawn and innocents wept. Mike had come to Chula Vista first because homeboy Billy Lansing had been one of the principal players in the Los Angeles pageant. It was ten-thirty now, and Mike was due back in San Diego at one o'clock. He had no time to waste on the bit players. What he hoped to get here was not only further confirmation of the date of Lansing and Freeman's arrival in Los Angeles, but perhaps some piece of gossip about their original intention—*real* intention, not the public relations flummery of Freeman's radio announcements. Lansing had been an asshole, and the first rule of the game was that assholes ran their mouths.

When he pulled off the freeway, Mike looked for a 7-Eleven or shopping center with telephone booths—*and* telephone books. He had to settle for a Mexican *cantina* where the customers stared balefully as the fat bartender directed him to the old-style wooden booth in the rear, beyond the dull green of the unlighted pool table. Mike's first call was to the number in West Los Angeles that Marge had given him. This is what he had forgotten to do in San Juan Capistrano.

"Harcourt Pryor," a smooth voice said.

Mike rocked back. Suddenly his palms were itching. "This is Bob Wills of the *Herald-Examiner*, Mr. Pryor. I want to ask you why you were in a telephone conversation with the late LAPD detective, Dan Crawford, on the tenth of April."

The man snorted. "You're not Wills. I spoke to him two days ago."

Mike was silent, and Pryor hung up. Mike began to grin. *Two days ago!* Pryor's name had not been in Wills's story on Maxwell's real-estate holdings, but what else would Wills have had on his mind? Dan had said at the Clown Club that Pryor held the mortgage on the bungalow on Norma Place. Mike remembered the way Dan had identified Pryor. *In the society pages*. Then Dan had paused. Now Mike knew that Dan had been thinking of his own contact with Pryor. *Yeah*, Dan had said, *Pryor is on the business pages, too.* Dan had not wanted to talk more about Pryor. Dan had never mentioned the Brandon family, whose business Pryor managed.

Mike called Frank Kennedy. Kennedy's machine answered. Mike said that Maurice Constantine would know in the next hour or two where to reach him, and that Kennedy should leave any messages with Constantine. Now Mike was running low on quarters. The telephone book showed two Lansings in Chula Vista. There were a half-dozen Freemans between San Diego and the border, and almost a half-page of Browns. Mike went up to the bar where the customers glowered at him over their *cerveza*. The bartender waddled up. The bartender was fatter below the belt than above. Now Mike saw that he was the only guy in the place without a mustache.

"I need to find the library," he said.

"Oh, library. Sí." The bartender turned to the nearest guy and asked him in Spanish for the best way to get to the library. The guy turned to his drinking buddy, and now all three were talking at once. A guy at the other end of the bar got into it, then *his* partner. Everybody knew where the library was, but each was talking about a different street to take or direction to go. Then the bartender turned back to Mike. "Ih's ten blocks op, two blocks righ'. Just go two ligh's op, turn righ'. You can' mees ih."

Mike said thanks and left. Ten blocks north, two blocks east, was a one-story brick building behind an American flag flying from a thirty foot pole. Only one car was in the small parking lot, and the curb was empty from one end of the block to the other. Mike parked the car at the foot of the concrete walk. The sun was getting stronger and the air wasn't moving at all.

The librarian was a tall, gray-haired, sad-eyed woman of fifty wearing a tailored blue suit and a soft, ruffled white blouse. Her upper lip was creased with vertical lines that disappeared when she smiled at the sight of his badge. She looked him straight in the eye as he told her quickly about the multiple murders in

L.A. and that he wanted all the information on Lansing and Freeman he could get, including the names and addresses of relatives and friends. "It's a quarter to eleven now," he said. "I'm due up in San Diego at one, and I'm hoping I can be back here at a quarter to three. So I'm trying to save time and locate names I found in the telephone book. I've got to talk to people."

She took a deep breath, never breaking eye contact. "I remember a piece in the *Union* last week about Lansing—an interview with his stepmother, I believe." She stepped around the desk, talking over her shoulder. "Last week's papers aren't on microfilm yet, but we have them in the back. If you want to use the telephone, please keep the calls in the immediate area, where we have unlimited service. My name is Muriel."

"Mike Gallagher."

"Are you going to be in town long?"

He smiled. "I don't know." She was hitting on him. He'd learned soon after his divorce that the sexual mentality of some fifty-year-old women was everything fifteen-year-old boys dream about. And Muriel was okay. She smelled good, too. Still, he thought he would have passed even if he had never met Laura Demming. Muriel's unhappy eyes gave her away: she had too many problems.

It took him only five minutes to find the article she remembered. He had the stepmother's new name and address. Fernandez. Geraldine Fernandez. In the article Fernandez spoke bitterly of Lansing, calling him "vicious" and a "mad dog." Mike knew all that. Muriel was standing right behind him. He gestured to the address. "Is this far from here?"

"Only a few minutes."

"I'm going to take a run over there. In my business, it's usually better not to call in advance. Besides this stuff, can you think of any other materials you have that might point me toward people who had contact with Lansing, Freeman, or Marylou Brown—she was another victim, and she was from this area."

"Well, if they went to high school in the area, their home addresses at that time would be in the high-school records. The high schools will give that to me. Old addresses, though."

"It might help, although I think Freeman is originally from

El Centro." "I can get addresses for you while you see Mrs. Fernandez."

"Are you sure I'm not imposing?"

"I was only going to shelve books. Librarians are supposed to answer questions for readers. We go to college for that."

"Brown is from National City. Freeman, too, now—I think."

She smiled. "Chula Vista has diplomatic relations with National City. Some people don't think so, but we do."

Maybe her eyes were the result of a bad choice of parents. She was a day too late—or he was. It was pretty funny. One day after making a promise to a woman for the first time in many years, he meets a possible grandmother who makes the thought of a quickie against the wall an interesting proposition. "Leave me the number here. If I can't get back, I'll be calling you."

"All right. I'll take my lunch at one o'clock, while you're in San Diego. I close at six."

"You'll hear from me." He held up the paper on which he had written Mrs. Fernandez' address. "Okay, how do I get to this place?"

Muriel gave directions and in another ten minutes Mike found himself on a street of run-down clapboard and stucco bungalows, the yards bare or weeded over or turned into parking lots. No one in view. The temperature was going up, and Mike wanted to loosen his tie, but felt he couldn't. He missed the address the first time up the street, turned around, and cruised back more slowly. One of the clapboard places, the front door open, the living room a shadow through the old, wood-frame screen door. Mike had to park two doors down and walk back. He rapped on the screen door.

"Yeah, who is it?"

A guy, with the hint of a Mexican accent. A big guy in dark pants and a sleeveless undershirt lumbered into view. He had a gray mustache, and a full head of steel-gray hair. His eyes looked puffy. So did his cheeks, neck, and shoulders. Mike flashed the badge. Without a hitch in his movements, the guy flipped the hook on the screen door and turned away." Come on in. She's out in the back. I'll get her. We figured we'd see you guys a couple of times, but you're getting to be a habit. I'm her third husband and don't know shit, if you don't already know that by now.

Mike waited alone. The newest thing in the living room was the television set, a remote control job. The remote control box was on a scarred coffee table in front of a sagging couch. The couch had slipcovers, and on the wall above was a painting of a sunset over the ocean. The water was still and in the middle distance was a sailboat that had no sails. No people either. Mike decided the name of the painting was *Futility*.

Geraldine Fernandez weighed about eighty-five pounds. She was not an especially short woman either. She looked, in the old phrase, consumptive. Her cheeks were hollow, and there was no color in her skin except for ominous circles under her eyes. Billy Lansing had been thirty-four. Geraldine Fernandez could be any age between fifty-five and seventy. The circles under her eyes were so deep and dark that Mike was ready to believe she had cancer. "You're a new one," she said. "It's getting hot. Do you want a Coke?"

"No, thanks."

"It's not Coke anyway, it's the Von's house brand. We have to watch our pennies. Victor's on disability. Hurt his back—no lie. Still, we're trying to clean the garage today. I thought I told everything already."

"There may be something else," Mike said. "When was the last time you saw Billy Lansing alive?"

"I did answer that," she said. "I told the federal cops that I saw him in early April."

Mr. Fernandez had said that the cops had been coming around here lately like kids on Halloween, so there was no point in asking her when she had seen the *federales*. Mike said, "This is LAPD business. When you saw him who was with him?"

"It was only that one night. There was a carful, headed down to T.J., they said. I thought they were going for drugs. There was Billy, Dale Freeman, that girlfriend of Billy's who lived, that girl of Freeman's who thought this place was beneath her— you know, she had her nose in the air, hoity-toity. She didn't kid me. That Dale Freeman has a stink onto him that would gag a maggot. There was another bimbo, a drug addict if ever I saw one, and the fellow that was with her. He thought everything was slightly funny. Good-looking guy, but I thought there was something a little loony tunes about him."

"How so?"

"He was wearing an undershirt like Victor's, and suspenders. Now *that*'s crazy. No shirt at all. He was another one who thought he was hot stuff. Always grinning. I thought it was an act."

"Do you remember his name?"

"Not an American name, I remember that."

"But not Mexican either," Mike said.

"No, no, I'd remember." She laughed. "I should have married a Mexican years ago, it would have saved me a lot of heartache. Victor's the most easygoing man I've ever known in all my life."

"Let's go back to the guy in suspenders. Tell me everything you can remember about him."

"Well, he was always grinning, as I say, and he was jumpy, too, like the girl with him. They were both jumpy, like they were on something."

"How about Billy?"

"He was always on something. I gave up on him years ago. He was hitting me when he was in high school. His father had taken off, and I felt sorry for the boy. I must have been crazy myself. I thought he'd give as good as he got from me. Like father, like son. Just as soon as he was old enough, he was gone. Oh, that hurt. Into the service, that's where he went. He came back worse. I tell you, sometimes I was in fear of my life. He would come around whenever he needed money, or a place to hide, or just food. One time he wanted me to hide him because he thought some people were going to kill him. That was Billy. That was the kind of man he became. This didn't surprise me."

"Dale Freeman's girlfriend, Marylou Brown—"

"That wasn't her name."

"What was it?"

"It was one of those fancy Hollywood names. I didn't believe that either."

"The guy who thought everything was funny. Is it possible he had a German name?"

"Yeah, that was it. Not Fritz. This is upsetting me, and I've shed enough tears. Hans. His name was Hans."

"Dale Freeman is a big, fat guy, isn't he?"

"You better believe it. Really, there's only so much I can take." She was guiding him to the door.

"I understand," Mike said. "And the girl he was with: do you think her name could have been Valerie Moreland?"

"Yeah, something like that. I think so."

"Broad hips," Mike said. She had the screen door open.

"I don't look at women's bodies, mister."

"Thank you," he said, stepping out. The door closed quickly behind him, and he heard the hook being slipped into its eye. He didn't look back, cursing himself for not closing on her sooner. What she had said was a long way from a positive ID of Valerie Moreland. She had liked big guys; Dale Freeman was a big guy; Ben Hollister had met Moreland next door to his own place, which was to say, the murder house, but nothing yet absolutely said that Valerie Moreland had *known* Dale Freeman, not even the clothing found in her apartment, the kind of clothing you bought at Zody's or even a supermarket, unless Mike went back and found a hair on it.

It was twenty to twelve. Mike could return to the library, but there wouldn't be time to start on anything else Muriel had lined up for him before having to leave to be in Old Town at one. He didn't want Muriel thinking her interest in him, however she chose to characterize it, was reciprocated. It only stood to reason that Lansing and Freeman had known Hans Roehrig. Daisy Nunn had been doing business with Bernie Maxwell. Mike had seen Roehrig with Jack Skelley, Maxwell's partner. Roehrig and Barranquilla had met with Maxwell the Saturday evening before the murders. Roehrig spoke to Donnie Jackson on the telephone. And Jackson knew Hollister, who had known Valerie Moreland. There was a pecking order: Dale Freeman, Valerie Moreland, the victim, and others, up perhaps half a step to Hans Roehrig, up a full step to Jack Skelley, another full step to Bernie Maxwell. And then—still not fully established—a *big* step to Harcourt Pryor, Maxwell's mortgage holder. The ladder went higher still, to Randall Brandon. Brandon went to presidential inaugurals.

And what had Maxwell and his gang—that's what they were, even though nowadays clowns like these were pleased to call themselves a *family*—what had they been doing lately that was different from what they had done before that caused the great, shapeless Washington beast to grunt and stir itself? Mike was no closer to that than ever. And he wasn't sure he was any closer to the reason for Dan's death. Or why somebody was checking to see if Mike was home at night—in the day, too, at least yesterday, the day of Dan's funeral.

He couldn't find his way back to the freeway. He pulled into a gas station, but nobody came out from the service bays, and he didn't want to blow his horn to ask for a favor. Mike was walking in when he saw a telephone on the wall of the office. Muriel could tell him the way to the freeway. She could also tell him of the progress she'd made, and he'd be better able to budget his time for the rest of the day. With luck.

"Oh, I'm glad you called," she said. "Is there any possibility that you're being followed?"

"As a matter of fact—" He let his answer trail off.

"Well, when you left, I walked to the door. I never met a police detective before, and I wanted to see what kind of car you drive. Is that clear enough for you?"

"Sure, I like cars, too."

"You're a Virgo," she said.

"September first" he answered correctly, but thinking, *Another dingbat*.

"Virgos can be acerbic. In any event, you drove off, and then a moment later, I saw a car pull away from the far corner. Two men were in it, and as they passed me, the one in the passenger seat was looking at me while the driver was pointing toward you."

Mike turned slowly toward the window of the gas station office. "Tell me what kind of car."

"A green four-door sedan. I think it was a Chevy."

He didn't see it. He told her where he was, and she gave him directions to the nearest on ramp. He asked, "Have you made any progress?"

"I think I've found Dale Freeman's sister. She still lives in National City."

"How do you know she's his sister?"

"Another article, in the San Diego section of the *L.A. Times*. I have it here, let me read a little. 'San Diego police sources say that Dale Freeman, Lansing's partner, was to be a victim in the massacre, but somehow evaded the killers. Freeman's sister, Mabel Reiner, of National City, says she has no knowledge of her brother's whereabouts.' There are three Reiners in National City, one is an old man who lives alone, and the second is a woman with a heavy German accent, and the third is listed as Sam Reiner, but a young woman answered when I called. I hung up."

As he took down Mabel Reiner's address, a green Chevy Caprice cruised by. Two guys, studiously not looking at him. He didn't recognize their faces. "That's just fine, Muriel. If the two guys in the Chevy come back, play dumb until they describe me, then tell them that I only asked to see the old newspapers. You can tell them I showed my badge. I want to know what they say."

"I haven't been able to learn anything about Marylou Brown. The high school in National City didn't have anything in its computer."

"How about the local Catholic high school?"

"My God! Do you always think this way?"

When I'm working, he thought. People were concerned that he was down here. People were concerned that he would come here. There were a limited number of people who knew that he would be out of the office today and tomorrow. He would make a mental list of them—*after* he got rid of Heckle and Jeckle in the Chevy. "I'll call you later. If someone's hanging around making it difficult to talk, call me Mildred."

"You drip sex, Mike Gallagher."

"And the doctor said it wouldn't show. Have a nice lunch."

He disconnected with his hand, keeping the receiver up to his ear. His car was facing the direction the Chevy had taken on its pass-by. The Chevy could be parked within sight of the car, but out of his field of vision. He had to decide if he wanted the Chevy's occupants to know that he knew he was being followed.

Mike had not forgotten that Don Grant had told him that the guy he was meeting wanted protection. Ten to twelve. Suddenly Mike had gone from having too much time to not having enough. He put the receiver on the hook and walked out to his car, looking neither left nor right.

On the freeway north he kept up with the traffic and paid no more than his customary attention to the rearview mirror. He got off near the downtown high-rises and headed toward them. What he wanted was a large, full-service hotel on a busy street, or better, two of them. He'd make no attempt right now to elude his pursuers—that would make things only more difficult later. Mike made two turns, sat through too many red lights, endured too much traffic, and then saw a hotel with a doorman. Perfect. Mike pulled up in front of the marquee. Twelve-twenty. He opened the trunk as the doorman hurried over. ''I'm checking in, colonel. Is there a good restaurant in here?''

''We think so. Shall I garage your car?''

''Sure, I won't be using it until after lunch.''

At the desk he told the clerk he was in a hurry because he wanted to take a shower before lunch. ''Is that your best restaurant over there, or do you have a better on the top of the building?''

''The food's the same, sir,'' the kid said, ironing Mike's credit card.

''Maybe I ought to make a reservation from my room,'' Mike said.

''That's the best way.''

In the elevator he peeled a couple of bucks from his roll for the bellboy. ''What's the best thing on the menu in this barn?''

''The cold poached salmon. I always try to get some of that myself.''

''I worry about fires in hotels.''

''We got smoke alarms, fire extinguishers, hoses, fire stairs. We can even handle the Big One—steel-reinforced concrete.''

''That's a relief.''

In his room, Mike dialed the downstairs restaurant. ''This is Mr. Gallagher in room 423, and I want to make a reservation for two at one-thirty. Do you have the salmon today?''

"Yes, we do. Do you want us to set some aside for you? It might be all gone by the time you get here."

"No, I might just change my mind." He hung up and turned on the television set and stepped out into the hall. The bottom of the fire stairs opened onto a side street service entrance. A uniformed guard looked startled.

Mike flashed his badge. "Did you see two young guys in business suits?"

"No. No, I haven't."

"They're driving a green Chevy sedan. I want you to be careful with them. They're involved in that big murder case up in Los Angeles."

"I gotcha."

On the sidewalk, Mike headed back toward the hotel's main entrance. On the next block was a bar, and the bartender had a taxi company's telephone number committed to memory. Mike had left a false trail wide enough to handle a landing 747. It would be a quarter to two before Heckle and Jeckle began to get the idea—and if they went upstairs to listen at the door to his room, they'd be that much longer getting off the dime.

Casa Rosarita was at the downhill end of the long slope that had been the site of the original San Diego, one of the city's premier tourist attractions—there were, in fact, genuine old buildings among the restaurants and gift shops of Old Town, including an authentic eighteenth-century hacienda, and the print shop that had founded the city's first newspaper. Casa Rosarita was in a building modeled after the hacienda, enclosing a tree-shaded courtyard as big as itself. The courtyard was jammed. In one corner four characters wearing sombreros and serapes were playing guitars, and the maître d' gave Mike a mellow "*Buenos dias, señor.*" Mike told him that he was looking for Pablo Kerrigan. The maître d' lit up. "One of our favorite people, Señor Kerrigan. He is here, let me show you to his table."

Mike tried to pick him out in advance. Even in Southern California there was a tendency to forget that Mexico had taken its share of Irish immigrants in the nineteenth century, and when

Don Grant had said the name, Mike had had to suppress a smile. Kerrigan saw Mike before Mike saw him, because Mike saw him getting to his feet, some twenty feet away, a short, smooth-skinned, black-haired man perhaps a few years younger than Mike, wearing a three-piece, light blue glen-plaid suit, a medium blue silk shirt, and a tan silk tie. He had a full mustache. He was wearing a 187 pin. On the table was a bottle of Corona Extra from Mexico City, arguably the best lager beer in the world. Kerrigan smiled without showing his teeth as he extended his hand and said Mike's last name. "Don Grant said you were a little guy with no hair." He glanced at the bandage on Mike's left hand.

"That's Don Grant," Mike said. "How'd you know me?"

"I read lips. Beer?" Kerrigan's eyes were so brown they were almost black. He had eyelashes as long as the kind women glued on. Mike decided not to tell him he read lips, too.

"No, thanks. I'm running on no sleep. I'll have some coffee, though."

Kerrigan gestured to the maître d'. "A message for you," he said when they were alone. "Your new partner, Marvin Burgess, wants you to know that Bobby Michaels has left L.A. Your partner called Don Grant and Grant told me. Your partner thought it was important, urgent for you to know."

Kerrigan's fingernails were professionally maintained. On his little finger was a small diamond ring, and his watch was a Rolex Cellini. Mike said, "Michaels entered Mexico on Tuesday. He's probably on his way to Oaxaca." He watched Kerrigan's eyebrows rising. "The sooner he's picked up, the sooner I can turn up the heat. The information's reliable."

"Why don't you do this yourself?"

"My first priority is Dan Crawford. I'm not supposed to know about Bobby Michaels."

"But you do." A waiter brought Mike's coffee and the menus. Kerrigan sighed. "I knew Dan. I liked him very much. A different kind of man from me, but I liked him. I could see he was a good cop. I've been told that you're a good cop. In San Diego I am known as a great cop. I would never get mixed up in something fishy."

"You married?"

His eyes were fixed on Mike's. "I was, but my wife died. I have a little girl who just started school. My wife was twenty-two years old when she was wiped out by a drunk driver. No jail term for him—they just took away his license for a year. She was visiting her mother, who was in bed with the flu. That was three years ago, and I'm still not completely myself. You asked because I dress too well for you, don't I? A married man isn't supposed to be able to afford to dress so well—at least not a cop.

Mike sat back. "My curiosity was aroused."

"It isn't now?"

"You just told me some things I didn't expect to hear. I'm sorry about your wife."

"You surprised me with the information about Bobby Michaels. I'm sorry about Dan. I understand your priorities. My clothing is my trademark. I want to be instantly recognizable. Down here, all the assholes know me. When they see me, and they're doing something wrong, they get very nervous very fast. People wet their pants when they see me. You see, for years here in San Diego we police have tried to integrate ourselves into the community. We have had classes in conflict resolution and all that liberal shit. In my opinion, it's the reason the San Diego Police Department has suddenly developed the highest death rate in the country. I never went along with it myself. The more I study the criminal mind, the more a law-and-order man I become. There used to be complaints about me using excessive force, but not since I began to dress for the job. How can such a well-dressed fellow kick dope dealers in the balls, the way I kicked Billy Lansing and Dale Freeman? They were on the floor and I kicked them again. This was after the state drug investigators flipped Lansing. It happened in the county, not here. I knew right away what had been done, so I decided that they would work for me, too. I didn't get much out of them, but I could see in the newspapers that the state guys were working them good. I thought they were very unreliable, myself. A real crook never gets a break from me, and all of them know it. I could rid this country of illegal drugs in a year, but nobody wants to listen to the way I would do it."

Mike grinned. "I'm game."

"I would go after the users and the dealers right here in America. Interdiction at the source is bullshit, but it increases DEA's power, which is more important to DEA. The drug problem is our problem. Anyone with so much as a crumb of marijuana on him, a grain of coke or smack, should go to jail for two years. Dealers—anyone with more than an ounce of weed, a gram of coke—go to the gas chamber. I would allow users to turn in their dealers, but beyond that, no exceptions, no copouts. I'd put the executions on television to educate the public."

"You're an angry guy," Mike said cheerfully.

"You should be," Kerrigan said. "You're as much a victim of all these animals as I am." He waved to the waiter. "Let me order. I'm paying. And don't worry about where I get my money. I saved for years before I got married, and invested in my brother's construction business. This is a boomtown. I saw it coming. *Dos Especials, por favor,*" he said to the waiter. "This is a lovely dish, Mike. Sautéed shrimp in cream and a little wine, on orange rice in half a pineapple. If you're tired, you need the sugar. Are you a parent?"

"Not yet."

"As a parent, I've had to learn all that stuff."

Mike wanted to regain control of the conversation. He was still feeling the sting of Kerrigan's comeback about anger. Thinking that Kerrigan was the first guy he had met who was angrier than himself was too easy, Mike decided, and just a way to slip the hook that Kerrigan had put into him. And with his investment in a construction business, Kerrigan could be thought as much a despoiler of the land as any other moneygrubber— but that didn't cut it for Mike either. Kerrigan lived with a *level* of anger Mike had not been able to bear—if anything, Mike could tell Kerrigan about what it meant to be angry, to learn to live with an anger that had been plunged into the heart like a knife. Sure, Kerrigan's solution to the drug problem would work—if the general population could submit to Kerrigan's own mind-set, his anger-fueled self-discipline. Without that anger, Kerrigan himself might succumb to the despair that moped on the street corners of every American city, including San Diego. Kerrigan's anger was a defense against himself. Mike thought he would give the man his privacy in the life that he lived alone, at night, in bed with the lights out, with nothing on the screen of his imagination but the movie he made with his memories. One did not have to be a genius to know who played the female lead. Mike didn't want to know, for Kerrigan's sake, just how well Kerrigan could still feel the dead girl's lips, or hear her small cries of pleasure. "Tell me about Lansing and Freeman," Mike said.

Kerrigan had known them for years. Lansing and Freeman had been bad boys, just bad boys, in spite of Freeman's radio protestation to the contrary. Freeman had as much anger in him as the two talking about him put together, a goofy, picked-on kid, a young man who enjoyed the thrill that accompanied the power over people that his physical strength gave him, a rapist before he was twenty-five even if the victim had not pressed charges, quick with his fists against all comers, a habitual drug user. He had never had a job, as far as Kerrigan knew.

Lansing was only worse, a true sociopath who had welded Freeman's inchoate brutality to his own cunning, a slithering creep who enjoyed pitting people against each other, who had drugged women to put on obscene shows for him. Mike added that to his stepmother's truncated account of having been beaten by the high-school-aged Lansing. In that, Kerrigan's law-and-order position was correct: nobody who had power in this society wanted to face the reality of such scum. Kerrigan had gone up against Lansing and Freeman years before Lansing had beaten the murder rap. Mike had to take Kerrigan as a real tough guy: Kerrigan had put Freeman in the hospital, and had made Lansing beg. Civilians never understood this, which was the real police work: when you had one of these pigs, you had to cripple his psyche, if you could, better, deeper than twenty years in the joint could do. Call it administering the fear of God. There was no rehabilitation for these people; they had made up their minds too early in life that all their fellow creatures were to be used for their pleasure and gain.

The food arrived, and it was delicious, as Kerrigan had said. He wanted to bring Laura Demming here, too. He remembered thinking, Another dingbat, when Muriel Library had guessed his sun sign. Laura wasn't a dingbat; if anything, all that stuff about meditation and the trick she had done with her hands had been an hors d'oeuvre before a more substantial and surprising meal than the guest had been led to hope for. The trouble with Laura Demming was that Mike wanted more of her. The trouble with Laura Demming was that she was in Los Angeles while he was in San Diego. In *A Man and a Woman*, Jean-Louis Trintignant drove all over France like a maniac and still had the energy to attempt to suck the melanin out of Anouk Aimee's freckles. Laura Demming was a head shorter but a lot rounder than Anouk Aimee, and she had freckles and was no less a love object for the stupid bastard who wanted to trust her. Laura seemed to be paying closer attention to his business than he had thought at first, but that was the natural curiosity of an active mind. Only a paranoiac would have second thoughts about a woman who had made herself an accessory after the fact of Barranquilla. She had cleaned up Barranquilla's last filth. But she had said, *Think twice*, and he had heard genuine fearfulness in her voice. What did she have to fear?

Kerrigan had last seen Lansing in January, in a joint on Pacific Beach. Lansing had seemed particularly pleased with himself that night and Kerrigan had wanted to know where Lansing had been. In L.A., Lansing had replied. Kerrigan had told him he thought the L.A. drug scene was too tough for small fry from San Diego.

"Then he said something you want to hear," Kerrigan told Mike over coffee. "He grinned, you know, the way the assholes grin, and said, 'This is heavier than drugs, a lot heavier.' He wanted me to ask, but I never give these guys any satisfaction."

The maître d' approached the table and whispered in Kerrigan's ear. Kerrigan sat up straight. "He's at the bar?" he asked. "Okay, I'll take care of him when I'm done here."

"I was hoping you'd be able to give me a lift back to my hotel, or near it," Mike said.

"Oh, sure. This is a guy whose supposed to stay out of this place. If anybody else in the San Diego department was running Lansing and Freeman, I don't know about it. They were supposed to keep quiet about me anyway, but I don't know if they did or not. As I said, I considered them unreliable—worthless. We're a clean police department, I believe, but I make it a rule not to let other people know too much of my business." He wiped his mouth, put thirty dollars on the table, and stood up. The maître d' rushed over.

"On the house today, Señor Kerrigan, please!"

"Split it with the waiter," Kerrigan said.

The maître d' looked abashed.

"Either way," Mike said to Kerrigan, "thanks for lunch."

"My pleasure. I have to do something now. Maybe it would be a good idea if you stayed at the door of the bar."

Mike nodded, uneasy with having to take orders. The maître d' followed them, and he was joined by the cashier. The bartender saw Kerrigan from the far end of the bar, and tilted his head toward a very big guy in a Hawaiian shirt in animated conversation with a well-tailored character in his late twenties. Kerrigan was shorter than both of them, but Kerrigan had the attitude of command, and the crowd at the bar moved aside for him. The business suit noticed Kerrigan coming at them before the guy in the Hawaiian shirt, who was slow turning around. He decided to tough it out. Kerrigan grabbed the shirt with both hands and kneed the guy in the balls, the knee coming up so swiftly that only the guy's face, emptying of everything but sadness and pain, confirmed that anything at all had happened. Kerrigan grabbed the other guy's necktie and pulled him forward and past the Hawaiian shirt. The two were heading so quickly to the front door with Kerrigan behind them that the confrontation was over before the tourists realized something was happening. Mike was ten paces behind, suppressing a grin. Through the doorway he saw the big guy pitch hard down the stone steps outside. Kerrigan was full of tricks. He told the business suit to stand still, pointing toward a spot on the ground as one would do with a dog. Kerrigan picked up the big guy, whose face was bleeding, and pushed him toward a small Japanese sedan. Kerrigan was talking now, but Mike was too far away to hear what he was saying. The business suit was as motionless as a hypnotized chicken. Hawaiian shirt was doubled up, in pain. While he talked, Kerrigan opened the rear door of the car, rolled the window all the way down, and closed the door again. Mike had no idea what was coming next, but it didn't take long for him to find out. Kerrigan grabbed the big guy by his hair and threw him into the open window and then kneed his butt so hard that he was wedged tight. Kerrigan motioned to the business suit. "If I see you in this place again," Kerrigan said to the business suit, "you'll get worse than this guy. If I see you with him again, I'll put his shit on you and bust you." Kerrigan tore the big guy's pockets off his pants, and a half-dozen white packets spilled out onto the ground. "You got any of this shit on you?"

Business suit shook his head no. "Just the money to buy it, you cocksucker. You got a business card? Give me your fucking business card. I own you now," Kerrigan said. "You'll do everything I tell you, or you'll wish I'd tear your head off and shit down your neck. I *will* do worse." The guy produced his card. "Now get the fuck out of here." Kerrigan cuffed the big guy and pulled him out of the car window, opened the door, and pushed him into the car. Then he ground the packets into the dust with his shoe. "Motherfucker bleeding all over my car. Get in, Mike. It's a good thing I've got vinyl seats." Inside, he said, "Keep your head up back there. I don't want to get another carpet." He turned the key. "This will take about ten minutes."

"Okay," Mike said.

"My nose is broken," the guy gasped as they rolled away.

"Shut up! What did I tell you last time?"

"Stay out of there."

"What else did I tell you?

"That you'd have all the witnesses and evidence."

"Did I lie? You think those people in the restaurant wouldn't testify against you? Answer me. Did I lie?"

"No."

"Now I'll tell you straight: if I see you in San Diego again, I'll kill you. I'll put a bullet in your fucking drug-baked brain. Do you think that's a lie?"

"No."

They were on the freeway that ran out through Mission Valley. At the I-8 Kerrigan swung north past Jack Murphy Stadium and out of the suburban blight into high scrubland. Five more miles, and then Kerrigan pulled onto the shoulder. He opened the door behind Mike. "Get out," he said to the big guy.

"I need a doctor, man."

"Find one up north, or east." As Mike leaned forward, Kerrigan pushed the guy out of the car facedown onto the gravel. Kerrigan got out to retrieve his handcuffs. Mike heard him say, "We have to go down to the next exit to turn around. If I see you doing anything but walking north, I'm going to come back. You want me to come back?"

"No."

From the corner of his eye Mike saw Kerrigan move quickly again and the guy groaned. When he got back in the car and put it in gear, Kerrigan said, "I kicked him in the hamstring."

"I know, I do that myself."

"You know how many times I've busted that guy? Good busts, too. Always back on the streets again before I'm done with the paperwork."

"Still, you're taking a chance."

"Once I got him a year. He did nine months. What the fuck is that?"

Mike wanted to get him off the subject. "I like the trick with the back door, but I don't think I'd do it with a car of mine."

"I'm not a big guy, like you; I have to move fast and hard and throw a scare into them."

"That's the way I was taught," Mike said, remembering Dan.

"I know karate, but I never use it," Kerrigan said.

"Why not?"

He smiled. "Too dangerous. I might hurt somebody."

Three minutes later, heading south, they passed the guy in the Hawaiian shirt hobbling north, holding his leg, his pants sliding off his ass. Kerrigan was telling Mike what he knew about Jacumba, laying it all out for him.

If the guys from the green Chevy were waiting for Mike in the hotel lobby, Mike didn't make them. No matter. It was two-thirty now. Don Grant had said it was necessary to preserve Kerrigan's security, and Mike had done it; now he knew enough about Jacumba to feel more confident about getting Dale Freeman. Upstairs, Mike turned off the television set and called Maurice Constantine.

"I didn't know you were going to use me as an answering

service, Mr. Gallagher," Constantine said good-naturedly. "It's a good thing I have a tape recorder with me. There's been some action at Jackson's. Apparently Jackson tried to reach that guy Hollister last night, and this morning he went over there. Hollister has cleared out."

"Jackson could be misreading what he found," Mike said.

"I don't think so. Jackson didn't find anything except Hollister's furniture. Clothing, video stuff, cameras—all gone."

"You're sure about the clothing?"

"That's what Jackson said."

Hollister must have come back for it. "All right, what else?"

"I'm still telling you. Jackson is really losing it. He's going nuts. He's afraid that Hollister had some stuff that was important, incriminating. I played back the conversation last night between Jackson and Hollister, and Jackson asked Hollister if he had anything in his house."

"I remember."

"Anyway, Jackson's convinced now that Hollister did, and took it with him when he split. Jackson is scared to death. He called Hans Roehrig, and Roehrig told Jackson he had nothing to worry about."

It sounded like Roehrig thought he was controlling Jackson. "What do you think?"

Constantine said, "I think Jackson is in very bad shape. The blonde, Jenny, was out of the bedroom for a few minutes, and he just went ape, growling, hunched over like an animal; at one point there I thought he was going to chew on the furniture."

"More power to him," Mike said. "Anything else he's doing?"

"He's very rough on her," Constantine said. "She's so pretty."

Mike took a breath. "I've seen her."

"Tits to die for," Constantine said.

"You've seen them," Mike said.

"I told you yesterday when she was wearing only a T-shirt. Today she's wearing shorts. Who knows tomorrow it may be shoes." He laughed through his teeth at his own joke.

"Have you heard anything indicating anything heavier than drugs?" Mike asked.

"Just what I told you about Hollister, if that's heavier."

"What are the messages?"

"The first is from Frank Kennedy, and the second is from your partner. He called only a little while ago." Constantine hit a switch. "The sound is fuzzy because I didn't do a good connection," he added quickly.

Frank Kennedy's voice: "I have that background you wanted on Randall Brandon and his family, but it's too lengthy and maybe too ordinary to go through on Radio Free Constantine. As for Bob Wills—the question I just found on my machine— Wills will be happy to meet with you anytime, anywhere. He's being a little prick. Wants a quid pro quo. If you're straight with him, and answer some questions he has, he'll be straight with you about the connection between Bernie Maxwell and Harcourt Pryor, which I think is hot. You can call me anytime, and I mean anytime." And he left his home telephone number.

Marvin Burgess: "Ruppert was around a few minutes ago— I mean, at eleven-thirty. He got a call from Cutler's office. A body was found in the bottom of a canyon off Mulholland, on the Valley side. Ruppert thinks that because Cutler called him that we know something about it, or rather, *you* do. You were the one Ruppert was talking about. The other thing is that one of the boys who works with Marlon called me, and that Kiku got out on bail this morning. What this guy heard was that Kiku told his boss, Bernie Maxwell, that he was going to get his own lawyer and go for his own best deal if Maxwell didn't move his ass. I don't know what Cutler has on his mind, if anything, but it's all the more reason to be very, very careful. I'll talk to you later."

"That's it," Constantine said. "I can get back to either one of them, if you want."

"No. We'll talk again at nine o'clock," Mike said, and hung up.

He dialed Muriel Library. Two rings before she picked it up.

"Hiya, it's Mike Gallagher. I wanted to find out if you had anything on Marylou Brown."

"Oh, *hi*, Mildred. No, I haven't. Not a thing. I've done what you said, but I have two gentlemen here. Can we talk later— this evening?"

"Sure, give me your number at home." He wrote it down, thinking he was getting the chance to shake the two characters for good. He'd check out of the hotel now. He'd tell the bellboy, clerk, and doorman he had finished his business early and was heading back to L.A. The gag might work a second time. Why not? It even made sense.

18

"THE LAST TIME DALE CALLED ME, ABOUT A MONTH ago," Mabel Reiner, Dale Freeman's older sister, said, "he said they were about to fuck things up for this fellow Maxwell, just as they were supposed to do. It was why they had been in L.A. so long. He sounded very optimistic and hopeful. You have to understand about Dale: he's capable of forgetting bad things in a way that I'm not. If there's a shred of hope to cling to, he has his hands on it. I thought he was involved in something up in Los Angeles much too complicated for him, but he saw it as a way of getting his life straightened out once and for all. He was in love with that Valerie. I was very skeptical of her from the start, but Dale was in love. He's like that, likes to think he's rescuing a woman. It's how he knows he's in love."

Mabel Reiner had told all this to federal investigators last week; she thought Mike represented LAPD in a similar investigation of its own. Burgess's message about Barranquilla's body

being found had left Mike feeling tense and anxious, and what
he was learning was making him worse.

She was talking from the kitchen of her double-wide mobile
home in the middle of a tightly compressed acre of such structures, tiny, neatly trimmed gardens, and toyland streets. Mike
was sitting in the living room, decorated in the chintz and panel-
ing that was apparently obligatory for mobile homes. She was
getting coffee for herself—he had had enough today. The Reiner
place was neat, clean, and comfortable, the result of real effort
and perhaps sacrifice. Mabel Reiner was coarse-featured and
dark-haired, in her mid-thirties, a tall woman who might have
been heavy once. She was wearing a short-sleeved salmon-col-
ored blouse and black slacks. The two Reiner children were in
school, Reiner up in San Diego at the Navy shipyard. An older
man, Mabel had said. It was clear to Mike that she loved Reiner
and was grateful to him, but Mike wondered if she had ever
been *in* love with him. There was no doubt in Mike's mind that
that consideration did not matter to Mabel Reiner, whose careful, constrained demeanor suggested she was glad about what
she had. She had already told Mike that she and her brother had
had an abused childhood, their drunken father brutalizing both
of them, Mabel in ways that Mike construed to be sexual. The
mother had known, it seemed, and had chosen to keep silent.
Brother Dale had not been all that kind to Mabel, either, but as
Mabel was saying, he was both forgetful and ever-optimistic.
Mabel had already said that her childhood had had her screwed
up for years. With their father dead and their mother in a mental
institution, Mabel was all the family Dale had, and he clung to
her, now calling her "Sis." Mike found her view of Valerie
Moreland instructive, even if prejudicial: Mabel thought Vale-
rie was using her brother. Mike had not told Mabel that Valerie
Moreland was dead. Valerie wanted the fast lane, Mabel said,
and Dale was easy access, a pigeon for someone who thought
she knew how to put on the dog. Dale thought Valerie had class,
Mabel snorted, adding that Valerie was a pig wearing perfume.
Mike was remembering what Azzolini had told him about
Moreland being drawn to big guys, and chances were good that
his truth was as true as Mabel's. All Mabel Reiner said about
Dale Freeman and Valerie Moreland was that they weren't as

smart as they thought, and not cut out for a life against the rules, a thing that could be said for just about everyone who had ever lived.

Freeman and Lansing had left San Diego last October, setting themselves up in a house rented for them—Freeman's words—on Mulholland Drive. According to what Freeman had told his sister, Lansing met with "important people" about what he called "the operation"—Freeman liked to talk like that, full of himself, Mabel said. The deal was better than the one they had been getting in San Diego, he had told Mabel; the police down here had been squeezing them, forcing them to take chances. Lansing had been a problem for the police here, Freeman knew, often double-crossing them or going off in his own directions. As Freeman had been given to understand the Los Angeles "operation," he and Lansing had had one target, Maxwell, and once they had hit him, they would be free of police control thereafter. Lansing's girlfriend was up in L.A. for weeks at a time, Freeman had told his sister. To Mabel it seemed that her brother had met Valerie Moreland within a month of his arrival in Los Angeles. Azzolini had said she had been a regular in the Clown Club at that time. Freeman might have met Moreland in the Clown Club, but it really didn't matter: Hollister had met her in the house where Freeman's partner had later lost his life. Lansing's stepmother had seen Moreland in April in Chula Vista. No shadow or fuzz on it now. This was May, and a well-triangulated, clear chain of evidence put Freeman and Lansing in Los Angeles *and* involved with the Maxwell menagerie continuously for at least six months preceding the killings, not the two months of the official account.

And involved for a purpose—an *assignment*. Mike was more than anxious now, he was frightened. Only a fool wouldn't be, even without two guys in a green Chevy two and a half steps behind him. Mike couldn't be sure he had outfoxed them. He couldn't be sure Muriel Library had told him the truth about what she had told them about him. One thing he could be sure of: even if he could consider backing off—which he could not— it was impossible. Backing off was just another way to invite disaster. Mike knew too much. He had not thought of it this way before. More than defending himself, he had to pursue this to the finish simply to survive.

"What did your brother mean, that Maxwell was their 'target,' and they were supposed to 'hit' him?"

"Dale really didn't say," Mabel Reiner said. "He just gave me some nonsense about Maxwell being a heavy dude. My brother likes being full of himself. If you knew him, you'd know what I mean."

Mike had the idea. "Now, we both know that your brother *and* this character Maxwell were involved in drug trafficking. Was there anything else your brother ever mentioned *besides* drug trafficking, in addition to it, bigger than it?"

"Hints."

"What kind of hints?"

"Dale said Maxwell was the first really evil person he'd ever come across. My brother has a low set of standards, so make of that what you will. Dale thought there was something good inside Billy Lansing. I never saw it. Billy Lansing would have cut the heart out of an infant if he'd thought there was something in it for him, like a laugh."

"What do you think went wrong in Los Angeles?"

"Oh, *Lansing! He* went wrong. I don't know who gave those people up there the idea that he could be trusted. If there's any part of this I can't understand, it's that Billy Lansing had any role in it whatsoever. He wore out his welcome down here a dozen different times. He wasn't feared, he was just hated. And my brother? My brother is below normal in intelligence. He's not retarded, but he *is* so dumb that he laughs at people who are smarter than him because he doesn't know what else to do. He can't imagine what the world is really like. He never outgrew those movies we saw when we were kids—he *couldn't*. My God, he was even seeing himself as some kind of undercover law enforcement operative. He went from crime to anticrime without blinking an eye, like Elvis Presley taking drugs and hobnobbing with the FBI. My brother Dale was still doing cocaine while he was talking about getting rid of this guy Maxwell as a service to society!"

Mike stood up. "And you haven't heard from your brother since the murders?"

"No. I didn't hear from Valerie either. She had my telephone number. I suppose she just moved on to the next dope." Mike was moving toward the door, but she saw something in his eyes. "What happened to her?" Mabel Reiner asked.

Mike shrugged. "Same thing that happened to the people in the Rainbow Drive house, and at about the same time." She looked jolted. "Your brother didn't do it, and I don't think the guy who did the people on Rainbow Drive did her either. One other thing: Marylou Brown. I'm having trouble getting a line on her."

"I didn't know her. She was so much younger than the others."

"Your brother said he knew her."

"There were an awful lot of people he knew that I never met. Thank God."

"Your brother never mentioned her, even once?"

She shook her head.

"To the best of your knowledge, he was all wrapped up in Valerie Moreland?"

"That's one way of putting it, yes."

"Wait a minute, I've got something I want you to hear." Mike had all but forgotten it—forgotten he had the radio station's cassette, and where he had stashed it in the glove compartment of his car. Now it was under Hollister's videocassettes. Mabel Reiner was holding the aluminum screen door open for him when he returned. A mobile home was nothing but aluminum, vinyl, and polyurethane posing as wood; if the designers ever submitted to the materials, mobile homes might become truly popular, even trendy, as superefficient instant hi-tech, where spring cleaning could be done with a garden hose, and the occupants, watching a satellite television transmission from Belize, could wonder why the laws of gravity still applied. Mike told Mabel Reiner only that he had gotten the tape from a talk show in Los Angeles. He had not listened to it before, and now he found that five minutes of the prattle of the show's host preceded the hillbilly's call.

At last the hillbilly, with all his crap about the victims being good people. "Is that your brother?" Mike asked.

Mabel Reiner nodded. "See what I mean about him being full of himself?"

Mike didn't answer, because he was thinking of the last thing Freeman had said: *Marylou Brown, . . . like a song.* The tape went blank, hissing.

"I never heard of her until this moment," Mabel Reiner said.

"He never mentioned her to you, you mean," Mike said.

"Yes, that's what I mean. I never heard of her before the murders. You say Valerie was murdered, too?"

"Yes. Actually her name was Ethel not Valerie. I think your brother was crying for her when he made that call. Does that make sense to you?"

"Do you mean, could he do that?"

"Yes, that's what I mean. You said he was dumb, but there are trees that must be that smart."

She looked as if he had hit her with the back of his hand. "Yes. Yes, he could do that. Say one girl's name while he had another in his mind."

Mike rewound and collected the tape, thinking that everyone in Hollywood was an actor. Twenty-four hours or less after her death, Dale Freeman had known that Valerie Moreland was dead. How? By the time of the radio show he must have been in police custody participating in the cover-up. He'd said *two months*, parroting the police story. Mike turned to Mabel. She was in tears, but her mouth was twisted in a crooked grin.

"Ethel? That's worse than Mabel."

Mike had his card ready. "Call me if you remember something, or anything else comes up." He let himself out and returned to his car. He had thought of saying, *Her throat had been crushed with a tire iron.* It made him wake up. *Same weapon, different killer.* Not Brother Dale. Not Lansing, who was already dead. Not Barranquilla, who would have beat her to death—that was the way he'd tried to take out Mike, like his Rainbow Drive victims. No, a *different* killer. Jackson had been in on it. Bobby Michaels. And Roehrig. The blood in her trunk said Valerie Moreland had been killed someplace else and then brought home. Mike still didn't know why, but he'd get to that later. Of the bunch who had double-timed down the hill, if he had the players right, Jackson was now the most frightened, and

Bobby Michaels the one who possibly had some real affection for women. Roehrig? Of the survivors, Roehrig was a sociopath. Mike had seen him, knew his record at Huntsville. Roehrig was a pervert who would do anything if he thought he could get away with it.

As Mike drove away from the mobile-home park, he was supposing that Valerie had been up the hill at Roehrig's house, waiting, not knowing, not suspecting that she, too, was to be a victim. She could not have heard the cries in Daisy Nunn's house from Roehrig's place. When the gang had shuffled back up the hill, under Mike's nose, Valerie had gotten hers. All right, Mike asked himself, almost aloud, why?

She had known the victims, and Dale Freeman best of all. She had done costumes for Hollister.

Nah. Not good enough.

But Hollister had run for his life last night after Mike had confronted him. Maybe he had run because Mike had shown his face, but that wasn't what had made Jackson nervous earlier. Jackson had made a rare trip out of his house to find Hollister, the man who worried him because he might have had something at home that Jackson didn't want him to have, something heavier than dope. Moreland had run around with Freeman, who thought Maxwell a truly evil man. He had blabbed a lot to his sister—what had he told Moreland? Was *that* it, something he told her? From what Dan had said, what Bob Wills's recent interest in Pryor suggested, Maxwell had been involved with Harcourt Pryor in real-estate investments. *Very* indirectly Harcourt Pryor had allowed himself to be vulnerable to a bigdreaming female jerk who may or may not have found sexual satisfaction with a full-of-himself country lunk who more often than not needed a bath. Not even Harcourt Pryor was as smart as he thought, or cut out for a life against the rules.

But none of that explained what the sons of bitches were really up to, or why Dan had had to die. About the latter, Mike was getting an idea: in its own way, small potatoes, and that made it only worse.

How? How do you kill a man in his car without touching him or the car?

Four-thirty. Mike was heading north on the freeway, back to

San Diego, and not being followed. He wanted to check into another hotel and get some sleep before he started east along the border. He wanted to talk to Kennedy, he wanted to talk to Laura, even if it was much too early for her to have information for him. As much as anything he did not want Pablo Kerrigan getting any more under his skin than Kerrigan had gotten already. *In San Diego I am known as a great cop.* Mike had wanted to tell Kerrigan to go fuck himself, but then Kerrigan had Saran-wrapped those two geeks in the bar, getting one to stay motionless with a command while he rolled down a car window to improvise a seventeenth-century stock for the other, talking all the while. Element of surprise. The whole episode had made Mike crazy, not because it had been so dangerous, but because Mike had not been in on it or had known what was coming next. This was the wrong time in his life to be shown that he did not know all the tricks. Kerrigan may not have recovered yet from his wife's death, and maybe the drunk who had killed her had caught no time, but Kerrigan himself had not failed her or her memory. He had a little girl who had just started school, a little girl who would never have the problems of a Mabel Reiner. All Mike had to show for his life was a hope for a woman he had just met. Kerrigan reminded Mike too much of his own failures, all of them. As much as Mike needed sleep, he did not look forward to what he might dream, or the way it would leave him feeling afterward.

His eyes snapped open and he sat up quickly, turning his watch into the dim twilight seeping through the gap in the drapes: a quarter to eight. He was in a hotel room in Mission Valley, he remembered. According to the map, Jacumba was at least thirty miles from here, mostly over a two-lane county road—but he couldn't leave here until after nine o'clock, when he was scheduled to talk to Burgess and Constantine. No time to eat. He'd have to find a supermarket, too, for a package of big plastic garbage bags. Kerrigan had given him an idea. Now Mike stood up and shuddered, still struggling with the confusion created by sleeping in a strange place at the wrong time of day. He could have slept around the clock—but he doubted that he would have felt rested even after that, given his frame of mind. He stretched, trying to wake up, thinking: *Kennedy. Laura*. He had put off calling them. And Muriel Library. He wanted to hear what Heckle and Jeckle had said to her. He was rattled—ragged. . . .

He called Kennedy at home and told him he was just waking up.

"I was wondering when you slept. You missed the news, I guess. That big guy, Kiku, is out on bail."

"I knew that."

"Parker Center announced that he's not a suspect in the Rainbow Drive killings, but that his boss, Maxwell, is still the subject of investigation. *Your* bosses seem to be letting out a story bit by bit. The heat is very definitely on. Late this afternoon one of my federal friends told me that a little Latino was found with his head crushed in a car in a canyon off Mulholland this morning, and the police won't speculate even privately on a connection to the other killings."

"Did you get his name?"

"No name yet pending notification of next of kin. My federal friend downtown says that the body was picked clean of ID and that the car had been sold months ago, but not reregistered. Don't hold your breath for his name."

"Given the number of hours that passed between the discovery of the body and what your friend was able to tell you, can you make an educated guess about how close to the case the federals are?"

"That's a hell of a good question," Kennedy said. "Damned close, I'd have to say. No, let me correct myself. They're as close as it's possible to get. They are *there*."

Mike decided that there was no point in telling Kennedy that he thought so, too; it would only invite questions about how he had formed his opinion. "Tell me about the Brandons. I want to talk to you about Bob Wills, too."

Kennedy had gotten his information on the Brandons from the very social ex-wife of a dead television actor. She was in constant need of money, always trying to sell him information for the supermarket tabloids, and she knew that anything she ever told Kennedy that turned out to be untrue or even exaggerated would make her worthless to him. At first she had not wanted to talk about the Brandons because of their immense power, but Kennedy had softened her up with a tease about her memoirs, which she wanted to have written for her—a guaranteed best-seller, she thought, because she had been laid by every man who had achieved any kind of show business fame in the last forty years. It was probably the only noteworthy thing she had ever done, but Kennedy doubted that the book would get written even by a ghostwriter, because the woman had the attention span of a gnat.

According to her, there was no proof that Randall Brandon had done anything intelligent in his life. He had been an awkward, lonely child, dominated by his mother until he had gone away to college, where he had fallen in love with the first girl to smile at him, a large-breasted blonde probably no brighter than he was. Mother had opposed the marriage, and now that it was over, Mother, long-widowed, was pleased. Mother, in fact, had been the powerhouse in the family since the early thirties; Randall Brandon had inherited his father's brains, which was to say, he was cerebrally bankrupt. According to Kennedy's informant, Randall Brandon was still an awkward klunk, and she, the informant, figured that the Swede now in the Brandon beach house had seen her opportunity and grabbed it. The Brandon marriage, never a healthy one, was stone dead; it had struggled along for twenty-three years. Two children: a daughter, Barbara, twenty-one, described by the informant as a sullen little tramp; and a son, Randall III, a fourteen-year-old interested in computers—he might be the one in the family with his grandmother's intelligence, if not verve.

Randall Brandon had inherited not only a fortune of more than three billion dollars, he had inherited the man who had been groomed for more than two decades to manage it, Harcourt Pryor. Kennedy's informant had seen Pryor over the years at galas and charity dinners, always at a distance, and she had watched his transformation from a very junior partner in the Brandon family's private legal firm to the firm's man in charge. The transformation had been marked by a profound personal and social development. Harcourt Pryor had gone from a relatively shy, even grim young manhood to a sophisticated, urbane, even graceful maturity. A very classy guy, was the way Kennedy's informant described him. When Kennedy asked about Pryor's personal life, she could only say that Pryor was the personification of discretion and privacy. She had never heard a word about Pryor with women, although she had seen him in Chasen's, Perino's, and La Toque with beautiful, stylish women—*smart* women, not bimbos, or the kind of hags with whom a closet queen surrounds himself. Kennedy's informant prided herself in always having been able to spot a fag. Pryor was no fag, secret sadist, or anything that women on her social level gossiped about quickly enough. Harcourt Pryor had been part of L.A.'s establishment forever, and there never had been a bad word about him. Some women found him too opaque, but others found that opacity beguiling. He was attractive, not overweight like so many middle-aged men, and rich in his own right: but the real center of what was sexy about him was his power. No single individual in Southern California was as powerful as Harcourt Pryor, with the possible exception of Randall Brandon himself—and that exception was only possible, not probable.

"The indispensable man," Kennedy said. "Brandon would be in terrible trouble without Harcourt Pryor, while Pryor would probably do pretty well for himself without the Brandon power base."

Mike was trying to match the voice he had heard this morning with Kennedy's informant's description. Harcourt Pryor was not only comfortable with his power, he *believed* in it: he would not have told Mike that he had spoken to Bob Wills two days ago if he were not as sure of his power as the Russians of their historic destiny. Pryor didn't think he was indispensable, he thought he was untouchable. Mike decided not to tell Kennedy about his brief contact with Pryor. Dan had had more than a brief contact. A conversation—after other conversations with someone in the Brandon household. And after that conversation, the others had stopped. To Kennedy, Mike said, "See if you can have Bob Wills where I can reach him tomorrow morning. I don't know what time I'll be able to call, so tell him it's in his interest to keep himself available."

"Do you have something newsworthy to trade? Wills can be a bastard at times, and I have to do business with him."

Mike sighed. "I'll have the stuff. One other thing. Pryor's office: that's on the West Side, isn't it?"

"Century City. His firm has a whole floor near the top of the north tower. His own office has an unobstructed view of Brentwood, Bel Air, Beverly Hills, and everything east to downtown and the mountains. There was a big spread about it in *Los Angeles* magazine last year."

On Mike's income, upscale consumer magazines were only depressing. He said good-bye and dialed Laura. No answer. He checked his watch while letting the phone continue to ring. Eight-thirty. On impulse, he tried Maurice Constantine.

"I'm on my way over to your place, Mr. Gallagher. Let me pull over so we can talk. I'm on Ventura Boulevard in Sherman Oaks and the traffic is pretty heavy. Something happened at Jackson's this afternoon that you want to know about. I have it on tape and I'll play it for you if you want. You might be able to figure out who installed the television transmitter."

"That was Bernie Maxwell," Mike said. "There's a Hughes Market at the corner of Coldwater with a very big parking lot. You can pull in there."

"I see it. How did you know it was Maxwell?"

"It's his house and he moved Jackson in there in a hurry. The cops had the infrared. When they busted Maxwell the other night, they hit his office at the same time and found the television receiver. That explains why the infrared was turned off. If it had been my operation, I would have figured out the special frequency business and then left everything as it was, but I don't know if the people running the show are that smart. Originally I thought Maxwell had put Jackson in there to keep track of him, but television is an expensive way to do it. Now I think Maxwell wanted to keep an eye—literally, an eye—on something else."

Constantine chortled. "You don't need me, Mr. Gallagher. You have it all figured out."

"Maxwell dropped in on Jackson today, didn't he?"

"Well, Jackson called him, and Maxwell came right over.

Hold on, I've got to wait for this gal in front of me to make the turn into the lot. Boy, it's crowded in there.''

"Today's the day the newspapers print the double coupons, and Hughes takes everybody's. Tell me about Maxwell."

"Jackson called him at three o'clock and told him that Hollister was gone. Maxwell and that Japanese bodyguard showed up twenty minutes later. What made *me* think that Maxwell set up the television transmitter was that he stood with his back to the camera so that there was nothing on the screen but his head and shoulders and a little bit of the room on either side. I saw Jackson open the closet door and then the Japanese guy went in and out a couple of times. They didn't talk about what was going on—''

"They talked about Hollister," Mike said.

"And Roehrig. Maxwell was really tense. From what I understood, he's on the outs with Roehrig and wants Jackson to kind of keep tabs on him. 'Listen to what he says, don't argue, but tell me what he has to say when we talk again.' I remember that exactly. I'm in a parking space now. Do you want me to play the tape?"

"No time. What did Maxwell say about Hollister?"

"He said, 'Do you think this fellow Hollister has any of these?' He jerked his head toward the closet. Then he added, 'He was supposed to have destroyed the ones he had left.' Jackson said he didn't think Hollister was a problem either way."

"And you say Kiku was going in and out of there? Where was the girl?"

"They sent her up to Power Burger for food. She was so doped up that I was thinking that she really couldn't handle going out. Jackson told her to take an hour. He's one nasty bastard, I'll tell you that."

Mike said, "Even though you couldn't see, was it possible that Kiku was carrying something out of the closet?"

"Well, Kiku made more than one trip, and Maxwell said *these*. So it was more than one thing."

"Was there any way you could tell if those *things* left the bungalow?"

"No, but I don't think they did. At one point, Jackson said, 'That's an awful stink,' and Maxwell said, 'We'll turn on the attic fan and it will be all gone by the time the girl returns.' If they didn't burn whatever they took out of the closet, they poured acid or something on it, because when Maxwell finally moved out from in front of the camera, Kiku was wearing a mask the way they do in Tokyo when the pollution is bad. After Maxwell was gone, Jackson was out of the bedroom awhile, and I heard a door open—not the front door, because I know that sound— and then after a while, the door closed and Jackson came back to the bedroom. My guess is that he took out the garbage. When the girl came back, he was real sly with her, as if he had a secret.''

"But he didn't tell her anything," Mike said.

"He told her she wouldn't be seeing her friend Roehrig anymore. There must have been something between Roehrig and the girl, but I tell you, Mr. Gallagher, I'm sure Jackson put her up to it. He's that kind of guy. He was getting rough with her again.''

Mike was thinking about Roehrig. Apparently Roehrig had been able to make the kind of new deal for himself that had Maxwell alarmed enough to try to defend himself. Of course Maxwell's position was more than seriously eroded now—only a fool would not know it. Given Roehrig's proximity to, and probable involvement in, the murders, Roehrig had not made his deal with the police. He would have had to go another way, a way that threatened Maxwell. Mike wanted to remember that Maxwell hadn't known him during the raid on his house on Woodrow Wilson Drive, the night after Mike had taken care of Barranquilla—that had been three nights after Dan's death. And for *these,* the only *these* that Hollister could have had that Maxwell would have known about were the videotapes now in Laura's house. Hollister had taken off not only because he thought Mike had been involved in the murders, but also because the tapes had been missing when Hollister had returned to his place last night. You kept such things because they were valuable, and perhaps potentially more valuable later as a true life insurance. You destroyed them when they had lost their value, even had become a threat. *That* was how badly Maxwell's situation had deteriorated. All that had changed, besides Roehrig's allegiance, that Mike knew was the discovery of Barranquilla's body, but Maxwell's reaction to Mike on Tuesday night had shown Mike that Maxwell had had no knowledge of what Barranquilla had been trying to do at the time of his death. The discovery of Barranquilla's body had tipped Maxwell not only to the fact that the little guy had taken the assignment to hit Mike from somebody else, but also to the idea that Barranquilla's pal Roehrig was working for that same party. Now Mike gave Maurice Constantine Maxwell's address. "I know that there's a line of sight to his house from across a canyon. You're going to have to get a map and figure it out for yourself. If you have any energy left after you see Marvin Burgess in a few minutes, start tonight. Otherwise, pick it up tomorrow. Somebody's greasing Maxwell's skids and he still thinks he can hang on. I want to hear it when he can't anymore. And you be careful. Maxwell still has fangs, and you don't want to be spotted by anybody else interested in this."

"I understand, Mr. Gallagher. You don't want me to mention this to Mr. Burgess, do you? I haven't told Mr. Kennedy what I'm doing."

Mike gave a little shudder. "Yeah, that's the way, I'm sorry to say."

Constantine giggled as if from under a quilt. "I'm enjoying watching you work, Mr. Gallagher. I don't know how you had all that figured out about Jackson and Maxwell, so you must be a pretty good cop."

"Maxwell made himself Jackson's landlord, that's all. I watched another cop at work today," Mike said. "He said he was considered a great cop. Now I'm not so sure I know what a cop is."

"I wouldn't be surprised if you were a little tired, Mr. Gallagher."

Mike said thanks and good-bye. He dialed Muriel Library's home number. She was one of those women who sang hello over the telephone.

"It's Mildred, Muriel. This is the first chance I've had to call you."

"Well, hello! I'd just about given up on you!"

"There was a moment between us today that I'm not in a

position to do anything about. Since that's the only thing stopping me, I thought you'd like to know.''

"You're not married," she said firmly.

"As a matter of fact, no. I just met a woman who may have found the zipper to my heart.''

She laughed. ''Thank you for your honesty. Your friends came back a second time. Are you in some kind of trouble?''

"You tell me.''

"It seems so serious, I'm not sure I should—I mean, I'm not sure I should get involved.''

"I showed you my badge," Mike said. "My partner was killed and I want to know all about it. Those men you saw today don't really know what they're doing. They're obeying orders. Do you want to hear more?''

"I don't think I should.''

"There's been one attempt on my life already," Mike said.

"The only reason—no, *one* reason—I've told you as much as I have is that the two men were less than polite with me the second time they were here. Maybe I'm not the actress I think I am in my fantasies, but when they returned and I told them the same thing I told the first time —which was what you told me to say, by the way, that you showed your badge and wanted to see old newspapers—one of them said, 'We don't want to find out that you've lied to us.' They were more like the Mafia than the police. This has been a very unhappy day for me, I must tell you.''

"What kind of police?''

"Los Angeles, like you. I thought you knew that.''

"I did. I wanted to be sure. They showed their badges?''

"Oh, yes. They never said that you've done anything wrong. Maybe they were more like the KGB than the Mafia. They were in a very agitated state the second time, could hardly stand still. When one was talking, the other was looking out the window, as if you were going to roll by.''

"Did they say anything to each other that you weren't supposed to hear or understand?''

"I know what you mean. I thought of it when I heard one of them say something to the other, and the other said something back.''

Mike took a breath. "Let's pretend I don't want to come through the telephone at you to find out what that was."

"Your lady has her hands full," she said coolly. Muriel's feelings about him were a long way from where they had been this afternoon. "I really didn't get what the first one said. After the second said his piece, I just froze. They wanted to see the newspapers you looked at, so I gave them the right ones. They looked at them, wrote down some things, and left. What the second said was, 'I wouldn't want to be in his shoes. He's as good as dead.' I think they were talking about you, Mr. Gallagher."

"Did they give you their cards? Do the cards say what division they're with?"

"Yes, they gave me their cards, and no, the cards just have their names, if that means anything. I'm to call their office in Los Angeles if I hear from you again. Are you as good as dead?"

"Only if I slow down." Cards with no division identification indicated something, all right: Internal Affairs—Cutler's men. Mike asked for their names and Muriel read them off. He didn't recognize the names any more than he had recognized their faces this morning. Mike had no time to waste on niceties. "I'll see you, Muriel." He hung up and dialed Laura again. If Heckle and Jeckle had worked their way to Mabel Reiner, there was a chance that Cutler or whoever was directing them had the Jacumba move figured out already. Hammond might figure it out, if he remembered what he had said to Mike the other night. It was remote, but it was *possible*. And Mike sure couldn't trust Muriel not to drop a dime on him—not now, he couldn't. This time Laura picked up on the first ring. "Are you naked?"

"Yes, as a matter of fact. The telephone's in the bathroom with me. I got in ten minutes ago and I've been hoping you'd call. The dog is outside the bathroom door, and I've got a little protection right here on the sink."

"That fourteen-shot automatic?"

"No, that's still in the drawer of the corner table in the living room. This is a sawed-off, a real alley cleaner, my father called it. He made it for me."

"Why all the ordnance?"

"The tapes. I started watching them this afternoon. Girls,

Mike. One after the other with a lot of blank tape in between. They were showing their stuff, pulling up their skirts, taking off their blouses, opening negligees, taking instruction from someone off camera. Some were drugged, others just as obviously not too bright. I looked at twelve or fifteen girls on three or four tapes, and I *did-not-like-it!* They were *scared,* some of those girls. The tapes are like the ones that actors have of their performances to show what they can do. One girl after another, most of them young, a lot of them street girls, no more than fourteen, fifteen years old. One might have been even younger. What do you want me to do, Mike? I really am unhappy about this."

"I'm sorry. Were they numbered?"

"Yes, on the cassettes themselves. One through six, seven through thirteen, and so forth."

"I'd like you to see if there's a number seventy-four. It's important. See if it's on the tape. Please. Has the dog sounded off tonight?"

"No. Don't play games with me. I'll do what you ask, but— anyway, I have the right to say I don't like it."

"Yes, you do, and again, I'm sorry. Keep that dog close to you. And the shotgun. Did you get to the college?"

"Yes, that's where I just came from."

"Were you able to compare Greg Novak's signature last week with the signatures in the preceding weeks?"

"Yes." He thought he heard her hesitate again. "They match, Mike. It's all right."

"You sound like you're not sure."

"I am sure. The signatures match. It's just not for me, this sort of work. The tapes really upset me."

"What do you think they are?"

"Hollister is a pornographer, isn't he?"

Her voice was unsteady. Maybe he had asked too much of her. If she wasn't as tough as she hoped, he was just as glad. "Do you think you can describe one segment of tape in detail? I'm sorry about this, Laura."

"I'll try. There's one I remember, a blond girl about sixteen years old. Some of these girls are prettier than others, but all of them are attractive. This girl had blue eyes, a sweet face, a little baby fat, soft shoulders, full bosom, curvy hips. She stepped into the range of the camera with her eyes on the man giving the instructions. She was a little glassy-eyed, a little frightened. You can hear his voice in the background—''

"Tell me about it."

"He had an attitude. He could have been high himself. He was derisive."

"You're saying he was laughing at her."

"To himself, in a degrading way. He had her move to the right a little, then to the left. She pulled up her skirt to show her knees. Not all of these girls wore skirt, blouse, full slip, stockings, and garter belt, like her. Some were in costume or sexy underwear, as if they were different men's fantasies. He told her to pull her skirt up higher, and she did—reluctantly."

"What do you think was the effect that was to be conveyed by the outfits?"

"With few exceptions, or unless you looked very closely, you had the impression you were looking at nice girls who were not too bad or tough. Some of them were quite timid in the way they responded to the off-camera instructions. Often he'd say, 'Higher,' or 'Put your hands down.' The blonde cried a little when she was told to take her blouse off. She turned around and slipped off the shoulder straps of the slip. Then she faced the camera again with her arms over her breasts. He told her to put her arms down, and she did. I remember this one because she was so completely submissive. She didn't want to do it, but did anyway, and the off-camera voice showed some positive emotion—*he* liked it. That's the effect they were going for, men's dirty pleasures."

"With all of the girls?"

"Yes. That's what makes me so upset. For men who have fantasies about girls submitting to them—''

"What do you think it means?"

"Well, it's only a *tease*!"

He didn't answer.

"That's what it is, isn't it?"

"Laura—''

"What do you know about this, Mike? It's horrible!"

She was in anguish. He wanted to ask if she thought the

costuming looked professional, or close to it, but he didn't believe she could handle any more conversation. "I don't think I know much that you don't—just Hollister's connections, and you already have an idea who they are. I'm sorry I got you involved in this. I feel that I've abused your trust."

"You haven't—but your voice is so flat! What's happening?"

"It's me," he said. "I'm tired of playing the cop."

"As long as there's nothing wrong between us."

"No, there isn't."

"Don't launch yourself on a guilt trip. You didn't get me involved in anything and you know it. You've kidded me about the guns here. Do you believe that I know how to defend myself? Whatever you believe, say it."

"Okay, I have the idea." He remembered that he had to stop at a supermarket before he headed out to Jacumba. Heckle and Jeckle might not have given up searching for him. If they had chosen to canvass San Diego area hotels and had spotted his car, they could be downstairs waiting for him. He had paid cash and signed in as Barney Phillips, but all he had been able to do about the car had been to park it behind the building—where a cop as good as Mike Gallagher would have found it. Now Mike thought getting to see Dale Freeman was more important than ever. "Look, I want you to do everything that needs doing to stay safe, do you understand?"

"Yes, Mike. I've become attached to you, too."

"No, it's just that talking to you reminds me of what real life is like, that's all."

She laughed again. "I suppose there's a compliment in there somewhere. Call me when you can."

At five after nine, Mike dialed his own number. Marvin Burgess picked up. "Hold on, Mike. Maurice wants to get on the line."

"Okay." He felt awful, as if he were coming down with something. Girls. Teenagers: fourteen and fifteen years old, younger, drugged, frightened—it was an expensive way to tease. The telephone on the other end clattered.

"Mr. Gallagher, give me your number down there. We want

to call you back in five or ten minutes. Do you want your messages? The machine has some on it.''

For a moment Mike didn't understand. He sighed. He felt like a man in one of those rooms in which the walls close in, rumbling even closer. He gave Constantine the number and said he would be waiting by the telephone. Constantine said they would be as quick as possible and hung up.

He peered out the window. The parking lot was illuminated by those damned purple lights that made even July and August look as cold, abandoned, and forbidding as winter. This was not Mike's best time of day anyway. After his father's death, early evening had emptied of all pleasure as Mike had watched his mother's downward spiral into drunken bitterness and rage. . . .

The telephone rang in seven minutes. It was Constantine on the line. "Something told me to check your line voltage, Mr. Gallagher, and it's low. You're being tapped. The line was clear the other morning when your little girlfriend was visiting, but it's not now. We're in a drugstore where the telephones are in a quiet corner, so we'll be all right—''

"What kind of tap do you think it is?" Mike asked.

"Nothing fancy, just a wire between your apartment and the central office. Somebody with earphones listening or a tape recorder activated every time you opened the line. A guy on duty would be able to disconnect on a moment's notice. Of course, I said enough to you just now from that telephone to tell the tappers that we're on to them.''

Constantine had been using his head tonight. "Is our tape ready?''

"Oh, sure.''

"I want to hear the conversation, if I can.''

"You'll be able to hear us, all right, Mr. Gallagher. We've got adjoining booths here, and the cords on the handsets are long enough.''

"Let's do it," Mike said. In a moment he could hear Burgess hitting the touch tones connecting him to the hotel in Jacumba. "It's ringing, Mr. Gallagher.''

"This is Larry Hammond's office, LAPD," Marvin Burgess

said. "Put us through to the room where we're holding the prisoner."

Mike heard the response faintly.

"Uh, just a minute."

There was no way to tell if the hesitation meant anything. Cue the tape, Mike thought. Again, faint: "Hello?"

Constantine hit the *Play* button. "This is Larry Hammond, with special instructions—shit, I'll put my assistant on. Pay close attention." There was a click: Constantine had taped the sound of a line being put on hold! Thank *God* he loved his toys! Mike thought he heard the guy on the other end mutter something. Now there was another click: Constantine had thought of the sound of the reconnection, too. Marvin Burgess started talking.

"Yeah, hiya. Look, a guy is on his way down there with some papers for Freeman to sign—the DA wants it done. Be sure that you can see not only his badge, but his ID. His name is Phillips. We want you to take this extra precaution because we have this problem with a guy—"

"Yeah, we heard already. Gallagher, from Hollywood Homicide."

Mike thought he could hear Burgess swallow. "The important thing is the prisoner. Phillips should be down there in the next hour or so, and he shouldn't take more than five minutes to get his job done."

"That's too bad. The excitement down here is after midnight, when the Mexicans start thundering across the border."

"Oh, yeah, do you know what Gallagher looks like?"

"Big guy, medium brown hair."

"Phillips has got brown hair, too, but he isn't that tall."

"That's a help, I suppose. All right, thanks for the information. I doubt that we would have shot Phillips anyway, except out of boredom. Do you know they're still showing 'The Untouchables' on San Diego television? When you're out of town, you might as well be on Mars."

"Well, take care of yourself," Burgess said. Mike heard the handset to which he was connected being moved. "Were you able to hear that, Mike?"

"Yeah, you did great. I think I can try it."

"You're letting your ass hang out. When they mentioned your name. I figured I had to do something. Have your knees bent when they open the door."

"I'll think of something. Since they're looking for me anyway, I can play it just as hard as I have to."

"How did they get on to you?"

"They followed me down here. My taking vacation days set off alarms. You can see that they have something to be afraid of."

"Take care of yourself, will you?"

"Sure. I've got things to ask you. Did you read Wednesday's papers about the raid on Maxwell's house?"

"That was in the late editions. Yeah, I read that in the *Times* and in the *Herald*."

"Do you remember seeing anything about the confiscation of videotape cassettes from Maxwell's safe?"

"No. No, I didn't. There wasn't a thing about them. I'd remember."

"The Brandon telephone bills—were you able to get a look at them?"

"Yeah. There were maybe a dozen calls to Dan's house over the last six months, and another ten or so to our number at Hollywood Division. Some of the calls to Dan's place went on for a while. The last one was in early April—"

"I have the idea. Okay, put Constantine on, will you, please?"

"Yes, Mr. Gallagher."

"You said I had some calls."

"Oh, right. Bob Wills of the *Herald-Examiner.* He said he'd call you back. There were two hang-ups—I hate it when people do that—and then a lady named Gretchen. She said she's winding up her business in L.A. and wants to talk to you before she goes home, which she figures will be sometime late next week. That's it, Mr. Gallagher."

"You did a great job today, Maurice. You did things that I hadn't thought of, and I really appreciate it."

"Well, this is how I make my living, Mr. Gallagher."

"It's a very spooky way to do it. Do you have the energy to do the other thing?"

"For a little while."

"I'll be calling you. As you know, things are happening fast. Tell Marvin that if he doesn't hear from you or me by six o'clock tomorrow morning, he should call Frank Kennedy and arrange with him to get what we know—all of it—to Bob Wills of the *Herald-Examiner*."

"Will do, Mr. Gallagher."

Mike was almost afraid to put down the telephone. Dan was so clear in his mind. It wasn't difficult to come to a conclusion about which of all the clowns in the Brandon household had been talking to him. According to what he had told Mike, Dan had met only one of the Brandons, the daughter, Barbara. Dan had been too good a father not to have been willing to serve as father confessor to a screwed-up kid not getting any guidance at home—that is, until Harcourt Pryor had imposed his love of power onto Dan's gentler, more humane value system. Maybe Pryor had only been running Randall Brandon's errand. Mike would find that out.

And the tapes. Tapes of young girls. If Maxwell had had duplicates of Hollister's tapes at the Norma Place bungalow, what else could have been on the videocassettes in the paper bag in his floor safe? If the tapes in Jackson's closet had been so valuable and then valueless, would the tapes in Maxwell's home have been something different? Of course not. Maxwell had been concerned that Hollister hadn't had the copies. The newspaper stories had not mentioned the tapes in the safe, the tapes Mike had seen. Had Hammond—or somebody else downtown—destroyed the Maxwell set, or kept them for himself? Maxwell's statements and behavior this afternoon at Jackson's told Mike that there was another interested party beyond the police, the individual who now had Hans Roehrig's loyalty. Maxwell had had dealings with Harcourt Pryor—Pryor had talked to Bob Wills two days ago. And Laura had the only copies of the tapes that Mike knew of—except for the one that had fallen out of Valerie Moreland's dashboard. He had wanted to call Laura again anyway; now he wanted to tell her to get rid of the damned things. But he couldn't do that, not until he understood exactly what had happened to Dan. Laura said she was safe: Mike had to believe her. . . .

He carried his suitcase down to his car—when you paid cash

for a hotel room, you kept suspicions muted by having luggage. There was no one around, and the car bore none of the usual marks, like chalk on the tires, that police used when they wanted to know if it had been moved. Mike felt terribly uneasy, but he had to hang in—he had to hang tight. He rolled out of the parking lot slowly, and when he had driven a quarter of a mile, he pulled over and watched the traffic behind him: no sign of Heckle and Jeckle. But that was no proof that Hammond or Cutler had not prepared a surprise for Mike at Jacumba. After another mile, Mike saw what looked like a shopping street, and he turned in. Two blocks down was a supermarket, with telephones outside. When he paid for the big garbage bags he wanted, he got a roll of quarters and called Laura.

"I meant what I said about feeling like I'm returning to real life when I'm around you."

"That sounds better than the way you said it the first time. Take care of yourself and don't worry about me. That's really why you called. I can hear it in your voice. I'll be all right."

"Okay, I'm sorry I bothered you."

"No, no. You just said something I wanted to hear. Call me anytime you want. Collect. Yes, tonight. Let me know you're safe."

He wanted to ask why she thought he was in danger. "You don't know what I'm doing."

"The way you've been going since I met you, nothing would surprise me. Just call me, okay?"

"It's a deal."

He got on the I-8 eastbound and stayed with the traffic until the exit for state highway 94. The map indicated that 94 would eventually squeeze down to two lanes, but for a long way in the San Diego sprawl it remained a freeway, and Mike thought he would arrive in Jacumba earlier than Burgess had told the guy on the telephone. This country was rugged, hilly, and parched, but at the rate San Diego was expanding, all of it would be subdivided before the end of the century. Mike could not help thinking of Pablo Kerrigan again. With his money in a building contracting business, Kerrigan was a cop making his own work. At least he was doing it honestly. The only way Maxwell's desire to destroy the videotapes made sense was if he believed—or hoped—that the Norma Place copies were the only ones still in existence. As of Tuesday night, that had not been true. So someone connected to the Maxwell investigation—*maybe* Hammond—had destroyed the tapes that Mike had seen in the safe.

When the traffic eased, Mike went back again to everything that had happened. He still couldn't understand Judy's behavior at the funeral. He had lived with that woman, and from everything else he had seen since the divorce, she had not changed much. Something had been on her mind at the cemetery—she had *known* something. As soon as the service had ended, she had run off. Then Mike had talked with—whom? Don Grant. Somebody else first. For a moment Mike had to go through his memory to place that person: Ira Rosenberg. All that goofy ignorance from all sides about funeral customs. And then something else.

Mike could see it.

Yes, something had passed before his eyes, and then Ira Rosenberg, walking behind the group of cops, being polite, had said something about things coming full circle. Why? What had it meant? How do you kill a man in his car without touching him *or* the car?

On a deserted stretch of freeway. At a time of night that had all but guaranteed privacy. They, whoever they were, had wanted that: the *friend* had made sure that Dan had stayed in town until very late. And Dan had made it that much easier—Mike wasn't sure that *easier* really was the operative word—by stopping at Norm's for a dinner salad. He had cleaned up. Cleaned up the car. The friend had told him that he had called Triple-A. Mike was no closer to the answer to the question of the friend than ever. If it had been someone outside Hollywood Homicide, Mike might never find him—Mike couldn't think of anyone outside Hollywood Homicide besides Marge who had been that close to Dan. Cutler had asked the question the wrong way. It really was: what did you have to do to a man behind the wheel of his car in the middle of the night on a deserted stretch of road to make him swerve so violently that the resultant accident killed him? Involving a friend: that was the blinding part, the thing that caused Mike to swerve off his intended line of thought . . .

To the girls. The *tapes* of girls, the kind that were drawn to Hollywood year after year. In all the time Mike had lived in L.A., there had always been plenty of new arrivals. Young, pretty. The only variants among them were talent, brains, and character. The entertainment industry was full of women with talent, no talent; brains, no brains; character, no character. Many of the successes said that luck had been the determining factor in their lives. Sometimes people wondered about the failures, but not enough to find out what happened to them. One *supposed* that they drifted off, went home, married, moved to the suburbs, took up the needle or fell into the bottle or the gutter. No one really knew. Cops saw only the wreckage—a woman dead in her apartment for most of a week, like Valerie Moreland, was an example of only one of many worst-case scenarios.

Mike wanted to think about Dan in the car again. Mike was going to call Ira Rosenberg tomorrow and ask him what he had meant up on the road in the cemetery, but for now Mike was going to think about Dan. The conditions were nearly the same now as they had been at the time of Dan's death. Mike put himself behind the wheel of Dan's car and tried to imagine what Dan could have seen that would have made him step on the brakes, swerve, and plunge to his death. Dan may have died quickly, but not completely painlessly. He had felt the impact at the bottom of the canyon. For only a split second, but still, he had felt the pain of having his chest crushed. Maybe Pablo Kerrigan carried his anger closer to the surface, but that didn't mean it was more intense than Mike's—than Mike's *right now*.

What had Ira Rosenberg meant?

Don Grant had described Jacumba accurately. Without the hotel, there was no town. The hotel was being refurbished, Grant had said. You had to wonder why it had been built in the first place. Except for San Diego, all the action down here was on the other side of the border. Tecate was a big town, Mexicali a real city. Mike drove past the hotel and then another mile for insurance. A helicopter roared overhead, then arched along the border, searchlight on. Even if the police in the hotel were not expecting Mike Gallagher, Mike figured he would be better off if he surprised them. He made a U-turn.

He pulled into the parking lot quietly, and when he got out of the car he did not lock it. Inside the hotel, there was no one behind the desk. In the office an overweight young woman in slacks and a San Diego Chargers T-shirt was watching a small black-and-white television set with aluminum foil wads wrapped around the ends of the rabbit ears. Mike wanted to get her attention without making noise: he leaned over the counter and waved until she saw him. He produced his badge.

"One seventeen," she said. "It's down the hall on the left."

When he was out of her view, Mike took out the Magnum. He knocked on the door.

"Who is it?"

"Phillips." Mike had the badge out, in front of the bag containing the garbage bags. He had the gun in his other hand, behind the bags. The door opened.

"We're supposed to see your ID."

Mike let the guy see the gun. *"Buenas noches."* The guy backed up. In the corner a color television set was showing "Hill Street Blues." The other guy made a false start up from the couch, but then stopped when he saw the gun. Freeman was sitting on the couch, too, and his jaw dropped open.

"The badge is real, Freeman, so don't get strange." Mike turned to the guy near him. He was young and wearing a T-shirt and jeans. "I'm Mike Gallagher and I'm investigating the murder of Valerie Moreland. Make this easy on yourself and tell old Dale there where you and your partner are keeping your handcuffs."

"Cutler is going to rip your ass."

"Handcuffs."

"In the bedroom" the other guy said. He was a little older, almost Mike's age. "They're in the top drawer, Dale."

"I don't want to go with this one," Freeman said. He was six three and weighed two-fifty, most of it beer gut. He was barefoot and his unbelted pants hung on his hips. His short-sleeved sports shirt looked as if he had been wearing it for two or even three days.

"He's not going to hurt you," the one on the couch said.

"He wouldn't have told us who he was—not that we had any trouble figuring it out."

"I just want to ask you a few questions," Mike said. "It's just not their business."

"Do as he says, Dale."

Freeman was in the other room when the guy at the couch said to Mike, "We've put a lot of work into building that goon's trust."

"Yeah, but you don't know why." Mike motioned the younger guy toward his partner. "One at a time, your guns on the coffee table. Play it straight, because this thing can take your leg off."

The older guy smiled.

"What I'd really have to do is kill you all," Mike said. "And with what I've got on the department, Cutler might even have to eat it. Believe me."

His eyes on Mike, the guy put his gun on the table. The younger did the same. Freeman returned with the handcuffs. His body odor soured the air in the room.

"Cuff them together, back to back," Mike said. When Freeman was done, Mike said to them, "All right, sidestep into the bathroom and get into the tub."

"You have it all worked out, eh?"

"Dale and I are going to have a private conversation." Mike picked up the guns and unloaded them. In the bathroom, keeping his distance, he handed the garbage bags to Freeman. "Put one over their heads. Pull it all the way down."

"This is crazy," the young one said as the bag went over his head.

"All right," Mike said to Freeman, "turn on the shower, then close the shower door." Even outside the bag, the sound of the water splattering on the plastic had the volume of a tropical downpour. Mike backed out of the bathroom. "Come on. Close the bathroom door, too. Now we can talk. They won't hear anything for a week." Freeman was watching him warily. "This is between us. I don't give a shit about you or the deal you've cut with Cutler or the DA. If you don't tell me what I want to know, I'll kill you right here—the two in there, too. They know I'm not kidding. You went up to Los Angeles with

Billy Lansing last fall, rented a house on Mulholland, and then proceeded to get as close as you could to Bernie Maxwell. Lansing had his girlfriend, Ellie Gordon, with him most of the time, you met Valerie Moreland at the Clown Club, you had money to spend, enough drugs to fill all your body openings, and the freedom to run any damned scam you wanted. Hog heaven. More people are learning every day that you were flipped by state cops in San Diego County. You worked for the state and the city of San Diego. Given everybody's record, it's awfully clear who you were working for in Los Angeles. You were in deep shit in San Diego because of Lansing. They wanted to get rid of you. Didn't it occur to either of you that you were being set up in L.A.—at the least, that you were expendable? Now that you've seen what else has gone down, with Maxwell busted by the L.A. sheriff *and* LAPD, you must be able to see that you were the smallest part of the operation. You and your buddy, one of those good people you mentioned on the radio, didn't amount to cock cheese to the guy you were reporting to, Larry Hammond—Hammond was in charge of the Maxwell investigation.''

''He's taking good care of me!''

''Only because you happen to be alive. You're supposed to be dead, the way Bobby Michaels is supposed to be dead. Let's talk about Bernie Maxwell, Donnie Jackson, Hans Roehrig, Barranquilla, and Valerie Moreland. I know it was her you were crying for on the radio, not Marylou Brown. Hammond put you up to that, too. You ran to him for protection. Now, which one of those bastards killed her?''

''Roehrig, I'm sure of it.''

Freeman was subdued. Mike knew that it was time to push. ''Tell me what happened. Tell me why you're sure. Where were you when the others died?''

''I was at her place. I was waiting for her. She called to say she was going to stop at Roehrig's before she came home.''

''She was working for Hollister that night?''

''I assume so. She didn't say.''

The noise from the bathroom had not changed: it sounded like a bunch of teenagers doing something lewd on a high-school-cafeteria steam table. "You were there when she met Hollister. What did she tell you she was doing for him?"

"Costume design."

"Of course. She was a costume designer. I've seen the tapes. What was she doing that *for*?"

Freeman took his eyes off Mike for just a moment as he glanced toward the bathroom. "Oh, man, I can't discuss that with *anybody*."

Mike hit him. Dan had taught him this for emergency use only, a quick, short chop to the brow, downward: it opened the skin; the wound would bleed buckets. It always scared the shit out of the suspect, Dan had said; the guy thought he was going to bleed to death. Freeman went halfway down, his hands coming up to his head; as he rose, Mike uppercutted him so that Freeman went backward on the couch. Mike was over him, the barrel of the Magnum pushed into Freeman's cheek. The guy's stink was making Mike's eyes water. "Don't *fuck* with me! Do you know what happens if I shoot your dick off? Answer me!"

Dale Freeman shook. The blood poured into his eye; he blinked.

"Nothing!" Mike yelled. "Nothing happens! It doesn't get reported in the papers! Nobody will say anything to you! When you wind up in Folsom or Q, as you're bound to someday, and take your showers with the rest of the guys and they start asking what happened to your dick, *the-fun-begins! Now* you tell me what Valerie Moreland was doing for Ben Hollister or you'll be pissing all over your leg for the rest of your life!"

Freeman was in agony. He wiped at his face with the bottom of his shirt. "Oh, I stayed clear! After I got an idea of what was going on, I didn't want to *know!* I know I'm not bright, but I'm not completely stupid. Oh, man, please. Please. I'm bleeding." He glanced at the bathroom again. "Don't do anything more to me."

"Tell me about Roehrig!"

"She went up to his place that night. He called her when she was at Hollister's. He told her to come over, that he had some toot that he wanted her to try—you know, a freebie. You had to know Valerie. She loved to party. I thought something was up. After what we did to Maxwell, I could tell there was something in the air. It was just a matter of time before he caught up with the whole bunch of us. Billy didn't want to listen. He wanted the music to keep playing, know what I mean? If what you say about us being set up is true, Billy fell for it completely. He believed the good times weren't going to stop. He *wanted* to believe that. Of course, I was never in on the big picture, as he called it. Billy said that Hammond said that everything was okay.''

There was a box of tissues on the coffee table. Mike motioned to them, and Freeman pressed a wad against his brow.

"Tell me about this big picture. It was Hammond who gave Lansing his instructions, wasn't it?"

"That's the name Billy said. He didn't even want to tell me that much, but they made him. If there was ever trouble, I was to call Hammond. That's what I did—how I got here. You had to know Billy. He loved being cute about what he was up to. He'd never tell me what we were supposed to do. He'd say, 'I met the man today. Something's going down.' Or, 'Something *big* is going down.' He said that before we gave up the Mulholland house and moved in with Daisy and them. I know they were working on Daisy for a year, setting her up for us. Billy told me that much. I wasn't really there that much of the time. I was at Valerie's every chance I got, and that was okay with all concerned.''

"Going through all those drugs at the Nunn house, running up that big debt with Maxwell—that was all part of the plan, wasn't it?''

"I guess. When I saw what was happening, I said to Billy, 'This is going to be trouble.' He said, 'Don't worry about it, we're covered'. You have to remember, those were fast times, and once you start going like that, you don't want it to stop.''

"Where did Billy meet Hammond?"

"Different places."

"But he told you where. He told you the places, the neighborhoods.''

"It was always off the turf—downtown, Santa Monica, over in the Valley. Places like that.''

"Did he ever mention Panorama City?"

"Where is that?"

Freeman wasn't lying. A lot of people had never heard of Panorama City. The only thing panoramic about it was a brewery. "How well did you know Azzolini?"

"Who?"

"Azzolini, the bartender at the Clown Club."

"I didn't go in there that much. I know who you mean now, though. A big guy with curly dark hair and a beard."

"You met Valerie at the Clown Club, didn't you?"

"Oh, sure. That's really why I didn't go in there that much afterward. Billy wanted me to stay out of there—I knew that it had to do with what we were doing in L.A.—but I didn't want to go in there because it was Valerie's old stamping ground. Once I went with a gal who took me to the places she used to hang out, and I wasn't really comfortable with all her old boyfriends, if you know what I mean."

"Did Billy ever mention Azzolini?"

"No, not that I recall."

"I want you to tell me about that young girl who was killed in Daisy Nunn's house, the one you called Marylou Brown."

"I didn't hardly know her at all."

"Don't give me that shit! You saw her enough! What was her *real* name?"

"We all called her Bobbie."

"Bobbie. For Barbara?"

"We knew her as Bobbie."

"Tell me about her."

"There's not much to tell. She was kind of your basic coke hog. She worked her way down to Daisy's from other people."

"You mean like Donnie Jackson."

"Among others."

"*Which* others?"

"Well, Billy had her."

"For one. Who else?"

"Roehrig. Roehrig worked his way through them all. Even Valerie, for that matter. That was something that happened. I didn't like it, but it happened. She said he got her high."

"You didn't stop her from going to Roehrig's that last night, though, did you?"

"I couldn't stop her from doing anything she wanted, especially when it came to drugs. I definitely wasn't the boss in the family. It was the only way I could do business with her. You have to understand, I had a real case for her.''

"You said Roehrig killed her.''

"I said, she called me to say she was going there, and then I called Roehrig's a couple of times, but he had his answering machine on. I figured he was having at her again, but there was nothing I could do about it, because after the first time, Billy told me, 'Let it go. Don't make that kind of trouble.' Billy told me it could screw things up. So I hung around her place, and about nine o'clock the next morning, the morning of the murders, I was looking out Valerie's window and saw her car come along. Roehrig was driving it, and she wasn't in the passenger seat. I knew something was wrong, because after he drove her car into the underground garage, I saw Barranquilla come along—''

"What kind of car was he driving?''

"He has that old white Toyota.''

"So what did you do?''

"Well, that's when I got scared—as I say, I knew something would be going down after what we did at Maxwell's. So I went up to the roof and hid there until I saw Roehrig and Barranquilla drive off about an hour later.''

"And then you went to the police.''

"Well, I had this phone number that I was supposed to call in case anything happened, and ask for Hammond.''

"So you called the number, and then found yourself in custody.''

"I guess so. That's one way to put it. They told me to be at Sunset and Vine, and I was, and this unmarked car came along.''

"And the next morning, you got on the telephone and said on the radio show that Marylou Brown was your girlfriend and in the wrong place at the wrong time.''

Freeman stared at him.

"You're going to tell me about the raid on Maxwell's.''

"I can't.''

Mike hit him hard on the point of the shoulder with the butt of the gun. Freeman slumped and whimpered. "My partner is dead because of scumholes like you!'' Mike screamed. "Don't pick at me! You answer!" Mike kicked him in the shin. *"Answer me!"*

"Daisy had this deadline from Maxwell, but it didn't seem to amount to much. We were still doing what we felt like, but we were really out of drugs. I mean, we were starting to score from Frank Thomas's old friends. You know, off the street. Then Billy went to one of his meetings, and came back with this plan to rip Maxwell. I thought it was pretty nuts, but Billy said we had nothing to worry about. He said we were being watched, I remember that. And later, after we had the meeting with Bobby Michaels, Billy told me that all we were really supposed to do was get Maxwell pissed, get him to do something stupid. As crazy as I thought the whole thing was, I never thought it would develop into what it did."

"Were you supposed to hit the safe?"

"There was never a word about a safe."

"Did Bobbie, the girl, ever say anything about her family?"

"Just that they were all assholes. You know, they were interested in their own things. I recall that she said something about her father having a girlfriend. That hurt her, I remember."

"You said people passed her around?"

"Oh, sure. She and that Jerry Chambers had a little thing going the last week. Billy was saying that they were well-suited, because they were both such terrible dope addicts. Well, she wasn't an actual addict, but he was. Frank Thomas got him on smack. Now that I think back on it, I see that the whole thing had to have a big finish, but nobody expected what happened—and I mean *nobody*."

"You mean, including Hammond."

"I'm afraid to say. Don't hit me anymore. You are one mean son of a bitch." Freeman curled up, and Mike felt pity for him—but it was the same pity he'd felt for Hollister, just before Hollister punched him in the mouth. Mike pushed the gun barrel into Freeman's cheek again.

"They said that to you, didn't they, that they hadn't expected it."

"Yes!" It was a wail. Mike backed off.

"Now—*now* tell me what you know about the girls."

"They were doing something with girls, that's what I know.

It was a regular business—I got that from Valerie. She wasn't supposed to talk about it with me. I know it was nasty. One time she came home real upset, and when I asked her what was wrong, she told me that she had made sure she was all right— she had a little insurance now. 'I have a little insurance now,' she said. I do know that Roehrig was in charge. He told Valerie what kind of look he wanted with each girl, and she went out and bought the stuff.''

"Did she say what happened afterward?"

"No. It was only every other week or so that they had any work for her. On the other weeks, Roehrig was out of town, more or less. I figured he was out of the country, because he's a pilot. He was a chopper pilot in Nam, and he told me he has a four-engine, commercial license. When I asked him if that meant he could fly 747s and stuff, he just looked at me and laughed. He has that way. He likes to laugh at people.''

"He speaks German, doesn't he?"

"He and Maxwell talked German together all the time. It was like their own private code, because nobody else could talk it. That drove Billy crazy.''

"You haven't told me why you said you thought Maxwell was the only really evil man you've ever known.''

"You saw my *Sis?*"

"That's right, and if you don't answer my question, I'm going to go back to that mobile home and play this game with her until *she* tells me what she thinks you meant.''

A look of utter hopelessness crossed Freeman's face. "It was the girls. I used to see some of them at Daisy's before that picture stuff at Hollister's, but I never saw them again afterward. I could see how scared some of them were, but I figure they went ahead because the money was good and there was always plenty of drugs. Roehrig knew how to keep women in line. Valerie liked Roehrig as much as any of them there. You have to give him that, he really knows how to do it.''

"Did Roehrig ever say anything to you that made you think that he was actually leaving the country?"

"No, but one time there—or, for a couple of days—he was talking about how he didn't need this country, that he could be very comfortable in any one of a number of South American countries. He was full of talk about how the Nazis had been in South America because so many of them were on cocaine. He knew that because he's from Germany, you see. A lot of people knew that over there. Another time he talked about the Arab world. He said it was a very expensive pay toilet.''

"About the dog—Ellie Gordon's dog—"

"It was *their* dog, Ellie's and Billy's. Billy loved that dog. He taught it to get high.''

"All right, on your feet." He gave Freeman room. "Into the bathroom.'' Mike got out his handcuffs. In the bathroom, he told Freeman to open the shower door. "Put one foot in the tub and both wrists over the top track of the shower door.''

"Hey!" one of the cops shouted from under the plastic bag. "Hey!"

Mike kept his attention on fastening the cuffs to Freeman's wrists. With his armpits exposed, Freeman nearly made Mike gag. "You guys will be all right.''

"Do you know how hot it is in here?''

"Be grateful I don't put Freeman in bags with you.''

One of them cursed, and the other quickly told him to shut up.

Mike got to the parking lot through the fire exit. Heading east, to the linkup with I-8 doubling back to San Diego and the freeway north to Riverside, Mike went back to everything that had happened to him. He had been at Gretchen's, across the street, when the murders had occurred. He had gone down to Wilcox, and when Dan had come in, they had made their way back to Laurel Canyon and watched the arrival of the coroner's van. In the afternoon Bob Wills had called him with the news, apparently public information by then, that five people had died. By Mike's own observation, the police had delayed sending the survivor to the hospital, seemingly in the hope that she would die before the doctors could save her. That night, Mike had called Judy and asked her to put him in touch with someone who could get him to the child who had been given the dog by the dumb uniformed officer. Judy had never called back. On Friday, Mike had answered the call on Valerie Moreland, and on Friday night, Saturday morning, Dan had died. Sunday, guns and Laura Demming. Monday morning, Cutler and Dan's car. Before many more hours had passed, Gretchen's picture had shut down and its male star headed for his Oaxaca retreat, satisfied with—or resigned to—the deal that had been cut for him by Norman Birnbaum. Apparently Gretchen was satisfied, too, not incidentally. Dick Albert had been a longtime friend of one of the suspects in the murders, Bobby Michaels. Michaels might have directed the killers to the Daisy Nunn house, but Mike thought Michaels had had nothing to do with the killings themselves, and unless eyewitness testimony to the contrary could be introduced, Michaels would be able to walk away free. Clearly, every other suspect was known to the police in charge of the investigation, but no moves had been made against any of them. Trying to match Kiku's blood to whatever sample had been found at the death scene had been a waste of time. Kiku had acted like an innocent man. Kiku was *one* kind of non-Caucasian, Barranquilla had been another. After a year of intense investigation, Barranquilla would have been known to the task force—by now, *someone* might have figured out that Barranquilla could have been on the murder scene. That none of this was being revealed was itself instructive. Marylou Brown—Bobbie—had been the first to get her autopsy, on Monday night, from Elmer Washington himself. Given what Mike suspected about the man accompanying Hammond on his return visit to Rainbow Drive that morning, concealing Marylou Brown's identity could have been the most important item on the authorities' agenda that first day. And given the time Maxwell was going to draw as a result of the LAPD raid on his home, the authorities were probably satisfied that their war aims against Maxwell had been achieved. Maxwell was out of action. Donnie Jackson and maybe even Hans Roehrig were small fry. Below them, as far as Mike could see, no one counted for much. Birnbaum was in on the cover-up: Harcourt Pryor had made him a director of the art museum as soon as Birnbaum had applied the tourniquet to the potential publicity hemorrhage of Dick Albert's connection to Bobby Michaels, which would have blown the story back onto the front pages and gotten people digging into it again. When there was more than one level of reality, above the surface and below, it was easy to make such payoffs. . . .

Mike stared through the windshield, remembering something he had thought last night: Mike's connection with the Rainbow Drive mess *preceded* that morning at Gretchen's when he had heard the victims' cries. It must have! Mike himself was the kind of cop who would have gone around a motel in search of a suspect's car. If he had been on a task force investigating a Bernie Maxwell for a year, he would have been damned sure of *everyone* around Daisy Nunn's house, the house being used by the police for a move against Maxwell. Mike would have checked the license plate of every car parked in the area, and he would have made it his business to know *why* the acting head of Hollywood Homicide was spending nights across the street, and after the murders, he would have stayed as close as possible to that guy. . . .

He thumped his fist on the dashboard and almost shouted out loud. *The sons of bitches!* They knew his deepest personal secrets—*somebody* did!

When Mike reached the I-15 interchange, he drove north until he saw a Denny's, and then pulled off and drove around the restaurant until he found a parking spot that would not be seen easily by passing police cruisers. They were going to be looking for him now, or soon. The cashier gave him some change and he headed outside and called the desk clerk at the hotel back in Jacumba. The tone of her voice told him that the cops in 117 still weren't free, so he told her that they needed her help. Next he called Laura collect and told her he was done for the night and safe. She said she had screened the cassette labeled 72-78, and that there were only six girls on it. "If the numbering is supposed to be inclusive, like ones I looked at earlier, there's one missing."

"Was there a girl in a stewardess's uniform?"

"No. Definitely not."

"That's it. You're done for the night."

"There's something I want to say, Mike. I've been thinking about what you've been able to accomplish in all you've been through. You're special and I love you. Don't feel trapped, please. I just want to be able to say it."

"I don't feel trapped. There's something I've been wanting to ask you, though."

A pause. "What's that?"

"How did you do that thing with your hands?"

"With my imagination and will. I'll teach you. There's so much more to human beings than they know, that once you get a sense of it, you begin to realize that the human condition is just one massive tragedy. That's why I've wanted to change my life. You'll know what I mean. I promise you."

"There's something else I want you to help me with," he said.

"What's that?"

"Wrapping my tongue around all your freckles at once. Sleep well." He hung up and called Maurice Constantine. "Let Marvin Burgess know I'm all right. Have you been able to zero in on Maxwell?"

"He's just told his bodyguard that when he's done paying the lawyers, he'll wind up with enough money to live comfortably for ten years if he lives that long. He said that. He said he's going to prison for five. He's got it all figured out."

"Or somebody's figured it out for him."

"That could be, too. He seems pretty resigned. He's pissed off, but he's calm. He told Kiku that he's had a pretty good run. He trusted the wrong people. He says he should have figured an endgame like this. That's from chess. He says he got into bed with the Devil, but forgot that the Devil would put sand in the Vaseline."

"Any idea of who he's talking about?"

"No. He's not concerned about Roehrig either. He mentioned Roehrig. He said he figures Roehrig had been really working for the other guy right along. One thing—I'm quoting—'Hans Roehrig is one of those men for whom the taste of blood means the loss of all control. Now that he's killed, he'll manufacture ways to do it again and again."

"These guys know each other pretty well, don't you think?"

"As a matter of fact, Mr. Gallagher, that's exactly what it made me think. You have to wonder why they bother with each other."

"They like it, Maurice. For them, there's no other way to

live. If there's no surveillance on Maxwell, and he's talking the way he is, the only people who haven't faced the fact that he's been reduced to nothing are you and me. After you talk to Marvin, go home. You said that Jackson was getting rough with the girl again. I owe you some money, but would you get back to that tomorrow, please?''

"I'm not worried about money.

"I appreciate that. Also, can you get a very private telephone number for me? I'm going to need several numbers, in fact."

"I've got a guy in the phone company, if that's what you mean. He'll be on duty tomorrow morning after eight o'clock. Sometimes I have to get into the computer banks, and I don't want anybody tracing it back to me."

"You scare me, Maurice. You seem like such a mild-mannered guy."

"I am. But when you want to know, I'll tell you how to neutralize a surveillance satellite. It's really pretty easy. All you have to know is exactly where it is, which it tells you with its radio transmissions."

Suddenly Mike was thinking of something else. "And then you blind it with a laser." *Sure, you blind it!*

"It's perfectly legal. A couple of years ago, Congress made it legal for government to use surveillance satellites over American territory, but it forgot to make it illegal to put them out of action. I do surveillance *and* countermeasures, Mr. Gallagher, and I told you, I have to keep pace with my field. You know when you go to the ophthalmologist and he shines that light at an angle across the surface of your eye? You can't see anything beyond it, and it's really only a pinpoint of light. It's in the accuracy of the aim, and with computers, that kind of accuracy at 22,500 miles is easy."

Roehrig had been a helicopter pilot, and there had been a robbery at the police helicopter facility in Van Nuys. Cutler wouldn't have mentioned it to Mike if he had known anything about Dan's death. At a police facility, just about the only equipment to be found that couldn't be bought through commercial channels were the articulated searchlights with the pencil-thin, blue-white beams. "So a helicopter shooting one of those searchlight beams through the windshield of a car to blind the

driver would be just another application of the same principle,"
Mike said.

Maurice Constantine was quiet for a moment. "Yes, Mr.
Gallagher—but again, the angle would have to be right."

"Did you ever see one of those lights come on?"

"Like the light in the bathroom, no start-up time. Bang, it's
on, full intensity, a couple of hundred thousand candlepower, I
think. Getting that full in the eyes in the middle of the night
from a short range with no warning would be one hell of a deal,
Mr. Gallagher."

"I'll call you tomorrow after eight." Now he wanted to call
Marge, but that would have to keep—if Cutler had been concerned enough about Mike's activities to have him followed,
then Cutler might also be concerned enough about the reasons
why to have Marge's telephone tapped. Mike wanted to talk to
Don Grant, too, but that call could wait until morning. There
could have been someone taking pictures at Dan's funeral. *Who's
that guy with Gallagher and Burgess?* Someone would know,
and Cutler would want to know why a Palm Springs cop was so
close to the center of the action in L.A. Mike didn't think he
could keep Cutler off his trail completely—but all Mike was
looking for was a little maneuvering room. There were a lot of
people he wanted to see tomorrow, and first on the list was Paula
Rogers.

Mike slept, but badly. It could have been the worst night of
his life—off the top of his head, he couldn't remember one
worse. He was in a hotel in Riverside, but when he lost consciousness—or rather, lost consciousness *again*, because he
awakened, it seemed, two or three times an hour—he found
himself surrounded by one of those funny buildings again (in
the dream, strangely, he knew exactly what he meant: he was
remembering the dream he had had in Laura's bed, the night
they'd met) —but this time Judy was in the dream, taunting him
with other men. What bothered Mike most was his aloneness,
his estrangement not just from one person, but all people. Alone.
Empty. Dead inside, which made him think of Dan. Mike woke
up at one point afraid that he was losing his mind, or had already
lost it; that, without knowing, he had crossed a line inside himself, one he could not find now. He did not have to think about

the case; the case had become his reality, which itself was insane—he knew it. There was so much that he knew now that he had never wanted to know. People looked toward the future as if it always had to be bright, or where brightness was always a possibility, if they did the right things. But that was not the way life was. Dan had told him that. There were traps. Dan had found that he lived a nightmare, the nightmare that surrounded Mike now. Mike had thought he had been simply acting crazy with Dale Freeman this evening. Now he wasn't so sure that his craziness had been all that much an act. When he asked himself where he had crossed the line, the first thing to come to his mind was Barranquilla in his apartment, sinking the butt of his gun into Barranquilla's skull—but then the second was finding Dan's body and going up to Marge to tell her that life as she had known it had ceased to exist some hours before. *I'm going to tell you that the world has gone mad.* That had been the real message.

Finally Mike got out of bed and sat in the chair by the window, looking through the heavy curtains down toward the asphalt parking lot, white-purple lights shining down on it, vaguely remembering the long, dead evenings of his adolescence. He did not want to think about Dan, and he could not let himself think, or dream, about Laura. He had to stay in the insanity. He had to hold his ground until it started moving again. He had no choice. All he could do was play the game, because there was nothing left to lose. The human condition was a massive tragedy, Laura had said. Right now, and for a little while longer, Mike wanted to play by those rules exactly.

BOOK SEVEN

19

DON GRANT WAS WAITING FOR MIKE ON THE SIDEWALK outside the courthouse in Riverside. He had not heard anything from Los Angeles, and didn't think anyone else in Palm Springs—or for that matter, Riverside County—had heard anything either about what he wanted to call "The Jacumba Caper." San Diego was probably looking for Mike, as well as Los Angeles—Constantine had given Mike that information, passing it on from Marvin Burgess. Cutler had called Burgess at two o'clock this morning, demanding to know where Mike Gallagher was. Constantine had said Marvin had a message for Mike from Cutler, too: *Turn in your badge immediately.* That was when Mike had told Constantine that the telephone number he wanted was the one to Cutler's private line. Mike wanted Maxwell's and Donnie Jackson's, too. Constantine had laughed, sounding like a cat trying to clear a fur ball from its throat. He would have the numbers by eleven o'clock.

Paula Rogers didn't flounce into court until ten-fifteen—and just as well. Grant had spoken to the prosecutor, and the prosecutor had spoken to Rogers' attorney. No problems. The prosecutor was happy to be rid of a lousy case, and the defense attorney was happy to oblige the other side when it meant that the case scorecarded a win for him. All he had to do was sell it to his client. Mike and Grant waited in the hall outside the courtroom while Rogers listened to the lawyer's pitch a few yards down the corridor. When they turned to Grant and Mike, the lawyer threw them a wink. Rogers' face bore the same sullen glare Mike had seen in the Clown Club the night of Dan's death. A psycho, Dan had said. Her perfume was overpowering. She was wearing red slacks and a red-and white-striped blouse. Maybe this was subdued for her, but she looked like a barber pole.

"Can we get out of here? This place is awful." She was rubbing her upper arms with both hands, as if she was cold. It was seventy degrees in the building. Mike hadn't thought that she would be a smackhead, but she was showing one of the symptoms.

"We'll be better off if we stay in the building. Let's see if we can find a conference room."

"I'd like to use the bathroom first," she whined. "I need to go pee-pee bad."

"I'm going to get a matron," Grant said.

"Hey, I'm not in custody! I'm helping you out!"

"You're not off the hook either, sweetie, until you tell us what we want to know." As Grant started away, she looked to the lawyer, who nodded to her.

"I'm going to be with you all the way," he said soothingly. "They told me what they want to ask you, and when you've answered those questions to the best of your ability, it's over. Finished."

"And I can't be held liable, right?"

"That's right."

"How do I know it's not a trick?"

"Because I'm an officer of the court, and a deal is a deal."

Grant was back with the matron. She led Rogers toward the ladies' room. Grant said, "I told her to watch the girl. I wouldn't want her overdosing now. Not that I think she will, but we don't want an accident.''

"I love cases like this," the lawyer said. "I may get in a round of golf this afternoon."

"Oh, she's going to want her money back," Grant said.

"Let her sue me."

Grant laughed. "I get chills just thinking about you guys. The doctors deserve having you wrapped around their necks."

"You're lucky we're not suing *you*—for police brutality."

"Would you want something like that spitting on you? How would you like to take her diseases home to Mama?"

The lawyer was ready with a comeback when the two women stepped out of the ladies' room. The matron indicated with a nod that everything had gone well. Now the lawyer led them to a conference room. Inside, Mike and Grant sat on one side of the table, and Rogers and the lawyer on the other. Rogers' makeup was thick enough to be scraped off with a knife.

"Can I smoke?"

"Sure." Mike clasped his hands. "I saw you last Friday night in the Clown Club on Sunset Boulevard with Jack Skelley, Bobby Michaels, and Hans Roehrig. There was another girl with you, and you, Roehrig, and the other girl left the place after nine and went up to Roehrig's place on Rainbow Drive in Laurel Canyon. I want to know about Roehrig that night. Tell me what he did."

"Hey, what somebody does in the privacy of his own home isn't any of your business!"

Mike nodded. "All right, so it was party time. What time. What time did the party break up?"

"Two-thirty the next afternoon."

"Was the action continuous?"

"You got a dirty mind?"

"No, I want you to tell me about Roehrig that night."

"Actually, we didn't get started until six in the morning. I mean, we were having a good time and all, but the real fun didn't start until after the sun came up." She gave Mike a leering smile. "Is that what you wanted to hear?"

"Why the late start?"

She was quiet a moment, wondering whether she should answer him. Mike was thinking that she liked being the center of attention. "He had to go out," she said at last. "He said he had to run an errand."

"We know he's in the funny business. Did he say what kind of an errand it was?"

"No, but he likes to be mysterious. He's a real asshole. Everything about him is supposed to be a big deal."

"So Roehrig went out. What time did he go out, and what time did he come back?"

"He had to wait for a phone call. When the phone call came, he left. That must have been around one or two o'clock. I'm not sure. Me and this other girl hung around doing drugs and watching one of my movies on the VCR. Come to think about it, Roehrig was pretty generous that night. You know, like he was high. Up. He was very charged. He wanted to make sure we were there when he got back. The drugs were like he was paying us."

"How did you feel about that?" Grant asked.

"I didn't give a shit. If somebody wants to be a sucker, that's his business."

Mike wanted to get back on the track. "Was he charged before or after—or both?"

"He was up beforehand, but very up afterward. Afterward, he said, 'I just made a lot of money tonight, the easiest money I've ever made in my life.' "

"Did he ever talk to you about his flying, or where he went when he was out of town?"

"He likes to bullshit, you know, talk about different things and places as if he's been there. I've always thought he was full of shit. We really don't get along."

"What do you mean, you don't get along?" Grant asked. "I just heard you say you were partying with him last Friday night and most of Saturday."

"That's true," she said.

"You have to know how things work," Mike said gently.

"That's right," Paula Rogers said. "You don't have to like somebody if he's paying for the party. You're there for the good time, and that's what counts. He and I kind of like the same things. That's the way it is."

"Can you remember where he's said he's traveled to?" Mike asked.

"Oh, all over. Really. Germany, Scandinavia, Europe—countries like that."

He wanted to stop her before the other guys burst out laughing. "All right, did he ever say anything about girls? Traveling with girls? Transporting girls?"

He had not spoken of this to Grant. He couldn't see Grant's face, but the lawyer's was something to behold: the lawyer was grinding his teeth, enraged, instantaneously. Maybe he knew something about what the law was for after all. Rogers looked blank for a moment.

"I remember something. This was awhile ago. I've known Roehrig a long time, since he got to town. But one night, two or three years ago, he was loaded, *mean* loaded—you know, nasty?—and he said to me, 'You know, I couldn't get ten bucks for you even in a toilet like—' I can't remember the name of the place, and I couldn't pronounce it then. I never heard of it before or since."

"All right, the girl who overdosed down in the Springs. Her name was Bobbie, wasn't it?"

"I thought we weren't going to talk about that!"

"You're free and clear on that. It *was* Bobbie, wasn't it?"

"Okay, it was."

"When was the last time you saw her?"

"A couple of weeks ago, maybe longer than that."

"Do you know Valerie Moreland?"

"Sure."

"When was the last time you saw her?"

"Oh, about a month ago. No, I saw her the same time I saw Bobbie. Listen, let's just forget about Bobbie, okay? I stuck my neck out for that bitch, and it's a miracle I'm not in big trouble now."

"Donnie Jackson and Jennie Wagner were with you when Bobbie overdosed. Don't worry, we're not going to get you in any trouble with Jackson over this. What I'm curious about is, why didn't Jackson come to your aid in this problem? You got his irons out of the fire, too."

"Tell me about it." She turned to the lawyer. "Can I talk to them?"

"Full immunity," the lawyer said to Mike.

It was nonsense. Cops didn't grant immunity. "I just want background," Mike said. "She'll be in no jeopardy from any side because of anything she tells me. I also want to ask her about the call she made to Bernie Maxwell."

"Immunity can't be any clearer than that," the lawyer said.

"He just earned his fee, girlie," Grant said. The lawyer's face was red with suppressed laughter.

Paula Rogers glanced around. "Well, I called Bernie after Donnie and Jennie took off. I kind of thought that he would help me out, know what I mean?" She glanced around again. "He told me to do the best I could, and he would cover me. But then things happened. I know how things work."

"Did he give you any idea that the people involved were in any way important to him?"

"What do you mean?"

"Politically, socially," She was still staring blankly. "It's okay," Mike said. "Who popped you out of Palm Springs—made bail?"

"Oh, Bernie did that. He had to. I was shooting a movie for him. I had to be on the set."

"Does Maxwell know Bobbie?"

"No, I don't think so. He didn't when I told him why I was in jail."

"How close was Jackson to her?"

"Not very, really. She just drifted in during this past year or so. You know, for drugs. She liked to party and she had money to spend. You have to know Donnie. But when I got back to L.A., Donnie told me that Bobbie was out of his life. He didn't want to have anything to do with her. She'd called him, and he let the machine answer for him. He kept the message tape. He played it for me. It was the most god-awful thing I'd ever heard, just words or even only bits and pieces of words, all gushing out at once. It sounded like her whole brain was *frying*!"

"And that's why Jackson wanted to stay away from her?"

"Yeah. He's another hotshot, like Roehrig. Sometimes he

does things just to be cute. I know some shit about Donnie Jackson.''

''Like waiting at the bedroom door listening to people in the living room? Like watching his girlfriend with other guys?''

''You've got the idea. Do you know Jennie?''

''Has she said anything to you about the kind of attention he's been paying to the murders?''

''Oh, he's glued to that.''

''And acting crazier and crazier.''

''You know all about it.''

''Is she thinking of leaving him?''

''Oh, she's always thinking of it, but she never will. He's got exactly what she wants: coke, and plenty of it. You've seen her, I can tell by looking at you. She's a real heartbreaker, but she doesn't give a shit. Inside, she's the pig of the world.''

Mike stood up.

''That's it?'' she asked.

''Have a safe trip back to L.A.''

''Another two hours on the freeway! Christ, I could have phoned this in!''

''Don't phone anybody about this,'' Mike said. ''If I get the idea that you've been talking about this, the deal is off. *All* deals will be off.''

''You've made your point,'' the lawyer said. He had her by the elbow. She was glaring at Don Grant.

''Now I remember you,'' she said. ''It took me awhile, because you don't make much of an impression—''

''That's enough,'' the lawyer said. ''Quit while you're ahead.''

''Don't tell me! Do you know what this fucker did?''

''Let's go,'' Mike said to Grant, who turned away, grinding his teeth.

''I don't want to see her in the Springs, I'll tell you that.''

The lawyer got her into the hall first. Grant took out his cigarettes and offered one to Mike, who shook his head no. Grant said, ''She's going to wind up murdered. After hearing all that, I don't know if you should get combat pay or the rest of us should nuke Los Angeles. Do you want some breakfast?''

''I could use some coffee. I've got to make a bunch of calls.''

"You want to be careful, youngster. You've got a head full of valuable information."

"If I get a little more time, I'll be able to move to Montana and do all my shopping out of the Sears catalog. Down at the foot of my road will be a sign: BUY YOUR BLUE BIRDHOUSES FROM THE MUTE. If you want a birdhouse, you get it in one color, and no arguments."

"I heard that from Dan," Grant said.

"We both heard it from another guy back East. Until then, I'd never met anyone as sour on police work as him. But since, needless to say, I've met quite a few. I've been thinking of Montana or someplace like it off and on for years. All I need is a little more time today, and I'll be gone—out of L.A."

"Cutler will have gotten a line on your car," Grant said. "Depending on how public he wants to go with this, your ability to get around will be that much impaired. Take my car. You can return it when it you're ready."

"Thank you. I hadn't thought of the car. My whole career as a detective is filled with things I didn't think of. I do want to start over. Reinvent myself. Most of all, I want to get out of that hellhole people have made for themselves. I'd like to know what the real world is like."

"It's a bore," Grant said. "What you'll find first is the real Mike Gallagher, and that the real Mike Gallagher is most interested in the problem of people fucking with the real world."

"Now *you* sound like Dan."

"We talked about this, he and I," Grant said. "Each of us had flat moments, just like you're having now. Well, not exactly, because it looks like your situation is permanent—and I'm sorry for you because being a cop is so much fun. Maybe I'm more sorry for you than I am for Dan. You're the poor bastard who lucked into the case that destroyed you as a cop if you solved it, or destroyed you as a man if you didn't. Consider yourself lucky that you've done as well—or badly—as you have."

"I have a gun under the dashboard of my car. I want to get it before we do the exchange."

Grant grinned. "Well, that's one thing you remembered."

Other things, too. The 9000 Building register, the evidence that connected Maxwell to Roehrig and Barranquilla—and the

Hollister tape that has Hammond and Randall Brandon coming and going on Rainbow Drive.

Mike followed Grant to a breakfast place Grant knew. Alone in his own car, Mike decided that the banter between them was too pleasant, comfortable, and seductive. He did not want to let his guard down. He had to keep his anger fueled. That he wanted to relax frightened him. Talking of Montana was premature—stupid. He *had* to keep his edge. He wanted to talk to Bob Wills. He had to talk to Cutler. But before he could talk to Wills, he had to call Kennedy. There was somebody else Mike kept forgetting, which he took as another bad sign. Ira Rosenberg.

After Mike gulped a half-cup of coffee, he left Don Grant reading the *L.A. Times* over his bacon and eggs. Mike called Frank Kennedy.

"People are looking for you," Kennedy said.

"I've been told. Tell me what *you* know."

"The federals want you. They won't say why. Talking to my friends the last couple of days to get information for you, I couldn't help giving them the idea that we had been in touch. This morning, my best connection called me and asked if I knew where you were. He was very tight and secretive. He wouldn't say anything more than that they want you. The way this has happened, it's clear that somebody on their end is pretty upset about something you've done recently. My friend did tell me that they've been watching you for some time. You're famous among them as a swordsman. They know quite a bit about you. They know that you were jumping some dame on Rainbow Drive not long ago."

Even though he had thought this through, allowing himself to see that people had been pawing through his private life like dirty-fingered burglars, the confirmation felt as if someone had reached into Mike's heart and squeezed it. "Is that the exact wording on that one?"

"Yeah. Look, I don't know what any of this means, but I'll tell you from my own experience on their side: if they want you, they'll find you. If you don't want to be found, find a deep hole and pull the top over your head."

"You've gotten an honest count from me, Kennedy. I've had to kick some ass lately, but I'm not now and never have been involved in any criminal activity."

"Swordsman or not, you don't think enough of yourself to be crooked. I've got Bob Wills waiting for your call. Do you want his number?"

"Did you give him mine? He called me at home yesterday."

"He has his own contacts at the phone company," Kennedy said.

"You don't have to tell your federal friend you talked to me, do you?"

Kennedy laughed. "Fuck that shit! I know my rights! You're my client, and our communications are protected by my professional privilege."

"It's all a game," Mike said. "All you have to know are the rules."

"What you have to know is how to play the rules to your advantage," Kennedy said as if he were talking to a kid. "Do you have a pencil and a paper to take down Wills's number?"

Mike was ready. In another moment, Wills's telephone was ringing. Wills picked up on the third ring and said hello softly, as if nobody ever called him. Anybody who cultivated a telephone *style* was an asshole. Mike said, "This is the guy you were expecting. I'm prepared to give you the name and address of the person who drove Bobby Michaels to Tijuana in exchange for information about the connection between Bernie Maxwell and Harcourt Pryor."

"You don't waste time on pleasantries, do you?"

"I'm in a hurry. You have my offer—take it or leave it."

"I can't *prove* the connection. If I could, I'd print it, understand? Now, the story of how Bobby Michaels got out of town—Tijuana, you say?—ought to be front page. Do you know where he was headed? His *final* destination?"

"I'll give you all of that stuff. It's front page. The individual I'm talking about is headed back to Los Angeles right now. The sooner you act on this, the happier I'm going to be. I want to make the biggest possible mess."

"If this is a good story, I don't want the Saturday editor fighting for it. You kill somebody in the Saturday paper, his soul goes to limbo maybe forever, understand? Even God doesn't read the Saturday paper."

"What the hell," Mike thought aloud. "The individual probably has other information about Rainbow Drive and the loonies involved. It's up to you to get it. I gave my word that there would be no jeopardy because of dealing with me."

"I think we have a deal," Wills said. "What do you know about Harcourt Pryor?"

"He's the smooth talker who runs the Brandon empire, a powerful man in his own right. He spoke to you last Tuesday, spoke to my friend in April. A very tough guy. He's been in the Brandon organization a long time."

"You don't know anything about Harcourt Pryor." Now Wills started talking as if reading from notes. Pryor had been raised in Silver Lake, when Silver Lake had been the westernmost suburb of the city, a genteel upper-middle-class neighborhood of big homes overlooking the downtown area. Pryor had come from a broken home, and after the Korean War, he used the GI Bill to put himself through law school. He went to work for Randall Brandon's father and had his teeth straightened, nose done, and religion changed from Baptist to Episcopal to prepare for the future. There was a story that he had a rival for eventual stewardship of the Brandon fortune murdered, but now too many years had passed for anyone to be able to gather proof.

Even twenty years ago, it had been clear that Randall Brandon would never be able to handle the day-to-day operations of the Brandon businesses. Old man Brandon, no great shakes himself, had been able to see that only too clearly. So Harcourt Pryor, clawing his way out of his parents' alcoholic nightmare, had gotten himself close to old Brandon, a classic bourgeois gladhander and adulterer. There was some evidence that Pryor had done a little pimping for both generations of Brandons he had served. Wills had gone back to old, old police records, he said proudly, for Pryor's background, making Mike decide that he disliked Wills with the same intensity he disliked Pryor for having a background so close to Mike's own. Over the years, Pryor had created and dissolved dozens of corporations, creating a labyrinth so complicated that it was not sure now that even he understood it. What Pryor did was make money, enlarging the Brandon holdings, expanding the Brandon empire. In the process, not surprisingly, he had managed to establish a smaller, but just as real, empire of his own. Harcourt Pryor was worth almost one hundred million dollars. A hundred million was nothing compared to the Brandon billions, obviously, but it was still enough to give Pryor some muscle in the local economy.

Wills had not been able to find the starting point of the Pryor-Maxwell connection, but he suspected it had existed at least a dozen years ago. The few available records suggested that Pryor was Maxwell's banker, never his partner, and always by remote control, through dummy corporations, beard men, and those small banks that were so useful as conduits for money to and from the wrong side of the law. In recent years Maxwell had been channeling his assets into North Hollywood real estate, probably at Pryor's instigation.

"What do you know about North Hollywood?" Wills asked.

"It's up for a rebuild," Mike said. "The subway is supposed to terminate there."

"North Hollywood is to become one of the new cluster cities," Wills said. "Another is in the West Valley, Century City is a third, Irvine a fourth. The idea behind the cluster-city concept is that people will work near where they live, that offices and light industry will be surrounded by appropriate housing. That's the concept, but it won't work because people tend to expand their horizons, not narrow them. And people aren't going to pick up and move closer to work simply because the politicians say it's the latest thing and a good idea. The politicians know better anyway. Right now the Ventura Freeway is the busiest highway in the world, with an average speed, solely because of the congestion, of around twenty miles an hour. What the politicians want to do is build another rail line from the subway terminal at Lankershim and Chandler on the existing right-of-way that starts on Chandler Boulevard and works its way northwest through prime suburb all the way to Chatsworth. North Hollywood will be the terminus of both the subway and what is now seen as a light-rail feeder line. The homeowners' associations in North Hollywood and Studio City are pressing for a moratorium on building on Ventura Boulevard all the way down to Barham Boulevard, but even if the moratorium goes through, it won't last for long. You can't have much of a home-owners' association if all the homeowners have been bought out and have moved away. That's been happening. Harcourt Pryor has been using all the money he can get his hands on to do exactly that—that's Brandon money, his own, Maxwell's, and others.''

"So you think Pryor touted Maxwell onto North Holly-wood,'' Mike said. "Is there any suggestion that Pryor agreed to buy Maxwell's holdings at a later date?''

"Not necessarily. Everybody will make out like sharks in a feeding frenzy. What Pryor was looking for was the creation of a power bloc.''

"Is it possible that Pryor was setting Maxwell up, or helping to pull his chain?''

"No. Do *you* have evidence of that? *That's* a story. Let me ask you a few questions, Gallagher. Do *you* have any informa-tion connecting Pryor to Maxwell's operations?''

"No.''

"Do you know of anything Maxwell was involved in besides drugs?''

"Like what?'' Mike said.

"Like porn. Maxwell is supposed to be a manufacturer and distributor. He has the world's largest porn mailing list.''

"Tell me about that,'' Mike said.

"Not all of the people who love hard core are willing to risk exposure at those adult bookstores or the porn theaters. They buy by mail, that's all.''

Mike had known that the lovers of porn in the closet far out-numbered those willing to frequent the sleaze shops. He just hadn't been thinking of it—or that Maxwell would have a mail-ing list of such suckers. People like his customers wrote letters, asking for more specific kinds of material, bigger thrills, hoping for the possibility of forbidden pleasures. Mike had seen reports claiming that the worldwide porn business was bigger than drugs. Who was to say that there wasn't another market below porn, one like kiddie porn, where people who were in a position to explore the real taboos weren't actually indulging unspeakable appetites? Mike asked, "Does Maxwell have an airplane?''

"To jump bail with, you mean?''

"Sure."

"No, but one of Pryor's companies leases jet planes to movie stars and touring rock groups."

"You mean, the big jobs with intercontinental capability," Mike said.

"Yes, 707s. Because they carry lighter loads than the commercial models, they're fitted with extra fuel tanks that give them greater range."

"How far?"

"Cruising slowly, to save fuel, almost halfway around the world."

"What would that cost?"

"I heard about one charter that went for a quarter of a million. In the luxury market, markup is usually one hundred percent."

Mike had talked to a guy—the same guy who had been in Beirut, and swore that L.A. had more guns—who had said that he had seen an Arab offer Arab-sized amounts to spend a single night with a slender American blonde. The Arab's first offer had been five thousand, but after it had been turned down, he had come back again and again until he had made an offer her husband had not been able to refuse: one hundred thousand dollars. Now Wills asked for the name, address, and telephone number of the individual who had driven Bobby Michaels to Tijuana.

"I don't have a telephone number. I have just one more question to ask you, and it isn't about Pryor or Maxwell. How do you know Greg Novak?"

"Who?"

"A cop. Hollywood Homicide. Blond guy, twenty-eight, six feet, cleancut."

"I never heard of Greg Novak. And I can't place anybody that age, coloring, and height. Did he say he knows me?"

"He said he saw you on Sunset Boulevard last week, and that you asked him about the murders."

"I don't think I was on Sunset Boulevard last week. Is this important? I'll check my notes, if you want."

Mike could feel his heart again. "Please." He heard the telephone hit a table with a clatter. Didn't know Novak. And the *federales* knew about Mike and Gretchen. He hadn't been with Gretchen in her home since the murders had occurred-*that* exact moment. He had a reputation with the federals as a swordsman. They had done some job on him—and for what reason, save that his car had been seen outside Gretchen's place while the federals had been surveilling Daisy Nunn's house? Hammond had been surveilling the same location but hadn't seemed to know about Mike being on Rainbow Drive. Perhaps the federals had been dogging Hammond, and had just been more thorough in following their leads than Hammond's people had been. Given what had happened on Rainbow Drive, that made sense. Mike could remember Novak's words—that he had seen that guy from the *Herald-Examiner*, what's his name, Bob Wills, on Sunset Boulevard. Maybe it hadn't been exactly that way, but that was close enough. The federals who knew so much about Mike were now casting about for information about where he was—why? Because they didn't know. *Why* didn't they know when they had been so smart in the past? Now Wills picked up the telephone again.

"I write down all my contacts, times and days, as they occur," Wills said. Mike heard pages turning. "I remember that you were the first person in Hollywood Division I spoke to, right after the word came in. I meant to get back to you anyway, because I wondered about the meaning of the fact that you didn't know squat about a quintuple murder in your own division. Since this is a big case, and a really good story will get me out of this newspaper-game one-horse town, I made sure that I had my notes in order. My notes show that you're the only person from Hollywood I talked to until Friday, when I talked to your dim-witted Captain Ruppert, and he told me that I should talk to Whatley downtown about any and all developments."

"I told you the same thing," Mike said.

"I had another conversation with Ruppert this week—"

"I know about that one," Mike said quickly, "and that subject isn't on our agenda."

"Let me have the information on your individual. I hope this pans out. Even so, I get the feeling that I'm on the short end of the deal." Mike gave him Paula Rogers' name and address and told him to ask her if Michaels was heading to Dick Albert's place in Oaxaca. Wills whistled. "I take back that last crack. That's page one, all right."

"What I'd like you to do is stay in touch with Frank Kennedy," Mike said. "I may have more for you, you may have something for me. Rogers is going to ask you where you got your information—she doesn't know it's me. You tell her that the police are looking for her. They will be, later today. That means you have to hustle."

"What's going on, Gallagher? What are you up to?"

Mike hung up and called Maurice Constantine. Constantine was tuned in on Donnie Jackson, who apparently had been awake all night. Jackson was in a vile mood, Constantine reported. He had Cutler's private number, Jackson's, and Maxwell's. Now Mike asked him to check on Bernie Maxwell again. Constantine said it would be no problem, and Mike disconnected, pumped a fresh quarter into the pay telephone, and lined up more. He stopped. He had been about to call Cutler, but now he was thinking of Ira Rosenberg. He didn't have to consult his notebook for the number of the coroner's building. The girl picked up and said that Rosenberg was unavailable.

"Tell him it's Mike Gallagher of Hollywood Homicide and that it's urgent. I'm calling long distance."

She sighed. "I'll have him paged."

It took Rosenberg almost three minutes to get to his own extension. "Mike, me boy! Top o' the morning!"

"I want to ask you about something you said at Dan's funeral. You're not going to think it's important, but it may be. I won't know until I have your answer." He asked Rosenberg to project his memory to the graveside ceremony and walking back to the cars afterward. "When we reached the road, a Niles Eberhart and Son hearse went by. You were standing behind me, and I heard you say something. Do you remember what it was?"

There was silence for a moment. "I don't remember what I said, but I know what I was thinking, and what I thought after I saw old Niles's body truck. I can't ask you not to take offense in advance, but I'm afraid you might. I told you, Mike, I'm not a brave man."

"This is business, Ira. It won't hurt our friendship."

"I hope not. When you told me Dan was dead, and later, when I was working on him—it was difficult for me, Mike; I didn't see Dan every day, but I liked him very much—I thought he was dead because the two of you had gotten involved in the Laurel Canyon killings. Maybe I didn't communicate to you how seriously the killings were taken, but they were—"

"You communicated that, Ira."

"Thank you. It may help to stem the flow of guilt. Anyway, that's what I thought. There was no way for me to prove it, but I don't think Dan's accident was accidental. Too convenient, if the two of you weren't minding your own business. You know that all my skill and training went into searching for a cause other than the trauma that was fairly self-evident—you know that, don't you?"

"I know. I really wouldn't have asked anything of you if I thought otherwise."

"I appreciate that. Anyway, that was my mind-set as we walked up the hill, and even though we were talking about the funeral, I was still thinking those thoughts that had started the previous Saturday. I saw old Niles himself the night before I saw you when you came down for the autopsies of the victims. He came with his driver to pick up that young girl, Marylou What's her name."

"Why did he do that?"

"I don't know. Maybe he wanted to see the bodies. He's a friend of Elmer Washington's. The Marylou job was his. He belonged here."

"So when you saw his hearse, you had it in your mind that it was our meddling in the same case that brought about Dan's death, and so you said that things had come full circle."

"That's what I said! You have some memory, kid! What does it mean?"

Now Mike was silent. He could see Don Grant reading Jim Murray's column while mopping up his egg yolk with a slice of toast. One of those big redneck hippies was at the cash register, reaching into his tattered jeans for money to pay his check. Tattered jeans, sleeveless red shirt, beat-up, curved-brim straw cowboy hat. Life was going on. Niles Eberhart had gone to the coroner's building for Barbara Brandon. He was the Brandon family garbageman. Full circle—Niles Eberhart. Mike had not even known that Eberhart was still alive.

"Mike?"

"I'm here. What you said turns out to be pretty interesting. And for your information—your information only—Dan would have been killed anyway. It had nothing to do with our meddling."

"He *was* killed?"

Now Mike was remembering Rosenberg's big mouth. "Yes, Ira. If I'm not clever, I'm going to die, too. Keep absolutely quiet about this for your own sake as well as mine."

"The girl out there knows that you've called." Mike could hear fear in his friend's voice. "If someone wants to know what you had on your mind, what should I tell them?"

"Tell them I asked you about the size of the irises of Dan's eyes."

"They were normal—"

"And at night, they would have been wide open to admit all the available light."

"Oh, Jesus, Mike, I really don't think I ought to hear anymore."

"That's the idea. Thanks for your help."

"Be careful," Rosenberg was saying as Mike hung up. Now Mike dialed Cutler's private line. Mike drew a breath and rocked on his heels. For a split second he flashed on his father's funeral, on the slim, sandy-haired man walking back up the hill toward the descending Niles Eberhart, the pile of raw earth of the open grave above and beyond their heads. Now Cutler said hello.

"It's Gallagher, Chief. Can we talk?"

"You fucking moron! You're fired! *Fired!*"

"Not yet, I'm not—"

"You drew a gun on fellow officers!"

"*Shut up!* Shut up and listen! I've got hard evidence that puts Larry Hammond on the scene of the Laurel Canyon murders between nine and eleven o'clock in the morning on the day of the crimes and a printout from the hospital computer that will establish what many of the press corps observed—that the survivor of the attack didn't leave for the hospital until late in the afternoon."

"You son of a bitch! What are you going to do with that stuff?"

"Shove it up your ass, if you don't listen! I want to know

what was taken from our helicopter facility in Van Nuys last week.''

''Who told you about that?''

''You did, Monday morning, when Dan's car was getting its autopsy.''

''Shit,'' Cutler muttered. ''Look, Gallagher, what do you want?''

''What any cop wants. Tell me what I want to know, or I'll lay everything I have on the table for the press. You don't want them to know that the federal government all but took over the investigation of Bernie Maxwell, or worse for you, the reason why it happened. Just as you don't want things known, the government doesn't want things known. I don't give a shit about any of that. My partner was murdered, and a bunch of self-serving bureaucrats aren't going to protect his murderers to save their own asses. I'm not kidding you, Cutler. If you don't give me what I want now, I'm going to pull the whole thing down on anybody standing under it—and you know that includes some people who are powerful enough to squash you like a bug.''

''All right, what was taken from the Van Nuys facility were helicopter parts—''

''*What* helicopter parts?''

''One of the searchlights, brackets to mount it. Why do you want to know this, Gallagher?''

There was a weariness in Cutler's voice. Mike said, ''You know why Dan was killed. He told me the story of Barbara Brandon running down that guy on Tampa Avenue, how he called you, how you were at the Brandon place up in San Marino waiting for him. He told me that someone called him before the week was out and set up a meeting at Alphonse's in Toluca Lake, and that while Dan was in the restaurant waiting, somebody put a paper bag in his car. *Dan played the game,* you bastard—''

''Don't blame me. I know he did. What happened to Dan was a mistake—''

''Not a mistake so much as the kind of decision made by someone drunk on his own power. You know that, too. I want you to stay clear, do you understand me? You've already told me all I need to know.''

"Don't go taking the law into your own hands—"

"There's no chance of getting justice your way. We know who they are, how they did it, and why. Nobody's going to touch them in this community and you know it. When Larry Hammond identified Barbara Brandon's body in that house on Rainbow Drive, he ran like hell to Randall Brandon to see that Brandon was served and that his own position was improved thereby—"

"I know that, Gallagher."

"And then Brandon told Harcourt Pryor to take care of things through the normal channels. That meant dealing with you. Brandon didn't want to deal with a geek like Hammond. I was in your office when Brandon called you. By then, Thursday, the wheels were turning smoothly again, and you, Brandon, and Harcourt Pryor knew it."

"I had nothing to do with Dan Crawford's death, and I resent it if you're implying that I did."

"Somebody set him up, and when I find that somebody, I'm going to kill him."

"On that we're agreed," Cutler said.

Mike was surprised. "You mean, if I don't, you will?"

"No, I mean, first come, first served. You don't run this department, Gallagher, and you have only a dim idea of how this city works. Dan's death broke a fundamental understanding between the police and the powers that be. You people are out on the street risking your lives not so you can be cut down from behind by the assholes you're supposed to be protecting. Get me? I know that Hammond went over my head on the Brandon thing, and like you, I believe I know why Dan Crawford died. But there's a lot more at stake than that, and many more lives. I don't know what else you know, Gallagher, but this has been a big problem for a lot of people for a long time. I really do appreciate what you've been through, but it doesn't change anything. You pulled a gun on officers of the law, *my* officers, and that puts you up shit creek without a paddle. You're out of a job, I've told you that, and you're now carrying a firearm illegally and almost certainly with criminal intent. We want to talk to you about the body of a Latino found in a canyon off Mulholland. Now if you don't turn yourself in at the nearest law enforcement agency—*within the hour, damn you!*—I'm going to move against you with extreme prejudice!''

"Don't bullshit me, you old turd! You know you're in deep trouble! The only reason you'd shake up Hollywood Division is to scatter the people who might have some knowledge of the Laurel Canyon mess. But it won't work! I have Hammond on videotape! The tape shows him leaving the scene and returning with Brandon, Brandon coming out of the house—a crime scene, for Christ's sake!—in a distraught condition and being driven off by Hammond again. According to the organizational charts and what the press and public understand, *Hammond is your boy!* Now if you want to take your chances with that against you by playing tough with me, go right ahead!''

"Then that's the way it is. We'll both take our chances." And Cutler hung up. Mike went back to the booth. Don Grant looked up from his newspaper.

"If I'm picked up in your car," Mike said, "it could be a real problem for you."

Grant looked out toward the parking lot, then back again. "Suppose we say that you told me you had car trouble and needed to get back to town today. You said you were going to return my car tomorrow or Sunday."

"If they ask you, tell them I said I bought a tank of bad gas. It happens often enough."

"My family back East say they never heard of such a thing as water in the gas," Grant said. "You take care of yourself." He picked up his paper, and Mike thought he heard Grant utter a curse.

Mike put Hollister's videotapes and the 9000 Building register under the seat, and the .38 in the glove compartment. Grant's car was one of those big old Ford wagons that rode like a balloon floating down a stream. Out here in the desert the air was perfectly clear, the sky blue, the barren mountains in bold, brilliant relief in the sunshine. The traffic was flowing smoothly on the freeway in both directions. Mike realized that something in him was trying to commit the picture to memory—more insanity. Every step he had taken since he had heard the footsteps outside Gretchen's window had brought him deeper into an un-recognizable world—but unrecognizable, he knew now, only because of its unfamiliarity. It was the world he had been thrust into as a child and from which he had been running ever since. Now his life had become a matter of survival, and if he had done anything to bring that about, it was to have stopped running. Nothing more. All he had done to Barranquilla was go out in the hall to wait for him. Mike wanted to talk to Barranquilla. It was Barranquilla who had initiated the combat between them.

And Bernie Maxwell hadn't sent Barranquilla, Mike was sure. Bernie Maxwell had no beef with Mike Gallagher, no reason to fear him.

Mike was still carrying four guns. He was closer to using one than ever, and he could see that the more he thought about it, the more he would fix on just how insane the idea really was, even in self-defense.

But that was the kind of thinking that would kill him. The evidence he had might keep him alive a little while longer. If he turned it over to a lawyer to be used in the event of his death, then he would die, because there was no lawyer in the world who would go up against this kind of power. Another deal would be cut and then it would be business as usual. Again. Mike's evidence could give him only what he had thought he needed, a little more time today, enough perhaps to draw those who could protect him into doing it. For that, power had to shift—those who could protect him had to find themselves in *his* situation: no choice. Cutler was there already, even if he could never admit it to Mike. Mike's evidence was now more important to Cutler than Mike, and Mike had to be approached with the same caution one reserved for a ticking shopping bag under a bench in a mall. Now Mike had to spread the word—make sure that everybody involved had the message. The people against whom Mike could use Hollister's other tapes did not need to know that Mike did not have those tapes absolutely in his possession-*shit! He wasn't thinking at all!* He knew enough about the tapes to say any tapes were Hollister's. That would work for just long enough. . . .

Mike's mind was working again. There were more calls he

wanted to make, but there was no point in pulling off the freeway now when he would have to do it again later. He was going to wait until he was closer to town. . . .

And he still had to be concerned with tapped telephones—like his own. Nothing was sacred. Dan, Valerie Moreland, Marvin Burgess's nephew—Mike knew he was exhausted, and that one of exhaustion's symptoms was paranoia, but he had to think this way. The public could not imagine the nature of undercover work. A lot of cops had trouble dealing with it. Mike had been told that shooflies had been working Hollywood Division, and he had promptly put the information in the file-and-forget box of his mind. *Think twice,* Laura had said, in another context, one he still didn't understand. *Yes,* he almost said aloud, think twice. . . .

In Pomona he turned north to the 210 Freeway, which took him through Pasadena toward the Valley. In Glendale he pulled off at Brand Boulevard and headed down to the Galleria, which some locals called "The Mall That Ate Glendale." Every three or four years came a new proposal to tear down more of the city for additional parking for the mall, or a new wing on the structure itself. Judy had lost her car in here once, and even with the help of the security people, had spent four hours looking for the thing. She'd been told that it happened regularly, every week, but that hadn't lessened her rage—and neither had Mike's laughter. That had been a long time ago, and Mike had not thought of it since the event had faded from his short-term memory. Laura, on the other hand, seemed to know when the joke was on her.

It took him ten minutes to get parked and into the mall, and then another ten minutes to find a home electronics store and buy five VHS videocassettes. With another handful of quarters, he found a bank of telephones. First he called Maurice Constantine.

"Maxwell's driveway is full of cars, Mr. Gallagher, but the house is quiet. I can hear people breathing. One of the faucets is dripping, which it wasn't doing last night. I have a feeling that Maxwell was up late. Where he's going, there aren't an awful lot of all-night parties, so I guess it's understandable."

"Time for a wake-up call," Mike said. "Ring until somebody answers, ask for Mr. Maxwell, and if he doesn't come to the phone, tell whoever you've got that you're a real-estate dealer and want to show the house to a prospective buyer. But try to get it to Maxwell. Play it straight. If you're asked who told you the house was up for sale, answer that you're not at liberty to divulge the name. We're going to have to hope you're effective, because you won't be able to hang around for his reaction. If you don't mind, Maurice, would you go down to Century City next, the north tower, and see if someone is doing an infrared job on an office on one of the upper floors? The people who did Jackson would be using the same technology on this guy. I'll be getting back to you on it as quickly as possible, but if you get ahead of me, go over to Jackson's again. I want to do to Jackson the same thing we're doing to Maxwell. Call Jackson and tell him you're from San Francisco, or Phoenix, and you have some videotapes that once belonged to a Mr. Ben Hollister. Tell Jackson that you've screened the tapes, and there's some tape of Hollister incriminating Jackson, among others, in some very serious business. Then tell him to stay where he is, and that you'll be in touch. Then see what he does next."

"You know he's still on television, Mr. Gallagher. If somebody is tuned in, all of it will be heard."

"That's what I want, Maurice."

"It'll be safer for me if I kept my distance from Jackson's place. If I go up into the hills, I might have a direct line of sight on the Century City address—*or* the source of the infrared on it. If I can, I'll tune in on Century City, too."

"Don't take any risks, Maurice. This is the only play I've got, and I have to run it now."

"I think I have the picture, Mr. Gallagher."

"I have your address, Maurice. After I make another call, I'm going to stop at a stationer's for an envelope and mail you some cash. Will a grand cover it?"

"It's close enough. Is there anything else I can do for you?"

"Kennedy told me that if somebody asked about me, he didn't have to say a word. That will be enough from you, too."

"Take care of yourself, Mr. Gallagher."

The second call was to Marge. Mike gave her the number of

his pay telephone and asked her to go up to the Burger King as Dan had done so many times in the past.

"I was going to suggest it anyway, Mike. There's been a telephone truck up at the corner for the last three days. Even if Dan hadn't told me to be suspicious of telephone trucks that wear out their welcome, I'd be suspicious of this one. I've known the old people at the corner for as long as we've lived on this block, and they're on Lifeline service—you know, thirty local calls a month. They don't need three days of telephone repair even if they could afford it, which they can't. I'll call you right back."

"We don't have a lot of time. I want to tell you what I've learned—except for a few loose ends, it's the whole story."

She hung up. For a moment he was motionless. He didn't know if she had meant to say something, but he had heard something, a gasp, even smaller, almost silent, as deeply internal as the receding of a memory.

20

A DREAM WORLD—IT WAS LIKE ENTERING A DREAM world. Mike thought he was reasonably safe in Glendale and Burbank, on the Ventura Freeway heading west toward North Hollywood, Griffith Park, and then Forest Lawn rising on the left, the Valley spreading off to the right, west, and north in a bleak urban sprawl. Mike's father had been dead twenty-three years. There was no one in Mike's life who gave a damn about Jerry Gallagher now except Mike himself. The head office of Niles Eberhart and Son was in Van Nuys, not far from where Mike had grown up, not that far from where he lived now. Los Angeles had been sold to America on the notion that filth and corruption were not part of the fantasy of its palm-lined boulevards. Los Angeles was the world's first modern desert community, the so-called island on the land, the place Israel had once studied for clues to how it should be done. Years ago, L.A.'s palm trees had been brought in from the desert, and with them, rats. All old Angelenos knew that the palms were penthouses for rats. . . .

And so here it was, vivid under the rare clear sky, the newest big part of it, the last spoiled dream, so many swimming pools that from the air the Valley looked like it sparkled with jade, but containing as much alcoholism, drug addiction, wife-bashing, and depravity as any other place in America—or, for that matter, anywhere in the vodka-soaked Soviet Union. The filth and corruption were in the human beast, part of its nature: the Pryors, Maxwells, Jacksons, Azzolini's landlady, Mike's own mother—and father. When people stopped believing they were going to live forever, they began to insulate themselves from death in any way that made them happy, numb, or able to believe the lies they told themselves. Mike wasn't sure that that was what Laura had meant by "massive tragedy," but it would do. Somewhere out in the middle distance was an old man who might remember something about Jerry Gallagher's death, which mattered now because the thoughts it still evoked in his son had pointed to the role Niles Eberhart had played for the Brandons just days before the death of Dan Crawford. Probably Tom Cutler had some insight into, if not evidence of, the Brandon-Eberhart connection, but Eberhart's place was almost certainly the last where Cutler would be looking for Mike.

A quarter to two. Constantine needed more time. Mike wanted Eberhart to confirm only what Mike already knew in his bones: that Marylou Brown—known to her killer and fellow victims as Bobbie—had been Barbara Brandon, whom Dan had delivered to Tom Cutler the night she had run down and killed a man on Tampa Avenue. Maybe Mike would have to scare Eberhart, an old man now, and maybe the old man would be in jeopardy if Mike somehow failed to finish what was still coming together in his mind. If that happened, old Eberhart would be the least of Mike's worries. Mike wasn't afraid he was going to start feeling sorry for Eberhart. There were a lot of people higher than Eberhart on Mike's list of people to feel sorry for—*if* he ever felt in the mood again. Mike knew that this whole experience had changed him, and that he was changing still. It might be years before he had a sense of himself again. If he lived.

He took his time getting close to Eberhart's, looking for any sign of a surveillance. He didn't want to have to kill anybody—he could see that he was trying to forget what he had done to Barranquilla. He didn't want to have to kill anyone who didn't *need* it. He decided to park Don Grant's car in Eberhart's lot and save steps to the solid-brick, too stately structure rising out of a fringe of immaculately manicured shrubs. Undertaking was a racket, of course; with prompt burial or cremation, even embalming was unnecessary. Mike had never seen Eberhart's bill for his father, but he had assumed ever since the day of his father's funeral that Eberhart was some kind of crook. When Eberhart had stopped to speak to the man walking up the hill to him, *something* had happened between them, because Eberhart had looked as if he had been caught at something dirty. It had been a look Mike had seen frequently later as a cop, when he had caught respectable businessmen waving their wienies at girls on Sunset Boulevard. A *sick* look. When Mike had begun to see it on Sunset, he'd had to go back to Eberhart to remember where he had seen it the first time.

Everything in this place was identical to every other Death Dump Mike had ever visited, from the hotel-lobby-like directory inside the front door to the vapid little geek in the black suit, white shirt, and silver tie stepping out of the shadow to assist him. Mike let him glimpse the badge. "Niles Eberhart, kid, and don't tell me he's become his own best customer."

The guy took too much offense to think about anything else. "This way, please. Quietly. People are mourning."

Two characters were in the hall outside one of the rooms, whacking away on cigarettes. Mike wanted to tell the geek to get a liquor license; the place could charge half-price for Unhappy Hour. At a door at the end of the hall, the guy paused, turned to Mike, and put his fingers to his lips.

"He ain't mourning," Mike said, and wrapped his hand over the guy's on the doorknob, and squeezed as he turned it. The guy rode in as Mike swung the door open. Niles Eberhart, in an open-collared, short-sleeved shirt, rose from behind his desk, as pale and squat as a toadstool. Mike turned to the assistant. "Now you see that we're not disturbed."

"Mr. Eberhart is not a young man!"

"In my line of work, neither am I," Mike said. "Get the fuck out of here."

"Who are you?" the old man gasped.

Mike got out the badge again. "Gallagher, Homicide." He waved the geek off.

"Is it all right, Mr. Eberhart?"

Mike pushed him, hard, in the solar plexus, so that the small man flew out into the hall. Mike closed the door, saw a lock on this side, and turned it. Old Eberhart's mouth was hanging open. Mike saw a gleam of spittle forming in the corner. Mike said, "Call somebody and tell him we're not to be disturbed. Come on, pick up the telephone or I'll sink it into your skull."

"What's wrong? You're a detective?"

"Yeah. So was my partner. *Pick up the phone!*"

Trying to keep his eyes on Mike, old Eberhart complied. "What did you say your name was?"

"Make the call first."

The old man's hand was shaking. He wasn't a big man, and he was almost as wide as he was tall, his gut having settled almost completely below his waist, his belt buckle glowing heavenward like a beacon in the service of Eberhart's soul, which Mike took to resemble the old fart's body: Eberhart wasn't so much white as a canvas of muted, obscene halftones of gray, yellow, blue, purple, and even blotches of brown. His hair was so devoid of life that it looked like wet toilet paper clinging to the side of a bowl. He had the narrow slit of a mouth of a dead man, and his eyes were the color of overcooked cauliflower, mushy-looking, as if the slightest pressure would cause them to lose whatever surface tension that held them together and they would burst, sad-looking, and flood down his cheeks in a dull, thick ejaculate. It was all a fake. Eberhart only looked near dead. He had been down to the coroner's building to pick up the kid's body. There was enough life in Eberhart, despite appearances, to take charge when necessary.

"We don't want to be bothered in here," Eberhart said into the telephone. He listened. "No, I'm all right. Don't bother, my son." More listening. "I'm fine, I tell you. Call back in five minutes, if that will make you happy." Now he hung up. He gave Mike a look that said, *What now?*

"Sit down," Mike said. "I want to talk to you about Randall Brandon, Harcourt Pryor, Tom Cutler, Larry Hammond, Elmer Washington, and Barbara Brandon."

Eberhart folded his hands. "What's to talk about?"

"You picked up Barbara Brandon's body from the coroner's building the Monday night before last."

Eberhart blinked.

"I can *prove* that you were part of a conspiracy to falsify official records, a felony and cause to revoke your license to practice this witchcraft. After the lawyers are done, there won't be enough for your kid to bury you anywhere but your own backyard. This isn't my idea of a good time, Eberhart, but if you heard what I said about my partner, you know that it's what has to serve for the duration. If you don't tell me exactly what happened, how you know the people I already mentioned, and what you know *about* them, I'll throw you to every newspaper and television station in the city. When they're done, you won't be allowed to bury cat shit."

"What did you say your name was?"

"Gallagher. My partner, Dan Crawford, was killed a week ago because somebody was afraid he'd stumble onto the real identity of the Marylou Brown killed up in Laurel Canyon. My partner got her out of big trouble once, and Cutler, Pryor, and Brandon knew about it. All three of them knew that he could identify her even from the coroner's photographs—"

"I didn't kill anybody, Gallagher. My customers have to figure out how to die on their own—and they all manage somehow."

Mike opened his jacket. "My customers aren't that smart. You don't need an IQ test, do you?"

Eberhart snorted. "You don't fool me—"

Mike was on his feet, gun drawn. He grabbed Eberhart by the ear and pulled him forward onto the barrel of the Magnum. The force knocked Eberhart's upper plate askew. "Fuck with me! Fuck with me, old man, and you'll know you're dead before your brains hit that window behind you!"

The old man blubbered. "Don't kill me! Don't hurt me—*please!* I didn't hurt your friend!"

"How did you know he was my friend?"

"I didn't! I just assumed—"

Mike held Eberhart by the ear and fished the upper plate out of his mouth with the sight of the gun. He had an idea. Eberhart's hand came up to catch the plate but it didn't fall from the gun barrel. It rocked, dripping drool, and looked for a moment like something from an animated cartoon, trying to bite the gun in half. Eberhart's face, by contrast, looked collapsed, like a rotted jack-o'-lantern. "Give me that phone," Mike said.

"Who are you going to call?"

"A guy I know." Mike deposited Eberhart's denture on his side of the desk, then dialed Maurice Constantine. "Hiya, it's Gallagher. I know I haven't given you time to do everything I asked, so just tell me what you have been able to do."

"I got through to Maxwell," Constantine said. "He hit the roof. He wanted to know who had told me that his house was up for sale. He cursed me out, and then he said he had an idea who had put me up to it. I figured you wanted me to rub salt in the wound, so when he was done, I asked him when he thought the house was going to come on the market and what he thought it was worth. He bit. So then I told him that I thought the market was too soft for the kind of money he was looking for. Then I asked him if it was legal for him to carry paper on the place while he was in the can. He went nuts."

Because of Eberhart, Mike had to conceal his smile. "Were you able to get to the next location?"

"The clear air gave us a break, Mr. Gallagher," Constantine rumbled. "I took Mulholland west to stay out of the traffic, and when I got up above Beverly Hills, there was Century City, clear as a bell. So I took a look. This guy's office is on the north side of the north tower, right?"

"If it would give him a view to the north and east, yeah. I was told he can see all the way around to downtown."

"He sure can today. Anyway, there's a beam on him slanting up from the north side of Wilshire. It's all residential down there, and it wouldn't be too difficult to locate the source. My guess is that it's a van, like mine, parked on one of the streets down there. Do you want me to go have a look?"

"That wouldn't do any good. I have what I need. I'm having a conversation with a guy here—"

"You want me to record it?"

"That's the ticket."

"Just put the telephone someplace between you. I can enhance the quality of the sound later."

"How do you pick up so fast, Maurice?"

"Actually, Mr. Gallagher, it's the other way around. I don't think I've ever had a client make faster, better use of the stuff I can do. You have to be a very smart man."

Laura had said something about his intelligence—now Mike remembered: that while he acted as if he had only average intelligence, he seemed surprised by evidence that others could think, too. He put the telephone on the desk.

"You can get out of this without more trouble, old man, by answering all my questions as completely as you can"

"Dish ish illegal!" Eberhart said, spitting on himself. Furious, he grabbed for his handkerchief. "You'll go to shail!"

Mike sneered. "Barbara Brandon was killed at dawn Monday of last week. When were you informed that your services were required?"

Eberhart wiped his brow. "I want to get out a here! I don't have to do thish!" He started to get up. Mike pushed the gun barrel into the soft opening of Eberhart's mouth, then used the gun to push the old man down into his seat.

"Let's get something straight." Mike seethed. "Your pals conspired to keep an injured woman from getting necessary medical attention for most of a full day in the hope that she would die so that Barbara Brandon's identity would remain secret, because the Brandon family power would be seriously threatened by the knowledge that one of the children had been a common junkie who had been passed around sexually by every scumbag doper on the West Side. It might have come out that she once ran down and killed a man, and that the Los Angeles Police Department helped cover that up—for the same reasons of family power. If people start asking questions, those questions might not ever stop. The best thing that can happen to the people responsible for my partner's death is that they'll go to jail. If you want to protect these slobs, I'll make you pay promptly and in full, you motherfucker!"

Eberhart was staring at the gun barrel, his eyes almost

crossed. "I heard—I got a call in the late morning. They didn't tell me who it wash at firsht, but I figured it wash important."

"Who are *they?*"

"Harcourt Pryor and Elmer Washington. I had no contact at all with Chief Cutler, although the other two do, I know that. I never had any dealings with Randall Brandon over the yearsh, and I don't know who that other man ish. I never heard of him."

"Hammond."

"Him. I never heard of him."

"All right," Mike said. "Tell me everything that happened from the time you got the first call to the last contact you had with any of them."

Eberhart pointed to his teeth. Mike shook his head no. Eberhart said, "Harcourt Pryor called me at about eleven o'clock lasht Monday. He shaid that he had another job for me, the mosht shenshitive he could give me, and that he had to have absholute dishcretion. Well, he knew he'd get that. He told me to call Elmer Washington and that Elmer would tell me what needed doing. Elmer told me to bring that wagon down to the Esh level entrance that night. I got there at about ten o'clock— that's what Elmer shaid. I shaw her on the shlab. They were shewing her up again. I shtill didn't know who she was. The only mark on her wash in her shcalp. Jusht one. Elmer shaid she died eashy. We went back to hish offish and he called Pryor. The idea wash that I wash shupposhed to get inshtructionsh from Pryor. He told me who she wash. Now that I knew, I could undershtand why they wanted to do it that way. Pryor told me that the family wanted the coffin closhed and the funeral to be conducted the nexsht day. They had a minishter. They had a plot, too, the family plot. I did the embalming job that night myshelf. My shon didn't even shee her. The shervish wash in Chapel Shee right here at noon the nexsht day, and only her parentsh and Harcourt Pryor attended. The man who drove the hearsh didn't know who he had. A lot of kidsh dead from drugsh get that treatment becaush the family'sh ashamed, sho there weren't any queshtionsh, and there won't be in the future either."

"Tell me about the death certificate."

"Elmer shigned it. It shaid she died of a sherebral hemorrhage. Everything elsh wash routine. Nobody would notish. There are hundredsh of deathsh every day. I didn't ashk how the family intendsh to deal with the legal aspectsh—I'm ashuming that shome of the family property wash in the girl'sh name. There are waysh, and Pryor knowsh them all.''

"You've had a lot of dealings with Pryor over the years,'' Mike said.

"Well, a few. I've had dealingsh with other people, too. That goodlooking young fellow who ran for congress a couple of years ago. I buried two of hish boyfriendsh. That'sh how he got beat. The other guy had the goodsh on hish private life and how he sholved that problem.''

"You helped the other guy find out that the candidate had killed two homosexual lovers''

"Not directly. That wash Pryor. He'sh very powerful—*very powerful.* You'll never be able to use thish, you know. It's jusht too shtrong to be allowed to get out.''

"Pryor saw to it that the other guy had the goods on the candidate,'' Mike said.

Eberhart shrugged. "It'sh the way bushinesh ish done. I'm not important in the shcheme of thingsh, Gallagher. I jusht eshtablished yearsh ago that I wash shombody who knew how to do bushinesh—''

"What's wrong?''

"Nothing.''

Mike leaned in. For a moment, Eberhart's eyes had widened. Something had passed through his mind. Mike's palms itched. He put the gun away. He had a bad feeling, a terrible, awful feeling, and didn't know why. "I want to know who else you've buried for Pryor.''

"I'm not going to tell you that.''

"You've been the garbageman for years. Have you buried any girls?''

"What?''

Mike was fishing, hoping Eberhart wouldn't realize it. "Girls. Young girls. Good-looking ones. Laid them out, boxed them, and shipped them down to the airport and onto one of Pryor's big jet planes—''

"No—no, I never did anything like that! Ash God ish my

judge, I never! I shwear it! I don't know anything about anything like that!''

Mike grabbed his ear again. ''Then why did you look at me that way? It was when you said my name—'' His voice failed on its own, it seemed. ''You buried my father,'' he whispered. ''You connected the names.''

Eberhart's eyes bulged with terror.

''I saw you that day,'' Mike gasped. ''A guy met you halfway up the hill. I watched you. You noticed—*you remember it even now!*''

''You *were that kid!*''

Mike twisted his ear. ''Was Pryor involved in that? Was he? I know my father was murdered! Was Pryor involved? You established years ago that people could do business with you—*you just said it! Was Pryor involved*?''

''You're hurting me!''

''I'm going to kill you if you don't answer!''

Eberhart was cowering, his arms up to protect his head, his eyes squeezed shut. ''Yesh. He wash the one.''

''The one on the hillside with you?''

''Yesh.''

Mike flung him back in his chair. Mike's heart was pounding wildly. He flailed his arms. He wanted to kill—not this old man. He wanted to destroy the heart of this life he had been living for twenty-three years. Sound was coming from the telephone. Mike picked up.

''Are you all right, Mr. Gallagher?''

Mike drew his breath. ''Did you hear, Maurice?''

''It's all on tape, Mr. Gallagher. Can you get hold of yourself? I'll come over there, if you want.''

''No. No, I don't think it's necessary.'' He was looking at Eberhart, who was trying to push himself deeper into his chair. Eberhart was quivering, as if on the verge of shock. Maybe Mike was supposed to feel sorry for Eberhart, but he didn't. He couldn't. That idea he'd had: he picked up Eberhart's handkerchief, reached across the desk, and removed Eberhart's lower plate. ''What I'd like you to do, Maurice, is play the tape—all of it—to Frank Kennedy, and then ask Kennedy to call that guy you just reported on and pull the stunt you pulled. I think Frank will go along with that, don't you?'' Mike had the dentures stacked on the desk.

"My teep!"

"He talks funny," Constantine said. "Why does he talk like that?"

"It's a long story. Tell Frank I want that other guy as crazy as I can get him."

"I understand, Mr. Gallagher. Is there anything else I can do for you?"

It took Mike a split second to remember what Constantine had not done yet. "No, that's it. I'll be calling you again soon." He hung up. Using the handkerchief like a pot holder, Mike picked up both dentures, carried them to the door to the hall, and stacked them on the carpet two feet from the door. He unlocked the door and motioned to the guy at the other end of the hall. He closed the door again and turned to Eberhart, who was struggling to get out of his chair. "Sit still," Mike said. "You're getting off easy, considering what a miserable little turdlet you are. This is one way to keep you from calling people."

The guy outside knocked.

"My teep! Pweash!"

"Come on in," Mike said.

Eberhart wailed. The door opened and the guy stepped in—and on the teeth, which broke like a teacup. The guy didn't know what he had done. Mike had a twenty-dollar bill peeled, and stuffed it into the guy's breast pocket. "Get your boss a pizza—and make sure the crust is extra crisp." And he pushed past him, walking briskly.

At first. By the time he reached the foyer, he felt as if he were walking underwater. *Warm* water. He was sure people were watching, that they could see that something was wrong with him.

And outside, he burst into tears. For his father, who would have been sixty-one years old, if he had lived—if he had been *allowed* to live. *Pryor!* He had *seen* Pryor. But what had Frank Kennedy said? Harcourt Pryor had changed everything about himself. Mike would not know in fact if he had actually crossed paths with Pryor in the past two weeks. Did Pryor know that

Mike Gallagher was Jerry Gallagher's son? Mike saw that the answer was yes, of course. Pryor might not have known it last week, when he had conspired against Dan, but he knew it now—and had known for some days. *Oh, yes.* Mike sniffed, like a kid. And just that quickly, he wasn't crying anymore. It was twenty to three. Mike wanted to get away from Eberhart's. He wished he could have arranged for some eavesdropping at Pryor's—but that would have been risky for Constantine, as well as asking too much from him. Mike wanted to talk to Kennedy, too: he was thinking that there was something else Kennedy could do for him, if Kennedy had the juice to get it done.

Heading down to Ventura Boulevard, Mike passed enough fast-food stands to be reminded that he hadn't eaten since early morning. Dan had always been ready to eat. To Dan, there had been no such thing as junk food. Mike knew that if he stopped for a couple of burgers and a mess of fries, it would be like taking a sleeping pill. He couldn't go to Winchell's for doughnuts and coffee—the amount of time L.A. cops spent in Winchell's was a citywide joke. But he was hungry and had to do something about it. The car needed gas, too. This was Friday. The traffic on the Ventura Freeway overpass in front of him was stopped cold. Traffic would be heavy in all directions and wouldn't begin to clear up until nearly eight o'clock. Mike pulled into a gas station, up to the full-service island, told the kid what he wanted, and went into the office to load up on candy bars—and change for the telephone. There was a stand of telephones out at the corner, where people using them could be seen from all sides. He'd find out soon enough if Cutler had every cop in town looking for him. He called the school in Laurel Canyon.

"Let me speak to Laura Demming, please, it—"

"Who? Is she a student here?"

Again, Mike thought. "No, she's a teacher. This is a police emergency."

"Hold on." Her hand covered the mouthpiece: he could hear her voice, muffled, but not her words. But then he heard a word as her voice went up a half-octave: *emergency!* There was a moment's silence.

"Helloo-oo." Another voice—another woman who gobbled on the telephone.

"Hiya," Mike said. "I'm just trying to get hold of Laura Demming."

"Did you say police *emergency?*"

Mike hesitated. "Yeah."

"May I ask what this is in reference to?"

"No, you may not. But it's important."

"Ahh—she'll have to call you back. Will you give me a number where you can be reached? And your name, so I may say who's calling?"

"You know, in the time we've spent talking to each other, somebody could have gone down the hall and gotten her. I've seen that school, and it isn't that big—"

Her tone turned cool. "She'll have to call you back. Now if you'd like to give me a number, fine—"

He'd alienated her somehow; now his only chance was to press. "I *said* police *emergency.* Doesn't that mean anything to you?"

"I'm afraid—" She stopped. "We'll do it my way or not at all. Now—"

Mike hung up. All he'd done was create a problem for himself with Laura. *I had a fight with somebody at your school, probably your boss.* . . .

He dialed Constantine.

"Mr. Kennedy is making that call to Maxwell," Constantine said. "He has a message for you, too. I'm in range of Donnie Jackson's place, so if you hang on a second, all I have to do is find a place where I can receive the signal, and I'll tell you what's going on."

"My ass is hanging out here, Maurice."

Constantine chortled. "Mr. Kennedy told me that all the cops in the world are looking for you, Mr. Gallagher. I'm going as fast as I can. You still want me to make that call to Jackson about Hollister's tapes, don't you?"

"Yeah. Is that what Kennedy said to you word for word? It sounds like him."

"Yeah, it does, doesn't it? It's what he said. I didn't ask for details. Okay, I know I can get a picture here. Hang on, now I have to park." Mike could see a police cruiser on the cross street on the other side of the boulevard. All he could do was turn his back to it and hope for the best. Constantine said, "Jackson's on the telephone. He's standing, and the blond girl is standing in front of him. Wait a minute, he's holding her there. I told you, it's a fuzzy picture." Mike heard the traffic start up. He didn't think there was anything about his behavior that could attract attention—except self-consciousness. The assholes made themselves obvious when they tried to *act* normal. Mike knew something about acting: the best acting was *being*. In the same situation without his awareness that the police were looking for him, Mike would be watching the kid gassing his car—which is what he did. Then he looked the other way, back toward the intersection. The traffic was moving freely, which meant that the cruiser had passed him. When Constantine started talking again, Mike was taking the chance of looking for the cruiser itself: it was at the next block—but making a turn. Constantine said, "He's got her by the shirt—the front of it, you know, bunched up in his fist."

"Who is he talking to?"

"A woman, I know that. He just called her a bitch. He's yelling at her. He's doing all the talking, Mr. Gallagher."

Mike had a bad feeling about the cruiser. Eberhart might not have called the police, but he must have called Pryor, if only to lie about what had happened between Mike and him. And then Pryor would have called Cutler—even if Cutler knew exactly who had ordered Dan's death, he was still looking for Mike. Cutler wanted information about Mike no matter where it came from. "I'll call you back, Maurice," Mike said, and hung up. He walked quickly to the Ford wagon, peeling off bills as he went. The kid wasn't quite done. Mike gave him the money and pushed him aside to put the cap on the gas filler. Traffic was moving down the boulevard again—only the flow of cars would keep the cruiser from making another right turn so its officers would see Mike. From behind the wheel of the wagon, Mike now saw the cruiser's fender poking out behind the building line. If Mike was to escape if only for a while, he would have to get out of the gas station before the police themselves saw him in the wagon. Even so, he would have to separate himself from the wagon soon, because the gas station attendant was about to give the officers information that would connect Mike to the vehicle. A line of cars was forming on the side street to block the only route that was out of view of the cruiser. Mike shifted into gear and moved down the sidewalk to the midblock fire alley, turned in, and stepped on the gas hard. Horns blew behind him. At the next street, Mike turned right. He'd last even longer if he could get the wagon out of sight. The nearest public indoor parking that Mike knew of was at the Galleria in Sherman Oaks, about a mile from here. He could call Laura at home from the Galleria, but he couldn't ask her to come down and trade cars with him: the police would pick her up almost at once—and that would be a lot more trouble with her boss than Mike had made already.

He zigged and zagged down two, three streets at a time, angling southwest toward the Galleria, watching the rearview mirror, pushing the wagon through the stop signs. Frank Kennedy had a message for him. Mike wanted to know more about Donnie Jackson—*and* his reaction to the call Constantine still had to make to him. But Mike had to be careful about calling all of them now. Kennedy had said that the federals were looking for him, and he had said, too, that they knew that he was in contact with Mike. Mike had no idea if the federals and the city cops were working together, or in a race against each other. It made no difference: the effect on Mike would be the same. He would be in custody, and everybody else would figure out some way to continue business as usual.

Ten blocks north of the Galleria, Mike was on a side street at the stop sign waiting for a chance to make a left turn when a cruiser roared northward through traffic, lights boiling, sirens howling. A minute later, Mike was nosing out into the traffic lanes when he saw another cruiser, same trim, screaming his way. Mike threw the wagon into reverse and scooted back into the side street. When a break in the traffic finally came, Mike had to burn rubber to get to the southbound side of Sepulveda Boulevard. Seconds more, and he was in the Galleria garage.

Hollister's tapes of Rainbow Drive the day of the murders. Five brand-new blanks and the 9000 Building register. And one more gun than he could carry. Mike slipped the gun in the side pocket of his jacket, stacked the rest of the stuff like a schoolgirl's books, locked the car securely, and started for the escalator.

He still didn't know what he was going to do. At the top of the escalator, on the left, was a camera shop, empty, with two kids in open-collared, white dress shirts behind the counter. As one approached, Mike flashed his badge. "All right if I use your phone?"

"Something tells me I'll have a richer, happier life if you do."

Mike smiled in spite of himself. "It's not that bad." He started to dial Kennedy and stopped. "Let me have some privacy."

The kid raised his hands and backed up, grinning. He had blue eyes and thick, dark, close-cropped hair. "Go ahead," he said through his teeth, "I won't stop you."

Mike was listening to Kennedy's telephone ring when he realized that the kid had been doing Bogart in *The Maltese Falcon,* when Peter Lorre as Joel Cairo had insisted on searching Bogey's office. Kennedy said hello and Mike identified himself as he turned his forefinger and thumb into a gun and shot the kid, who doubled up with laughter. Kennedy said, "Yeah, that's some tape Maurice played for me. I just finished giving Maxwell the business about when his house is going on the market. He's wise—knows he's being fucked with, but that isn't making him calmer or happier. He said, 'Stop the crap. Just get to the punch line.' I played it straight. Anyway, I told Maurice that I had a message for you. Call Bob Wills. He remembered something about the guy he talked to about the killings. He said, 'It took awhile, but I *did* talk to somebody.' He said it like that, if that means anything to you. Wills said he was calling from outside and wouldn't be back to the number I already gave you for another hour or so. He's talking to that dame you threw to him. He told me that. As for you, the heat's up a couple of notches—I can feel it myself now. The boss of the guy I talk to downtown called less than an hour ago and told me I didn't know what I was dealing with, being associated with you. I told him the truth, that I had no knowledge of your whereabouts; and then he told me that life for me could be made very uncomfortable if he found that I was withholding information."

"Did you get any sense of what he meant when he said that you didn't know what you were dealing with?"

"No, it was just one of those blank threats. They can't bullshit me. I told him to go fuck himself and hung up on him. Another bureaucratic dickhead. If you ask me, if there's anybody who doesn't know what he's dealing with, it's him."

"Why do you say that?"

"You know as well as I do. It's the way things work. You're told what they think you need to know, and then they expect you to go out and blindly obey orders. That's the situation he's in. He doesn't know squat."

"There's something I'd like you to do," Mike said. "How far are you from Laurel Canyon?"

"If I have any luck in the traffic, about twenty minutes. If the luck is bad, figure forty."

It would have to do. Mike explained that he wanted Kennedy to go up to Rainbow Drive. "Oh, and in this traffic, you'll know soon enough if you've made new friends."

"I'll let you know that, too," Kennedy said. He hung up. Mike dialed Constantine. Out of the corner of his eye, Mike saw the kid take notice.

"Are you all right, Mr. Gallagher?" Constantine asked. "You kind of scared me there."

"Everything's all right now, Maurice. You were telling me that Jackson was on the telephone with a woman while he was holding his girl by the shirt."

"I told you it was a fuzzy picture. He was holding her by the skin. She's bare to the waist, as it turns out. She's got an awful-looking welt between her breasts. I have a lot of stuff for you, Mr. Gallagher. Let me get it all out. I almost started to make notes. And I got to keep my eye on Jackson. He's in the middle of a shitstorm, and I figure you're the weatherman."

"He better not be in the middle," Mike said. "That spot is reserved for somebody else."

"Maybe you're right. Jackson sure as shit doesn't know what's going on. Anyway, when we were talking last time, I told you he was on the phone with a woman. That turned out to be Paula Rogers. That's a positive ID, Mr. Gallagher. I'm afraid this could turn into a real mess. Anyway, Jackson was having trouble hearing Rogers. She couldn't speak in her normal voice—you know, whispering. I don't think she was alone at her location, somebody in the other room, something like that. She was all pissed off because she thought Jackson or Roehrig tipped the cops to her going to court in Palm Springs today because a cop was waiting there for her with a lot of questions about Jackson and Roehrig. She's one dumb cunt, Mr. Gallagher. In a situation like this, she thinks she can get away with teasing, as if these guys won't throw her to the sharks. Well, Jackson got real upset with what she was saying, and when I thought he was twisting his girlfriend's shirt, he was twisting her flesh. Over the phone he warned Rogers to keep her mouth shut—that's all he said, or had a chance to say. She hung up on him, and right away he called Maxwell, but Maxwell said he'd call him back, he was on the other line. I figure Maxwell was talking with Mr. Kennedy. Anyway, while Jackson was waiting for Maxwell to call him back, the girl went to the closet for more drugs, saying he had to calm down, and he just exploded. He said they were running low on stuff and that they might have trouble getting more—he really made it sound like a nightmare. And then he wanted to know why she was always trying to get him high. The truth is the other way around. He kicked her. I've never seen an animal kicked as hard as he kicked her, but she seemed to know what to do. She curled up in a ball, and he kicked her butt and her hip. Just awful. To tell you the truth, if I'd known I was going to have to look at stuff like this, I might not have taken the job. That's when Maxwell called, all pissed off, too, I guess because of what Kennedy and I did, but also at Jackson for calling him. That makes you right about who installed the TV equipment in Jackson's place, Mr. Gallagher. The way Maxwell talked, I could tell that he knew they weren't private. Jackson didn't cop to that. He's a bumpkin, just country-cruel. Maxwell asked him if anything funny was going on, and Jackson said that Paula Rogers had been blabbing to some cop in Palm Springs and she was up to something even as they spoke."

"But Jackson didn't know what that was," Mike said. At the other end of the counter, the kid was trying not to pay attention. His pal was staring at Mike. Mike turned away. "Were you able to get that call in?"

"When I saw how upset Maxwell was with Jackson calling him, and that that Rogers dame was up to something, I figured I'd wait until Maxwell hung up before I called—Jackson's got Call Waiting, and I would have been butting in. Maxwell was making it clear that he didn't want to hear from Jackson, and from everything else you've been doing, I figured you wanted Jackson stewing over the message you wanted me to give him."

"You figured right," Mike said. "You did good."

"So I told Jackson I had Hollister's tapes, that I was from Vegas, and that he should wait until he gets another call."

Mike heard Constantine draw a breath before he continued. "Then I hung up. I watched him bash the receiver down, pick it up again, bash it down again, and break it in half. That's when he screamed. I mean *screamed!* I told you about the other day when he growled like an animal. This was a hundred times worse. Even the girl got scared. She ran into the bathroom and locked the door. It's a good thing for her that's an old place, Mr. Gallagher. Jackson went for the door and punched it a couple times, but it's not one of those modern hollow-core jobs, and I guess he broke a couple of bones in his hand. He sat down on the bed and cried like a kid—well, not quite; *almost* like a kid. I don't have a lot of experience with crazy people, but I'd believe it if an expert told me that Jackson is one."

"What's he doing now?"

"There's more, so let me tell you. I figured you'd want to know whether his phone is working or not, so I called him again. It rings, he can transmit, but he can't receive. People can call him, but he can't hear what they're saying. So then he tried to get her to come out of the bathroom, begging and pleading, moaning about his hand—the whole shot. Finally she came out and looked at his hand, but he pulled away and went into the bathroom to tend to it himself. The phone rang again —it wasn't me—and she picked it up, not knowing the handset was being held together only by its wires. She laughed and he went ape again. It wound up with him throwing money at her and telling her to go get a telephone, a job that may be too tough for her. It's not that she's that stupid, but she's that drugged and beat down by him. She's out now looking for a telephone, and he's sitting on the bed looking at his hand like a monkey—when he isn't packing his nose or telling callers that the phone isn't working and they have to call back later.''

"Do you know where she went to buy the telephone?"

"He told her to try Adray's down on Wilshire Boulevard."

"See if you can find her and talk her out of going back to Jackson's, at least for tonight. And if you can, keep calling him every five minutes. How far will you be able to pick up the transmission from his place?"

"Oh, I ought to be able to get the sound on Wilshire, even with all the buildings in the way."

"Go for it. I'll be calling you." As Mike hung up, the kid came down from the back of the store.

"It's been nice having you, but if you keep calling Rangoon—"

Mike laughed. "One more—and then you have the chance to pick up a fast twenty bucks."

His eyebrows went up. "How fast?"

"I'll need you for most of an hour. You got a car?"

"Yeah. Look, you have to take care of my friend, if he's going to cover for me. So make it thirty."

"Five for your friend."

"Ten. I *meant* friend."

"You've got a deal. Privacy again, eh?"

"I don't *want* to hear," the kid said, heading back to his friend to tell him how he had just skinned a cop.

Laura wasn't home yet. He hung up and waved the kids forward. He found a twenty and two fives in his roll and distributed them. The one who had done all the talking came around the counter.

"No matter who asks for me," he said to the other, "the story is that my father's car broke down and I had to go and rescue him before he got hysterical again."

Now they were headed down the escalator, stepping down the treads, the kid leading the way into the garage. "I'm taking Beverly Glen, it's faster than the freeway."

"I need a post office," Mike said. "Wrapping paper first— or a bank of lockers."

The kid eyed the tapes. "There's always a checkroom in a department store, and there are plenty of those in Century City.

Under the Twin Towers is one of those mail service stores. They'll wrap, stamp, and send.''

It was close to four o'clock. Mike had to get himself together, call Kennedy, Wills, Constantine again—and Maxwell, and Pryor. He had to get into the mail service store even if he didn't know to whom he should send the package. He was still hiding from himself, hiding from what he had learned from Eberhart. Maybe it wasn't possible to run and think at the same time. If that were true, he owed it to himself to stop running long enough to think his way through what he was going to do next. He had started the day with the idea of pushing people to the limit, the people he thought could be pushed. The equipment required to kill Dan had been stolen from the department's Van Nuys facility, and if Cutler's anger during the teardown of Dan's car last Monday morning had been authentic, Cutler had not known the reason for the robbery. That was Monday. Today, Mike was sure, Cutler had the whole story, including the name of the man who had flown the helicopter to which the equipment had been affixed, the name of the man the first was working for—and the name of the man who had set Dan up. Mike had thought he wanted that guy most of all, but now he wanted Pryor, too . . . and the helicopter pilot, and anybody in between. He didn't give a damn about Maxwell or Jackson or any of the people around them . . . no, that wasn't quite true, either: he wanted to get the blonde away from Jackson before his roof fell in on him; and Mike would even the score for Marvin Burgess's nephew with the bodyguard Kiku if given the chance. . . .

That was later—maybe. Right now the kid was flashing his best wheelman stuff, whipping up the switchbacks crisply, pacing his advance on the car ahead, for far up the hill could be seen the traffic clotting at the Mulholland light. On the other side where the road narrowed, he downshifted to third and let the engine braking reduce the car's speed, still almost ten miles over the limit.

"Sometimes there's a cop down here."

"You're not a danger to the republic, kid."

"Thanks for telling me. I'm going down to Olympic and then head east. It should be a smooth and steady trip."

Mike was thinking that he had to send the register and tapes—

all of them, even the new, blank ones—to Marge. If he failed, if he never saw her again, at least she would have some proof that her husband's death had been the result of a conspiracy. Mike would write a note—he had to figure that out, too. A lot to do in Century City, and not the least of it was staying clear of Pryor and anyone else who knew Mike Gallagher.

The kid pulled the car up to the curb outside the ABC Entertainment Center and Mike said good-bye and hurried through the crowd across the sidewalk and down the steps to the plaza opening out upon the two high-rises on Century Park East—triangular buildings facing the plaza, they looked like King Kong's stereo speakers. The kid hadn't known what time the mail service store closed, and it was getting too late for Mike to take chances. Century City was the future as it had been imagined twenty years ago, massive buildings surrounded by plazas, gardens, and fountains, all of it oversized and difficult to negotiate. Mike was trying to hurry without being conspicuous, and it made him more anxious. Another three hours of daylight remained. He didn't know if Pryor was in his office. It might even be better for Mike if Pryor were not—although Mike did not know how.

He need not have hurried. There was a line in the mail center, but it wasn't going to close for another hour. Constantine, he was thinking, Kennedy, and Wills. And he wanted to call Maxwell. . . .

Kiku.

No mistaking him. Mike caught only a glimpse as Kiku passed in the hall outside the windows, but it was he, in a dark T-shirt and chino pants, swinging his huge, bare arms, parting the crowd like a tugboat churning through a river of ducks. He was headed toward the north tower. Last in line, Mike stepped out into the hall to watch Kiku make the turn toward the escalator, head and shoulders above the crowd, some of the people looking around and up at him. Kiku had seen Mike during Hammond's raid on Maxwell's place, but there was no way to know if Kiku remembered Mike. Kiku had not looked into the mail center, Mike was reasonably sure of that. When Mike had first seen him,

Kiku's eyes had been straight ahead, and then had stayed that way. For all the uncertainty, there were two things that Mike knew now that he had not known before.

The first was that Pryor was in his office.

And the second was that Mike couldn't stay here for long, not if more people were on the way, people who had seen Mike and might have better memories than Kiku's seemed to be.

On the other side of the street where the kid had let Mike out was the Century Plaza Hotel. Mike would be able to make his calls from there.

Kiku? Pryor had business with *Kiku?*

Maybe Maxwell was already upstairs, or on his way over from Woodrow Wilson Drive. The way these buildings were laid out, it was impossible for one man to know with certainty who was entering or leaving. Mike was at more of a disadvantage here than he had realized, more of a disadvantage now than ever.

When Mike stepped onto the plaza again he could see the passage of time in the changing of the light. He was aware of how vulnerable he was, how exposed to the windows above. He remembered that Kennedy had said that Pryor's own view was to the north and east, and that Constantine had picked up the infrared beam rising from the Beverly Hills flats to the north side of the building—but that didn't mean that Pryor's office windows didn't extend around to the west, or that Kiku hadn't seen Mike down in the arcade, in spite of Kiku's behavior afterward. Because he was now carrying the police .38 that had been in the dashboard of his car, Mike now had enough firepower to take out all of the L.A. Lakers *and* the bus they rode in, but it did not make him feel more secure. He did not like guns—he did not trust them. Mike took that as a sign of fear. Of course he was afraid. He did not think he was tough. He did not even know what tough *was*.

In the hotel he bought another roll of quarters for the telephone. The first call was to Kennedy.

"I just got back—well, five minutes ago," Kennedy said. "There's nobody at the address on Rainbow Drive that you gave me. I looked for an old Volkswagen bus up and down the street. Finally I went up to the door and knocked, figuring that if somebody opened, I'd say that I was interested in buying the property—I have fake business cards. No answer. The place is dark. Nobody followed me in either direction, incidentally."

Mike was silent. Roehrig was on the wind. Mike had a way of seeing if Roehrig was down here, time-consuming as it was: if Roehrig was with Pryor and Kiku—and probably Maxwell—somewhere in the five levels of garage under Century City was Roehrig's old bus with its souped-up motor. Mike said, "Try Maxwell again. I'll get back to you."

Mike called Constantine.

"Mr. Gallagher, I didn't catch up to the girl until she was headed into the store—she was going to Adray's for a telephone, in case you forgot —and something funny happened. She was pretty blotto. A civilian wouldn't be able to tell, but it was obvious to me. Two guys were a few steps behind her. I made them right away. No doubt about it. Young guys in good suits, matching haircuts. They were paying too much attention to her and each other to pick up on me. They followed her into the store and I watched through the doors from outside. They were awful close to her. They knew what she was supposed to be doing, because when she got lost in the store, they laughed at her together. The only way it makes sense is if they were watching Jackson and her on television, and the two of them, Jackson and the girl, are supposed to run out their string. What I mean, Mr. Gallagher, is that something's going down. It's not just in the air, it was in the way those guys behaved."

"So what happened?"

"She figured out how to buy a phone and paid for it with a hundred-dollar bill, left the store with the two guys behind her, and drove back to Norma Place. They followed her and I followed them. It was no problem. They didn't bother to see if she turned in at the driveway—I was the one who saw that. They went straight on to the 9000 Building. How about that? Real clowns."

"Your best guess, Maurice: who were they?"

"Not LAPD. Young LAPD plainclothes have a certain dumb, grim look on their faces."

"I know what you mean. So you figure they were federal?"

"State, more likely. I've seen state guys before. They can't play on my team."

Mike knew what that meant, too. "Were you able to hear what Jackson was up to?"

"Yeah. While she was gone and people called, he kept telling them that the telephone was broken and that it would be fixed in just a few minutes. He can't take much more, Mr. Gallagher. While she was gone, he was whimpering like a baby. The people who called him were able to hear. Since he couldn't hear them, he had no idea of how he was coming across—"

"And that changed when she came back," Mike said.

"Oh, yeah. He got tough with her right away. I think I've learned something about these guys on this case, Mr. Gallagher. The women, too. She wanted more dope as soon as she got in the door, and as I said, he had to play tough, so it got a little sick. She's a pretty girl, Mr. Gallagher, but that's all. Anyway, he talked to his usual customers, and then, a few minutes ago, Maxwell called. Actually, another guy called, and said he was glad that the telephone was working again. Then he told Jackson to hold on for Maxwell, and Maxwell got on—"

"Let's stop, Maurice. Who was the guy who did the calling? Did he identify himself?"

"He had one of those deep voices, like he was a big guy. I think Jackson called him Keego. I have it on tape. Do you want me to play it for you?"

"Did he say anything else? It will save some time."

"Well, Jackson asked him how long he'd been trying to get through, and this other guy said about half an hour."

"So he heard Jackson coming unglued," Mike said.

"*Being* unglued, Mr. Gallagher. He's too far gone now to make any kind of quick comeback, although he thinks he can. I've got video again. Jackson's sitting on the bed, having the d.t.'s. Have you ever seen that?"

"Yes, I'm sorry to say." Mike's mother, a couple of times, paralyzed with terror, seeing things that weren't there, not recognizing the things that were. "Did you get any idea of what Maxwell told him?"

"Oh, yes. Jackson's supposed to stay right where he is. Not leave the bungalow. If he gets another call about Hollister's tapes, he's supposed to call a number Maxwell gave him. It's new to me. Can you take it down now?''

Mike had reached for his notebook when Constantine had said he had a new number. He found the Harcourt Pryor number that Marge had given him. Constantine's number was a match.

It made no sense. Maxwell knew that the television camera was installed in Jackson's bedroom and still working—the police were going to hear everything Jackson and his caller said about Hollister's tapes of the girls. ''Hang on,'' Mike said. He wanted to think it through. Maxwell was with Kiku, in Pryor's office. Roehrig, not at home, was probably there, too. Pryor, Maxwell, Roehrig, and Kiku. Cutler had wanted Mike to turn himself in. Almost certainly Pryor thought he was safe working with Cutler—he would be out of town if he thought otherwise. If Cutler had told Mike the truth—that he believed that Dan's death violated a basic understanding between the police and the establishment, then Cutler was concealing that from Pryor. Hammond was in this somewhere—he had to be. Maybe Hammond didn't know what Cutler thought either. Constantine had said something was going down. Cutler *still* wanted to cover up what had happened on Rainbow Drive. There were the federals, too. As long as no arrests were being made, Mike had to conclude that all concerned wanted the tapes destroyed.

But all of them wanted something more—and different from each other. If Mike was to believe that Cutler had told him the truth, Cutler was using Pryor—just as Pryor was using Maxwell, and Maxwell was using Jackson. And if Maxwell was being fooled by Pryor it was not completely: Maxwell had told Jackson to keep an eye on Roehrig, the Vietnam helicopter pilot now apparently in Pryor's camp. . . .

''Mr. Gallagher?''

''I'm here. Maurice, what I'd like you to do, if you will, is make yourself as secure as possible and tape everything that happens at Jackson's place this evening. If you can't bear watching it, don't; and if you don't want to hear it, rig up your equipment so the recording is done without the sound going through a speaker. I know you can do that.''

"That's just flipping a switch, Mr. Gallagher. I'm concerned about you, if you want to know. From what I've seen so far, these people will do anything—"

"You don't know the half of it, Maurice. If you don't hear from me, get in touch with Bob Wills. You won't be the only one."

Now Mike called Frank Kennedy again. Kennedy said that Maxwell wasn't answering.

Mike didn't bother to say that he knew where Maxwell was. "One last thing, Frank. In half-an-hour—let's time this—call the number I'm about to give you and tell the geek who answers that you want to talk to somebody important about Hollister's tapes. The geek will know what you're talking about, and if he does what his bosses told him to do, he'll ask for your number or call him back. Call him back but anything else he tells you to do, forget. You're not going to discuss the contents of the tapes over the telephone, and you got them from Ben Hollister. If you're asked how, allow it to be understood that you squeezed them out of Hollister's nose."

"I don't have to know any more than that," Kennedy said. "My watch says it's a quarter to six." Now Mike called Wills again. He got the answering machine. Mike left his name and said he would call back later.

He had told Kennedy a half hour because he had wanted time to talk to Wills—it would take only ten minutes for Mike to get from here to the north tower. Something was going down, Constantine had said, and Mike had wanted to know what Wills had remembered. Mike still needed all the information he could get. He didn't know if the *federales* were aligned with Cutler, against him, and he didn't know how much of their surveillance of him had been passed on to Cutler to help him find Mike.

The federal people didn't have much to report of the last two days. If they had, they wouldn't have been bothering Frank Kennedy. . . .

Kennedy had told Mike that the federals knew about Gretchen and him. He'd met Gretchen months ago. Suppose they'd checked him out then, and given him the pass he'd deserved? How soon after the murders could they have started to listen to him again? The night of the murders—that first Monday night.

From home, Mike had talked to only two people, and one, Dan, was dead.

The other was Judy. Mike drummed his fingers on the metal shelf under the pay telephone. He had time to call Laura.

He stopped.

Judy had stared at him, then hurried away from the funeral. She'd been reasonable enough, for her, on Monday. She had said she would think about his request. And then Laura started calling. Suppose somebody had heard that Monday-night conversation with Judy?

He had not seen any surveillance on him. Kennedy had reported this morning that the federals were looking for him. Mike assumed that their difficulties with him had started yesterday—when he'd left town. Laura had been with him as late as Wednesday night, when she'd accompanied him to Hollister's. The night before, she'd been in his bed while he'd been out with Hammond, at Maxwell's place. And on Monday, she'd come up to Mulholland after he'd gotten rid of Barranquilla's body. . . .

And he met her the day before; she'd called on both of the preceding days. Pretty quick. What would the federal people have learned about him *after* they'd learned he loved women?

Not a hell of a lot.

He'd called Laura twice at the school. Both times he'd had to hold briefly while his call was transferred from one woman to another, and each time he'd been told that Laura would have to call him back: he had the same experience *exactly,* except for one point—this afternoon, the first woman had not heard of Laura at all.

Now he remembered her hanging up the telephone Wednesday night after he'd returned from checking on Agnes. She'd been alone in his apartment for hours the night before, and when Constantine had checked his telephone in the morning, it had been clean. . . .

He didn't like what he was feeling. He almost believed it now, but he still wanted to believe *her.* If this was not all conjecture—paranoia—she had done some job on him. Freckles and big, round glasses. He'd never seen a cop who looked like that before. Guns and the quick flashes of intelligence and improvisation, always helpful and getting closer to him so that he thought nothing of it Wednesday night when she'd asked how he knew what was going on with Jackson when he'd spent the morning at Dan's funeral, and the afternoon at court. . . .

He'd been under surweillance! It took him a minute to find the number of Judy's office in the directory, and then when he asked the switchboard to connect him with her, her secretary was the one to pick up.

"May I speak with Mrs. Gallagher, please? Tell her it's her ex-husband calling."

He was put on hold, and then the wait was a few seconds longer than he'd expected. It was the secretary again.

"I'm sorry, but Mrs. Gallagher can't come to the telephone right now."

"Tell her it's a police emergency, please."

She pushed the hold button. Now he was afraid he had spent too much time here. Just about twenty minutes to Kennedy's call. What had Wills remembered? Mike was not ready to see the man who had been at his father's funeral, who had elevated himself over the years to a position where he took care of so much of the Brandon family business that he'd called Dan . . . what else had he done? Mike wanted to compose himself — collect his energy. The line opened. It was the secretary again, which braced him only a little for what she said: "Mrs. Gallagher told me to say that she's acting on the advice of a lawyer, and then she told me to hang up." And the line went dead.

It took him a moment to get the handset back on its cradle. His hand was shaking. If what he was just told was fact, it only *fit* his theory, it didn't *prove* it—that his call to Judy was overheard, that federal people contacted her, that Laura Demming was put in place, and that she had run a number on him. She would have known exactly how to push his buttons. All that stuff about being a daddy's girl had covered an awful lot of ground for him—and for all he knew, her information had been piped to Cutler. She could have even known that. . . .

No proof!

He had to get going. Outside, the light had changed again. The shadows were longer, the sky darker, and the Twin Towers still gleamed in the sun. The wind had changed, too: now there was an onshore breeze. It was going to be a beautiful night, a great night to be alive.

Pryor, Maxwell, Roehrig, and Kiku—Mike had to get his head clear. Pryor had made his climb from one crime to the next, insulating himself from common human decency with the results of his own outrageousness. Now his power was so immense and far-reaching that he had reason to believe he was safe no matter what he did. Mike could feel himself being drawn back into the feeling he'd had after his father's death, a feeling of wanting to hide, something very old inside him. It had begun, in fact, when he had been watching Pryor and Eberhart together, on the cemetery hillside, and had continued through those years his mother had drunk herself so close to death that Mike had had no choice but to run into the Marines.

He had been a good marine. He was a good cop. He thought he was a good detective—except maybe when it came to Laura Demming. He was no killer. Barranquilla had been self-defense. He had only inconvenienced Eberhart, only embarrassed Freeman and the cops guarding him. That was why Mike wanted to hide. He didn't know if he was tough enough. He wasn't very tough with Laura, not tough with himself.

He was halfway across the plaza again when he felt a presence behind him. It was less than ten feet back. Mike stopped, then turned around. Roehrig grinned at him. He was bareheaded, wearing a light windbreaker, with his right hand in his pocket, holding something. If Mike didn't want to believe it was a gun, the chance was his to take. Roehrig's smile was the studied grin of a guy who thought he was good-looking.

"You look like a worried man, Gallagher. Got something on your mind?"

Mike was looking into the sun. "Where's your hat?"

"Ah, you remember me, too. That's evening wear. Clothing is part of the lingua franca of the global village. Police wear uniforms. In earlier times, the rich had private armies to protect their property. Now the rich make the poor pay for those armies with their taxes, and the armies protect the rich against the poor. No rich man ever went to jail for stealing bread. It's a wonderful system."

"Thanks for your insight. Where do you place yourself in this picture of the world?"

"We're only animals, and so-called civilization is only a metaphor of the jungle from which we sprang. Once you understand that, the illusion fades, your real senses sharpen, and the world is yours to enjoy to the full for as long as you last."

"Like teenagers," Mike said.

"I love teenagers—and they love me back. I don't think you could possibly understand. We've got you because Kiku spotted you in the arcade. He remembered you, too. He's better than people think. We're interested in the items you just mailed, and to whom you sent them. You were headed in the right direction, so why don't you just keep going? If you turn around, you'll see Kiku watching us from inside the building. Walk—you'll have a chance at living if you do. If I have to kill you here, I'll be in the building before people get to you, in the building and down to the garage."

Mike turned and walked. Kiku even opened the door for them, then led the way to the far elevator bank. There were a few people in the lobby now, all of them moving as quickly as possible, headed out or down below—Roehrig had had it right; he could have moved very quickly. Watching Mike, Kiku touched the elevator call button. Doors at the far end of the bank opened at once. Mike felt Roehrig prod him in the back. Kiku's eyes moved toward Roehrig, but Mike knew that trying to resist was pointless, if not suicidal. Kiku let Mike enter the elevator first— and then punched him, with a fist that felt like a sledgehammer, solidly in the left kidney. Mike cried out and thumped against the back wall of the elevator like a sack of pineapples. He was sliding to the floor when Kiku grabbed him by the collar. He was almost unconscious, momentarily beyond pain.

"Can you hold him up?" Roehrig asked.

Kiku did it with one hand. The elevator bolted upward. Roehrig patted Mike down, getting first the .38 in his side pocket, then the .22 in his ankle holster, and finally the Magnum under his left arm.

"A lot of guns," Kiku said.

"More for us," Roehrig said. "Want one?"

"I don't need no fucking gun," Kiku said.

"I like this cannon. Whip him around." Kiku did it, and Roehrig stepped within inches of Mike's face. The pain was starting, stabbing Mike's kidney. He could feel his bladder open. Roehrig's breath was foul. "Make this easy on yourself," he said. "My adrenaline isn't flowing. I don't want it to, and neither do you. Just to know that I have that poison in my blood will make me angrier. I have the same sadistic streak in me that's in every other human being, only I've had more opportunity to explore it. If you bring it out, I'll blame you."

Mike closed his eyes. There was nothing left of him. One punch had done it. The pain was incredible. If he lived long enough—another hour —he would be pissing blood; and if he lived a week, maybe it would stop. He didn't know how long Roehrig had been behind him. He hadn't cleared his head before leaving the hotel. *Think twice*, Laura had said. Mike had been thinking too damned much, and Roehrig had gotten him. The elevator stopped and Roehrig stuck his head out and looked both ways. He waved to Kiku, who held Mike upright with one hand, and marched him along on his toes like a kid going to the principal's office. Mike tried to get air in his lungs without Kiku or Roehrig noticing—*that* was his true position; he hesitated to breathe for fear of making his situation worse.

They were in front of a door that looked as if it belonged on an Aztec temple instead of a business office. Roehrig knocked, and after a moment, Maxwell opened. He had circles under his eyes, and his lightweight turtleneck sweater looked loose around his neck. Kiku pushed Mike through, not letting go of his collar. They went through a receptionist's area and a larger room full of secretaries' desks—all unoccupied: everybody was gone— then a private secretary's alcove to another Aztec-style door, and at last through that. Mike's back felt as if someone had stuffed a red-hot cannonball where his kidney had been; he couldn't straighten up, he couldn't reach around to put his hand on the pain. But he could see Harcourt Pryor rising behind his desk, slim and whitehaired, immaculately tailored in a light tan suit, white shirt, dark brown tie, and silk handkerchief emerging from his breast pocket.

"Where was he?"

"Coming across the campus," Roehrig said, putting the

smaller guns on the edge of the desk. "You were right, though. This was his next destination."

"Not exactly," Pryor said. "Given the time and place where he was spotted, he went somewhere else, perhaps to make some calls. Put him in the chair. Gallagher, who did you talk to? What were those videotapes you were mailing?"

Pryor's desk matched the Aztec doors in the outer offices. Beyond Pryor, under a nearly purple sky, was Beverly Hills, the Hollywood sign, and beyond that, the dark, jagged crest of the Angeles National Forest. In between was Forest Lawn, where Mike's parents were buried. Sitting—or, more accurately, slumping to avoid contact with the back of the chair—left Mike gasping, with streaks of light shooting across the insides of his eyelids. He tried to get his weight up on his elbows. He didn't know what he was doing. He did not know how much time he had—how long they would let him live. There was no one else on the floor. If people above or below heard a gunshot, they wouldn't know how to look for its source—if they even wanted to.

"Wait a minute," Maxwell said, almost tiredly. He had moved over to a wing chair against the wall. "Kiku don't need to hear this." He looked up at his bodyguard. "Go find yourself something to do. Go down and have a drink."

Roehrig looked around from where he was sitting, facing the desk. "Go into the Sports Deli and get us some sandwiches, a half-sandwich for Gallagher—"

"Shut up," Maxwell said.

"I'll see what I want to do," Kiku said. "Don't worry about Gallagher. The punch I threw at him, I don't know why he isn't begging to be put out of his misery."

Pryor waved him off. Roehrig was still playing with the Magnum, not really pointing it at Mike, just holding it aimlessly: if it discharged, it would blow a hole the size of a football in Pryor's desk. Pryor was still behind it, his fingertips touching. It seemed like another minute before he spoke, although Mike doubted that that much time actually had passed.

"Gallagher, at best your situation is precarious. You know as well as I do that every police officer in the city is looking for you. What you don't know is why. They think you killed your partner; that, contrary to what you told Tom Cutler, you stayed in town and delayed Dan Crawford until your hired killer had positioned himself up in the canyonlands. Does that sound good to you?"

Mike tried to straighten up. He wanted a little more time. He couldn't look at his watch. When Jackson called, even fifteen minutes from now, Pryor would remember that Mike had been checking the time—Pryor was that smart and more. Maybe Cutler had told Pryor that his police thought Mike had killed Dan, but it was probable that Cutler's agenda with Pryor was better served if Pryor believed such a story. Mike drew a breath. If Cutler had told six thousand cops that one of their own had killed another, it would have been on the radio and television before Cutler had drawn his next breath. No one knew that better than Tom Cutler: even if he had thought Mike had killed Dan, he would not have told the six thousand gossiping adolescents working for him. They were looking for Mike, all right, but not because they thought he'd killed his partner. It was another story, just bad enough to motivate them. To Pryor, Mike said, "I know you're the one who arranged Dan's death."

"Gallagher," Roehrig said quietly, "I told you not to let my adrenaline flow.

Mike didn't move quickly enough. Roehrig flicked the Magnum in Mike's direction, and the barrel caught Mike on the point of the shoulder. Pryor made a face—but not one that Roehrig would construe as an instruction not to do it again. Roehrig knew about sadism, just as he had said. Mike rubbed his shoulder. Roehrig had found the one place that could hurt for years.

"Actually, I mailed two items," Mike said. He could tell the truth after a fashion, when the truth could be used against them. He told them about the 9000 Building register. He looked to Roehrig, hoping that the beam was still on the window, that the conversation was being recorded. "Your little Colombian friend signed in under the name that you all know, while you played it for laughs. But the handwritings will match."

For a moment, Roehrig's smile went glassy, then he glared. "What happened to Barranquilla?"

Mike smiled. "Do you want me to get into that in front of Maxwell?"

Pryor didn't—it showed in his eyes for just a split second. Maxwell didn't seem to see it, but he stood up anyway and pushed toward Mike, a vein in his skinny neck throbbing.

"What happened to Barranquilla?" he demanded.

"Your civilized friend here behind the desk thought it would be a good idea if I got dead, like my partner. I know you don't know anything about that. Barranquilla showed up at my apartment last Monday night at eleven-thirty with his tire iron and a knife. That's how I got this cut on my hand. I killed him and dumped his body into a canyon off Mulholland—not far from where you live, as a matter of fact. Crawford was killed because your big-time partners fucked up so big—"

"You've said enough, Gallagher," Pryor said.

"Shut up! I want to hear this!" Maxwell shouted.

"I don't want to get hit again," Mike said.

"He won't hit you," Maxwell said. Mike could feel himself bleeding in his lower abdomen. Kiku had a punch that could smash bowling balls. "Go ahead," Maxwell said.

"The other thing in that package I mailed downstairs was a set of videocassettes showing the murder investigation on Rainbow Drive. Never mind how I got them. A couple of the pictures show Larry Hammond giving Pryor's employer, Randall Brandon, a tour of the murder scene. He turned to Pryor. "Does Brandon know yet that your friend Roehrig and the others working for your partner Maxwell here managed to kill his daughter? Hammond's people found her ID. Hammond didn't know he was supposed to do Brandon business through you—for that matter, he didn't know about your connection to Maxwell—and so he went directly to Brandon. Before the day was out, Brandon told you to clean up the mess. That's the way Brandon wants things handled."

Pryor sat back. "Brandon knows how his daughter died. He doesn't want his family to know the truth—the whole truth. Tom Cutler knows what Brandon wants—do you see why you don't have a chance? The family thinks she died of a simple overdose. The coffin was closed. It's going to stay that way."

"You applied that thinking to my partner." He tried to get

his weight on his elbows again. "Because the girl had been in trouble with drugs for years, you thought there was an old problem that would have led to her identification at the murder scene. Dan never saw her. He couldn't have identified her, but you didn't know that." Now Mike told Maxwell about the incident on Tampa Avenue, what Dan had done, Cutler's intermediation, and the payoff afterward. "This past winter the girl got hold of my partner's telephone number and started calling him. He was a natural father and teacher. Maybe she was just curious about him, but what she got from my friend was help. He would have done that. Believe me, I knew him that well. But in April somebody caught on, and Pryor was told to scare Dan off. I have the records of the telephone calls. But then when the girl was killed last week, Pryor thought Dan could identify her, and given the way Pryor thinks—Dan had an opportunity for blackmail, or worse—Pryor orchestrated Dan's death. Hammond was in on that—for Dan's death, Pryor dealt directly with Hammond, not through Cutler as he's been doing for years. Another guy was in on killing Dan, somebody working for Hammond. Hammond thinks he's done exactly what was necessary to be made chief. When Dan got up to the canyonlands before dawn, there was Roehrig in a blacked-out helicopter with a stolen searchlight mounted on its nose, hovering a few feet over the roadway. No traffic. In that darkness, all it took was one long flash of that light, close up, to make Dan swerve off the road." He looked to Roehrig. "That's right, isn't it? The easiest money you've ever made in your life." Roehrig's blank expression told Mike that he didn't remember saying that. If Mike said he had a witness, and then didn't get out of here alive, Paula Rogers was as good as dead. Now they were glaring at him, but Mike let his own eyes move away from them as he eased himself up again and unbuttoned his jacket.

Maxwell said, "I want to know about Pryor working with Cutler. There's been a task force after me for over a year."

Mike was looking at the Magnum in Roehrig's hand. Roehrig was capable of something stupid—impulsive. He was already a killer. Now Mike was thinking of why Roehrig had killed Valerie Moreland. Moreland had figured out what they were doing with the girls, and thought that the possession of one tape would protect her. Quite the opposite. The tape of a woman undressing needed some explanation, and without anybody around to do the explaining, the tape would be seen as just another sample of homemade porn. "Doing business with Cutler has always been part of Pryor's territory. Pryor couldn't have put you in business without Cutler going along. Maybe Hammond was the bagman—"

"He was," Pryor said. The telephone rang. Pryor picked up. "Yes?" He handed the receiver to Maxwell. Silently, he formed the name, *Jackson*.

"Yeah, go ahead," Maxwell said. He listened. "What do you mean, another guy? Different from the first, you mean? What did he sound like?" Maxwell's eyes rolled. "Listen to me! When he calls back, tell him to call this number! You're in no fucking shape to talk to anybody, you asshole! Why don't you lay off? Lay off the fucking shit for an hour! *Just an hour! And don't move from there! Don't leave! We want to get those goddamned tapes back!*" He gave the handset to Pryor, who put it on its cradle. "The sooner we make direct contact, the better." He waved his hand toward the telephone. "That lunatic is a problem in his own right."

"He's your boy," Pryor said smoothly.

"Don't give me that shit!" Maxwell screamed. "You're the one dumb enough to kill a cop! Don't you know *anything?* Do you think I didn't know you were selling me down the fucking river all these months! I got the message the first time I had trouble getting you on the goddamned phone—when was that, last summer? Do you think I didn't spot Lansing and Freeman, those two San Diego jokers, right away? There's a rule in this business: don't make new friends! After I sensed things going wrong, I knew it was just a matter of time before they showed up. Don't you think I have contacts in San Diego? What's the matter with cops? I checked on those guys! People in S.D. were wise to them! Lansing was an insult to my intelligence, the way he hung around, doing little favors, and coming up with little *ideas* for making more money." He turned to Mike. "But don't blame me for anybody's rich-bitch daughter, or killing a cop!"

Roehrig was on his feet, pointing the Magnum at Maxwell. Mike took Chino's pen out of his pocket and wrapped his hand around it. "Sit down," Roehrig said to Maxwell. "This will make a hole in you that will swallow your fist."

"Sit down," Pryor said soothingly. "Let's all just sit down." He looked to Mike. "Now, suppose you tell us where you mailed those tapes?"

"Who did Hammond get to set up my partner?"

"I haven't the faintest idea," Pryor said, with a smile.

"Did Brandon know what you were doing with the girls?"

Pryor shook his head. "You wouldn't ask that question if you knew anything about Randall Brandon. Don't click that pen, please; it's a kid's habit."

Roehrig sat up, "What pen—"

Mike was moving—slowly, but he was moving. He thrust his right hand out toward Roehrig's face and depressed the button at the top of the barrel of the pen with his thumb. The pen made a noise like a snapping rubber band, and blood appeared on Roehrig's right cheek. His eye bulging slightly, Roehrig slumped back. The heel of Mike's right hand was stinging as he reached for the Magnum on the desk. Pryor was on his feet. Time seemed to crawl. Mike hurt so badly in so many places that it took him a moment to get control of the Magnum. Maxwell was on his feet again. Mike sidled toward the desk, where he gathered up the other guns and pocketed them. Roehrig was motionless, blood trickling down his cheek, his glazed eye staring downward. Pryor and Maxwell were still standing, their hands away from their bodies.

"Sit down!" Mike commanded. *"Go on, sit down, or you'll be dead before you hit the floor!"*

They lowered themselves into their chairs. Maxwell motioned toward Pryor. "He has to be the one who set up your partner. I didn't know a thing until I read it in the papers. I didn't even connect anything until that guy in the chair"—he pointed to Roehrig—"started getting scarce, like Pryor."

Mike moved toward him. Mike wasn't standing straight. He couldn't. The pain in his right hand and the shoulder where Roehrig had hit him were meeting in the middle of his arm. "That doesn't change the fact that you put together that gang of morons to go into the house on Rainbow Drive and bash in the heads of all the people inside. And you did that only to protect yourself—''

"They changed the game on me! They expected me to take the jolt alone! Racketeering charges—it was a gag. I was supposed to smile while they did it to me! Maxwell pointed to Pryor. "He was in on it with me! He made a fortune out of it! *We used his fucking planes!* I don't know who he kicked back to, but we were covered, he said—''

"Selling girls to perverts? Don't be stupid. Nothing covers that. You never were supposed to come out the other side in good order. From the moment Pryor put you in business, he was looking at the back end, knowing that someday he'd be glad to be rid of you." Mike turned to Pryor. "Tell him."

Pryor was looking at Maxwell. "We'll talk about this later.''

"You're the guy who put him in North Hollywood real estate," Mike said. "You never had any intention of letting him keep it. Tell him. Tell him!''

Maxwell rose, screaming. *"You bastard!"* He reached into his jacket. Mike had to hold the Magnum with both hands, he hurt so badly. Mike shot him in the neck, breaking his spine and killing him instantly. Maxwell hit the chair hard; his head went back against the wall and then flopped forward again so that his face turned upside down against his chest. A bloody splinter of bone stuck out of the back of his neck. A revolver fell out of his hand and into his lap, where blood spilling from his neck began to cover it. Mike turned to Pryor again.

"What about my having to know Randall Brandon?''

Pryor frowned. "Let me sit down. I'm a little shaky.''

Mike was, too, but he stayed on his feet as he waved Pryor down. He moved closer to Maxwell to discourage Pryor from thinking about going for Maxwell's gun.

Pryor drew a breath. "The Brandons live in a very special kind of pressure cooker. Do you know how much money is involved?''

Mike knew he was listening to something Pryor had said many times before. "I think so.''

"Well, so that I know that you know, let me say that the money increases so rapidly now that it isn't possible for *all* those who have access to spend it on themselves and their pleasures so that it ever decreases, no matter what they buy, no matter what it costs." Pryor was glancing at the gun every once in a while as he tried to get hold of himself. "But the Brandons don't buy things like that. They already have everything. There's a warehouse out in Temple City that contains nothing but old cars and furniture. The Brandons don't throw anything away because it will be worth more in the future, and they can afford to store it. No Salvation Army tax deduction can do them any good anyway. The Brandons pay taxes, but—let me put it to you this way: not even their taxes make a difference."

"What's the point of all this?"

"The point is, they want for nothing. The only thing they have to fear is death itself, but they never even think of it. Do you know why that is, Gallagher?"

"I haven't the slightest idea."

"They don't think of death because they aren't smart enough. Under it all, they're very ordinary people. I remember reading as a child that George Washington had done the country a favor when he refused the crown of the United States. According to the research, his direct descendant was an ordinary plumber, no more qualified to manage this country than you. And so it is with Randall Brandon. An ordinary man, mother-dominated in his youth, married to the wrong woman through most of his adult life, and now, at the age of fifty, he suffers from impotence. *That's* what worries Randall Brandon, Gallagher. He can't get it up anymore, and like many another rich man, he's found a solution to his problem in a young woman who is skilled at fellatio. It's nature's little trick that, while some older men can't get or maintain an erection, they're still capable of pleasure and ejaculation. Randall Brandon has that young woman, Gallagher, because I introduced her to him. He's not smart enough to realize that I spent a lot of time and money searching for her."

"If you're waiting for Kiku—"

Pryor shook his head. "You have the gun and he doesn't. I don't want you to make a mistake. *Listen to me, Gallagher:* I don't work for Randall Brandon or his family! They're *television!* Dad's dick doesn't work, Mom's nonorgasmic, daughter's a junkie—*was* a junkie—and Junior has withdrawn from it all into the world of science and hi-tech. *I work for the fortune itself, Gallagher!* It is one of the great power centers of this country! When it comes time to throw Randall Brandon into the sausage machine, I will do it. With that money, and through that money, Southern California itself has been made possible. That money *builds* things! We're going to have more people here than any place in the country by the end of the century. That money is jobs and homes, transportation—we're going to have a city running from the Mexican border through Santa Barbara into the middle counties, as far east—''

''I have the picture. So you don't know who Hammond got to set up Dan Crawford?''

Harcourt Pryor looked startled. ''That's all you've got on your mind, isn't it? How do you *know* he was trying to help her?''

''I knew that man! I knew what was in his heart!''

Pryor began to rise from his seat. Now Mike could smell his cologne, subtle and expensive. ''For God's sake, man, I've been trying to tell you that this fortune belongs to anyone with the strength and opportunity to take it! It will give you the world— *the world!''*

''Would you have gone near Dan if you had known in advance that he was my partner?''

''What do you mean?''

''The real reason you had Roehrig recruit that little geek Barranquilla to come after me. You recognized my name when you read it in the papers. You know who I am. Maybe you've known for years where I've been, maybe even asked yourself if I became a cop in the first place because of what you did to my father—''

''Now listen, Gallagher—''

''You've got a chance here, Pryor. Tell me a good one, one I can believe. I remember my father telling my mother that there wouldn't be any public housing in L.A. the way there is back East, that millions were to be made. Sure enough, that housing isn't here—oh, a few token developments—''

''We were putting in the freeways, they had to come first. They lead to the outlying districts, to great parcels of privately held land. Do you think I made the decisions so many years ago? I was a nobody. Your father had been walking around in a daze for months. Your mother told me that it was all just too tough and cold-blooded for him, the business decisions that were being made, and that there was nothing else bothering him, but I never believed that. I saw him—he went out of his way to *make* people think he was unreliable. He knew—''

''What are you talking about? How did you know my mother? What did my father know?''

Pryor's face was inches from Mike's own. ''She must have told you. The two of us. You know what kind of woman she was. She made the first move. We had an affair—''

Mike screamed and shot him in the heart. Pryor fell back, his arms flung over the side of the chair. Mike wanted to shoot again. He knew he was on the edge of sanity. Just trying to do nothing made him shake. He had to get out of here.

He didn't want to go into shock. Mike put away the Magnum and drew a slow, deep breath. There was no point in trying to obscure the evidence. At this moment, the more Mike looked at his situation, the more he welcomed the thought of a gaudy arrest and major-league trial. If the federals had had an infrared beam on the place earlier—Constantine would testify to that— they'd have to say why they had discontinued it, if that was their explanation of why they hadn't come to Mike's aid. The sky was darkening, lights coming on. He wasn't going to worry about legal consequences now anyway. He had to worry about staying alive. Even with the Magnum, Mike felt he would lose another argument with Kiku, who was out there somewhere. Mike couldn't walk around with the gun in his hand in the expectation that he'd see Kiku first. He moved out of the office, not bothering to wipe the doorknobs. He hadn't touched anything in the room. He took a step away from the closed door, then stopped. Something was wrong, something he could feel. He went back to the door and opened it. Roehrig was struggling to his feet. He'd only looked dead—he'd been *acting*. He turned around, his right eye still bulging, and smiled. His face, neck, and shirt were covered with blood.

''Stupid bastard,'' he said. ''The bullet's in my cheekbone. I can feel it.''

As quickly as he could, Mike crossed the room and drew the Magnum, grabbed Roehrig by the hair, and pulled him back down into the chair. Roehrig quit fighting. Mike shoved the barrel of the Magnum in Roehrig's ear. "What do you know about the guy who set up Dan Crawford?"

Roehrig was still smiling. "Not my department."

"But you killed him" Mike said. "You killed Valerie Moreland."

"Fuck Valerie Moreland."

"What about my partner? You killed him!"

"Fuck your partner, too. What are you going to do about it, kill me in cold blood?"

Mike let his eyes go over to Pryor just long enough for Roehrig to see. Roehrig's grin faded at last. Mike was flying apart inside, but he could not stop what he was doing. This was what he had promised himself for Dan. Roehrig squealed and flailed, but Mike screwed the gun deeper into Roehrig's ear and pulled the trigger. For just a moment, Roehrig's head ballooned to the size of a pumpkin, vivid red, spraying blood, cheeks bulging, tongue protruding. Just that quickly, Mike felt as if Roehrig's hair were attached to a sack of bait. Every bone in his skull was shattered. Mike knew if he thought about it, he would be sick. And now he remembered something else. If he wanted to get away, he had to search Roehrig's corpse for the keys to the only vehicle he knew in the garage below. He'd have to find a raincoat in Pryor's closet to wear through the lobby. And Kiku was down there somewhere; Mike was no better off. . . .

Before he left, Mike wiped the Magnum and put it on the floor under Roehrig's right hand. He found the splintered pen under a chair, wiped that, and put it on the desk in front of Pryor's body. The weapons made a pretty picture, if those investigating the deaths wanted one, but that's all it was, a pretty picture, useful in another cover-up. . . .

Five levels. Not even a Roehrig had found a way to hustle a parking space on the top level near the escalator. It took Mike half an hour of wandering ever downward, watching for Kiku at every corner, looking behind him as he crossed the parking levels, before he found the Volkswagen bus. He was sniffing like a child, trying to hold back the tears. He couldn't let himself think about his mother, not now. When he started away, he forgot the souped-up engine. The clutch had the bite of a Doberman. The sky was going to be black now. Mike was thinking of Hammond. He wanted to call Constantine. Wills had a message. . . .

Only the north exit of the garage was open. Cars were streaming down the entrance ramp—it wasn't that long until curtain time at the theater. Three cars in front of Mike were waiting to get to the toll booth and freedom beyond. Another car pulled up behind him—he hadn't seen it coming. He was trapped—he had let himself be trapped. Why hadn't he thought of walking away from the complex? The door on the passenger side of the car behind him opened and a man got out, a big man. Mike struggled to get the .38 out of his jacket pocket, then quit as a meaty fist rapped on the passenger window of the VW. The door opened—it hadn't even been locked.

Azzolini got in and slammed the door shut. "Let's ride," he said. The cars in front moved forward. "Keep up," he said, reaching for his pocket. He handed Mike a twenty-dollar bill. "Let me cover this." He shifted his big frame and slapped Mike smartly on the knee. "So, Gallagher, how've you been doing?"

21

"L.A. GOT LOUSY FOR ME WHEN THEY CLOSED THE drive-ins," Azzolini said. "Turn right here." He meant Santa Monica Boulevard, the main route through Beverly Hills into West Hollywood. No earring now—instead, a simple gold band on the ring finger of his left hand. "If there was a drive-in around here, we'd be able to pull in and get something to eat while we talk. We can't even go into a fast-food joint, not the way you look, which isn't as good as you think. You look like you're in pain."

"I fell in the shower."

"Most accidents happen in the home, Gallagher. You have to be careful."

Mike didn't answer. Azzolini had shown no ID. He'd said they'd picked up Kiku in Harry's Bar—Mike was supposed to figure out who *they* were. What Roehrig said about adrenaline was making sense. Azzolini didn't want to know how little patience Mike had for games. Mike wasn't in custody—no ques-

448

tion of that: he would have been disarmed, cuffed, and read his rights. What Azzolini wanted was control of the situation, maybe complete control. A drive-in would have been perfect: Mike wouldn't have been able to make a telephone call without encountering resistance from Azzolini. He wanted to talk, he said. If he wanted to talk about what had just happened, that would be a violation of Mike's civil rights—a GET OUT OF JAIL FREE card. The best thing Mike could do for himself was let Azzolini talk. For now, Mike still didn't know if Azzolini was going to let him live. Mike didn't even know where they were going.

"This mess goes back a bit, Gallagher. Do you know how long I've been in on it?"

"You moved into the Panorama City apartment last September. Six months before that? I don't know how you guys operate."

"You're close enough. This has been a big project. The special appropriation was buried in a farm bill. We were able to do that because a senator on one subcommittee is chairman of the other full committee. He waved it through. He's got the juice to get something on his say-so—*and* he's a good guy. I'm a good guy, and so are you. The last thing in this world I want is to hurt you. I'm not alone in that feeling, but that doesn't matter. Now you become a team player or we kill you. We really have no choice. If what your little playmates back there in that office were up to becomes known to the public-at-large, there's going to be a demand for war, or at least revenge, and we can't do that. If we turn on our friends, such as they are, the Russians will take advantage of the opening."

"You yourself told me to burn those guys," Mike said.

Azzolini smiled. "At the time I said that, no one had the faintest notion that you could come anywhere close to them. You solved a lot of problems for us, and believe it, we're grateful—let's say, relieved. What we spent on the investigation, you saved for us on the trials. That's not what the Founding Fathers had in mind, but that's our America. We have what you did on tape, of course. What wasn't self-defense was temporary insanity. Nobody will ever hear that tape after tonight, certainly not with that authoritative report on the status of Randall Brandon's pecker. Pryor was telling you the truth about the power of the

Brandon fortune, if not Brandon's own capacity to lever it. Of all the people in this city who claim to have access to the president, Randall Brandon alone can say he has real power. He's got so much power, he won't even know the tape exists. For that matter, neither will the president. That's real power, Gallagher, when people anticipate your needs and wants, and insulate you from unnecessary pain. One of the things we're not going to learn is whether Randall Brandon had any knowledge of what Pryor and Maxwell were doing. I don't think so. The only information we have comes from people who say that Brandon has always turned a blind eye to Pryor's independent ventures. There are a lot of things we're never going to know, Gallagher; you'd better get comfortable with that.''

"I want Hammond," Mike said.

"You can't have him."

"He set up Dan Crawford!"

"Yes, he arranged the setup for Pryor. Just as he'd gone directly to Randall Brandon to ingratiate himself with the power in this city, he answered Pryor's call when it came—by then, Hammond had learned that there was a hierarchy and chain of command. Of course Brandon and Pryor told Tom Cutler that Hammond was going around him, or trying to. Cutler didn't know right away that Barbara Brandon was one of the victims, but he was told quickly enough, within an hour. Apparently Hammond was transparent with Brandon, and Brandon, uncomfortable, called both Pryor and Cutler, who definitely didn't want Brandon to know of Pryor's connection with Maxwell. And that was the end of Hammond as far as Brandon was concerned. Pryor just didn't tell Hammond that he was only continuing to use him, just as he didn't tell Cutler he was moving against Dan Crawford. Cutler figured out days ago what Hammond did to Crawford, and why, and for whom. We don't think Brandon was in on Crawford's death; at least, we don't have any evidence connecting him to it. Cutler wants Hammond—he wanted Pryor too, but you got there first. We had to make a deal with Cutler on Hammond. I'm sorry, but you have to live with it.''

"Hammond knows the man who kept Dan in town!"

"Hammond's taking that secret with him. It's the way things

have to be done. Turn up Beverly Drive to Sunset. We're going
to the 9000 Building, but we can take our time getting there. I
want to tell you about all of this, more than my agents know. I
hope you understand I'm trying to meet you halfway. The girl
who went to the hospital died two days ago, by the way; not
even chasing after her damned dog could snap her out of her
coma. If you come out of this in good order, there's a job waiting
for you, working with someone you know is very, very good.
You *do* need a job. Cutler wasn't blowing smoke up your ass
when he told you to turn in your badge. In his own way, the old
fart isn't a bad administrator. A thief, but also not a bad administrator."

"Who will I be working with?"

"Pablo Kerrigan. He's already said yes—he has a lot of respect for you. You start in a month. Pablo wants to take his
daughter down to Mexico City to visit her grandparents. You'll
like Pablo, he's just what he seems to be."

Now Mike was thinking of Laura. He had a lot of phone calls
to make. Only for the last quarter mile, the stretch of Sunset
just entering West Hollywood, were there places where Mike
would be able to telephone. They were on Beverly Drive now,
rolling from one stop sign to the next. The lurching of the van
was crushing Mike's kidney. They were coming up on the Beverly Hills Hotel.

Azzolini said, "We don't know how Pryor and Maxwell got
hooked up in the first place. It could have been Cutler who
brought them together, or one of Cutler's predecessors. In any
event, we know that the association goes back to the sixties,
and that Maxwell operated with impunity from then on. Of
course, Maxwell was mobbed up, but many of his operations
were outside the mob. We believe, too, that Maxwell functioned
as Pryor's pimp—not that Pryor had any kind of track record as
a pervert—"

"I wouldn't want to hear it anyway." The light changed and
Mike drove straight across Sunset to the long, curving ramp up
to the entrance of the hotel.

"You're not dressed for the Polo Lounge, Gallagher."

"I just want to make some calls."

"You don't quit, do you?" Azzolini looked out the window. "Just don't be an asshole. That would disappoint me."

"These calls are confidential. I'm not working for you yet."

Azzolini shook his head. At the entrance, the parking valets opened both doors at once, and the one on Mike's side gasped as Mike got out. The bloodstain on Mike's pants was the size of a dinner plate. Mike showed his badge. "I'm all right. We have to use the phone. Keep this wreck where it will be handy."

"You need a doctor," Azzolini said.

Mike walked slowly, Pryor's raincoat closed in front of him. "I'm not bleeding now. It won't take me a month to get healthy anyway."

"Back off. You don't have to prove yourself to me."

"I have to work. I just lost a pension." In the lobby, Mike looked around. People were arriving for some kind of formal affair, wearing clothes he had worn twice in his life, at weddings. Mike didn't know if he'd live through the night. For all he knew, Azzolini was only setting him up again. Mike shuddered. For most of the last hour he had been living in the expectation of sudden death. Days ago he had resigned himself to the idea, but he hadn't tried to imagine it—he hadn't tried to *feel* it. It was unbearable, worse than Vietnam, much worse than police work, regular police work. He didn't trust *anyone*. . . .

Azzolini stood at a distance from the phone booth, his back turned, while Mike dialed Wills. This time Wills picked up. Mike identified himself.

"I want to thank you for putting me onto that Paula Rogers," Wills said. "She talked—told me what Bobby Michaels said to her on the way down to Chula Vista. He walked across the border with two hundred dollars in his pocket. Michaels told her that he had been in on a robbery of Maxwell's place with a couple of the victims before the murders on Rainbow Drive. I have it all on tape, although she doesn't know it. It's page one, I'm sure of that. Michaels told her that Maxwell figured out who had done the robbery, grabbed Michaels, and made him lead Maxwell's revenge squad—no names; she insisted she didn't know them—to the place where the other robbers were staying. That's it, that's all. Rogers never even asked who gave me her name. She loved the spotlight.

"As for what you asked today, I remembered something. I *did* talk to someone about the killings, but it wasn't anybody named Novak and it wasn't on Sunset Boulevard. It was a guy named Bradley, and I talked to him outside Parker Center. I did a story on him when he was fresh out of the academy and working undercover in the high schools, making small drug buys. This was four or five years ago. I did a piece on him and what it was like to be a cop going to high school again. He said he still had trouble with math. Anyway, outside Parker Center, he looked different, filled out, older, different hairstyle. Usually I'm able to keep up with people, but this guy just dropped out of sight after that assignment. I asked him about that and what he'd been up to, but he kind of shrugged—"

"You mean he was evasive."

"All right, if you want to characterize it. I asked what he was doing these days, and he said homicide."

Novak had done high-school undercover. Mike's head hit the side of the booth. Wills heard it. Azzolini came running. Mike waved him off.

To Wills, Mike said, "That description I gave you this afternoon—"

"I know what you're asking. I thought about it; Bradley had darker hair."

"Darker than what?"

"Well, you said blond, right?"

"Yeah, like a surfer's. You said Bradley had different hair last week. How was it different?"

Wills was silent. "Oh, Jesus," he whispered. "That's one of the things that was different. It was shorter, but it was also lighter—but not that much, I thought. When he was doing the high-school gig, his hair was down to his shoulders, dirty blond. Jesus Christ, Gallagher, I let my mind fool my eyes. I saw what used to be there. I thought I was a trained observer. He didn't call attention to the changes in him, so I just hammered what I remembered into what I saw."

Mike hung up on him and closed his eyes. He could feel himself bleeding again. Azzolini was pushing the door open. "You all right?"

"Better than you, you son of a bitch." Mike kicked the door closed and called Constantine.

"Mr. Gallagher," Constantine mumbled, "Jackson has been getting more calls—not the usual kind, I mean. Somebody's trying to drive him nuts. He's been calling that number Maxwell gave him, and there hasn't been any answer after the first call. Now the phone just keeps ringing."

"What kind of calls is he getting?"

"Sometimes they don't say anything at all. He yells hello, and nobody answers. Sometimes they just breathe loud. One time the guy called him a murderer. Jackson slammed down the receiver. He's going to break this new phone before he's through."

"What's he doing now? How many calls have come in?" Mike looked at his watch. An hour had passed since Jackson's call had come in to Pryor's office.

"I can count them if you want because I have them on tape, but off the top of my head, I'd have to say there's been at least six. Two of them have been silent jobs. He yells back. On one of the others, the voice said he was alone now with nobody to turn to. That really got him."

"Harassment," Mike said.

"Torture is more like it. You asked what he's doing now. The answer is, as much drugs as he can stuff into his body openings. She's right there along with him. You're like me, Mr. Gallagher. A pretty girl just opens you up like a farmer's wallet, but forget this one. He's so stoned he hardly knows where he is, and when she's not sneaking even more drugs, she's trying to get him hot. Everybody's got a mind picture of what it must be like to be crazy, and I'm looking at it now. Even the room looks crazy. Stuff is smashed, there's food spilled. I really wouldn't want to have to breathe the air in there."

"But somebody's pushing him," Mike said. "Is there any sense that the person or persons calling him are also part of his television audience?"

"Well, yes. The calls seem to come in when he's off balance, distracted—whatever. They're coming in when I'd make them, if I were trying to make him do something really loony. He's totally wrecked. On his own planet. All *she* can think about is getting his dick up, and that's a lost cause. He's ranting about Maxwell and the murders in Laurel Canyon, and she's working on him. And when they're reasonably straight, as I've seen them when customers pass through, they argue that drugs are perfectly okay. They ought to see themselves now."

"Will you stay on the job, please, Maurice? You were right, something is going down. It could be very important to me."

"I think I have the idea, Mr. Gallagher. If I don't hear from you, you'll hear from me. Don't worry, I'll be able to find you."

"Keep yourself covered, Maurice."

He cradled the receiver and got to his feet. When he opened the door, Azzolini reached for him supportively. "You can quit, Gallagher. You don't have to do another thing."

"Forget it." The 9000 Building—he couldn't tell Azzolini that the subject of his surveillance, if that's what it was supposed to be called, was ready for plucking. Mike wanted Constantine's videotape recording for insurance. Marge had two valuable pieces of evidence, the 9000 Building register and Hollister's tapes of the crime scene. He couldn't be sure of anything else.

Azzolini got behind the wheel now. They rolled down the drive with the parking valets staring after them. Azzolini said, "I'll go as gently as I can. I want to drive slow anyway. One of the reasons we've been at this so long is because we haven't been able to let anybody in on it. That's what Tom Cutler has on us—why we have to do business with him. He secretly tapped a few of our meetings, and now he can prove that we kept him in the dark about criminal activity in his jurisdiction. Say what you will about Cutler, he's a crafty bastard. So what you're about to hear, I tell you on the understanding that if we discover that you've ever breathed a word of it to anyone, even as pillow talk ten years from now, you're dead. Heart attack, stroke, swift-acting cancer—no one will give your passing a second thought." The light changed and he made a slow, sweeping left turn onto Sunset. "For us, this started over two years ago, when an oil worker in Southeast Asia wandered into one of our embassies with a story about an American girl being held prisoner in a cathouse in a village in the interior. The proprietor was quite proud; he'd bought her from the owner of a plantation in an even more remote area. That was the information our ambassador forwarded to Washington. He took it upon himself to send someone to the village to check it out, and that man actually saw the girl, who was in bad shape, and very, *very* frightened. Not a bright girl. She gave the man her first name and the city she had come from, Louisville, Kentucky. We found out that a girl from that city with that first name was in fact missing, but by the time we were able to get anyone back to that village, the proprietor of the establishment said that the girl had moved on of her own accord. He claimed to have been dissatisfied with her anyway. Congress specifically forbids us from acting like cops in other countries, and no law of that sovereignty had been broken. So that was it.

"But six months later, we got a tip that an American girl had been buried in a cemetery outside the capital, and long after a lot of string pulling, we got permission to dig. The remains didn't match the description of the Louisville girl, but the dental work was definitely American. The weasel who had given us the tip told us that he had heard that she had belonged to a rich man, a well-known pervert who was related by marriage to the wife of the president of the country. In Washington it was concluded that we had found the girl at all only because the agency that had given us permission to dig hadn't had the right inside information—just a bureaucratic fuckup. Since there had already been positive ID of one American girl in that country, a real effort was made to identify the second. According to her parents, in Bangor, Maine, she had gone to Los Angeles to pursue a career in show business. That's when I got into it. The decision was made on the highest level to reconstruct the movements of both girls prior to their American disappearances. The first girl had been a runaway, and the last tantalizing telephone call received by her maternal grandparents, who had raised her, had been from Las Vegas, where—we learned later—she had been working as a hooker. In that call, she told the old people that she was going on to L.A. You know the procedure of the LAPD: it won't take a missing persons report on an adult until twenty-four hours have passed, and in both cases, the files showed that the girls had been living on the edge here. Prostitution in one case, drugs in both, no steady employment records. Girls like these disappear pretty easily—they're made to order.''

Azzolini was doing twenty miles an hour up Sunset; Mike thought the bleeding had stopped again, but there was only one way to be sure, and this was not the location for that. He was in pain, sick, and thinking about what had been done to him. He knew he should be thinking about what was to come.

"We went back to the original sources with new people—undercover," Azzolini said. "We wanted to make contact with their suppliers. It was good work, Gallagher, and it took a strong stomach. We learned that there is a worldwide stratum of society that believes anything is permissible. They're in touch with each other, passing information around on what is available. Both Maxwell and Pryor knew these people—their weaknesses or appetites are useful in business. It's impossible to say whether Pryor or Maxwell took the first steps, or whether they were together at the start, but it doesn't matter. Roehrig became an integral part of the scheme as soon as he arrived in California. Given his record in Huntsville, it's possible that the other two recruited him from there. In any event, that's how far back it goes, and gives you an idea of how many girls have been involved. We *think* we've identified eighty-eight. There are more. As I say, they're made to order: already runaways, girls without families, girls with histories of drug problems, criminal records —girls whose disappearances were not surprising, noteworthy, or particularly interesting to people in our line of work. One way or another, Roehrig would get them in front of a video camera to show their particular best qualities. Some were promised show business opportunities, others thought it was some kind of sex game, still others were drugged, and one small group knew they were being victimized from the start, even if they couldn't imagine the full extent of what was going to happen to them.

"We do know that in the fall of 1982, Roehrig delivered three women to a man on the Arabian peninsula and was paid a million two for the lot. Four other girls brought a million apiece. A satellite picture shows a blond girl inside a walled estate in Paraguay. There are five girls there, and some of them may be others Roehrig delivered, but we know that the blonde is a twenty-year-old named Sharon, from New Mexico. Her parents hired a private detective a couple of years ago, and he told us that they swore that their daughter was a virgin when she'd disappeared—out of a shopping center in Albuquerque. If it's any comfort to you, in the course of this investigation we've had to kill three of these motherfucking buyers. The situation is so sensitive, however, that in Washington they're still debating whether they can bring any of these girls home. If what's been done to them ever came out, people would want to drop A-bombs on the people involved. *I* do. We've had reports of three suicides among the girls.

"We have a record of every flight that Roehrig made, every overseas telephone call made by Maxwell and Pryor in the last eighteen months, every trip to a safe-deposit box by any of the three. If a cop's satisfaction was all that was required to put people in jail, we had this case made a long time ago. But we were functioning under strict directive to be quiet, which is what you've just been told.

"And that's what gave us so much trouble. Because we couldn't bring any locals into our confidence, we had to get them to help us put a stop to people who've been feeding them all these years. For years Cutler knew about the Maxwell-Pryor connection, but until recently nothing about this. Hammond knew even less: as Cutler's bagman, he picked up payoffs on drugs, prostitution, and after-hours joints being made by Pryor to Cutler, but he always picked them up from a Pryor underling who kept his boss's identity a secret. And Maxwell thought he had his own lock on things, knowing how so many were connected, even if most knew nothing about the human air-freight business. What he couldn't understand was that we were getting him for something we can't tolerate, not the drug crap that we can. Did Pablo Kerrigan give you his rap on how he would clean up the dope trade?"

"Oh, yes."

"Well, we don't kill the dealers because we'd rather live with the results of drug use, especially in the ghetto, than have to deal with the anger that would surface from all those people if they were straight and able to see clearly the part of the world that this society keeps them boxed in. Now you *know* that you're never going to hear a more honest explanation of why drugs are tolerated in this country.''

"I suppose not.''

"I don't like it any more than you do,'' Azzolini said. "I think it's on the same level as thinking it might be better to leave those girls where they are—you know, when they get too old to be interesting to these guys, they're going to be sold again or just passed on to somebody else or simply killed. They're property now. If you don't think so, ask the man who owns one.

"Maxwell figured out only this past fall why we were after him. He was sincerely pissed—he thought it was okay, not worse than drugs. He said he was going to bring everybody else down with him. That's when Cutler cooked up the scheme—with our consent—to bring Freeman and Lansing up from San Diego. The idea was, *always* was, to draw Maxwell into a criminal act that would put him in a courtroom situation where he simply would not open his mouth about everything else. To us, it was a reasonable deal. Cutler put Hammond in charge of the day-to-day handling of the Lansing-Freeman thing. Now you know, and I know, that what Cutler was doing was setting himself up to be free and clear if something went wrong. And in fact, when it did, he was. The robbery of Maxwell's place that Lansing and Freeman perpetrated for the purpose of provoking Maxwell was approved in Cutler's office. If you can prove it, fine. But even if you can, it won't play in this jurisdiction. The people out here who support Cutler want to believe that if he could put on a cape after hours and fly around the city rescuing puppies, he'd do it. The Bobby Michaels trial for murder and conspiracy to commit murder will be a fake. He won't testify against himself, and he'll walk. The San Diego guys were only too eager to get rid of Freeman and Lansing. What Cutler didn't figure was that Maxwell would outsmart him at the same time he escalated the battle to the bloodbath across the street from where you were spending nights with Gretchen Heidl.''

"I know you know that,'' Mike said.

"We had to do it,'' Azzolini said firmly.

They were rolling into West Hollywood. Friday night, the traffic was heavy, and the sidewalk in front of the Clown Club was filled with skinny kids with spiked hair and lipsticked cheeks. When the word got out that someone had all but shot the head off the Clown Club's owner, the kids would be carrying away souvenirs. Azzolini said, "What went wrong was far worse than any of the principals could have imagined. Randall Brandon's daughter was one of the victims. Pryor didn't know that your partner would have been able to identify Barbara Brandon by only the most farfetched accident. If Pryor had left well enough alone, your partner would be alive, and so would everyone else—including Harcourt Pryor."

In his anger Mike kicked out at the front of the Volkswagen. He kicked again, a third time, until the headlight popped out like an eyeball hanging by its tendons. Mike still couldn't think about his father and mother: it was that, too. He was hurting terribly again. He doubled up and cried out with pain.

"You going to be all right?"

"If I had killed Pryor slowly, would you have stopped me?"

"Personally? No. Professionally, I'd have had to try. Look, we thought we could keep the reins on you. Obviously, you don't rein easy. We didn't think that Pryor would send Barranquilla after you, but then we didn't know that Pryor knew who you were. Obviously, we're still learning how good you are. Cutler didn't tell us where he had Freeman, and we had no idea of how to look for him. You don't know what a chase you led us—"

"Those guys who were following me were Cutler's," Mike said.

"Yes, but the guys behind them were ours. We didn't catch up to you until Old Town, where we saw Pablo Kerrigan's little floor show. You can understand why we hired him on the spot to work for us. Then you gave us the slip again—with Kerrigan's help. You got only a glimpse of Kerrigan. When my people identified themselves, he took the badges out of their hands and stuck them in a bowl of bean dip. He doesn't do other guys' police work, he told them. When I called him, he told me what to kiss and where." Azzolini turned into the underground garage of the 9000 Building. Twenty minutes ago, Jackson and the girl were loading up as much as their bodies could bear. If Azzolini was telling the truth, Jennie Wagner was as expendable as Valerie Moreland. Azzolini had been clear enough in his

comment about pillow talk being fatal even ten years from now.
Azzolini knew about Moreland—he'd known about her when
she was alive. If they were still debating in Washington about
what to do with the girls overseas, then there was no question
about what to do with the camp follower of a junked-out Hollywood dope dealer. Azzolini wanted Mike to see something.
He had offered Mike a job—*maybe:* Mike didn't know whether
to believe that or not. Mike felt misgivings about Constantine
being exposed to what was coming—but Mike had no other
insurance. Pryor and Maxwell had woven a durable web of evil:
even as their bodies began the process of mortification, their
web continued to attach itself to people. Mike had to continue
to protect himself. He had absolutely no idea what anyone was
planning to do.

Four guys were standing at the elevator bank—Mike had no
doubt that they were turning civilians away. Their eyes on Mike
and Azzolini, they moved aside as the two drew near. One man
pushed the button that opened the elevator door. As the car
headed upward, Azzolini said, "There was a break-in here the
night after your partner was killed."

"Hell of a thing."

"The description of the guy fits you pretty well."

"I'm a popular type."

"There was some vandalism upstairs, but the only thing that
seems to be missing is the book people sign when they're working late."

Mike shrugged. "Could have been a private eye working for
a woman who wanted to know what her husband was doing."

"He had a badge, Gallagher."

"People are finding badges in bowls of bean dip these days
You said so yourself."

"You're not going to give me a break, are you?"

"I want to see what kind of a break you're going to give me,"
Mike said.

"You and Kerrigan deserve each other."

"Don't count on anything," Mike said. "Let me have the
keys to Roehrig's Veedub, too. He's not going to report it stolen."

"You need medical attention."

"I'll take care of it." Mike had his hand out. After a pause, Azzolini gave him the keys. The elevator door opened and Azzolini led the way down to the Maxwell-Skelley office. He knocked, and a guy on the other side asked who was there. Azzolini said his name and the door opened. The room was dark.

"It's getting pretty wild down there," the guy said, heading toward a television set on a wide table. Tom Cutler stepped out of the shadow of the far corner.

"Give me your badge, Gallagher."

"Shut up and fuck off," Azzolini said. "You'll get his badge with a letter of resignation, which you will accept with regret."

Cutler was glowering at Mike. "What happened to you?"

"He fell in the shower," Azzolini said. "What's going on down at the house of mirth?"

A guy sitting at the table in front of the television set said, "Jackson's almost drifting into word salad, like that tape of the girl he was playing for a while."

Mike remembered: Barbara Brandon had called Jackson, babbling, her brain burned on drugs.

"Where did you meet Azzolini?" Cutler asked Mike.

"I found him in Century City," Azzolini said.

"At Pryor's office?"

Azzolini was watching the television screen. The image was as blurry as Constantine had said. When the figures moved, they left ghosts of themselves behind that took seconds to fade. Azzolini said, "Pryor's dead."

Mike was watching Cutler. Cutler asked, "What about Maxwell?"

"He's dead, too," Azzolini said. "Kiku's in custody."

"What about that Roehrig?"

"Dead," Azzolini said. "They all fell in the shower together. Gallagher was lucky he lived." Azzolini turned up the volume of the television set. The sound was fuzzy.

"And then we, let me tell you," Jackson was saying, rocking on the edge of the bed, "and then we, I hated Oklahoma, we just spent the night up there, you know? I should have been a star, but I got chicken-fucked. Those guys were just crazed, the way they used to get on Rainbow Drive. Roehrig just got that bar against her neck; boy, did she kick and punch—"

"You mean Oklahoma, don't you, baby?" the girl asked. She was sitting beside him, trying to take his hand, but he kept pulling away, rubbing his arms and shoulders like a smackhead with chills.

"Has he been talking about Rainbow Drive long?" Azzolini asked.

"No, this is new," the guy sitting in front of the set said. "We didn't miss anything anyway. It's all on tape."

Azzolini turned to Cutler. "Do you have everything ready?"

"I don't want Gallagher here."

"Gallagher works for me now. Something you ought to know: Gallagher has enough evidence to make this city drop Parker Center on your fucking head. Now let's get on with it."

The guy at the television set passed Cutler a walkie-talkie. Cutler said to Mike, "For me, this is nothing, nothing at all."

Mike didn't answer.

Cutler turned again to the guy at the television set. "Stop that tape recorder."

The guy did, and leaned back so that Cutler could see that the machine had been turned off.

Cutler had the walkie-talkie up to his ear. "Let me talk to Hammond," he said quietly. He waited. In the silence, Jackson's fuzzy voice seemed to grow louder.

"Did you ever fuck a chicken? Those women in that house screamed—screamed terrible. Jews, spicks, and niggers are the ones supposed to funny in this drug. That spick swung that steel like he was stamping cantaloupes. Use cantaloupe in a sentence."

"Donnie, you're scaring me."

"Get set," Cutler said into the radio. Azzolini picked up a telephone and tapped out a number. The telephone on the bed on the television screen began to ring. Jackson picked up and said hello.

"Your friends are dead, you hillbilly asshole," Azzolini said quietly. "Now we're coming to kill you."

Jackson screamed and slammed the phone down. The girl

tried to get away but he grabbed her by the hair. "Use cantaloupe in a six-pack!"

"What?"

"He's got guns in there," somebody said.

"He can't retain a thought from one second to the next," the
guy in front of the television set said.

"It would be better if he had a gun in his hand," the first one
said.

Azzolini punched the telephone buttons again. The telephone
on the bed began ringing. Jackson had the girl's hair in both
hands. "You have to hold the wings! Hold the wings! One-
legged dagos canna hop, but day cantaloupe!" He was shaking
her and she was trying to bite his wrist. Now she screamed.

"That's it," Azzolini said. "We can't wait for him to get a
gun."

"Go," Cutler said into the walkie-talkie.

"The danger's there," somebody said. "The girl's in fear of
her life."

It looked as if Jackson was about to break her neck. "Then,
when you come, you let go of the wings! They flap! Get it? *They
flap!* THE WHOLE BODY FLAPS! IT MILKS YOU DRY!"

Jackson was yelling at the top of his lungs. Now there was a
gunshot offscreen. Mike thought of looking away—he wanted
to, but he couldn't while he had Constantine on the job. It wasn't
fair. Now Jackson was getting to his feet, pulling the girl up
with him by her hair when the volley sounded, rapid-fire. She
was the one who was hit first, falling against Jackson in that
ghostly slow motion. Her head jerked, and while he was looking
at her, dumbfounded, a single small hole appeared in his forehead, a dark spurt erupting from the back. He went backward
onto the bed, pulling her with him. Now the screen was filled
with the image of a guy in a baseball cap.

"Larry Hammond was hit," he said. "We need an ambulance. It looks bad."

"How bad?" Cutler asked into the walkie-talkie. The guy in
the baseball cap didn't have a walkie-talkie. The telephone on
the bed was still ringing. Finally the guy reached over the bodies
and picked up the telephone. He said hello.

"How bad is Hammond hit?" Azzolini asked, holding the handset so Mike could hear.

"As bad as possible," the guy said. "Behind the ear."

Azzolini passed the handset to Cutler and then turned to Mike. "Need more?"

"No."

"Let me go downstairs with you. You may have trouble getting out of the garage. You can still change your mind about hanging tough. It's not necessary."

Mike didn't answer. He was thinking about Novak. Word of Hammond's "accident" would get out soon. Novak would know what had really happened, and unless he was completely stupid, he would run. There was no protection available for him, not now. But it would be difficult to communicate why he was wanted, or give him what he deserved. Mike might be hunting the guy for years, haunted by him maybe even the rest of his life.

Mike had to call Constantine, too. He had to make sure for both their sakes that Constantine was clear of the area. And then he was going to get straight with Laura—or Laura was going to get straight with him. But he couldn't call anyone until he was clear of the area. The route home would take him through Laurel Canyon—much of the way on the same streets on which he had followed Roehrig's Volkswagen bus just a week ago, the last time he had seen Dan alive.

In the elevator Azzolini asked if anything in Century City made it impossible for his people to construct a scenario of murder-suicide involving those still in Pryor's office. Mike said no.

Walking to the Volkswagen, Azzolini said, "Late next year, early the year after, Cutler will resign. He just wants to get out with his public reputation intact."

"I don't give a shit about Cutler."

"How do I find you if I want you?"

"If I'm not at home, I'll be at Saint Joseph's Hospital in Burbank." Mike was thinking that the one place on his route to make his calls was the Canyon Country Store, in Laurel Canyon at the foot of Kirkwood Drive. Outdoor telephones—no one would take notice of him at this hour. He was still afraid. He was afraid that all he had just seen had been some kind of show designed to lull him, whether or not Hammond had really been shot. Paranoia was like the flu in that it took you awhile to get completely healthy. If you ever did. Mike wasn't sure it was possible.

He was stiffening up. Even his right hand, the one that had held the pen gun: he was unable to close his fist. The traffic on Sunset had grown heavier, almost bumper to bumper. There was a space-cadet radio in the Veedub's dashboard, but Mike left it alone. He had to tell Don Grant that it would be a few days before his station wagon could be returned. Grant was one of the many people who would want to know the whole story. Burgess was another. Juan Lopez. Captain Ruppert. Kennedy. Not even Constantine knew everything—good thing for him. If Mike wanted to think that Azzolini wasn't as calculating a user of people as Tom Cutler, all he had to remember was the blond girl, Jennie Wagner, slumping against the unlamented Donnie Jackson. Maybe what she knew had to stay secret, but was there no other way to do it?

Probably not. Mike was going to have to figure out what he'd tell people.

He wouldn't want the responsibility of deciding what to do about the girls overseas. Even if they could be retrieved, they could not be kept quiet. And then what? The other governments would not take the embarrassment well. Mike had to believe that a lot of Maxwell's customers were people important in their own countries. The love of power was like that: after you tasted control over people, you wanted to control them absolutely. Faced with exposure, many of those men wouldn't simply kick and thrash like conventional American scum-sucking politicos: no, they'd bury the evidence—*alive,* if necessary. Maybe that thought made the Washington deliberations easier. Mike had thought he would be haunted by Greg Novak. He was haunted already. He'd be able to talk about Novak, at least to a few people, but anytime he did, he'd only remember what was really deep inside him. What Pryor and Maxwell had done was the kind of thing that made healthy human beings sick. It made them crazy.

Maurice Constantine was already well away from West Hollywood. Mike told him that he had seen what he had asked Constantine to record.

"Then we don't have to discuss it, Mr. Gallagher. I did the job and you paid me. If there's a balance, I'm sure you'll settle it in cash—please. If you want the tapes, I'll be happy to send them to any address you care to give me. But make sure you give it to me clearly and correctly, because the return address I'm going to put on the package will be a phony. I know we've been through a lot and didn't know what was coming, so I know you won't take it personally if I tell you that that was the most horrible thing I've ever seen in my life. We both know that you shouldn't call me again. Let's just leave it at that, okay?"

"Burn the tapes, Maurice. In a few days I'll call you from a safe number, and you'll tell me if I owe you any money. You did a good job and I'm grateful for it."

"Thank you. I wish I didn't have these fucking wires in my mouth, 'cause all I want to do is go out and get shitfaced drunk."

"Take care of yourself, Maurice." Mike called Laura. She didn't pick up until the fourth ring. "It's me," he said. "I'd like to stop by. It's time to talk."

"I think that's a wonderful idea," she said.

"I just saw people die, Laura—"

"Look, bring in some cigarettes, will you? I've been out for over an hour, but I've been afraid to go down to the 7-Eleven because I didn't want to miss your call. Benson and Hedges Menthol, don't forget."

He started to speak, but she was gone. The money dropped into the coin box. She didn't smoke. In the store, the guy behind the counter saw the blood on his pants. The guy opened the cash register.

"You want the money? Take it!"

"Don't be stupid."

Mike threw a bill on the counter. It turned out to be a five— the hell with the change. He grabbed the pack of cigarettes and headed for the door, the corner of his eye picking up the clerk's sudden wily grin. Mike cursed him.

In the Volkswagen, he checked his guns, the .38 and the .22.

She wouldn't have asked for the cigarettes unless she had wanted to warn him. But of what? He couldn't be sure. Who knew her? Cutler could have been following him for days. Somebody had been calling Mike at home—he still did not know who that had been. It could even be Azzolini's people at Laura's place. Laura had not known about Hollister's tapes of the girls, or what they meant. She had said she had decided to change her life: maybe she was expendable, now, too. Everybody's situation would be a lot more secure if Mike was off the planet. And if Laura was now a problem, the two of them together made one neat package.

Asking for cigarettes had been not only a warning, but a code. The person or persons with her didn't know she didn't smoke. What else had she said? He still had no proof of who or what she was. She wanted him to come over, but she had warned him, too.

He had no choice now but to do exactly as she'd asked—meaning he had to arrive in a way that aroused no suspicion. He could not appear to have hurried. He had to play *dumb*.

No problem: he'd been dumb all his life about his parents' adult reality. A son didn't understand such things, but a cop did. Now all he could do was forget it. It had nothing to do with him. He had his own life, and he was proud of it. . . .

There was nothing unusual outside her house. Her Toyota was in the driveway, and Mike recognized none of the vehicles parked at the curb nearby. He pulled the Volkswagen up behind her car, killed the engine quickly, and listened. He could not take much time at this. Now he heard Agnes. The dog was in the backyard, barking steadily, the kind of barking that drove neighbors nuts. Mike walked up the drive. Lights inside the house were on. No movement in the windows. Mike had his right hand wrapped as tightly as possible around the .38 in the pocket of Pryor's raincoat, the cigarettes in his left hand. He pushed the doorbell with his thumb. After a moment, the dog started barking louder and faster, and then the door opened. Laura's eyes were on his, not wavering.

"Hi," she said. "I missed you."

He held up the cigarettes. She took them. He was about to kiss her when he heard Greg Novak say, "Come inside, Mike. Close the door behind you."

Laura stepped back. "He's been telling me that a Professor

Popejoy was staring at him in class this evening. I don't know what he's talking about. He came here because this is where he traced you Wednesday evening, after we went over to Laurel Canyon together. He said he knew you'd turn up here eventually."

Mike was moving deliberately, carefully. Novak stepped into view. "I heard you say the name of this street over the telephone Wednesday afternoon. Let me have your guns, Mike. Be careful. I know the pressure's on. We have to talk."

Mike produced the .38. "The pressure's all the way off, Greg, Hammond's dead."

The coat fell open and Laura winced at the bloodstain on Mike's pants. Novak took the .38 "You carry a backup, Mike."

"Ankle holster Let me sit down" He put his arm around Laura's shoulders. "Where do you want me to sit, kid? I don't want to bleed all over your parents' furniture."

"Can you make it to the dining room?"

"Sure. I was thinking about your father. He must have been very proud of you."

"He was. Fit to bust." She took his hand and kissed it. "Did you win this one?"

Novak was behind them. "Yes," Mike said. "You want to know this, Greg. The guy who put you and Hammond up to killing Dan is dead, too. So is Maxwell and the guy who actually killed Dan. All that can connect you to Dan's death are the signatures on Popejoy's attendance rolls. Last week's doesn't match the others, does it?" Mike settled into a chair at the table. He saw Laura blink, but Novak didn't.

"Go slow, Mike. I want the gun."

"You'll get it. You're the guy who's been calling me, who looked for Randall Brandon's card in Dan's Rolodex. You've always been working for Hammond, part of his private army or something."

Laura went around the table and sat down, watching both of them. She had the cigarettes in her hand. Mike raised the .22 toward Novak with the tips of his fingers. Novak took the gun. He sat down opposite Mike.

"I didn't know what Hammond was doing," Novak said. "I swear to you, I didn't know what was going on."

"Who disabled Dan's car?"

"I did—but I was doing what I was told. I came up in Hammond's command. He taught us that we were always part of his team. He was going to be chief and take us up with him. Last week, all he told me was to keep Dan in town as long as I could."

"And to call somebody when you couldn't keep him any longer," Mike said. "What the fuck did you think they were planning, to steal his stereo?"

"I didn't know!" Novak cried. *"They used me!"*

"That's something I can understand," Mike said. "There's been a lot of it going around lately." He felt Laura's eyes on him. She was opening the cigarettes. "But what did you have in mind tonight, Greg? Hammond being dead doesn't change anything for you. You couldn't have done anything to us either way. If Popejoy couldn't put it together, others would. Do you see what I'm telling you? Put the gun on the table and slide it over to me, then get up, walk out, and keep on walking. Try Vancouver, Winnepeg, or Sydney, Australia. You get a running start, about as much time as you'd get if you killed us."

"How can I believe you? How do I even know that Hammond is dead?"

"Time to trust somebody," Mike said. "I belong in a hospital. Give *her* a break. She's just a teacher."

Laura said, "Can I get my lighter? It's in the living room."

Novak glanced over. "Stay in my line of sight."

Now the telephone rang. Halfway to the corner table, Laura stopped. The phone was in the kitchen. It rang again. "Let me get that, will you? It's my girlfriend, and she's going to let it keep ringing."

It rang a third time. She hadn't moved. Novak was trying to keep Mike and her in view. Mike opened his palm. "Give me the gun, Greg. Don't make things worse than they are."

The phone rang again.

"Answer it," Novak said.

Laura strode into the kitchen, out of sight. "Hi! I thought it was you! Hold on, will you?"

Novak was confused. Laura returned, caught his expression, waggled a cigarette, and pointed toward the living room.

Mike moved his hand to the middle of the table. "Give me the gun, Greg. Please!"

"He was your partner!"

"You were used," Mike said. "You made a mistake. For all you know, nobody will be after you." He didn't want to look at Laura, hoping that he wasn't giving anything away. "After all that's happened, people may be relieved to let it go. You don't want to know more about it—"

Laura was at the table.

"Greg! Give me the gun! Now!"

Laura turned, crouching, presenting the smallest possible target, the nine-millimeter in both hands. Her teeth were bared, her expression fierce. "Hey, *Novak!*"

Mike watched Novak turn toward her, his mouth open—he didn't figure anything like this at all. Novak's gun was pointing away from Mike only because he had moved his body around in the chair. She fired—filled the room with sound: *Pop! Pop! Pop! Pop!* Novak flopped backward, arms in the air, his blood hitting Mike in the face. Now she turned the gun toward Mike— then straightened up, the gun lowering to her side. *"Are you all right?"*

He swallowed. He hadn't moved from the chair. "Yes," he breathed.

"I'll be right there." She ran to the kitchen. "Azzolini? Did you hear that, you son of a bitch? No, Gallagher's fine—or in the condition in which you let him leave you. Why didn't you get him an ambulance? It was the other guy, that Novak. He was here for an hour. Get an ambulance here *fast.*" Mike heard her hang up. He was looking at the floor. He saw her feet and ankles in front of him before he looked up again. She was still holding the gun at her side. He took it. Her lip was trembling when she tried to speak.

"They'll be here in a few minutes, so you have to listen. This job did it for me months ago, when we were spying on what seemed to be half the city, including you. I didn't know the reason for it until last night, when I figured out what those tapes of the girls really were—a catalog." She took his face in her hands, but then glanced over toward Novak—and looked away, shuddering. "I don't want to see him. When I tried to resign last fall, Azzolini said not until the job was done. All the police work since the murders has been fake, just a show. They've always known who was in the Rainbow Drive house that morning. Maxwell's timing and thoroughness surprised them, that's all. What's been done since the murders has been designed to get everything flushed down the toilet—"

Her eyes darted again to Novak, and Mike got to his feet and moved to block her view. Now she looked up. "They needed a volunteer for you. I'd heard your private business, but I didn't care. You were what I'd been asking for—I've been telling you the truth about my inner life. That's why I told you to think twice—"

He had her by the arms, she was trembling so badly. "You don't have to say these things—"

Laura shook her head. "I had to lie to you about Novak's signature. By last night, Azzolini was afraid you were going to tear the city apart. He used me right along. He knew I liked you. He just played the card, he said. He used you, too. After he found out you were working the Valerie Moreland case, he told me to push you. O-orders from Washington, he said. He was supposed to wrap this thing fast."

"He just said he was trying to keep a rein on me. He offered me a job."

"Understand what you're getting!" she cried. "The game he's in is clean, so he thinks he can play it as dirty as he wants! You'll be doing the same—" The sound of a siren seemed to take that much more out of her. The sound was still a long way off. He put his arms around her. "I *am* quitting," she said, as her chest began to heave. "I-I can't do this job anymore. I never wanted to kill—"

"You had to kill him," Mike said. Now there was another siren, out of phase with the first. "There was no telling what he was going to do."

Telling her she had done her duty would not keep her from going into shock. He was thinking that he did not want to let go of her when he heard the sirens coming down the street. She was holding him tightly, the spasms of her weeping growing more violent. Red lights flashed menacingly against the curtains, and Mike could imagine the neighbors running to their

windows. They would want to know what had happened here.
Somebody somewhere, Mike was sure, was figuring out exactly
what to tell them.

ABOUT THE AUTHOR

RODERICK THORP is the author of eight other novels, two works of nonfiction, and newspaper and magazine articles and stories published in this country and around the world. A recognized expert on crime and police procedure, Thorp also traced cocaine trafficking from South America to southern California in a twenty-one-part series in the Los Angeles *Herald-Examiner*. He has been a college professor and a consultant to a leading California bank. Thorp is currently at work on a screenplay and two more novels, one set in Los Angeles, the other in New York. He has two sons.